MEG HENDERSON

Ruby

BLACK & WHI

First published 2010
This edition first published 2011
by Black & White Publishing Ltd
29 Ocean Drive, Edinburgh EH6 6JL

1 3 5 7 9 10 8 6 4 2   11 12 13

ISBN: 978 1 84502 335 5

le

For our granddaughter, Sophie Ruth Henderson:
Owner and Supreme Ruler of the Universe

AUTHOR'S NOTE
AND ACKNOWLEDGEMENTS

Like most of my books (the last two being exceptions) this one is a collection of obsessions that have taken root in my memory, and it's set in two of my favourite places.

Four generations of my family had lived in the great melting pot of the Townhead/Calton area of Glasgow, before our crumbling tenement collapsed one rainy June night in the early 1950s. We were re-housed in Blackhill, a place I loved. Despite the many lurid and mainly fictitious tales told about Blackhill, I have never regained the sense of safety and security I felt in that community. The housing was poor and there were no shops and no work, it was, after all, just somewhere to dump troublesome, slum-dwelling Irish Catholics, or those with Irish names, which to the Glasgow of that time meant the same thing.

My mother still went 'home' to Townhead to do her shopping where she had grown up and I remember as a very small child waiting at the bus stop on the return journey back to Blackhill and looking at two rows of tenements in High Street. Though they were only a few hundred yards from the demolished, dilapidated Balmano Brae tenement I had been born in, they were another world away in every meaningful sense. The Bell o' the Brae tenements were built of red sandstone and were incredibly beautiful, even as a child I noticed that, though I didn't know about the history of the area my family came from.

Across the street from the Bell o' the Brae tenements in one direction and the bus stop in another, was a railway goods yard, and as

I waited for the trolley bus I watched the comings and goings of the little scarab lorries, buzzing about and dodging the horses and carts that were still around then, as they loaded and unloaded the steam trains I could hear hissing in the background. That picture has stayed in the back of my mind ever since and it has taken this long to weave a story around them.

And those memories are where Ruby McLean came from, though this is story of the Bell o' the Brae community she lived in as much as it is about Ruby. It was the kind of place I grew up in, the fabled one where everybody knew everybody else and where lives were intertwined, and where women like Ruby were the unsung heroines and the backbone of ordinary life. As the book opens, Ruby has retired to live in Largs, a little place I've always been fond of, and that's the only reason I sent her there. There have been times when I've travelled long distances just to have a coffee in Largs, and not just because of Nardini's fish suppers and cakes, though they helped!

I now have an old friend who lives in Largs and who carried out various bits of research for me as questions arose, and questions always arise, so my thanks to Patricia Lock, or Pat Dolan as she was when we were at school together, for her patience and willingness to trot off every time the call came to check out locations and facts.

My main problem when working on a book is that I over-research everything, and with that thought in mind I'd like to thank Dr Irene Maver of Glasgow University and Elaine Murray of Glasgow's Caledonian University for their help in understanding a little of the social history and housing needs of Glasgow, and how and why the Bell o' the Brae tenements came to be built. The trouble with this is that, as ever, I got too engrossed in the history and had to be dragged back to work, but though they gave me too much information to use in this book, it will fester away in my mind and surface in future books.

I am always amazed at the readiness of complete strangers to find out whatever bizarre piece of information I have decided I need, as did Susan McGann, Archivist of the Royal College of Nursing, and Donnie Muir of the Compass Local Housing Organisation. Donnie was only too happy to climb onto one particular balcony in High Street on my behalf to inspect the view from it, to seek out people with memories and he may also identify with one character in the book as a result of our chats.

Someone not a complete stranger though is my old pal, Alistair Macdonald, ex-policeman, Deputy Lord Lieutenant, former Provost of Clydebank, all-round man of the people and a fervent 'Bankie', despite really being a teuchter. Alistair, though he's busy enough already, happily squirrelled about in obscure places for answers to my fresh queries about the aftermath of the Clydebank Blitz, for which I'm grateful.

Thanks also to various employees of Glasgow City Council, 'the Corporation' in my day. They helpfully passed on photographs and assorted information about the Bell o' the Brae tenements and the protocol for winding-up Corporation clocks during WW2. My grateful thanks to all the railway enthusiasts who gave me a jigsaw of snippets about the training of steam engine crews back then, especially Andy Munro who had all sorts of helpful snippets of information.

Lastly I have to thank the staff of Clydebank Library and the Glasgow Room of the Mitchell Library, as ever, for their knowledge and their constantly good-natured assistance. They know everything and pass on their knowledge with unfailing generosity.

To anyone left out I apologise, my only excuse is the old one about over-researching everything, and often many people tell me the same piece of information, for which I am always grateful.

1

It was only a tiny piece in the *Evening Times;* one of those paragraphs on an inside page no one ever reads, so she had no idea why she had noticed it. Maybe the address had caught her eye without her being consciously aware of it, because she had moved on to the Births, Marriages and Deaths near the back before she had taken the words in. At her age, the Deaths were often the only thing in the papers worth reading, not even Lobey Dosser to cheer you up these days, it was all lying politicians on the make and the human rights to do whatever you pleased, everywhere.

At least the Deaths columns hinted at peace, at a natural order of things, and every now and again it might be someone she knew or had known, though, if pushed, she couldn't have said what good that would do her. Perhaps it was like a visit from an old friend, someone you had lost touch with years ago, without being obliged to have tea with them only to discover you have nothing in common with them after all, and spending hours in polite conversation before you can escape, with promises to keep in touch in future, promises neither had any intention of keeping. Better to have your memories at a distance. She was that age, she supposed, scanning the names. One day soon she would see her own name there, she thought with a wry chuckle. Someone at Rarity's, the undertakers, would trot out the usual 'sadly missed' form of words for the *Evening Times,* because there were precious few relatives left to do it. There was her daughter, of course, but Ruby had decided long ago that nothing would be done when the time came to inform Frances she was an orphan. Not that she would care anyway. Just in case she died in the night, Ruby had long ago made sure there were no clues in her flat that might lead anyone to her daughter's whereabouts, which made that unopened letter in the orange glass bowl a bit of a worry. She'd have to see about that. If anyone asked – Paddy Keenan next door, mainly – she simply said her daughter lived a long way off. That was an age thing, too, preparing for a sudden exit, an elderly version of her mother's insistence on always wearing clean knickers in case you got knocked down, she thought with a laugh. And as for the others – nieces and nephews – they were scattered all over the globe. She rarely heard from them and wouldn't recognise them if she passed them in the street. Changed days. Then there would be the details of her cremation at Greenock, some twelve miles from Largs, where she stayed now, and that would be that. She couldn't really care less what they did with what was left of her afterwards. She had no time for lavish shows of grief. From what she had seen, and she had seen a lot in her nursing days, the process of dying was just that, a process, and once over no one should feel obliged to prolong the agony for the sake of form. Far better to give people some attention before they died than to pile it on when they were gone and could make no use of it. And those dreary hymns! She had never met anyone in the throes of real grief who could raise their voice in song, so what were they actually for, other than form once again? It kept down the unemployment rates among ministers and priests, she supposed.

As for the current fad of 'celebrating the life of', it seemed that no one was allowed to die any longer and no one was allowed to mourn if they did. They had to celebrate the life of, and not in the way of the old wakes, not a real celebration as her parents' generation would have understood it, but everyone slapping on big grins and pretending to have 'beaten' death. She would like to meet the first one who managed that. Indeed, she often thought she should plan her own 'celebration' and tell the truth, instead of some anonymous minister standing up and spouting a lot of nonsense about someone he or she had never set eyes on, far less actually known. She had sat through enough of those. She could record her last goodbye on her tape machine, though now that she had got the hang of it at last it was almost obsolete, a bit like herself really. Her generation was a vanishing breed now. Last thing at night she would put on a tape of *The Navy Lark,* or *Hancock's Half Hour,* and drift off with a smile. They were her barriers against too much thinking, regretting and guilt, as much as entertainment. Her goodbye tape would be played on the day. 'This is what's left of Ruby McLean,' she would say, 'a wee pile of grit that was no great shakes as a wife and mother and achieved so little in her life that she *won't* be sadly missed. Now there will *not* be tea and sandwiches at the Willowbank Hotel afterwards,' – or the Brisbane House Hotel which was a bit grander, and she felt she deserved not to be celebrated there at least as much – 'so the one or two of you who wandered in here out of curiosity can forget about looking sad and pretending I was a saint while you fill your faces. Thanks for coming. You can get on with your shopping now. 'Bye!' Of course they even had after-funeral receptions in pubs these days, though she wouldn't stand for that, 'Not over my dead body!' she chuckled. Even if she were in fact lying down or had formed that little pile of grit, no pub would play any part in the 'celebration' of *her* life.

Then she stopped. What was that a page or two ago? She flicked back, looking for that tiny paragraph. Why was it always like that? Why could you never find the page you wanted when you had only passed it a few seconds ago? Was there some built-in gadget that, sensing you were turning back, suddenly festooned the pages with adverts for things you wouldn't want in a million years, that you then had to read because you weren't sure where you had seen what you wanted? She wouldn't be surprised. They would stoop to anything to sell you something these days. Ah, there it was. High Street. Some Housing Association had taken over various flats in what had been Glasgow's Bell o' the Brae tenements in High Street, apparently; the ones that hadn't been sold off. They had been busy renovating them and what should they find under acres of old wallpaper in one flat but hand-painted murals on the walls? It took the wind out of her sails. 'Uncle Jakey!' she sighed, lowering the newspaper to her lap and closing her eyes for a few seconds. Then she looked back at the words on the page. The young man in charge was saying the murals were of such high quality they didn't know what to do, no childish daubs these, but the work of someone with talent, someone who could paint, though no one knew who had done them. Ruby put the paper down on the table in front of her and sat for a moment, then she took out a Kleenex, one of the fancy ones with balm on them so that your nose didn't get red and flaky from constant blowing when you had a cold, and dabbed at her eyes. 'Daft old biddy,' she chided herself, blowing her nose severely to stave off any more nonsense. She knew who had painted the murals at 266 High Street. Her uncle, Jakey McLean. She could see him yet, brush in hand, eyes fixed firmly on his latest creation, with Wee Dug, his only and constant companion lying under the table waiting patiently for whatever Jakey planned next.

She had been dreaming about her family these last weeks, funnily enough, though she supposed everyone did, especially when the older generations had gone and the prospect of rejoining them was coming ever closer. She hadn't thought of them for a long time, yet there they were, invading her sleep in all their awful glory. It was probably the letter from her daughter that had started it off, the letter with so much writing and crossing out that there was barely any room for that latest forwarded address, but it had found her. She still hadn't replied to it and wasn't sure that she would, but it had stirred up the past and whatever it meant – or didn't – to be family. Only that afternoon she had been standing in the shop inside Nardini's Café down on the front, waiting to buy a few cakes to take home to share with Paddy next door as they discussed the letter. Maybe. She wasn't sure how much of her life she should share with Paddy. As her eyes strayed over the fancy things in the cabinet she had suddenly thought, 'My, but Bea would've been in heaven here, her and her sweet tooth!' She stopped, puzzled. Her sister Bea and the rest of the McLeans were consigned to a box deep in her memory that she had no wish to delve into, and Bea was very definitely double-locked away at the bottom, heavily welded with even heavier weights on top, just to be sure, though she knew Bea could breathe through solid metal. So why had she popped into her mind?

The McLeans of High Street were just an ordinary family like any other. 'Aye,' she murmured, chuckling, 'but only on the outside.' But for all she knew all ordinary families were like that, full of darkness as well as sunshine – 'Jakey,' she thought – discord as well as

4

harmony, bitterness as well as sweetness – 'Bea. Oh Bea for sure!'

She sat for a while, clasping the edges of the newspaper in her hands, looking out across the sea from her window. She loved the sea, it calmed her. That was why she had chosen Largs to retire to. She loved it when it was churning, the grey waves edged with a deep layer of white foam as they pounded the shore, like the lace trimming at the throat of an elegant spinster, or when they were blue and lazy, lapping the sand with a slow, reassuring rhythm, and on other days, the golden summer ones, when it lay there like a sparkling sheet of green satin. She had spent a day here as a child and had never forgotten the sea or the peace, and there had been precious little peace to be had living with the McLeans in High Street. From her window she could look across the bay and see Arran, the Cumbraes and, on a very good day, so she had been told, the lump of rock that was Ailsa Craig, otherwise known as Paddy's Milestone, to the south, standing midway between Belfast and Glasgow. Paddy next door always said it had been named in his honour and he always expected you to laugh as well.

She barely thought of the city these days, though she had been Glasgow born and bred. High Street born and bred. My God, how long ago it all seemed. How long it must be since Jakey painted his pictures. Poor old Jakey. He had been a popular local character, a real eccentric whose antics made everyone laugh, but he had a sad, lonely kind of life, if you knew where to look. Only his closest family had been aware that he needed looking after, a little protection, though they couldn't have explained why. Ruby blew her nose again and then laughed at herself, but the laugh betrayed her by turning into a sob, then she was lost. 'Ach, Jakey, son!' she whispered softly.

It was as though the words on the paper had been a key that had released him from wherever he was and brought him back to life. He seemed to jump out of the newspaper and stand before her, looking her squarely in the eye, and that was one thing Jakey didn't do, make eye contact with people. Everyone knew that Jakey was so shy that he only ever looked you in the eye for an instant, and that if he couldn't avoid doing so. All you would get was a fleeting impression of blue eyes that were so clear and bland that you sometimes wondered if he had a thought in his head. And yet she knew there was so much going on in there, it was just that he hid it well, or kept it to himself, which amounted to the same thing. What made people laugh were his odd ways. Jakey was always coming up with bizarre things to amuse everyone and he had a little chuckle to himself sometimes, as though he was party to some secret amusement. You couldn't help smiling when you saw him or heard him chuckle, he was such a character. Yet if you didn't know him, if you came from outside the confines of High Street, you would pass him without a glance.

His head had been bald by the time Ruby arrived in the family a little belatedly, 'a surprise', as her birth had been described, but a mistake she guessed it had been. There had been Bea, then George and, after him, Iris, all separated by a few years here and there, and more than a few years more down the line, Ruby. 'My last wee gem,' as her father used to say with a smile. George and Ruby had their father's dark hair and eyes, while Iris had their mother's colouring, reddish blonde hair and blue eyes. Bea was something else though. She had blue eyes, but more vivid than her mother's and, lacking Sarah's warm, gentle expression, Bea's glared and blazed under a thatch of wayward, angry-looking bright red hair. There had never been anything subtle about Bea, Ruby remembered with a sigh. Ruby had always been close to her brother but felt distant from both sisters. If anything, she felt more kinship with her pal, Flora McCreadie, who lived across the road in George Street, than with Bea or Iris. Flora was the kind of person people talked of as 'having a good heart,' and she had always been fond of Jakey. She thought he was special, even if he didn't look it.

Not that anyone would have known for sure whether Uncle Jakey was bald, because he wore a cap, a *bunnet*, that he never took off, indoors or out. He had never married and always lived alone, apart from Wee Dug, of course. They were well-suited, she had always thought, two misfits who had found each other. Wee Dug was a mongrel, an animal of indeterminate parentage many times over; 'a Heinz dog,' as Ruby's father, Harry McLean, delighted in saying, 'a dog of 57 varieties. Just the kind of wee dog Jakey would have.' One day he had followed Jakey home and Jakey had simply accepted him. Wee Dug was more of a description than a name. It was as near to a personal attachment as Jakey had been capable of, come to think of it, a sad little scrap of canine life so afraid of humans that he avoided all contact with them. He had a long, smooth-haired body that just cleared the ground, supported by four large, hairy paws with thick toes. The toes looked as though they belonged, by rights and by logic, to a much bigger animal and they splayed out in a semicircle as he trotted along beside Jakey. He had no tail, though there was enough of a stump to discern that there had once been one, and a big head with two folded-over ears, all as hairy as his paws. To Ruby, he looked even worse than one of her mother's infamous 'crochet things', in fact he looked like he had been hand-knitted by a whole crowd of people who had lost the pattern and were working from individual memories, all of them with more enthusiasm than ability. He was such an eccentric creature that looking at him made you laugh, till you caught sight of his eyes and saw in them his habitual, fearful, haunted expression, if, that was, you got near enough to see them under the bushy eyebrows. Wee Dug's eyes told you that he was forever on the edge of terror, an animal once so used to cruel treatment that he lived in constant panic of its return at any moment. Even after years of benign companionship with Jakey, if an ill-advised and uninvited hand stretched out to fondle him, Wee Dug would shrink away, shivering with fear. But he was a gentle soul; another animal as terrified as Wee Dug always was, would have barked, growled or even snapped when threatened, but Wee Dug simply tried to vanish into thin air by thinking himself small and staring desperately into the distance, trying to convince the owner of the hand that he wasn't really there at all. When Ruby, a frequent visitor to Jakey's flat, came to call, Wee Dug lay under Jakey's table, shaking with anxiety, his eyes darting back and forth in an agony of dread, until she had gone and the danger had passed. 'Poor wee creature,' she sighed, remembering, 'God knows what had happened to him before he adopted Jakey.'

The same could be said of Jakey, though. Two of a kind, right enough, she mused, a case of like attracting like, though no one made that connection at the time, nor had since, she supposed. Jakey paid him no discernible attention, yet wherever Jakey went,

Wee Dug went too, trotting along on his great big feet so closely at Jakey's heels that you were sure he would be trampled underfoot, the little dog's eyes still darting about, on the lookout for who knew what. They seemed to live separate lives, but together, not exactly compatible, but not in-compatible somehow, and that was enough for both.

Ruby's father used to say it was hard to tell whether his brother's solitary life had caused his slight detachment or was caused by it. Harry often made little comments about his brother, mixtures of justification, defence and mitigation, with a dash of reassurance, for himself as much as for others, all little signs, Ruby realised years later, that her father had sensed there was something not quite right about Jakey's existence. 'I've always thought it a shame he never married,' Harry sighed more than once, in gentle sympathy and regret. 'If he'd had a wife and weans it might've taken him out of himself. But what woman would entertain Jakey?' Harry was the younger McLean brother, he and Jakey had the same father but different mothers, Jakey's mother having died when he was very young. There had been plenty of death about in the melting pot that was Townhead, an area of more than normal socialist leanings in the socialist city that was home to Red Clydeside. As the twentieth century took over from the nineteenth, and even beyond, TB especially had claimed too many lives for any one death in Townhead to be singled out, and early death was so common that it was barely noticed, far less talked about. It was simply a fact of life that people were frequently widowed and not just once; Jakey and Harry's father had lost two wives before he was thirty.

In truth, it was also hard to say whether that slight distance between Jakey and everyone else was his choice or theirs, because he paid very little attention to personal hygiene, he just put on a veneer that hinted at respectability when it was required of him, but the smell of something not quite pleasant lurked about him, an unwashed whiff was never far from the surface, it had to be said. For instance, if anyone had got near enough to see him take his jacket off they would have discovered both shirt sleeves black with dirt, because when Jakey set his fire or put coal on it, he just crossed his arms and wiped his hands on the opposite shirt sleeves. When she got the chance, Sarah, Ruby's mother, would tidy up his flat and change his bed when he wasn't there, and put out clothes she had bought for him. Then she would steal away some of his old ones, wash them and sneak them onto the pulley in his flat to dry, but rather than wear something else, Jakey would put on his old clothes still damp, leaving the new clothes to pile up, unwanted and unworn.

On her wedding day, though, Ruby remembered seeing him at the back of St Mungo's, sitting alone as usual, save for Wee Dug beneath the pew, looking around so intently that he missed the bridal party passing on their way out. As Ruby tried and failed to catch his eye, she had noted that his face was covered in little red shiny beads of dried blood, a sign that Jakey had shaved in honour of her big day. She had been touched and amused in equal measure, because she knew Jakey didn't possess a mirror, wouldn't have one in the house, so it had all been done with a touch that was less than sure, but it had been done all the same. When designer stubble had come along all those years later Ruby had laughed. Uncle Jakey had invented it decades before. As she and Gerry made their way out of the church she heard Jakey chuckling quietly behind her. 'I quite agree, Uncle Jakey,' she thought, 'I would laugh myself if I didn't feel like crying. What a farce!'

Ruby closed her eyes again. Her wedding day, not the pleasantest of memories, it had to be said. Fair Friday, 1939, the Second World War was waiting in the wings and there she was, not yet seventeen and pregnant, and her groom just a year older. She had learned her lesson that you should never trust any man who said, 'I know what I'm doing,' or 'It'll be alright,' but too late, sadly. How could a boy like Gerry Reilly know what he was doing? Pity she hadn't asked that question sooner and she might not have been wearing the wedding dress bought by her sister, Iris, in a rash moment six months before. The object of Iris's transient affection had been Andy Morris, who worked in the Goods Yard with their brother, George. Andy's mother had been aghast at the prospect of her shy, pleasant son marrying Iris McLean and, by all accounts, had all but fallen to her knees, lit candles and offered up prayers of deliverance. Not that the Morrises were Catholic, but any port in a storm.

9

Maybe her efforts were responsible for Iris backing out, but Andy had never really got over being jilted. He appeared in the McLean home at every possible opportunity in the vain hope of re-awakening whatever emotion Iris felt that had made her accept his proposal in the first place, or maybe just to be near her, to see her, and always with an expression so lovesick that everyone wanted to give him a shake. Andy had been an aberration for Iris. Iris liked men, but other women's men. To be exact, Iris specialised in married men, so no one really knew why she had contemplated taking on the unmarried Andy Morris long enough to actually buy a dress, and a white dress at that. Now that would have provided the neighbourhood with much merriment, Iris McLean tripping down the aisle in white! Before she had got it home, though, the notion had worn off and her mind, if not her paws, were already on someone else's husband.

And so the dress had lain in a box, half-forgotten, before it got the chance of an outing in just as dubious virginal circumstances. Nothing was true that July day, Ruby remembered. Everything was as big a lie as Gerry's had been, so the dress was in good company. Well, company at least. No, there was one thing that had been true to character: Big Bea. Her eldest sister had dominated the entire day, as Bea always did. She had been gone many years now, but Ruby could still recall the sound of her voice, the awful, painful sound of her voice, a peculiar mixture of high-pitched whine and shrieking battle cry. Sweet of tooth, weak of stomach, harsh of tongue and bitter of nature, that was Bea. If Uncle Jakey made people laugh, Big Bea made them run for cover. 'Some woman, that,' the locals would say, and Ruby would nod with a tight smile. 'Only if you let her be,' she would reply. 'Let her be?' someone else would say. 'How exactly do you stop her then?' and everyone would laugh. Ruby never laughed, she just replied with her tight smile. Not that she was annoyed that her sister was being talked about, Bea didn't exactly invite loyalty, it was that slight hint of admiration in the voices that irritated her. There was nothing about Bea to admire, she was loud, selfish and constantly on the look out for trouble and she always found it whether it was there or not. In her mind, if she wasn't being cheated, badly done by or insulted at any particular

10

moment, then she soon would be, so she got her retaliation in first. There wasn't a family occasion in living memory that Bea hadn't turned into a battleground, it was as if Big Bea was part of an official programme of events. 'At 10 a.m. Gerry and Ruby will be married. At 1 p.m. there will be a wedding lunch followed by a reception at the McLean family abode at 252 High Street, at which Big Bea will perform her renowned "Screaming Harpy" routine at 3 p.m. sharp. All welcome. Be on time to avoid disappointment. Ear plugs are recommended.'

When Ruby thought back on her early life as a railway child living by the Goods Yard, she would recall the sounds and the smells. The sound of her father's whistling receding as he went down the tenement stairs in the early hours to start his shift as a train driver. 'Harry!' her mother would chide him from the doorway. 'Folk are sleeping!' 'Oh, aye, Sarah, I forgot!' he always whispered back, but before he had gone two more steps he was whistling again. The smell of his overalls when he came home again; a mixture of oil, smoke and sweat permeating every fibre so deeply that her mother could never get it out completely. There were the other noises, the steady rumble of trains arriving and departing, the clanking of wagons being uncoupled, the different sounds of steam escaping from the huge engines, of metal against metal, the angry grunts of the Scarab lorries with their little triangular cabs as they scuttled about like ants, servicing the trains, and the gentle clip-clop of horses and carts. And there was always that other noise in the background, the one nothing else could ever quite deaden, the noise of Bea's voice constantly raised in battle.

Ruby picked up the newspaper again and thought. She had an arrangement with Paddy next door. In the mornings he bought the *Daily Record*, read it and did the crossword 'across' clues, then gave it to her afterwards so that she could supply the 'downs', and in the afternoons she returned the favour with the *Evening Times*. Seemed simple enough to Ruby – they did the across clues in their own newspapers – but Paddy could never remember the plan and, being a man, blamed Ruby each time he got it wrong, thus leading to endless arguments, discussions and conversations. That was the real object of the exercise, Ruby was convinced. Sometimes she was the only human being Paddy spoke to all day and he preferred discord to silence. Still, even with Paddy's deliberate acts of crossword sabotage, it saved each of them money and satisfied the skinflint in both, but she didn't feel like one of his discussions or another walk down memory lane tonight. She sat for a moment, working out tactics. If she didn't give him his *Evening Times* tonight he would want to know why and was likely to come knocking on her door, so either way she would get his discussion. So she quickly copied down the few facts in the paragraph on a piece of paper and put it on top of her daughter's letter, both things to be attended to later, she thought. Then she opened her front door very carefully, tiptoed across to Paddy's flat and slid the newspaper through his letterbox as quietly as possible; she could always say that she had knocked but he hadn't heard her and accuse him of falling asleep in front of the TV again. But instantly the door opened.

'Were you standing behind the door waiting?' she demanded.

'Well, I was listening for you,' he admitted. 'I thought you said you wanted to talk about something?' he asked.

'Och, it was nothing important,' she said. 'It'll keep.'

'But we were having cakes,' he complained.

Ruby looked him up and down, from his old carpet slippers with holes where his toes poked through, and the ancient cardigan, buttoned wrongly, to the mane of silver-grey hair six feet higher up, and laughed. 'Look at the size of you. You're hardly a growing lad, you can last without a cake!'

'But they were Nardini's cakes,' he muttered.

'Okay, we'll have a cake,' she grumbled, 'but I'm too tired to talk much, does that suit you?'

Paddy grinned and nodded his head. 'Just as long as we have a cake,' he smiled.

As they headed across the landing to her flat she shook her head and laughed, he should be Patron Saint of Cakes, Paddy Keenan. He and Bea would have got on well together, if anyone could have got on with Bea, that was, and given the evidence she had her doubts about that. There it was again, she thought, a member of her family, and the least likely one at that, had popped into her head as though she had just been talking to her the day before. She filled the kettle, opened the Nardini's box and put the cakes on her mother's cake stand as Paddy made himself comfortable. Tomorrow, she decided, she would call the lad mentioned in the *Times* piece, Ian Somebody, and find out if she could see Jakey's murals just one last time. It had been years, decades, since she had been back to High Street, and she had no clear idea why she wanted to go back now, apart from a feeling that something was drawing her back there.

2

The Housing Association chap seemed quite excited by her phone call. Ian Fraser, that was his name, sounded like a nice lad, though these days anyone under sixty was a lad to her.

'And you really think you know who painted our murals?'

'Aye, son,' she smiled, 'it was my Uncle Jakey, Jakey McLean. He lived there for years with his wee dog, Wee Dug. He was an odd man in a lot of ways and artistic in a lot of other ways. But that was in a time when men weren't supposed to be artistic, you understand. Real men worked with their hands.' She let her mind wander about Jakey's flat. 'And as you've seen, he loved to paint. I probably watched him doing some of those murals. My family lived at 252 High Street, right on the corner there with Duke Street, the flat with the wee balcony outside and the clock.'

'That's one of ours, too,' he said.

'And my sister Bea lived further up on the bend on the other side, just before the Barony Church. Drove her mad not being able to see what was happening further down,' she remembered, silently reminding herself that it hadn't ever taken much to drive Bea mad. 'Have you done anything to them, the murals I mean?'

'No, not a thing,' he replied. 'They're on every wall we've stripped so far and they've been varnished over so to get them off we'd have to replaster the whole place. When we realised what we had we stopped to think over the options before stripping any more. The thing is, they're too good to destroy, I don't think we know what to do with them.'

'I was wondering if I might be able to have a wee look at them,'

14

she suggested, 'before you decide, if you see what I mean, for old times sake, I suppose?'

'Oh, aye, of course,' he said. 'Would it be okay if I told the papers? I'm sure they'd like to take a picture of you there.'

'Och, I don't think so, son,' she said quietly, then sensing his disappointment she said 'Maybe later. You have to understand I'm a sentimental old woman, I don't want the world to see me bubbling away there.'

He laughed. 'That's okay, then. Just you let me know when you'd like to come through. And how's the weather in Largs then?'

Ruby smiled. Largs was no more than thirty miles from Glasgow. Typical Glaswegian, anywhere outside the confines of the city, outside the confines of their own part of the city very often, was a foreign land. 'Oh, likely the same as you've got yourself,' she said.

'Aye, but you won't have this traffic though,' he replied. 'And is the Laughing Policeman still down there by the front? I loved that as a kid, spent a fortune on him. A good laugh with him, a Nardini fish tea, an ice cream and a stick of rock, even though I hated the rock and just sucked the red stuff off. Largs was a magic place when I was a wee lad.'

'Well I suppose it still is a magic place, but it's funny how you never forget where you were born, it always gets you in the end.'

She decided not to tell Paddy that she was going to Glasgow for the day, he would assume that he was invited and would be upset when she told him he wasn't. Paddy Keenan was an exiled Glaswegian like herself, but Paddy hadn't let go of the city. The minute she arrived next door he had found out she was a Glaswegian too and had clung onto her as though she was a life-raft. Any opportunity and he was on the train back there, as excited as a large, gangly puppy, then he talked about it for days afterwards till she felt like taping up his mouth just to get a rest from his chatter. Trips back to Glasgow were, for Ruby, few and far between normally, on a needs-only basis, and invariably left her feeling weepy and depressed. The changes in the city were like seeing a well-loved relative who had suffered some catastrophic accident that had left their face hideously disfigured by scars; you could see tantalising glimpses of the person you knew, but only here and there. The last time she was back was for the funeral of one of her father's old firemen and, integrated transport being a foreign concept to Glasgow, she had allowed herself the extravagance of a taxi from Central Station to Queen Street for the next leg of her journey. There was the wee orangey bus that shuttled people and luggage between the two stations but she would have to climb on and off with bones still stiff from the hour-long train ride, very undignified, and she refused to be branded as some arthritic old crone, even if she was one. First of all she had been aghast at the traffic congestion and then at the bizarre one-way system that forced the vehicles to take long detours to get to where they wanted to be and, more to her point, it pushed up the taxi fare well beyond the realms of extravagance. A chimp wielding a crayon could have organised things better, she thought, scowling at the rapidly increasing amount on the meter as the taxi approached Queen Street. Then she looked around at George Square and was so horrified at what they had done to it that her eyes teared up. The lovely old square had lost its grandeur, most of the flowerbeds had been covered over with ghastly red asphalt, which explained why the locals had re-named it Red Square.

As a child she had loved playing in George Square, watching the gardeners constantly changing the flowerbed layouts, sowing and weeding, tending to the place. Like all children she had climbed up to sit on top of one of the two big lions at either side of the War Memorial, for the sheer excitement of being chased off by the park keeper. 'That's a monument to men who died so that you could play here,' the parkie would yell angrily at badly behaved children, 'you ignorant wee buggers! You should have respect for the dead!' Of course it meant nothing to the children, they only did it to annoy the parkie then they would compare notes on what he had said to them, giggling at how annoyed he was. They would be much older, as she had been, before they understood why he had been so angry at their casual disrespect for the War dead.

Looking round she saw that the old post office on one side of the Square had been vacated, by progress, she had no doubt, and the imposing four storey building with its graceful arched windows had become a giant billboard, its elegant proportions swathed in an

16

enormous banner proclaiming the delights of some car or other. And talking of cars, they were everywhere, with their noise and their stench. The entire place was like a rat run and there were so many buses on the streets, each one carrying no more than a couple of passengers, that the city must be permanently gridlocked. Yet here and there were glimpses of those scarred old childhood relatives, buildings of real beauty from Glasgow's days as a major city of the Empire; deep red sandstone and white sandstone edifices, with carved details that no one ever saw these days, they were so busy looking straight ahead to where they wanted to be ten minutes ago. Some of the buildings she remembered were still standing, surrounded now by concrete blocks with windows, like elegant roses fighting through weeds and losing, not retained so much as not required in this round of demolition, but don't hold your breath. The city had vitality these days, everyone said so, and if that meant people rushing about bad-temperedly, then she would agree, but from the driven expressions on the faces she saw around her, she doubted if they took time to talk to each other in the street or on the buses these days. It was as though the citizens of her time had been conquered by another race entirely, Glasgow had been taken over by aliens.

Glasgow was a corruption of a Gaelic word meaning 'Dear, green place,' and coming in on the train earlier she had been surprised by the amount of greenery still around the city as it continued to expand and absorb what had once been villages on the outskirts, but once you arrived in the centre everything had been sacrificed to the all-powerful motor engine. Roads had been expanded with entire locations bulldozed to make it possible, and here and there, like spectres at the questionable feast, stood the remains of communities that had been swallowed up, evoking memories, and sadness that only memories were left. Paddy said she was just one of those people who disliked change of any kind, she was stuck in her ways and, anyway, he would say, pleased with himself, as she well knew, to her the glass was always half empty, whereas to him it was half full. 'The education some people get reading *Readers Digest* in the doctor's waiting room,' she sniffed. On that last visit some years ago, she had peered along George Street towards High Street, pleased for once that her old eyes had let her down and she couldn't see it clearly, and decided not to visit her old home, scared of what she might find. But now, thanks to Uncle Jakey, she was going back, even though she had no idea why, except that he was haunting her thoughts. Waking or sleeping she could see him standing there silently with Wee Dug at his feet, looking at her with his expressionless blue eyes and somehow she had to make him go back from whence he came. So what could she have told Paddy anyhow? That the ghost of her long-dead Uncle Jakey and his mongrel were calling her home? She thought it was mad herself. She had a fair idea what Paddy would have made of it.

Usually, if she was going to Glasgow, she would creep out of her flat as quietly and early as possible to avoid Paddy finding out what she was up to and come up with a convincing explanation for her absence afterwards. Sometimes it was worse than living next door to the Gestapo. This time, she would plan her journey better by creeping out while he was still asleep next door. When she arrived at Central Station she would heave herself onto the wee orangey bus and her creaking bones and dignity could go hang themselves, then would come the short hop and a jump from Queen Street Station to High Street, either by train again or by taxi – it was a straight run along to High Street, you could see it there at the end of George Street in the distance. How much could the fare be? One thing she hated was hanging about between trains, but she knew she couldn't walk the entire length of George Street.

She wondered how many pubs were still there, that was another reason not to walk along, even if she could, after the assault she knew would be inflicted by climbing on and off the wee orangey bus. Funny to think there was a time when she could run from High Street and all the way down George Street just to get to George Square. Funny to think she had ever run anywhere, come to think of it. But she had, sometimes with her best friend, Flora, other times alone. She still remembered the relief at getting past all the pubs in George Street, the nervous feeling in the pit of her stomach before she started out, then the joy at the end, tempered by dread at having to do it all again on the way home. Even if you had memorised closing times and carefully avoided them, there were always one or two men lying about outside. Either they had been thrown out or had run out of money and headed for home, but had got no further than the street outside, and they would lie there, vomiting and shouting incoherent abuse at passers-by. The drunks had always terrified Ruby. She hated those pubs and the fights and the fear as the men came staggering out en masse at closing times, ready to do who knew what terrible things to everyone, even a passing innocent child.

Once she had seen one man kick another in the stomach as he lay on the ground, already unconscious. In a panic and feeling sick she had run home and vomited on the stairs outside her flat. Her mother hadn't been best pleased, she remembered with a smile, it hadn't been her turn to do the stairs but was honour bound to clear up the mess her daughter had deposited there. All these years later she could still recall the sound of that kick, but it wasn't just the physical blow that had upset her, it was the atmosphere of violence mixed with the smell, the noise and the fact that drunk men were out of control, the knowledge that absolutely anything could happen. That feeling of drunken menace in the air had stayed with her all life. Drunk men were creatures she could not tolerate. Did not, in fact, as it turned out.

Flora, on the other hand, had never been fazed by the sight of the drunks at closing times. She could see her now, fair pigtails bouncing as she side-stepped the belligerent figures with a giggle. Flora had never been scared of anything in her entire life, never even been unsure of where she stood on any issue or been afraid of speaking out when others held their tongues. When they left school Ruby had worked in the paper shop down the road, but Flora had chosen to go into engineering because it was a challenge. She worked in a small private engineering shop in Paisley that her father, Ali McCreadie, a strong union man, had told her about. The owner was a brute who mainly employed women because they were cheap, efficient and didn't complain for fear of losing their jobs. They in turn worked for him because they needed the money and, knowing this, he did what he pleased with them. He banned them from speaking during working hours on pain of instant dismissal, frowned on them going to the toilet and timed them when they had to, and provided no heating, though the women had to work with their hands in cold water all the time. The business made small parts for car engines and Flora operated a capstan machine, making it her ambition to get a trade union established. That was Flora McCreadie, no windmill was too small or too big for her to tilt at, and she was the best friend Ruby ever had. Whenever she needed someone to talk to or a bit of sound advice, it was Flora she turned to.

When she arrived at Queen Street she saw a line of taxis and approached the first one. The driver glanced up at her, folded his newspaper, put it in his jacket pocket and shoved his pen behind his ear.

'Right, missus, I'm all yours,' he said, rubbing his hands together.

'Look, son,' she said to him, 'I want to get to High Street.'

'Well that's all right, missus, I'll stop and ask somebody for directions,' he replied cheekily, 'but I'm not going to get rich with you as a customer, am I? I mean, what happened to your legs, did they drop off or something?'

She glared at him, an insolent brute, she decided, far too smart-arsed and, on closer inspection, she noticed that his eyes were too close together. 'If I'd wanted a laugh I'd have picked the taxi with Jack Milroy at the wheel,' she said icily. 'What I want to know is how much it would cost to take me from here, along George Street and half way up the brae?'

'You can't get along George Street,' he said. 'You have to turn down Albion Street, along Ingram Street, back onto High Street and up to the brae.'

'But that's ridiculous! Why?'

'You've been away a wee while, I can tell. Welcome to Utopia, hen.' He indicated with his head towards the City Chambers. 'Blame them buggers,' he grinned, 'the wizards on the council.' Then he gazed skywards and rubbed his chin with a hand. 'Let me see now,' he said thoughtfully, 'what is it the day? It's either road works or this week's stab at one-way traffic, you lose track.'

'Well, how about along Cathedral Street and down High Street?' she asked.

'Aye, we could do that, but there's other drawbacks, hen. You can go along Cathedral Street, then you have to turn into Collins Street and into McLeod Street, brings you out opposite the Royal, then turn right. If you can get out with the traffic coming up Castle Street, that is. A black cab is a red rag to a bull as far as cars are concerned. We're a persecuted minority you know.'

'I can understand why,' she muttered sarcastically.

He glanced at her but didn't reply. 'Then, if they do let you out, it's turn right and down to the brae.'

'They negotiated the end of the War quicker than this is taking,' she protested. 'Does anybody here just get to where they want to go any longer?'

He screwed up his face in concentration, rubbing his chin again. 'Well, I heard tell somebody did once, 1987 I think it was, but I don't believe it. I think it was a mistake, a downright lie, or one of they urban myths. Anyway, the bottom line is it'll cost you about the same either way, and somehow I don't think you're the kind who'd cough up the spondulicks without a rammy, hen. You see the problem is that nothing's easy and nothing's cheap.' He stopped and looked at her.

'Is the philosophy and character assassination extra?' she asked.

'No,' he said, stony faced, 'it's all part of the service. So what do you think?'

'I'm still thinking, Einstein.'

'Tell you what, hen,' he said, taking his paper out of his pocket and his pen from behind his ear again, 'just take the train. It's not much of a walk from High Street Station to the brae.'

'I know how long it is,' she snapped back. 'I was born there.'

'Then you can walk down – up – memory lane at the same time. As they say, no experience in life is ever wasted. Tatty-bye now,' and with that he wound up his window again, his brow already furrowed as he resumed battle with *The Sun* crossword.

She climbed the stairs from the platform and turned right out of High Street Station, then stood for a moment to catch her breath, holding onto the railings with one hand and grasping her bag tightly to her with the other, in a pose she hoped passed for nonchalance rather than fear of passing bag-snatchers. Not a lot had changed really, she thought, looking around, not here, apart from the fear of bag-snatchers. The Goods Yard had gone, it was a car park now, but across from where it had been the College Bar still stood in all its black and white glory, a hangover from the days when Glasgow University had been there. Further up, towards the junction of George Street, Duke Street and the brae, the shops she had known were still shops, though not the ones she remembered. Within a few minutes she was looking at 252 High Street, right on the corner, the red sandstone tenement where she had been born and where she had grown up. She didn't remember it being so ornate, with its little turrets and carvings. The clock was still on the balcony outside her parents' bedroom window. Was that carved laurel wreath always there around it? And that wee face at the top, who or what was that? And she couldn't remember ever seeing the triumphant banner carved above, proclaiming 'City Improvement Trust. 1903,' though she supposed it must have been there when she was young, since it was part of the building. It must always be strange looking at your childhood home if you haven't seen it in many years and haven't kept up with the inevitable changes, she thought. Everyone who goes back in time says it all looks so much smaller, but High Street didn't, though it did look decidedly shabbier than when Ruby and the other McLeans lived there.

The Bell o' the Brae tenements had been built for the upper working class, for those who had solid and respectable trades or their own small businesses. They had been built with business premises on the ground floor and three residential storeys above, but the businesses now had a definite fly-by-night feel about them. Some were boarded up and even the ones with their windows intact were covered with tattered flyers advertising events and services long come and gone. What had once been bustling, busy shops and offices in envied positions looked now as though they changed hands regularly. There was nothing of permanence about them, as there had been in Ruby's day and, as everywhere else in the city, heavy traffic thundered past. Even so, the feeling of her family was so strong and vibrant that she thought she might see them if she turned her head quickly. This was solid McLean territory, their footsteps must be imprinted in every paving stone, the air must still resonate with the sadnesses and joys of their existences. And with that their voices came in a rush, like a warm wind in her ear, as though they were all shouting at her at the same time. In the clamour, Bea's voice pierced through everyone else's of course, that was only to be expected; it always had, like a shard of ice encased in molten lead. She thought for a moment. What, she wondered, would she say if she should meet her younger self? 'I'd tell her to run away and not to believe Gerry Reilly's lies!' she smiled ruefully.

Ian Fraser was waiting at the close mouth to introduce himself and show her into Jakey's first floor flat, where she stood at the window and looked down on the street below.

'That used to be David Scott's chemist across the road there,' she said softly. 'Old Doctor McGill's surgery was just down that lane on this side. You could always tell who'd been to see him by the angle they crossed the road to go to the chemist. When the bodysnatchers were taking bodies from the Ramshorn down in Albion Street, they took them to that same surgery. Different doctor, of course,' she said with a smile. 'All the kids loved the idea of it.'

He smiled back and nodded.

'And my sister Bea and her husband lived just up there, on the other side, you can't really see it, but we always knew she was there.' She turned towards him with a wry smile. 'She was a bit loud,' she explained. 'Everybody called her Big Bea, but she wasn't really that big, she just seemed it when she came at you shouting the odds. She had blazing red hair and eyes to match.'

'Not someone you'd like to meet on a dark night then?' he said.

'Or even on a bright day!' Ruby chuckled. 'Her husband was a passenger train driver.'

'Oh, the elite!' he laughed.

'Aye, he thought he was the bee's knees, but he was a wimp really. Never took a stand against Bea.'

'Sounds as though that might've been the wise thing to do!' he laughed again.

'A lot of folk thought that,' she replied. 'My Da wasn't a man for gossip, or even saying what he thought, but even he used to hint that he had moved through the links to driver too young, especially on passenger trains. People always suspected there had been funny handshakes behind it.'

23

'My father worked on the railways, too,' he said. 'In the sheds.'

'Oh, where did you live?'

'Springburn,' he replied.

'Ah,' she laughed, 'still part of the family but a foreign branch!'

'I worked for the railways once as well,' he said quietly, 'but in the office. I was in the part of admin that tried to do injured railwaymen out of compensation for injuries. I couldn't stick it, so I left.'

'Aye, they were good at that,' she sighed.

'I couldn't have looked my father in the eye,' he said quietly. 'He was one of those old-fashioned Communists, the most honest man I ever knew. I was brought up to recite the Ten Principles.' He laughed softly. 'Let me see. "All property is theft," though Marx just stole that one from a Frenchman, which is ironic when you think about it! I've never been able to buy anything that wasn't a staple of life without feeling guilty! When I bought my first flat I couldn't bring myself to tell my da. I kept picturing a look of disgust on his face and felt sick to my stomach. And "All good things are produced by labour, whoever enjoys them without working for them …"'

'… is stealing the bread of the workers,' Ruby intoned and they both laughed.

'You too?' he asked.

'You couldn't really avoid it in this area at the time,' Ruby said. 'And my best pal, Flora, lived down there in George Street. Her father, big Ali McCreadie was a Communist, the same kind of man as your Da.' She laughed. 'Every New Year the whole family stood at their window and sang "The Internationale", it was as much Ne'erday to us as "For Auld Lang Syne"! Flora was brought up never to forget her ideals, made sure nobody else did either, if you shopped anywhere but the Co-op she'd give you such a look! I'm sure she had her Co-op divi number etched into her heart! We went to the same school but she came in fifteen minutes later every day so that she missed prayers, I was always jealous of that. I could see her house from the corner window at 252, we used to shout across to each other, but once I moved higher up the brae I lost sight of her, she made sure I still heard her though!' She sighed, smiling.

'My father drove goods trains and my brother George was the Yard Master at the goods yard down the road. My Uncle Jakey, him that painted the murals,' she looked around without taking any of it in, 'he was a fly-shunter. And when I first got married I lived at 256. My husband was moving through the links to fireman.'

'A real railway family then,' he smiled.

'Aye, you know how it is.'

'So a wee fly-shunter did all this?' he asked, looking round. 'That's amazing! A hard old job, that,' he shook his head, 'running along, uncoupling wagons while they were moving.'

'Aye, I remember it well,' she agreed, 'the number of them that lost limbs. Jakey was an odd wee man, though, as I said. The railwaymen used to say he was fearless, but I've often wondered if it was just that he didn't quite take it in, if somehow he just didn't see the danger. It was just a job to him and he got on and did it. It never even seemed to register with him when some man got hurt.'

'The railways encouraged it, of course,' he said, 'time was money so anything that saved time was fine by them.'

Ruby nodded. 'Then they got out of compensating the men by saying it was against the rules, so it wasn't their responsibility.'

'Now you can see why I couldn't stick it,' he smiled sadly.

Ruby nodded. 'Aye, that was Uncle Jakey,' she sighed. The mental picture of him as he painted his masterpieces was so strong that she felt she could reach out and touch him, if he had ever allowed anyone to touch him that was. She looked round. 'There was a table, there,' she said, pointing. 'It was always piled high with paint and brushes and things and, while he painted, Wee Dug lay underneath. He went everywhere with Jakey, even to his work.' She laughed at the memory. 'And there was a big armchair just there. My mother had crocheted a thing, that was the only way you could ever describe her crochets, you never had any idea what it was when it started out, don't think she had either, it was just what she did to relax. Anyway, like everything else she did, it hadn't worked out just right. One of those square things, began with a few stitches in the middle then you increased the stitches and worked in stripes of whatever spare colours you had, and it just grew.' She looked at him and he nodded.

'I remember my mother making shawls like that,' he smiled. 'And covers for babies' cots and prams.'

'Aye, that's right,' she said, 'though my mother's efforts could never be called anything, they were just "Sarah's crochet things," as I say. But for some reason Jakey liked this one, even if it hadn't turned out exactly square. It had too many stitches on one side I think. She was never good at the maths part and, for some reason, never used a pattern. Maybe it was the colours he liked. Anyway, he used it as a blanket on his bed and sometimes you'd see it on the armchair and that meant he'd slept there the night before. And every now and again he used to go off for a few days when he was upset about something, and the only way you knew he had gone was that my mother's crochet thing was missing. He always took it with him.' She laughed self-consciously, afraid that she had said too much, wary of making Jakey sound like an imbecile. 'He was a strange wee man,' she said with a smile. 'He didn't talk to people much but he was happy enough. You'd hear him laughing to himself sometimes, like he had secret thoughts. He was fond of me when I was wee. I think he found kids easier to deal with than adults, they just accepted him without asking questions, and I was the youngest in the family. He used to write wee bits of poetry for my birthday, pinched my school jotters to do it, mind you. I was always getting into trouble from my teachers for the number of jotters I lost and I could hardly say my Uncle Jakey nicked them to write poems on. The most beautiful handwriting he had, copperplate I think it's called. Even as wee wean from my background I would look at it and know he was an artist, I really knew that.' She laughed, remembering. 'He left a will, you know,' she said.

'Did he have a lot to leave?' he asked. 'Apart from your mother's crochet thing, I mean?'

'That's why I'm laughing,' she said, and waved a hand around the room. 'This is all he had, but he left a will, though not an official one. He wrote out a note saying "I leave everything to my niece, Ruby," and got Tam McVicar, the local bobby, to sign it first. Then he took it to Betty Campbell who lived across the road there to sign it as well. It was the day before I got married, apparently. He left it with Betty and made her promise to keep it safe. Betty had no idea what was in his head, but she was a nice woman, she just put it in a drawer and kept his secret.' She sighed. 'Betty forgot all about it, she gave it to me years later and I never told him I had it. He left the thought and his lovely writing but nothing else, I didn't even get my mother's crochet thing, as it happened. It had gone!' She sighed. She had edited every detail of Uncle Jakey's death, she thought with a wry smile, including what became of her mother's crochet thing. 'I suppose it's the thought that counts, though, and the thought was enough for me, that's why I've kept it all these years. Worth nothing but worth the world, if you see what I mean. He was a great one for his secrets,' she laughed. 'When I was wee he used to hide sweeties in an old biscuit tin under a loose floorboard for me to find. It was our secret. A bit eccentric, always doing odd things that made people laugh. He didn't have much of a life though. People only see what they see, and nobody ever looks very deep, do they? Everybody has their own cares.'

There was a silence.

'Would you like me to leave you here for a wee while?' he suggested gently.

'If that would be okay, son.'

'No bother,' he said, looking at his watch. 'What I was thinking was that after you've had a wee look here, you might like to see where you and your family lived down the brae?'

'Och, son, that's awful kind of you!' she said. 'But are you sure you've got the time? I'm not being a bother?'

'No, no, not at all,' he said, with a wave of his hand. 'I've got people to see with all the work going on. There's nobody living at 252 at the moment, so I'll come back in half an hour. That okay?'

A kind boy, she thought, though he was probably a grandfather himself. It wasn't just the policemen who looked younger as you got older. Ruby looked out of the window again, mentally erasing the sight and the sound of the traffic. Across to the left there, above what in her day had been the old Co-op, was where Gus and Betty Campbell lived. Betty was a lady, that was the description that had always sprung to mind when she thought of Betty, small, dark, attractive and graceful, but he was horrible, though no one else in the family saw it, not then anyway. He was big and coarse with something of the beast about him; a tall, heavy set man with a large, fleshy face that leaned into you when he spoke, and all the time he watched everything that was going on with calculating, icy eyes that had just enough pale blue in them to avoid being colourless. He missed nothing. He was a fireman, but he had never advanced through the links to engine driver because he was colour blind. Funny, really, when you thought about it, that those all-seeing eyes, their glare so intense that you could almost feel them on you before you knew he was there, had let him down because they couldn't tell red for 'STOP' from green for 'GO'. Poetic justice, she had always thought.

The day after her wedding she remembered watching from the window of her new home as Gus Campbell came back from work. It was Fair Saturday when most of the city was on holiday, so the passenger railway services were busier than ever taking Glasgwegians 'doon the watter,' to the Clyde Coast for a day out, but Gus Campbell, like Harry McLean, worked on goods trains, so it was a case of business as usual for them. Earlier, she had been at her brother George's house in Parkhead with Gerry and on the way back he had gone to a pub to be stood a drink in honour of his marriage. The day before, Betty had left the party as Bea got into her stride and, knowing Gus wouldn't be at home, Ruby had salvaged a piece of wedding cake and taken it across to his wife.

'Oh, that was good of you,' Betty beamed. 'So how is married life?'

Ruby chuckled. 'So far so good!' she giggled, with one eye on the clock. 'I won't keep you, Mrs Campbell, I know you've got Gus's tea on. It smells great.' She gave an appreciative sniff.

'Aye, steak and kidney pie, his favourite,' Betty smiled. 'Gus likes his tea on the table the minute he comes in, and he deserves it after working all day.'

Standing at the window of her new home afterwards, watching for Gerry, she noticed a figure walking up the brae, Gus Campbell on his way home, carrying a bag along with his usual railwayman's bag. Instinctively she stepped back behind the curtains. Just as he reached his own close he turned and waved to someone further down on the opposite side, then he disappeared into the close to climb the stairs to his own home. She was surprised that he would wave to anyone or that anyone would want him to, but then she was the only one who disliked him at that time. To everyone else he was a friend and neighbour. Then she had crossed from the sitting room window to the kitchen, where she wrapped the top tier of her wedding cake in waxproof paper and placed it in a tin; it would be kept for the baby's christening. Looking at the remains of the bottom tier, the one that had been cut to offer to the guests, Ruby shook her head. There was plenty of fruitcake left over, but precious little marzipan and icing, the debris had Bea written all over it. Her sister's sweet tooth would be the death of her, she thought. 'How she can consume so much sugar and still be bitter as hell is beyond me,' she muttered, putting the crumbs in another bread wrapper to feed to the birds in the back green in the morning. 'And she has the cheek to complain about the odd upset stomach.' Then she went back to her mother's house, where Sarah was waiting for Harry to come home from work.

'Da must be running late. I just saw Gus Campbell going into his close,' Ruby remarked.

'Oh, Gus isn't working today,' Sarah smiled. 'He had a rest day owing. Here, set the table, will you?' She handed Ruby a pile of cutlery.

'Hey,' Ruby joked, 'I don't work here any more! How many?'

Sarah looked up from smoothing the cloth over the table and counted. 'There's your Da, me and Iris. She's been to the Shows. Are you staying?'

'Might as well,' Ruby shrugged.

'What about Gerry?'

'He went to see some pals,' Ruby smiled. 'He could be ages.'

'Well that's the four of us then. I don't suppose your Uncle Jakey will put in an appearance, but you could maybe take him up a bite when you go back to your place.' She stopped and chuckled. 'Your place!' she said. 'Sounds strange, doesn't it?'

'How do you think it sounds to me?' Ruby laughed back.

★

Standing here after all these years it still seemed like yesterday, she thought with a sigh. She had avoided looking round Jakey's flat too closely while the nice lad was there, but she couldn't put it off. It was what she had come here for after all, so taking a deep breath she turned and faced the walls. She had expected to feel emotional and was surprised at the overwhelming calm that swept over her. Jakey's paintings were as fresh as the day he had done them, the colours just as she remembered them. The workmen hadn't quite uncovered all of the murals, but she recognised the one Jakey had done of the Clyde, even with hard layers of wallpaper still hanging around the edges. Jakey had spent a lot of his time walking alone, except for Wee Dug, by the banks of the river. Sometimes he was gone for a couple of days. Funny to think that as she watched him re-create that scene when she was a child there was no portent of what was to come, but on the other hand, Jakey wouldn't have known himself. It was just a scene he liked. She remembered that before starting on one of his masterpieces she had to go through the ritual of finding a bar of Fry's Five Boys chocolate that he had hidden in the old biscuit tin under the floorboards. It never occurred to her to ask him why he did this. She was a child and children accept what they know. To Ruby he was just Uncle Jakey and that's what Uncle Jakey did. It was their secret and Uncle Jakey liked secrets. Besides, she knew if she did ask he would say 'A wee voice told me to,' tap the side of his nose twice with a finger and wink. That was his usual explanation of the inexplicable and his way of not replying to unwelcome questions. Folk would shake their heads at his latest escapade and say, 'That Jakey and his wee voices!' She would tear the wrapper from her bar of chocolate and settle down in silence to watch him paint, knowing from experience that conversation was pointless. When Jakey was working he heard and said nothing. Eventually she would hear her mother's voice calling her from an open window and she would leave without a word, knowing once again that Jakey wouldn't have heard her anyway; he was too engrossed in his painting. No chance of a mother's voice carrying these days, she mused, not above this traffic. She looked around, trying to remember where the loose floorboard had been, and paced about the frayed and soiled fitted carpet that hadn't been there in

Jakey's time, testing here and there, then laughed when something squeaked underfoot. Daft old biddy, she thought, even thinking it could be Jakey's old hiding place after all these years.

On another wall was a steam engine being driven through the countryside and she knew without examining it closely that every pipe, every valve was correct. He was a railwayman after all. And there were other, more fantastical scenes, of butterflies and insects too exotic to have ever lived, their wings covered in intricate designs and colourful patterns that were almost psychedelic, betraying an ordinary man with an extraordinary imagination as well as ability. And the thing was that no one who knew of Jakey's artwork thought there was anything odd about it. He was Jakey, he *was* odd. She shook her head, wondering how much different his life could have been if he had been born in another era, one that allowed his talent to be recognised and developed. But there were lots of people like that in the early decades of the twentieth century and beyond, she decided, who were educated far below their intelligence, or whose abilities, whose genius, were sacrificed to the need to make ends meet by doing exhausting physical labour for a pittance. She thought of Flora and how pleased her pal would have been at her recognition of the inequality of life for the working classes, and laughed to herself. It was a different world back then, in more ways than one, and she had to concede reluctantly that some progress was acceptable, even to an old biddy like herself.

There were no people in the paintings. She hadn't really noticed that before, though it didn't surprise her. Jakey didn't really like looking at people, not even in photographs. That had been one of his eccentricities. First of all, he had turned all his family pictures towards the wall or face down, then he had removed them and put them in a drawer, but as time went on he threw them out. He just got fed up with them, he said, and he knew what everybody looked like, so a wee voice had said 'Why bother having them cluttering up the place?' so out they went. After that, even neighbours with family photos on show noticed them disappearing after Jakey and Wee Dug had paid a visit and it became almost routine to remove them and put them in a safe place the moment he appeared. 'That Jakey,' they would say, 'he's a helluva character!'

'It's to do with him being an artist, I think,' Harry, Ruby's father, would say, putting down his evening paper and scratching around for an explanation of his brother's behaviour. 'I think he sees people as ugly.'

'Same as his thing about mirrors,' his wife, Sarah, would add, nodding her head from the other side of the fireplace, her mind on her latest awful piece of crochet work. 'He doesn't like to see himself reflected because he isn't as perfect as his paintings either.'

'Aye, that's it, Sarah,' Harry would say, content with this explanation, 'human beings aren't as nice as things he can paint, not even himself.'

Of course, by this time he had taken to removing other people's mirrors too, and Harry was constantly being approached by neighbours who wanted them back. 'It was a wedding present, Harry,' they would say almost apologetically, 'I'm sure your Jakey's got it, it went just after him and Wee Dug had been round. Just ask him for it, will you?' Not that Jakey came calling very often, but in those days families and neighbours were close and there were more shared social events. Jakey would put in an appearance and leave sooner than anyone else. Sometimes you only knew he had been there by the disappearance of some object. And Harry would do the necessary, with an occasional little hint to his artistic brother that one of these days somebody would give him a slap. But no one ever would, everyone knew that. It was just Jakey and his odd ways, he was a gentle soul, he meant no harm to anyone. Jakey wouldn't hurt a fly.

Sooner than she expected the lad was back.

'Quite something, aren't they?' he beamed. 'Must be strange seeing them again after all this time.'

'Aye, it is. In a way it's almost like I expect him to walk in and start doing another one. He used to forget to eat when he was working on his paintings. He was supposed to have his meals with my family down the road, but he didn't turn up very often, never one to feel at ease with people,' she smiled, 'not even us. Most nights my mother would send me up with his tea and something for Wee Dug, and he'd be so wrapped up in what he was doing that he didn't even notice me. I'd go back later for the dishes and find his tea still lying there, stone cold, but he always made sure Wee Dug was okay.'

'He didn't paint people though?'

For a moment she misunderstood and felt Jakey was being criticised. 'I don't think he was very interested in doing people,' she said, trying for casual rather than defensive. 'He was fine doing scenes and steam engines, but maybe he'd have needed some training to get people right. This,' she waved a hand around, 'came from him, you know, never had a lesson in his life.'

'No, I meant did he ever do portraits as well as his murals, portraits of the family, that kind of thing?'

'No, that's what I meant,' she lied, giving him her innocent old lady smile.

'He did the odd figure on his murals, right enough,' he said, walking over to the scene of the River Clyde, 'but not in much detail, not his forte, as you say.'

'Oh?' she asked, following him.

He pulled back a hanging lump of wallpaper. 'This looks to me like an Arab,' he said self-consciously, 'though it seems a bit out of place with the rest of his work, so maybe I'm seeing things.'

Ruby peered at it and laughed out loud, covering her mouth with her hand. 'It *is* an Arab! I'll maybe tell you that story one day!'

Then he pointed to the lowest part of the wall, right in the corner, at the bottom. Ruby bent to have a closer look, and saw two figures sitting on a bench on the bank of the river looking across the water. She looked again. Under the feet of one figure was a little bundle. 'My God!' she said, shocked. 'That's Wee Dug! And that's Jakey! And that's me!'

'Is it?'

'Aye!' She fumbled about in her bag for her reading glasses, put them on and examined the figures. Even from the back, one was unmistakably Jakey, his bunnet on his head, Wee Dug at his feet, and beside him was a small girl wearing a ruby-red dress, her legs dangling over the edge of the seat. 'That's me when I was wee!' The figures were looking towards the river so that their faces weren't visible and both had one hand resting on something small and dark between them. What was it? She straightened up in shock. The biscuit tin! You wouldn't have recognised it unless you already knew what it was, but Ruby remembered it so well from her childhood that she could conjure it up in her mind even without seeing it, with its black, red and gold willow pattern and its hinged lid. 'I've never seen that before,' she said quietly. 'He must've added the figures later.' She hurriedly took out a tissue, choking back a sob and the boy moved towards her. 'It's okay, son,' she said, blowing her nose, 'but now you see why I didn't want a photo taken! What a sight, eh?'

As they walked down to 252 at the corner of High Street and Duke Street, Ian Fraser said 'I never thought, but would you like to see round the flat at 262 where you lived when you got married? There are people living in it, but I'm sure they'd be happy to let you have a wee look.'

That was the last place she wanted to see again. She had deliberately averted her eyes as she passed it on her way up to Jakey's place, but she didn't want to discuss it. 'Och no, son,' she said, in a voice that sounded amazingly calm, even to her. 'I don't want to be disturbing people. It's not my home any longer, it's theirs.'

He nodded, probably relieved that he would be spared any more of her weepy old lady outbursts, she thought. Then, with a smile, he handed her the key to her childhood home at 252. 'I think you know the way,' he grinned, 'I'll call back for you in a wee while.'

'I was right!' she smiled to herself. 'The poor lad's scared!'

3

The house was bare, it had been stripped back to a shell, but even so she found herself stepping around things that were no longer there: her mother's display cabinet full of special things had been against that wall there; her sideboard against the other one, packed with tins of stuff during the War; and her father's chair had been by the fireside, beside a small table with the wireless on it. She remembered sitting there with her mother listening to Chamberlain's Declaration of War. When she was wee her father would come in from work and sit there while she removed his boots, then he would pad across to the hallway in his socks and take off his working clothes, layer by layer. She followed him with her eyes. First his bag and his cap, next his jacket, pausing to remove any loose change from the pockets and setting the coins down on the nearest surface. Then he undid his bib and brace overalls, first removing anything that might be in the big pocket at the front, and leaving the bib hanging from a thick leather belt round his waist, while yet more coins were taken from the side pockets and placed anywhere within reach. The scene was repeated every night, as he wandered back and forth, leaving little piles of cash wherever he had been, and following Sarah about the kitchen as they exchanged details of their respective days. Then he would head for their bedroom to remove the rest of his working clothes before going into the bathroom for a bath. The MacLean children had grown up with money lying about the place because of Harry's habit of emptying his pockets and leaving it behind. Eventually he found most of it again, but sometimes a little pile of coins would be discovered in some odd place and handed back to Harry, who would shrug, raise a quizzical eyebrow and put them in another pocket. Ruby looked towards Harry and Sarah's big bedroom with its bay windows overlooking the crossroads. Outside the window was a little balcony big enough for a child to stand on, then lean on the parapet with the clock at its centre. When she was small she would drag a chair to the window, climb out and yell to Flora, whose home was near enough in George Street to hear her and yell back. And while she was out there she would wave to neighbours and to the passengers on the trams as they passed by. When she was very young she thought they were looking at her, but they were looking at the time on the clock, and there was a little girl on eye level with them. Not that it mattered. They waved back to her, that was all she cared about, until the day a treacherous neighbour coming out of Cochrane's on the corner opposite had rushed up to tell Sarah. Ruby had been dragged back through the window by the arm and given a severe dressing down, ending with the inevitable 'Wait till your father comes home!' He was usually Da, but when an even more severe telling off was required all Das became 'your father'.

'Out on that wee balcony, she was,' Sarah told Harry. 'Anything could've happened. Have you ever heard the like? You'll have to see to her.'

'Och, she didn't come to any harm, Sarah,' Harry said, still divesting himself of the bits and pieces of his working day. Ruby had taken refuge in her usual hiding place, under the coats hung from hooks in the hallway. She was near enough to hear without being seen, she thought; it never occurred to her that her lower half was still visible and no one ever told her. Harry hung up his scarf and winked at her as she peered with one eye between the coats, then turned back towards the kitchen.

'But she could have,' Sarah protested, 'if she hadn't been seen.' There was a sudden silence before Sarah said accusingly 'You knew she did that, Harry McLean, didn't you?'

'She sometimes waves to me when I'm coming up the road from work,' Harry said. His casual tone was designed to indicate that all was well in the land, but there was also a hint in it of desperate and failed nonchalance, of impending doom.

'I thought she waited *at* the window for you,' Sarah replied, icy cool. 'Are you saying she was leaning over that balcony and you did nothing, Harry McLean? Your own daughter and you never thought she was in any danger?'

Harry wandered slowly back to the hall for his slippers, still clinging to a surface air of calm. 'Quick!' he whispered to Ruby. 'Give Flora a shout, get your skipping ropes and head for the back green till the coast's clear, and if you need anybody to play with you, I'm your man!'

As she slipped quietly out of the door she heard her mother still remonstrating with her father, accompanied by the sound of pots, pans and dishes being thumped down with more force than necessary, a feature of Sarah in a bad mood. Harry used to say he wished she would just bang doors, or better still, throw things. He had a chance to move a bit sharpish and maybe catch cups and saucers, even if he collected the odd bruise in the process, but they tended to break if she just banged them down, and broken dishes, unlike bruises, didn't heal. When it came time for bed Ruby was called up from the window, knowing that as always, the storm would have blown over. But she was never allowed onto the balcony again, if Sarah even heard the slightest suggestion of the chair being dragged across the lino towards the window she was there in a flash, and by the time Ruby was big enough to carry the chair she was also old enough to understand the danger, though she never forgave the neighbour.

She sighed. She had spent a lot of her time in this room once, she thought, looking around, placing people and reliving conversations. Her mother had died in this room. She had nursed her through those last months and when it was over she had laid her out with the help of Sarah's two sisters, Auntie Cissie and Auntie Dot – they wouldn't let any undertaker touch her; bathed her, washed her hair, changed her into her best clothes and put a dab of her favourite lavender water behind her ears and on her wrists. She had no idea why it had been so important to do it, it just was. The last thing she could do for Sarah, perhaps, a final service for her mother. It was only a room, a space but, as she stood there, she wondered if it was possible for something to be retained, imprinted, of the people who had lived there, of what had taken place in it over the years.

Then she laughed quietly and told herself off for being such a silly, fanciful old woman.

Just then the lad knocked on the door. A nice touch that, she thought.

'I'm really sorry,' he said, 'but it seems the workmen have to get in here after all. It's the electricians you see, if I lose them today I'll never get them back.'

'That's okay, son,' she smiled. 'I'll get out of your way.' The truth was that she suddenly felt drained, the whole thing had exhausted her. Funny how that happened as you got older, she always thought, you would expect to get more of a grip on your emotions, rather than losing it.

'I feel bad about this after telling you could have a good look,' the lad apologised again. 'How about I give you a call when the rewiring's done and you can come back? It should only take a week or so.'

She had been about to say it wasn't necessary, but she surprised herself by accepting. She didn't know why, maybe to make him feel better, or was that just an excuse?

'I'll give you a lift back to the station,' he smiled.

'Och, it's just a few steps down the road,' she protested.

'No, I mean the Central,' he said, looking at his watch. 'It's nearly two o'clock now, you'd be surprised how early the rush hour starts these days and we can't have you battling your way through the crowds.'

'If you've got time, son,' she smiled, though she knew it was an offer she had no intention of refusing.

He looked at his watch again. 'In fact, if you fancy it I could take you on a quick tour.'

Just up the road was where Bea and her husband, Dainty Davy, had lived, another tenement she didn't let her gaze linger on, and along from that, where High Street became Castle Street, stood the Barony Church.

'It belongs to Strathclyde University now,' Ian told her, 'it's their Students' Union,' and he laughed when she rolled her eyes.

She was pleased to see Provand's Lordship still standing on the left, remembering the row she had got for trying to fit inside the little wooden cradle in one of the rooms. On the right, the Royal Infirmary was still there, a place that came to play a big part in her life, and behind it Glasgow Cathedral and the Necropolis.

'That new building there,' he said, pointing, 'that's the Museum of Religious Life. It was built to look old, to fit in.'

'Pity nobody thought of that when they were vandalising the rest of the city,' she said. 'I used to work in the Royal,' she smiled. 'I used to go into the Necropolis in my lunch hour, I found it relaxing.'

'I always thought it was odd having a cemetery beside a hospital though,' he said.

'They used to put patients out on those balconies,' she smiled.

'Looking right into a cemetery?' he laughed. 'That was supposed to make them feel better?'

'It was supposed to give them fresh air,' Ruby replied. 'No chance of that now with all the traffic fumes.'

'Did you know there are deer roaming about in the Necropolis now?'

'Away!'

'Aye, right in the middle of the city. Odd, isn't it?'

As they passed the infirmary she thought that at least hadn't changed, it still stood there in all its gothic splendour, the sandstone still blackened by years of industrial pollution, though the industry that had caused it had long since disappeared. But when they reached further up Castle Street she saw the Lister Building was in a state of decay, the little figures set into the stone eaten away with the sandstone equivalent of leprosy.

'Look at it!' she said, shocked.

'I don't think they know what to do with it,' he explained, 'now that they've built the modern Royal round the corner up here.'

She closed her eyes. 'Don't tell me, let me guess, another slab of concrete?'

'How did you know?' he laughed.

'Is the Art Gallery still standing in Dumbarton Road?' she asked. 'I used to go there when I worked in the Western.'

'Aye, it's still there, and Kelvin Hall.'

'Well that's something, I suppose.'

'And the Western Infirmary, but they've built ...'

'Don't tell me, a modern bit onto it?'

He laughed and nodded and looked at his watch. 'Would you like to see them?'

'No, it's okay, son, I'll take your word for it. Maybe next time. Sometimes I think they'd be better knocking them down completely than building on these boxes, it looks so sad,' she replied, shaking her head.

Then he turned down Cathedral Street, now much altered, only the name had been retained, and drove through increasing traffic.

'I'll take you for a look at the Merchant City,' he said, 'you'll see a few changes there.'

'The what?'

'Round about the old Fruit Market and Candleriggs.'

'I recognise the Ramshorn and the Firemen's church,' she said, when they arrived, 'but where's the Fruit Market?'

'Moved to Blochairn,' he said.

'My God!' she sighed. 'When I was wee this place teemed with life, horses and carts, vans, people. And you could smell the fruit from streets away. What is it now?'

'Bars, restaurants, galleries and flats, they cost big bucks as well. This is where the rich folk live these days. You've heard of the Yuppies? They're called something else these days, but this is their stamping ground.'

Further along they passed the fire station.

'Where is it?'

'It's gone as well,' he said. 'It's bars, restaurants ...'

'... and flats. I get the picture.'

'I can tell you don't approve!' he chuckled.

'Just getting old, son,' she smiled wryly. 'I'm looking at this, but if I close my eyes I still see it as it was. I suppose I always will.'

Suddenly she felt oddly emotional, so she turned her head and looked out of the passenger window, blinking furiously without really seeing anything. Then they turned this way and that through the various failed attempts at traffic control, which meant meandering along those one way systems that had obviously been designed to increase journey times, no one could have got them so wrong by accident, she decided, until they came to Central Station. She thanked him and waved him off, looking round and realising that much of the city centre was as it had been, this area she still knew, and felt relieved that some of her memories were intact. It was still Glasgow, even if much of it wasn't the Glasgow she had known and kept in her mind.

On the train journey back to Largs she tried to block it all out of her mind for fear of doing something stupid like breaking down and looking a fool. Her head was full of so many memories and people she thought she had dealt with and consigned to the harmless past long ago, only now they were there in front of her, threatening her composure with a new intensity. For no reason that she could understand, the most disturbing thing of all was Jakey's little addition to his River Clyde scene; Wee Dug and the two figures with the biscuit tin between them. When had he done that and why?

She got home at 4 p.m. and before she could get the key in the yale lock Paddy almost bolted out of his flat.

'Where have you been?' he demanded.

'For Godsake, Paddy Keenan, you gave me a fright there!'

'And you gave me a fright,' he accused her. 'You could've been lying in there dead for all I knew. You never told me you were going away for the day.'

'Why the hell would I have to tell you that?' she demanded.

'Because when I came over with your *Daily Record* this morning and didn't get an answer I thought there might be something wrong with you,' he said.

'You usually put it through the letterbox if I'm not in, and how did you know I was away for the day anyhow?' she said suspiciously.

'Aye, well,' he replied, shuffling his feet, 'the postie said he saw you getting on a train this morning.'

'I swear to God,' she said sharply, 'is there nothing I can do that won't be noted down somewhere for questions to be asked later?'

'But you usually tell me if you're going away,' he whined.

'Not always, Paddy. Sometimes I'm daft enough to think I can please myself about when I come and go,' she snapped.

'Were you away seeing one of your ...' he wrinkled his nose to show his disapproval, '... dying people?' he asked. Paddy, like a lot

41

of people, was afraid of death, so if he mentioned it at all it was with a slightly contemptuous frown, to show it he wasn't afraid.

'If you mean the terminally ill,' she said snootily, 'then just say that.'

'Don't know why you want to be around them,' he shuddered slightly.

'Because somebody has to be with them, Paddy, that's why, and because I can.'

'There's something wrong with a body that wants to sit there reading to them hour after hour,' he muttered, 'it's morbid.'

'Well when your time comes I promise I won't read to you, you can count on that, Paddy Keenan!' she retorted, stepping inside her flat.

A long time ago she had learned to recognise loneliness, she saw it in Paddy the minute they met in fact. For Ruby, being alone meant enjoying her own company, but people were different and, to some, it meant being lonely. Paddy was one of those and she knew their sparring and banter kept him going; it meant there was someone there for him and with him. Working in the wards all those years ago she had realised that the worst loneliness of all came with terminal illness. As her life unfolded in ways she could never have imagined or planned, she discovered that death didn't frighten her and she was good with the terminally ill; there was no reason for it, it was just one of those skills that could have gone untapped, just as Jakey's had. She discovered that the dying often couldn't talk freely to relatives for fear of upsetting them, but they could to an outsider and, even after she had retired, she would sit with them and listen or read to them, if that was what they wanted.

She looked at Paddy again and, seeing his hurt expression, she said 'If you must know, I did go see to see an old friend who isn't very well in Glasgow.'

'Glasgow!' he shouted, eyes wide with hurt. 'You went to Glasgow without me, without even telling me?'

'Paddy, listen, son. It's a wee woman who has women's trouble,' – she knew that would shut him up, like most men of his genera-tion the mere mention of 'women's trouble', especially when said in a whisper with one hand to the side of the mouth, was enough to make him head for the hills – 'and you wouldn't have wanted to come with me, now would you? That's why I never told you, what was the point? I went there, had a wee visit and came straight back, okay? She had the operation, the first one, and that just made things worse, so they went back in again and …'

'Eh, well, that's okay,' he blustered, clearing his throat, 'you don't have to tell me, it will only upset you, Ruby. I thought you were a wee bit off last night, right enough.'

'It was just the thought of it, Paddy,' she said pathetically, bringing out her hankie to herald a possible attack of the weepies, a trick she found very useful against all men but, once again, particularly those of his generation. 'The poor soul doesn't deserve what she's going through, they took out …'

'No!' he replied, hurriedly, already turning back to his own flat. 'You don't have to go into detail for me, Ruby, as long as you're okay. That's all I was worried about, you know, and I see that you're fine.'

She fought to control her laughter. 'But look,' she said brightly, 'I brought you back an *Evening Times*, actually bought it in Glasgow for you.'

'Oh, that's lovely!' he said, suddenly beaming at her as he took the newspaper. 'All the way from Glasgow, eh? That was awful nice of you, it's bound to better than the ones we get here, isn't it?'

'Aye,' she thought, closing her door behind her, 'far better than the ones that come here on the train all the way from Glasgow.' She smiled. 'Men are such daft buggers!' she said to herself. 'I only wish I had known that years ago!'

4

It was over the Christmas and New Year of 1938 that Gerry and Ruby got together, though they had known each other all their lives. Christmas had never mattered much in Scotland. The Presbyterian mindset had long harboured a suspicion that there was a hint of Rome about it, and for most people even Christmas Day meant work as usual. Christmas was a time for children to be given an orange, an apple, and maybe a thrupenny bit. For adults, New Year was the big event north of the Border and always had been. By midnight on 31st December, all bills had to be paid or a debt-ridden year was sure to follow, and everyone in the house had to have a bath and don fresh clothes before the year was out. Whatever they took off was immediately washed, no home went into the New Year carrying dirt of any kind. In what was to be her last New Year as Miss Ruby McLean, though she had no idea of it, Ruby watched her mother doing what all the other women were doing, cleaning her house from top to bottom, then staying on alert by the fireside for the clock hand to creep towards five minutes to midnight. The fire had been allowed to almost burn out before twelve then the hot ashes had to be taken downstairs and emptied into the bins at the back of the tenement, for a new fire to be lit after the Bells. It was essential to go into the New Year with no ashes and a strong fire in the hearth. The traditional feast of sandwiches, steak pie and various cakes – shortbread, Black Bun, cherry, sultana and Madeira cake – had been prepared in advance, and in the dying seconds of the old year Sarah sat anxiously, duster in hand, in case a speck of dust should settle and blight her family and home for a whole year.

As 1938 became 1939, like every other Hogmanay that had ever happened, the men gathered at the Tolbooth to welcome in the New Year, cheering and singing when the Bells tolled. The boats on the River Clyde sounded their horns, while from the Goods Yard came the screeching sounds of train whistles in celebration. At the stroke of midnight, Flora's family in George Street opened their window and sang 'The Internationale' as usual. Even after Big Ali's death the rest of the McCreadies carried on the tradition in his memory. At the same time women everywhere threw open their windows to let the old year out and the new one in, shouting greetings across to each other. It was a memory that could reduce Ruby to tears for the rest of her life, the sound of the McCreadie's belting out the stirring old Communist anthem, mixed with the joyous sound of the women she had grown up among shouting 'Happy New Year!' their voices filling the cold air with their hopes and dreams. If they had clean homes and tidy finances, then Fate would smile upon them and allow their families to stay healthy, wealthy and wise during the twelve months to come. It was their desperate optimism that prompted her tears; the innocent, desperate optimism of those good, decent, selfless women, and their acceptance that the responsibility for their families' prospects lay on their shoulders. If she had known those New Years would never come again, she often thought, she would have fixed that last one in her mind, she would have looked around at every detail and memorised each one. But she didn't. Like the young of every generation she had simply accepted that life, as she knew it, would go on forever. Sarah would always be there, blue eyes shining, her once-reddish blonde hair twisted into a topknot of shining silver, smiling as she presided over her family and home. It had never occurred to Ruby to take a snapshot and keep it in her mind because she had no notion that it would ever end.

No door was closed to anyone at New Year, and dark-haired men were much in demand for the luck they brought to every household they first-footed. Ruby's older brother, George, was taller and darker than most, so from the age of fifteen every house in the vicinity waited for him to be their first foot over the door when he made his way back from the Tolbooth with the other men. Every year he groaned at the prospect, but there was no escape. That last year of celebrations before the War intervened, he had stopped off

45

at the Goods Yard to wish Happy New Year to the railwaymen who were working, including his father, Gus Campbell, the lovelorn Andy Morris and young Gerry Reilly from up the brae. They had walked home together to the McLean home, before George left alone to start his reluctant annual pilgrimage around the other tenements. He carried a lump of coal in hand 'so that your home will be warm throughout the coming year,' a piece of Black Bun, 'so that there will always be food on your table,' and a bottle of whisky, 'for good cheer.' At each house a nip had to be taken out of his bottle and a nip taken from the bottle kept in the house. George had no head for booze and never developed one, so by the time he got back every year any resentment over being the tallest, darkest man in the area had long since disappeared. An avid nature lover, it was the joke of the neighbourhood that when George was tipsy enough to start passing on delightful facts about bugs and things, it was time to send him on his way back to the party in his mother's house.

Gus Campbell from across the street had his own ritual, he went around kissing every woman he could lay hands on, except Ruby, who had suffered his wet lips at previous New Years and made herself scarce. He had a way of holding onto you by both wrists that seemed both affectionate and familiar, but was in fact painful and slightly threatening, his grasp too long and too tight to be on the right side of comfortable. Women would finally get clear of him, catch each other's eyes and grin wryly, while rubbing their wrists and wincing, as if to say 'That Gus, doesn't know his own strength, does he?' But Ruby had been convinced all her life that he did. When she was young she had been forced to put up with his massive paws on her and his horrible big face coming at her, because he was a family friend, but she was seventeen next birthday, old enough, she decided, to choose not to. She checked on where he was at one point and saw that her sister Iris was stuck with him and she laughed. 'Serves her right,' she thought, thinking of the number of men Iris had chased and the wives she had brought pain to. Then she caught sight of Andy Morris, watching Iris forlornly from the corner of the room and felt sorry for him, before her gaze fell on Gerry Reilly, the motherless boy from up the brae, a boy without a family. And that's when it had all started, Ruby remembered with a sigh, though for the life of her and after decades to think about it, she couldn't understand how or why. Maybe it was because she was feeling sorry for Andy but knew there was nothing she could do to help him, then her eyes had settled on Gerry, another lonely lad, and she thought maybe she could help him, if only by being kind and paying him some attention. Maternal instinct had a lot to answer for. Even so, she should have kept her good intentions at that level, but three months later she was pregnant. Pregnant and trapped.

After her visit back to where it had started, the days and nights, especially the nights, were difficult. Experience had taught her to control her thoughts and emotions by putting them in different compartments in her mind, it was the only way she could deal with them, one at a time. But after her visit to Glasgow they kept seeping out. She would be walking along the seafront to do her shopping, thinking about tea, milk and bread and, without any invitation, one of her family would be talking to her in her head. If she did manage to exert some determined control over them during the day, they lay in wait for her in her sleep. Wee Dug and the two figures sitting by the River Clyde, the legs of the little one dangling in mid-air, that was the first one she saw when she closed her eyes every night. Even those old stalwarts, Tony Hancock or Jon Pertwee, couldn't banish them. Then the others would appear, the Arab who became known to everyone as the Sheik of High Street, and the exotic butter-flies that danced through her thoughts at odd times. But always that scene came back, the two figures with the biscuit tin between them like some strange hieroglyphic that she felt she had to decipher. Sometimes in her dreams she would try to make them turn round so that she could see their faces – were they sad or happy? – but they remained resolutely with their backs to her. Jakey didn't like faces, she knew that, but why did he add the odd little quartet – Ruby, Jakey, Wee Dug and the biscuit tin – to his painting? Was he trying to say something? Maybe all the presence of the figures said was that Jakey liked being with his small niece and enjoyed their bond of the biscuit tin, but every time Ruby convinced herself of that explanation Jakey appeared in her mind again as though asking her to think a bit more.

And she dreamt about her home at 252, of walking round it again as an adult, but with everyone and everything as they had been when she was a child. Her parents' bedroom wasn't empty, as it had been when she went back that day. There was her mother's dressing table where it had always been, where she had often watched Sarah taking down her topknot and brushing her hair into a silver river that flowed down her back. She only kept it long because Harry loved it, she would say bashfully, but everyone knew it was her pride and joy. In the dream she sat down as she used to when she was small, and looked into the mirror, and suddenly it was her wedding day and there was her sister Bea behind her, arms crossed, looking self-righteous. She did a very good self-righteousness, Big Bea, you could say it was her natural stance.

When Ruby had discovered she was pregnant Bea had offered to set her up with a back-street abortionist, there were plenty about in the 1930s, and in her panic Ruby had hesitated for a second before shaking her head. It wasn't that she wanted a child at her age, or a husband, but she didn't want to be Bea's hostage for life either. Somehow she knew Bea would use it in some obscure way in her constant one-sided battle with their brother, George. Despite the age difference, Ruby and George had always been close and she sensed that Bea would use the situation to drive a wedge, however small, between them. If she had accepted Bea's offer of 'help' she would know something about Ruby that George could never know and probably would never want to. But even if he didn't, in the tortured recesses of Bea's mind there would still have been some kind of victory in 'being of help' in Ruby's situation, in knowing what George didn't. So Bea had taken Ruby's refusal as a snub. In some strange way it was one more thing to hold against the entirely unaware and unsuspecting George. In Bea's mind anyone who did not fall into line behind her at all times and on every issue was showing allegiance to George, even if it had nothing to do with George. It was mad but it had always been like that. On Ruby's wedding day the last thing she needed was to cross swords or words with Bea, but there was no way of avoiding it.

'I'm telling you now, lady,' Bea said, lips pursed, a perfect picture of triumphant hurt, there was nothing she liked better than for her good intentions to be spurned. 'You should've listened to me, I could've helped you.'

Ruby watched her in the mirror walking up and down, an imaginary army marching behind her. 'I know, Bea, I'm an ungrateful bitch,' she replied, fiddling with her hair.

'You're ruining your life, I'll tell you that now,' Bea told her, ignoring the note of sarcasm in Ruby's voice, determined not to be cheated of her moment.

'And it gives you no pleasure to tell me either, does it Bea?' Ruby said, concentrating on winding a rebellious ringlet around her finger. 'You're all heart.'

'Well, you're making a big mistake, but on your own head be it!' Bea said, throwing her arms wide, as though casting her wilful younger sister to the cruel winds of fate. She jabbed a stubby finger in her direction. 'Just remember that I tried to warn you, that's all!'

'And if I don't you'll be sure to remind me, Bea,' Ruby said. She waited, watching in the mirror as Bea crossed to the bedroom door, judging her moment carefully. 'Besides, we all make mistakes, Bea, don't we?' she smiled sweetly. 'I just hope I cope with mine as well as you cope with yours.'

Bea was a graceful woman in only one situation and this wasn't it. She spun round, nearly losing her balance, as Ruby knew she would. 'What do you mean by that?' she demanded. 'Are you saying something about me and my Davy?'

'Bea!' Ruby said, shocked. '*Is* there something to say about you and your Davy? Is there something I can help *you* with?'

As the door banged shut behind Bea, Ruby smiled. 'I'll pay for that later,' she thought, 'but it was worth it!' And pay for it later she did.

She woke up with a start and looked at the alarm clock, one of those that did so many things you didn't want it to do that you needed a degree in electronics to operate it, and therapy after you had read the instructions. It was coming up for 3 a.m. Why was she thinking about her wedding day again? That memory had been consigned to family history so long ago that she couldn't remember when she had last dragged it out to have a look at it, so long ago that it no longer even annoyed her but amused her. That whole day had been such a farce that she wondered how she could ever have taken it seriously, far less felt disappointment and anger.

After their little chat Bea had boycotted the actual wedding ceremony at St Mungo's. Instead, she had waited outside to make sure her disapproval had been duly noted by family, friends and the entire locality. She was wearing a green dress. 'Green for bile,' Ruby said under her breath as the wedding party passed her and Gerry laughed. At least they hadn't had to hear her voice inside the church. That little pleasure would come later. Once they had climbed into the car Gerry wound the window and threw a handful of coins out, and watching the waiting children eagerly pounce on 'the scramble', the thought struck Ruby that her new husband looked so boyish he should be taking part with them.

Walking back down the aisle moments earlier, magically transformed by Father O'Hanlon from a brazen hussy and a fallen woman into a respectable married matron, she nodded to Flora, who smiled at her and shook her head in exasperation at the same time. Being a Communist, Flora disapproved of marriage and of all religions, which ruled her out as Ruby's bridesmaid, so it was a mark of her affection for Ruby that she had ventured inside this place at all. Flora had been in full agreement with Bea that Ruby was ruining her life, though for different reasons.

'Do you really want to marry this daft boy?' she demanded when Ruby first told her.

'Flora, I'm expecting!' Ruby said frantically.

'Well that was just a stupid mistake. It's no reason to serve a life sentence, Ruby. Look at him, he's—' she put a hand on either side of her head as though trying to drag the right word out, '—well, he's gormless!'

'He's not that bad,' Ruby said quietly, 'he'll grow up.'

'So you'll have *two* weans to look after, is that what you mean?' Flora said scathingly. 'And you're marrying him at St Mungo's, agreeing to have your weans raised as Roman Catholics and you're not even one yourself! What's going on in your head, Ruby McLean?' she demanded archly.

'Gerry's religion means a lot to him,' Ruby shrugged.

'Oh, nonsense!' Flora replied. 'You know what they say about religion, that it's the opiate of the masses, designed to keep the serfs in their place. Well it's true in his case. He's just like the rest of the serfs, he doesn't believe, he just goes along with it because he doesn't have the intelligence to think for himself. It's not so much a conviction as a strong weakness. Just because you lay *with* him, Ruby, doesn't mean you should lie down in front of him completely!'

Ruby winced.

'Oh, Ruby!' Flora sighed heavily, a serious frown on her face. 'You've got a brain. Do you really think marriage is all you're fit for? Staying at home and looking after a man and a growing band of weans for the rest of your life? A man, *a boy,* you wouldn't have married except for circumstances, taking his ring and his name as though you were a cow branded by its owner?'

'But you know what a hard time children have without fathers,' Ruby cried.

'So that's why you're signing away your life is it?' Flora said softly, putting her arms around Ruby. 'So that this one won't be called a bastard, a meaningless name, by some idiot? Ruby, don't do it, please.'

Now, passing her in the chapel, Ruby returned her smile and gave a slight, helpless shrug and Flora nodded in return. Further down, on the other side of the aisle, she noticed the family double act of acid drops, her mother's two older sisters, Cissie and Dot. They were seated together near the back of the church, trading genteel insults as usual in the loud way the slightly deaf have, only this time their words reverberated around the old church for all to hear.

'I never thought it would happen to wee Ruby,' she heard Cissie say, every word echoing. 'She was always a nice clean wee thing. You know me, Dot, I never speak ill of someone if I can help it,'

'Oh, aye, we all know you, Cissie,' Dot muttered, searching in her paper bag of mint humbugs for the biggest one.

'But,' Cissie continued, 'I have to say that I always thought it should be their Iris that got caught, she's nothing but a whore, but there again, her kind know how to avoid it.'

'Well, you know what they say,' Dot boomed back, 'it's always the innocent ones it happens to. Sure, your Isa found that out.'

Cissie didn't respond directly to the barb. 'As you say, Dot, it's always the innocent ones,' she said gently, then she moved in for the kill, 'so it wasn't something that was ever likely to trouble any of *your* lassies, they were lucky in that respect, as every man in the district knew.' Before her sister could respond she added 'I wish you wouldn't get these minty things, Dot, they always make me belch.'

'Better out than in, Cissie that's what I always say, and better up than down.' Then, old stager that she was, she hesitated like a comedian setting up a punch-line, before adding with perfect timing, 'Though in your case, Cissie, we can never guarantee that, can we?'

And at the very back and well away from other people as ever, sat Uncle Jakey with his newly-shaven, blood-speckled face and, under his feet, Wee Dug.

Later, when Bea's retribution came and the shrieking started, Ruby, taking a leaf out of her father's book when unpleasant scenes threatened, left the sitting room and headed for her parents' bedroom. She sat on the bed and gazed out of the window, trying to ignore the mayhem she had left behind. The door opened.

'There you are!' Gerry said.

'Aye,' she smiled, 'here I am.'

'What's up?'

'What's up?' Ruby repeated. '*She's* up!'

'Och, it's just Bea, you know how she is,' he laughed, sitting on the bed beside her and putting an arm around her shoulders. 'Your Da's gone for a walk and Jakey's hiding in the bathroom.' He drew heavily on his Woodbine. 'You can set your clock by them,' he laughed. 'Now you're doing the same. You're some crowd, you McLeans.'

He looked so, well, young, she supposed, in his borrowed suit that was so big that it kept falling off his shoulders. 'Look at us,' she said sadly, 'what are we like? I'm not seventeen, you're not eighteen and here we are, wearing other peoples' clothes, married and a wean on the way.'

'You worry too much,' he told her, removing his arm to light another Woodbine. 'Sure, we were always going to get married anyway,

52

and so what if the wean's on the way a couple of months earlier than we planned? There's a lot of it about, you know.'

'Aye,' she sighed, 'but it's not exactly ideal, is it? We should've planned, that's the point, and we didn't.'

He put his free arm around her shoulder again and shook her gently. 'But look on the bright side,' he said encouragingly, 'we've got our own house. That's something most folk don't have when they're first married.'

'Aye, I suppose,' she said quietly.

And he was right; unlike most newly married couples they wouldn't be starting their life together in the bedroom of someone else's house. The minute Gerry and Ruby's shotgun wedding had been announced, his older sister married a widower from Duke Street who had been courting her for years, stopping only long enough to transfer the tenancy of 256 to the young couple. Agnes had raised Gerry after their parents died from TB when he was a baby, and she had taken her chance of freedom even faster than Gerry and Ruby had sacrificed theirs. Ruby laughed at the memory. Agnes seemed to have been there just long enough to apply the tricks of her trade as a seamstress to let out Iris's wedding dress so that it would fit the bride's expanding waistline. Then she had gone on to a life of her own without the slightest attempt to disguise her glee, so at least marrying Gerry had done something good for somebody.

'Well cheer up then, we'll be okay,' Gerry said, blowing tobacco smoke around her. She turned away, waving a hand in front of her, having discovered that the smell was one of her pregnancy aversions. The wedding ring on her finger caught her eye and she thought how odd it looked. The noise of raised voices was still coming from the sitting room.

'What started it this time?' Gerry laughed.

'Nothing needs to start it, she doesn't need a reason, you should know that by now,' Ruby laughed wryly.

'I think it was about George,' Gerry said.

'It's always about George, Gerry,' she replied, 'even when it isn't. Her excuse this time was that it was Dainty Davy's turn to sing and George had sung instead, so Davy had been insulted and if Davy was insulted, so was Bea. That's all it is though, an excuse, she's been planning it for ages. She's a selfish cow, her only enjoyment in life is to ruin everyone else's.'

'They're all going daft in there,' Gerry chuckled. 'Your Da and Jakey have bolted, your Ma's trying to stop the rammy, George is shouting at Big Bea to shut up, Iris is cowering in the corner, and old Cissie and Dot are having the time of their lives eating sweeties and tut-tutting.'

'Aye, they would,' Ruby laughed.

'Cissie and Dot,' Gerry laughed, 'they sound like a music hall turn at the Empire!'

'They *are* a music hall turn!' Ruby smiled. 'And I'll bet that big animal Gus Campbell's stuffing his face with as much food and drink as possible while he stares at what's going on.'

'You really don't like him, do you?' he chuckled. 'I can tell! But I can't see what it is about him that annoys you.'

'He's horrible,' Ruby shrugged. 'The way he leans into your face when he's talking to you, not that he talks, he yells and sprays you with spittle, and the way his eyes bulge, and he's always watching. That enough?' She shivered.

'It's just how he is,' Gerry laughed, 'he doesn't mean any harm.'

'I think he does, that's the point, he makes my skin crawl.'

Gerry shook his head. 'Anyway,' he said, changing the subject, 'I don't know what it is about your Bea and George, though,' he laughed.

'She's *not* my Bea,' she sniffed. 'And it's not about her *and* George or the rest of us, come to that,' Ruby corrected him. 'It's about her. We do nothing to her except breathe.'

'Aye, but she's some woman, isn't she?' he chuckled.

There it was again, that note of admiration that always annoyed her and, on this day of all days, she didn't want to be annoyed at Gerry. 'I think I'll go up the road, Gerry,' she said, getting up. 'The day's ruined and she'll go on for ages yet, and I'm a bit tired.'

He walked with her down the hallway to the front door. 'Are you not going to say cheerio to everybody?' he asked.

She noted the 'you', and realised Gerry had no intention of leaving the party. 'No, just tell them I'm feeling a wee bit tired,' she said, 'but you stay for a while if you like.'

'Aye, well, if you're sure then?' he said, already stepping backwards towards the sitting room.

Her heart fell slightly, even if she had given him the choice. 'Aye, on you go,' she smiled cheerfully. Then Uncle Jakey was coming down the hallway towards her from his hideaway, Wee Dug at his heels. Poor wee animal, she thought, he must be terrified with all that going on.

'That you away, hen?' Jakey asked.

'Aye, Uncle Jakey,' she said, 'it's been a long day and I can't stand that racket any longer.'

'What racket?' he asked innocently.

Ruby giggled. '*Her!*' she said, indicating with her head. 'Her and that voice of hers!'

Jakey looked around then turned back to face her. 'The thing about voices, Ruby hen,' he whispered, 'is knowing what ones to listen to and what ones to ignore,' and he tapped the side of his nose twice with his finger and winked.

Ruby laughed out loud. He was a wise soul, her Uncle Jakey. Then he surprised her by gently placing his hand on her cheek. Jakey didn't touch people and didn't like being touched.

'We were always good pals, you and me,' he said softly.

'We still are, Uncle Jakey!' she said earnestly. 'Just because I'm married doesn't mean you're not my Uncle Jakey.'

He shook his head sadly. 'Things change when wee people become big people,' he said.

With that he opened the front door and started down the stairs before she could reply and, by the time she had reached street level, he had vanished. She looked in every direction but Jakey and Wee Dug were nowhere to be seen. So she made her way to her first married home alone with tears on her cheeks, and wasn't sure whether they were for some half-understood sadness about Jakey's loneliness or the fact that her new husband had left her on her own on their wedding night. She was asleep when Gerry, dead drunk, was carried home by a crowd of merry neighbours and deposited in the marriage bed. Ruby had put a coat on over her nightdress when she heard them at the door, but when she saw Gus Campbell there she instinctively pulled it tightly around her. There it was again, that thing he did, fixing you with his eyes and holding the stare a little too long. When they had gone she put a basin on the floor at Gerry's side of the bed, just in case, and lay beside him, but making sure there was a distance between them. She dozed, the sound of his snoring keeping her sleep light, then she awoke fully in the dark with the acrid smell of cigarette smoke mixed with stale booze and vomit all around her. She got up and rushed to the bathroom, retching. This wasn't what she wanted, she thought desperately in the silence of the wee small hours. Flora had been right and so had Bea. She hadn't wanted to marry anyone, and certainly not this drunken man-boy. She hadn't wanted this life or this child, she was little more than a child herself. If anyone but Bea had offered her a way out she would have taken it, she knew that beyond a shadow of doubt and now she was stuck with the situation. Sitting on the cold lino of the bathroom floor she put her hands over her face and wept once more, suddenly feeling as lonely as Uncle Jakey himself.

5

Ruby dragged her mind back from the past, made herself some milky coffee and padded back to bed, hoping that this, combined with the sound of the waves lapping the shore, might lull her back to sleep. She blamed her parents, she thought, laughing to herself. Sarah and Harry had their usual disagreements, but Sarah was everything a mother should be, Harry was the same kind of father and their marriage was rock solid. A child growing up in that situation, surrounded by security, has no idea what the world is really like. She supposed that she, like her two sisters and her brother, had expected life to be as it had been with their parents; that they would marry and be happy and bring up equally contented, grounded children. Yet only George had managed it, George who had been the main focus of every tirade launched by Bea, was otherwise content. He was the Yard Master at the High Street Goods Yard. Everything that was hauled in or out by rail was his responsibility. That was how he had met his future wife. Marie's father owned a coffin-making business in Salamanca Street in Parkhead, and when a consignment of wood had gone missing for days Marie had chased it up with George, who found the wood and a wife. They moved to Salamanca Street, taking George well away from Bea, where they raised two daughters and were happy, which only added to Bea's inexplicable, fathomless ire.

And what to make of Bea and Dainty Davy, Ruby wondered? That was an enigma that had always puzzled everyone. Hard to believe, looking at the joyless Bea, but she was a fine dancer, that was Bea's great talent, though she had to take that to extremes too, no simple joy or even pleasure was ever allowed to creep into any aspect of Bea's life. She couldn't just enjoy dancing, she had gone in for competitions and had to win every one. More to the point, she had to flaunt her success in George's face as though she had beaten him, though George hadn't the slightest interest in dancing and was completely unimpressed by Bea's talent, which, of course, enraged Bea even more. Ruby shook her head. She could still see Bea's face, the determination, the complete lack of anything approaching happiness as she danced. The only difference from everyday Bea was that, as though by magic, her normal gracelessness was transformed on the dance floor, a woman who couldn't turn round without falling over became a thing of grace and beauty when the music played. Watching her dance you were transported and couldn't believe it was the same troublesome, vociferous Bea, until you looked at her face; that remained the same, unfortunately.

A local dance hall manager had hit on the wonderful idea of pairing her with another noted dancer, Davy White, Dainty Davy as he was known, a little man who was as vapid and characterless off the dance floor as Bea was vicious and loud, and something had clicked, as they say. Together they gave exhibition performances, portraying themselves as the products of the lessons of whichever dance hall paid them to do it, every one a lie, of course, but who was to know? And so Bea and Dainty Davy made money that allowed them to spend more time practising, and the more they practised the better they became. Soon they were champions of this and that, which in turn raised their value to the dance halls, until they cut out the middleman and started giving lessons themselves, thereby making even more money. Three times a week they hired a room from one of their former dance hall employers and with Betty Campbell, the odious Gus's nice wife playing the piano, they put their students through their paces, at the same time unwittingly discouraging them, because Bea and Dainty Davy danced so beautifully together that everyone watching despaired of ever matching them.

Eventually they married, though no one could ever remember anything approaching romance between them, so it was widely suspected to be a marriage of convenience for both of them. Besides, Dainty Davy had survived as a bachelor into his forties, so no one could understand what benefits he saw in marriage to Bea, nor, for that matter, could anyone understand what Bea saw in Davy, who was more than twenty years older than her. No one within the family made any comment about the age difference, because, Ruby supposed, they couldn't imagine anyone else ever wanting to marry Bea, given her poisonous personality. Yet, when you saw pictures of her, red hair, blue eyes and mouth still for once, perhaps with a transient smile coaxed out of her by a photographer of more than ordinary charm, you realised that she could be an attractive woman. Even when she wasn't actually screaming the odds her normal expression was one of angry discontentment, as she prepared for the battle yet to come. The aunties, of course, had their opinions, Cissie and Dot commented freely on everything.

'I suppose the thing was,' Cissie opined, 'when his mother died that created a vacancy for a housekeeper.'

'Can't imagine him having any other reason for hooking up with Bea,' Dot nodded.

'Or her with him, he's a right wee weed,' Cissie mused. 'His eyes are that deep set and nippy you wonder if he has any. A sign of a furtive nature, that.'

'All the better not to see her with!' Dot giggled. 'Though come to think of it, he'd be better with no ears, poor bugger.'

'Aye, everybody knows what Bea's like, but he's that furtive nobody knows what *he's* like,' Cissie said, warming to her theme. 'Mark my words, he's a sleekit wee bugger, and he's that old, you can't see what she sees in him, can you?'

'I don't think I'd like to get close enough to see!' Dot replied.

'And have you seen how he walks? No man walks like that, dancer or not, Dainty Davy right enough. I think there's something queer about that wee man.' Cissie shook her head, narrowed her eyes and held out her paper bag of sweets. 'Rosebud?'

'I wouldn't be surprised, Cissie!' Dot replied, and they both dissolved in giggles, flapping their hands at each other and wiping their eyes.

'But you can never tell, can you?' Cissie sighed, catching her breath. 'I mean the unlikeliest people get married and make the best of it, you see it all the time.'

'Aye, but their Bea,' Dot replied, 'I mean ...'

'And him ...' Cissie added, nodding, and the two old sisters shook their heads in unison and shuddered delightedly. 'But as you know better than most, Dot, who are we to judge?'

Dot stopped laughing and looked at her sister. 'What do you mean?' she demanded.

'Well, you know what they said when you married Danny.'

'What did they say?'

'That it would never work because he was too good for you, Dot,' Cissie smiled innocently, 'that give him a wee while and he'd be off with somebody better. But you proved them wrong, Dot. You brought him to your level without him even realising it, and the two of you have stood the test of time. These days you'd never know what he was like before he fell in with you, you've a lot to be proud of.'

Bea and Davy had no children, and whenever the topic arose George, the nature enthusiast, would cite examples from the insect world. The day after Gerry and Ruby were married, when they spent the afternoon at Salamanca Street with George and Marie and their family, the events of the previous day led to a discussion on Bea and Dainty Davy's situation.

'I read about it in a book, apparently there are some big spider females that eat the males during mating,' George said sourly, 'and there's a thing called a preying mantis that does the same, and when the young hatch they eat their brothers and sisters. I bet Davy knows about them too, any time Bea gets that look in her eye, I bet you anything Dainty Davy does a quick foxtrot out of reach. The wee man's probably never—'

At this point Marie intervened. 'The children, George McLean, young ears!' as everyone laughed. 'Say what you like about Bea, but she looks after Davy well, he's always perfectly turned out.'

'Aye, we all know that, Marie,' George smiled gently. 'She even presses his overalls.'

'She does not!' Marie gasped.

'She does!' George laughed. 'He's the only train driver I know who has fresh creases in the legs of his overalls every day. It's a great joke with the other men. He might be Dainty Davy to everybody else, but it's not exactly what the men call him!'

'Och, that's a shame in a way, George, maybe that's what Bea needs after all, a couple of kids to look after,' Marie said sadly.

'Isn't that what I've been saying? Isn't that what I'm driving at, woman?'

'We can see what you're driving at, George!' Marie chided him angrily, 'but there's no need to drive it home!' which made everyone laugh even more.

'I don't think wee Davy has ever driven it anywhere!'

'George!'

'What I mean is,' George sighed heavily, 'that wee Davy wouldn't have any problem getting an annulment, that's my guess.'

Marie shook her head disapprovingly. 'We all know perfectly well what you mean, any minute now and you'll be drawing diagrams for us, or would you prefer to do a mime?' Marie protested.

George jumped to his feet, laughing. 'Well, if you're sure?' he said.

'Och, behave yourself,' Marie replied. 'And you have to feel sorry for the woman, she has all that trouble with her stomach.'

'Aye, she's rotten in the guts,' George said, 'and the rest of her isn't too far behind.'

'Stop being horrible!' Marie whispered, checking on how closely her children were listening to the conversation. 'And as to the other matter, you have no idea what goes on behind closed doors.'

'Isn't that what I'm saying? I don't think *anything* goes on behind those closed doors!'

'I give up!' Marie shouted in exasperation. 'I'm not saying another word, and I suggest you don't either, George McLean, if you know what's good for you!'

Then there was Iris. What was anyone to make of Iris? A bit wild, that was what people usually said if they were being kind to her, no morals, an alley cat or, as they old aunties maintained, 'a whore.' All of it true. If there was a beauty among the McLeans it was certainly Iris though, gorgeous figure, beautiful eyes and cascades of chemically enhanced, perfect blonde curls. She worked on the cosmetic counter at Daly's, one of the bigger, higher class stores in Sauchiehall Street, an occupation that suited her perfectly. Iris could tell with one glance who was worth waiting upon – who had real money to spend – and who was to receive a dismissive, snooty glance – those with no money to spend and had just come in to browse and wish. She was also a fine advertisement for the cosmetic counter, her entire face was heavily made up like a film star and all her money went on keeping up with fashion. But she had no real need to earn money, she lived off whatever man she was seeing at the time and there were always men willing to indulge her, using money that should have gone to looking after their children, something Iris knew but didn't care about. Not that money changed hands, nothing as crude as that, but whatever Iris required was forthcoming. A whore once removed then. It was common knowledge that it had all started with the manager of the Co-op across the road when Iris was fourteen, but thereafter the delights of free bourbon creams were quickly overtaken and the manager – the *married* manager – was left behind without a second thought. She may have learned the wrong lessons, their Iris, but she picked them up fast, the lessons as well as the men.

When Ruby had been about eight or nine years old she had been shooed out to play by her mother, which meant something was about to happen that was judged not for her eyes or ears. Ruby knew from experience that these were usually the most interesting happenings or conversations, so she opened then closed the door without going out and tiptoed back to her usual place of concealment under the coats hanging in the hallway, and there she overheard a discussion between her mother and Iris. It must have been during or just after one of Iris's dalliances with someone else's man, the husband of a cousin, as it turned out, which explained why Sarah had intervened when normally she would have looked the other way and pretended it wasn't happening.

Iris was reading a movie magazine, *Screenland,* with Marlene Dietrich on the cover, a girl had to keep up with the newest, sexiest looks, after all.

'Your Auntie Cissie is really upset,' Sarah said quietly. 'I mean, Iris, this is her Isa's man. Why do you do this? Bad enough when it's someone outside the family, but him and Isa's got two kids.'

'Nothing to do with me,' Iris shrugged without looking up, flicking over the pages of her magazine.

'You mean it's not true?' Sarah's voice rose hopefully.

'What I'm saying, Mother,' Iris said very carefully, as though speaking to a child, and in an affected accent she had obviously heard somewhere, 'is that even if it is true, he's the one who married her, not me.'

'But she's your cousin!' Sarah cried plaintively. 'How can you do this to her?'

'You're not listening, Mother,' Iris replied with mock patience, and Ruby knew her eyes were rolling upwards. 'I'm doing nothing to Isa. If her man's playing around then that's up to him. *He's* doing it to Isa, not me.'

'If it wasn't for you he wouldn't be playing around!' Sarah said angrily.

'Ah, now that's where you're wrong. They can always find someone to play around with if that's how they're inclined.' Iris laughed out loud, trying for sophistication but sounding harsh. 'Anyway,' she said dismissively, 'Isa should be grateful it's me. At least this way she'll get him back. I don't want him.'

Ruby heard Iris throw down her magazine as she got up and the clicking of her high heels crossing the lino to the sitting room door, so she took a deep breath and held it, an exercise she always felt helped maintain her invisibility.

'And,' Iris said wearily over her shoulder as she passed Ruby, 'I don't know why Isa wants to hold onto him. He's nothing special, believe you me, though like all the rest he thinks he's Valentino. He falls short, Mother, very short, if you know what I mean.'

Iris collected her bag and, hips swaying, headed for the front door. When it closed behind her Ruby heard her mother crying quietly in the sitting room. She had never understood why Sarah wasn't more severe with Iris. Maybe it was embarrassment at having a whore for a daughter, maybe it was because she knew there was nothing she could do about her behaviour anyway. In her own way Iris was just as out of control as Bea, when you thought about it and, though she was quieter about it in terms of decibels, she certainly

63

caused as much mayhem among the neighbours, male as well as female. And even though in time she might get her comeuppance, sister or not, Ruby didn't think any punishment meted out to Iris could make up for the sum total of misery she had inflicted on other people throughout her colourful romantic career.

Then there was Gerry and herself, and their daughter. Ruby sighed. She didn't want to think about that. Her daughter's letter was still lying unopened in the old fruit bowl Sarah had won at the Glasgow Green fairground years ago, on the Monday after Ruby and Gerry got married, funnily enough. Ruby didn't even like it, a square piece of cheap orange lustre glass, and she had always hated the colour orange. She had only kept it when the house was broken up because it was Sarah's, though apparently it had become all the rage these days with collectors. She remembered Wee Ted, a teddy bear her father, a typical man when it came to giving presents, had won at another Fair Fortnight fairground long before Ruby was born and had given to her mother. Whenever a young McLean was ill they were allowed to have Wee Ted in bed with them for the duration. The orange bowl must be an adult version of Wee Ted, something belonging to her mother, she thought with a smile, that and Sarah's wedding ring on her right hand. And now the letter from her daughter was lying inside the bowl. Talk about bitter orange. It had been forwarded on from one previous address to another so many times before it reached her that she supposed her daughter would have given up expecting a reply, which was by no means certain even if had reached her at the first address. If the past, the distant past in this case, was anything to go by, it either contained a demand for money or it was an attempt to find out if the old dear had popped her clogs and there might be a few bawbees to collect.

Everything had been going along so well, her life was in balance, she was happy, or at least content, then suddenly, it seemed, it had been thrown into confusion on all sides. Her daughter causing turmoil, that she could understand; life had never been exactly easy where Frances had been concerned, but even after her pilgrimage back to High Street, Jakey was still there inside her head, looking at her. She reached across to the tape recorder and turned the cassette over. One day she must try listening to one of her tapes all the way through to find out how it ended. She had never heard the end of any of them, she always fell asleep long before they were finished. 'Let's hope the same thing happens now,' she thought, pressing the play button and settling back on her pillows.

6

The next morning, she busied herself making soup and when Paddy arrived with the *Daily Record,* she invited him in.

'I thought you might like some soup,' she said.

'What kind is it?' he asked. 'Is it from a tin?'

'No, it's my own,' she replied, 'what's the matter with you?'

'Your own chicken soup?'

'Aye, my own chicken soup. If that's not good enough for you,' she said testily, 'then just forget about it. I'm sorry I mentioned it.'

'No, no,' he grinned, 'you know I love your chicken soup, Ruby, it sticks to the ribs nicely!'

'Another compliment,' she muttered, working about the kitchen.

'You know what I mean, Ruby, you could dance on your chicken soup, it's a meal. I was just asking so that I could work out if I'd have to make anything to eat later, and now I know I won't. Not if I have your soup.'

She smiled grudgingly despite herself. It was true, no one could top her chicken soup, she was rubbish with every other kind but her chicken soup was spectacular. Seemed odd, given the years she had watched her mother cooking, that she hadn't picked up more of the knack, but there it was, she would have to be judged on her chicken soup alone. They sat down companionably at the little table by the window and she watched Paddy blowing on his spoonfuls then gulping them down anyway because he couldn't wait.

'Paddy,' she said, stirring her bowl. 'When you were married, were you happy?'

He looked up at her, his spoon suspended in mid-air. 'What in hell kind of question is that?' he asked. 'Is this what you wanted to

66

talk about the other day?' He was staring at her as though she had gone mad. 'Happiness?'

'No, I've forgotten what that was about,' she lied, 'I told you it wasn't important. I was just asking, that's all. You know how it is, you find yourself thinking.'

'Well I don't,' he said peevishly. 'If I ever feel a think coming on I do a crossword.' He sighed. 'I don't know, Ruby, you lure a person in here with soup and then you ask him a thing like that!'

'You don't need to get all embarrassed,' she laughed at him. 'It's possible to be a man and admit to being happy as well, you know. I'm not suggesting you like wearing a dress and stilettos or anything like that.'

He stuck out a large slippered foot. 'What? With these feet?' he demanded.

'They're nothing to boast about,' she replied, frowning, 'I'll grant you, but they'd look a damned sight better in a new pair of slippers.'

'There's nothing wrong with these ones,' he protested. 'What are you talking about, woman? These are fine, comfortable slippers!'

'They've got holes in them!' Ruby shouted back. 'If it wasn't for the holes there'd be nothing to hold them together! Your toes are so far through them all you can see are your big ugly bunions!'

Paddy put his spoon down in his bowl and shook his head. 'I don't know what the world's coming to,' he said forlornly. 'A man accepts an invitation to a bowl of soup and next thing his feet are being insulted and he's asked to discuss happiness.'

'Well, were you?' Ruby persisted.

'With Martha?'

'Well, Martha was your wife, wasn't she? Unless you had another one I know nothing about?'

'Oh, one was enough!' he muttered.

'So you weren't happy then?'

'I didn't say that,' he replied.

'As far as I can tell you haven't said anything.'

He sat staring silently into his bowl for a few moments. 'Aye,' he finally admitted, 'I was happy enough.'

'What does that mean?'

He shrugged. 'She was a good woman, a good wife, a good mother,' he smiled. 'How much more can you ask for?'

'But no thunderbolts, no fireworks?' Ruby asked.

'Och, Ruby,' he laughed at her, 'that only happens in films. Sure what would the likes of us do with thunderbolts and fireworks? It's enough to rub along as best you can and I suppose me and Martha managed that.'

'You make it sounds so romantic!' she sniffed. 'Wonder what it was like for poor Martha?'

Paddy shrugged and went back to his soup. 'She seemed happy enough as well,' he said, between spoonfuls.

'Did you ever ask her?' Ruby demanded.

'There you go again!' he muttered. 'Why would a man ask his wife a thing like that?'

'Oh, no reason,' Ruby said sarcastically. 'Heaven forfend!'

'And what about you?' Paddy asked, ignoring her tone. 'Were you happy then?'

'Oh, pretty much the same as yourself I suppose,' she smiled. Even though she was the one who had raised the question, she didn't want to go into detail. 'There weren't as many choices for us as there are now, nobody thought of soul mates in our day, did they?'

'No,' he laughed, 'we didn't go in for all that nonsense! But we got by without them, didn't we? And there were compensations, weren't there? I mean, I had my son and you had your daughter,' he hesitated for a second, 'even if you don't see much of her.'

'Probing!' she thought. 'Probing, and sneaky with it!' but she didn't rise to the bait immediately, she had learned well from the family acid drops. 'Aye, I suppose that's true,' she sighed wearily. 'I had a daughter.' Then she leaned over and smacked the back of his hand with her spoon. 'And it's not that I don't see much of her, if you must know, it's that I don't see anything of her and it suits me fine.'

'I wasn't being nosy,' Paddy replied primly, his attention returning to his soup.

'Aye you were!' Ruby said.

'But are you happy now?' he asked gently.

She waited a few moments before replying. 'I don't know, Paddy, that's the truth. I'm not sure I know what being happy means. How can you tell? I feel as though I'm just existing, that's about the size of it.'

'Aye, you're rubbing along, Ruby, just like the rest of us. What's wrong with that? Maybe that's happiness, did you ever think of that now?'

'Ach, away with you!' she sighed. 'It's just that recently I've been thinking about my family again for some reason and wondering what happened, how I ended up the way I am and where I am.'

'You mean not in Glasgow?'

Ruby laughed out loud. 'It's still the centre of the universe to you, isn't it? I don't know why you don't go back and live there!'

Paddy laughed back. 'I don't know anybody there now,' he said sadly. 'I came to Largs all those years ago after Martha died because my son and his wife offered me a home with them. Then they went off to Canada and I stayed here. They were good to me, helped me buy my wee flat.' He shrugged his shoulders. 'You know that feeling that you don't really belong anywhere any longer?'

She nodded. 'You could have gone with them to Canada, though,' she reminded him. 'They wanted you to go, you turned them down.'

Paddy shook his head. 'Largs is far enough away for me,' he smiled. 'I couldn't be bothered starting all over again in a faraway place at my age. At least from here I can nip back to Glasgow now and again, even if I don't really recognise it these days.'

'I know what you mean,' she said, looking at him. 'But it's gone, Paddy, the Glasgow we knew, it doesn't exist now.' There was a long silence, broken only by Paddy noisily slurping his soup.

'Dear God!' Ruby said. 'No wonder your son buggered off to Canada. He'll probably be looking around him at this very moment wherever he is and saying "Listen! My old man's eating soup in Largs." You're an uncouth creature, Paddy Keenan!'

Later, she turned the conversation over in her mind. Rubbing along, that was his definition of happiness, it was enough. But it wasn't, not for Ruby, it never had been, even though she had been forced by circumstances to settle for it and now she wondered why she had let it happen. What was it the papers called this mood? Mid-life crisis, that was it. At that rate she should expect to live till well into her 160s then. And she thought about the question she hadn't answered truthfully, about whether she had been happy in her marriage. The truth was that it was the worst mistake of her life. She had known that even before she had married Gerry, known it even as she protested otherwise to Flora. But that was what single, pregnant girls did in the 1930s, regardless of what Flora thought, they married pretty quickly or took the exit Bea had offered her. And having a slut for a sister had some influence as well, she worked that out long ago, she hadn't wanted to be tarred with Iris's brush. She had made one mistake and was prepared to face up to her responsibilities, she hadn't wanted to be known as Iris McLean's slut of a sister, one in the family was more than enough. A time machine, that was the answer, all this progress and technology blighting peoples' lives and no boffin had yet come up with a time machine. If she ever came across one she would jump at the chance to try it out, even if she did jar her old knees on landing. She would go back to New Year 1938, ignore Gerry Reilly and avoid the mess that had dictated her life thereafter, she wouldn't have to settle for just 'rubbing along'.

7

The child arrived at the end of January 1940, three weeks overdue. Old Doctor McGill had died the year before and there had been a succession of locums till his son, Donald, could take over the practice. Ruby had been in agony for a full day before a stand-in doctor could be found and it was discovered that her labour was obstructed, the child was the wrong way round with her spine against Ruby's. Afterwards she was told she had been lucky, normal delivery was impossible with the child in that position and the usual outcome was that the woman died with her baby. It was just luck that the family could afford the doctor and that he was skilled in the use of forceps. He had managed to grab the child's head, turn her and drag her into the world, and while her head would be misshapen for a few days, she was healthy. Looking at her for the first time Ruby wondered how much more trouble her daughter would cause. She had, after all, kicked so hard while in the womb that she had broken one of her mother's ribs. A portent of things to come, without a doubt.

When Flora arrived later, she looked at the baby, grimaced, looked away and said 'Have you heard? Bacon, butter and sweets have all been rationed.'

'Flora!'

'What? Oh, the baby thing? I was hoping you wouldn't ask,' she frowned.

'Why?' Ruby demanded. 'The doctor says her head will look okay in a few days.'

'Oh, it's not her head,' Flora said, glancing at the child again. 'She looks just like her father, she's ugly!'

'Flora!' Ruby exclaimed again, but then she laughed despite herself. She knew her friend didn't mean to hurt her, she always spoke the absolute truth as she saw it.

'I wonder what's next?' Flora mused, returning to the War again. 'Petrol first, now this. Your horrible old aunties will faint clean away when they hear about the sweets, won't they?'

'I'm sure they'll have a supply stockpiled,' Ruby smiled. 'My mother's been putting stuff away for the last year, we'll be able to open our own shop after the War.'

'Don't count your chickens, Ruby, it could be a long war.'

'Funny you should say that,' Ruby replied. 'My father and the others have built a chicken coop or whatever it's called, down in the back green beside the air raid shelter, so we'll have chickens and eggs.'

'As long as you take the chickens and eggs down into the shelter when the siren sounds,' Flora giggled. 'That ought to be fun to see, everyone dodging the bombs to round up squawking chickens!'

The two girls laughed, then Flora, wiping her eyes, looked at the baby.

'Look at the ugly wee thing,' she said quietly, 'fast asleep without a care and the world is exploding around her.' She looked up at Ruby, her face solemn. 'Well, you're trapped now, Ruby, hen. Rather you than me.'

Suddenly threatened by tears, Ruby changed the subject. 'So how's work?'

'Oh, I'm leaving that old sod in Paisley,' Flora replied, holding a hand up to block any discussion, 'and before you start, I know you'll say I'm deserting the struggle, but the struggle against the Nazis comes first for the duration.'

'Have you made any headway in Paisley?'

'None that I can see,' Flora sighed. 'The place is still so cold we have to break the ice before we can work. He doesn't allow us to say a word all day and he still won't hear of a union.'

'And you thought you could win him round!' Ruby laughed.

'Oh, I have a plan for him though!' Flora laughed. 'Just you wait!'

'So where are you going now?'

'Rolls Royce at Hillington, still a capstan operator, but working on parts for aircraft engines, doing *something*, Ruby.'

Ruby smiled, she had known Flora all her life and her eyes had always burned with belief. It was something she envied in a way. Now she was taking on the Nazis with full confidence that she would beat them.

Gerry was nowhere to be seen when his daughter arrived, the moment war was finally declared in September 1939 he had enlisted in the army. It had been brewing; Civil Defence preparations were already in progress and women everywhere had been encouraged to stockpile whatever they could, because there were bound to be shortages. Sarah had taken the advice seriously and there was scarcely a gap in the house, including under the beds, that hadn't been packed with tinned food, flour and sugar. 'If I bounce on my own bed,' Harry would joke, 'I land on tins of soup or garden peas!' So the entire country had been waiting for the declaration since the turn of the year and hoping it wouldn't come, all except Gerry Reilly, who had stated from the outset that he would join up the minute the off was sounded.

And sound it did, on a Sunday morning at the beginning of September 1939. For railwaymen, Sunday was just another day and the ones in the family were at work, so Ruby sat in her father's chair by the radio with her mother on the other side of the fire and together they listened fearfully to Chamberlain, aware that at 11.15 a.m. life had changed forever but not sure how or what would happen next. The entire country had been subject to blackout conditions two days before Chamberlain's announcement, but even so, everyone hoped it was a bit of sabre-rattling, a demonstration to the Germans that Britain was ready to take them on, to make Germany back off.

If Ruby had been looking at her mother she would have seen her eyes cloud over. Sarah and Harry weren't married when the men in her life had gone off to fight in the First World War. It marked a time of turmoil in her life that she tried not to think about, though sometimes it still came back to haunt her dreams. The patriotic swellings had been more intense in WWI and Harry had been among the first to go and, being young, Sarah saw it as abandonment and swore they were finished forever. Jakey went too, within days of Harry, and finally her only brother had enlisted. It was three years before she saw Harry again and they had married shortly afterwards. The War had changed him, made him more responsible and given him ambition. He handed over his half of his father's carter business to his brother Jakey and applied himself. He wanted to raise a family and for that he needed secure employment, something with prospects of advancement. So he joined the railway, starting out as a cleaner, and working his way through the links to fireman then engine driver. He drove goods engines, he never reached the pinnacle of commanding passenger locos, but he was content to have reached his own pinnacle. After the War, Jakey eventually gave up the old horse and cart too, but unlike Harry he just drifted, finally getting into the railways as a fly-shunter when Harry put in a word for him.

Sarah's brother, though, never came back. She put a hand across the middle of her chest, grasping her heart, remembering. Her parents were already long gone, so the telegram boy brought the message to her and she had stood there, staring at the envelop stupidly, knowing what it contained but scared to open it all the same. She could still feel the pain in her chest under where her hand was now resting, it had never gone away, it had only dimmed to a manageable level. His body had never been found, leaving the cruel, illogical yearning that one day he might walk through the door, large as life. Hope against hope, Sarah knew all about that, and even naming her only son George after her brother hadn't eased the gaping pain of losing him. Now here it was again, like some vicious circle that couldn't be broken, another war, and against the same enemy. As Chamberlain droned on Sarah did a mental calculation. Harry and Jakey were too old to be called up and George's essential job would keep him out of the forces, one George at least wouldn't lie forever in a corner of some foreign field, but Ruby had whispered 'Gerry will join up!' then fallen silent. Sarah looked across the hearth at her youngest daughter, only weeks married with a child on the way, and was so scared for her that her hand climbed higher and grasped her throat to stop a sob escaping. What she didn't know – how could she? – was that her youngest daughter had mixed feelings about her husband disappearing into battle.

By the time the men came home from work they too had heard the news. Harry McLean, a man who rarely voiced a thought far less an opinion, said he was glad he hadn't heard the announcement and would've switched the radio off anyway. He had, he said quietly, before retiring behind his newspaper in silence for the rest of the night, no wish to hear that idiot Chamberlain's voice. Harry had been through one war, he knew the brutal reality and could not forgive any of it, but Gerry's boyish face was alight with excitement. Working on the railways was regarded, at the start of the War as a reserved occupation, and even if railwaymen had been allowed to join up, the best they could hope for was to be sent somewhere else to work on some other railway.

So next morning Gerry and Andy Morris went to a recruiting station on the other side of Glasgow and volunteered, Gerry as an unskilled and unspecified cleaner and Andy as an office clerk, hoping that in the chaos no one would check up. They joined the 2nd Battalion Highland Light Infantry, that peculiarly Glasgow regiment with the hard-fighting, resilient reputation that the city identified with so closely. The men of the HLI were said by the other armed forces to be 'fearless in battle and in bars across the world, while showing prowess in the Dark Arts: thievery, piracy, smuggling and general lawlessness;' descriptions probably intended as insults but seized on with pride by Glasgow. Everyone knew Andy joined up to impress Iris, just as they knew Iris had forgotten he existed, but Gerry was a boy full of patriotic vigour, as most were at that point. He wanted to get at the Hun and, doubtless, he wanted an escape route out of the life that had happened to him, that of a teenage husband and father. More than anything he wanted adventure and he thought he would get it with a gun in his hands, even if there were others pointed at him.

And what had Ruby really thought of that? Well, the truth was that she was upset and relieved in equal measure. On one hand there was the feeling that he had got her into this situation and now he was leaving her to it, and on the other she would have her life to herself again, apart from the child, of course. The fact that he was indeed a boy had become increasingly apparent to her in the lead up to the wedding, as Flora had pointed out and, during their few weeks together before he enlisted, her worries had grown. In many ways, the important ways, Ruby came to recognise that she was much older than he was, and that made her more anxious. But there again, she was a very young first-time mother-to-be, she told herself, her life had changed drastically in a very short time, anxiety was only to be expected in her situation.

They lived in a culture where men drank heavily, though the men in her family never had, neither her father, Uncle Jakey nor George had a head for it. Maybe that was part of the problem, a thought she had mulled over countless times since, the fact that she was young with too little experience of the world outside life with the McLeans in High Street, and so expected all men to be like the McLean men. That was what Gerry said, anyway, that all men drank if they could, and he was a man, it wasn't his fault if the McLean men weren't. And besides, he would challenge her, when had he missed a day's work through drink? And he hadn't, that was true, but she knew he had often gone to work still drunk from the night before. She saw that he defended himself in the petulant tones of a child who knew, but couldn't admit, he had been caught out and was guilty as charged, and she realised that he couldn't discuss anything as an adult, though he demanded the right to drink like one. There was no reasoning with him though, and she didn't know what to do about it. She couldn't admit defeat so early in her marriage, not even to Flora, and she could just hear Bea's crowing if she found out. Nor did she want to worry her mother, who already had to cope with the outbursts of one daughter and the conse-quences of another's habitual immorality, so she waited and hoped alone. Looking back, she accepted that she knew even then that she, too, was hoping against hope, a family trait inherited from her mother, or maybe just one shared with women in certain situations through the ages. In those early weeks of marriage she would wait for Gerry to come home, meal ready, and when he eventually arrived the meal was ruined and he was too drunk to eat it anyhow. Every night repeated the pattern of her wedding night in that she lay beside an unconscious boy. Indeed, if she hadn't already been pregnant she could have had her marriage annulled. That thought made her smile wryly. According to George, Bea and Dainty Davy could have qualified for that too. Strange bedfellows indeed.

When men finished work they headed for the nearest pub, it was their tradition, and who would deny a man a little relaxation at the end of his daily toils? But Gerry didn't go in for a quick one, nor was he just slightly tipsy occasionally when he left the pub or, she suspected, pubs. Every night he arrived home with the help of friends and neighbours, or he crawled upstairs, falling down, disgustingly drunk. Sitting by herself waiting for him to come home, Ruby wondered if she had seen him entirely sober once since they were children playing in the back green. He had been drinking when they got together at New Year, and she knew for a fact that he was slightly merry when they conceived the child a few short months later, too. Sitting alone on those evenings, she began to wonder at the speed his older sister had taken to her heels when she heard Gerry and Ruby would have to get married. Having raised him, Agnes would have expected the role of mother to come to an end when he became a man. She must have yearned for the day he became independent so that she could lead her own life and, not that she had ever confided in Ruby, she could imagine Agnes's dark fears as she watched this get further and further away as his drinking got out of hand. No wonder she had been so delighted to hand over the house to them and go, and who could blame her? Ruby hadn't wanted this marriage and she suspected that Gerry hadn't wanted it either, they were both trapped, but she was at least trying to make it one, while Gerry wanted to go on as he had before, even with fatherhood looming. So when war became a reality and he joined the army she was no longer waiting to see what would happen next, wondering when he would be home and in what state. At least now she knew where she stood.

As soon as war was declared, existing plans for the evacuation of city children to the countryside swung into action. Some parents refused to let their children go, including George and Marie McLean, but shortly after Glasgow was a largely child-free zone. They left with labels around their necks and carrying their suitcases and gas masks, leaving weeping mothers, aunts and grandmothers waving forlornly on station platforms, to be met at the end of their journeys with sometimes kindness and other times downright cruelty. In common with other cities and towns, though, when the Germans failed to invade or bomb, the children began to return, most of them relieved to leave the alien countryside behind. It was the year of the dummy war, when German planes flew overhead on reconnaissance missions, taking aerial photos of future targets. Everyone knew they were German and eyed them suspiciously, but even though they still dutifully carried their gas masks and headed for the shelters when the sirens sounded, they soon stopped expecting bombs.

At the outbreak of war the men of the existing 2nd Battalion HLI were already in Palestine and had then been posted to Egypt. Gerry and the other fresh recruits were being shipped out to join them, but before that they were allowed embarkation leave. For Gerry this coincided with the week following the birth of his daughter, for Andy it meant a last look at Iris and, perhaps, a chance to make her his again. They both looked different, Ruby thought. Gerry wore kilt and spats while Andy was dressed in the more sober khaki battledress, and there was an indefinable something about their bearing. Gerry was openly disappointed he didn't have a son, but announced, to the approving laughter of all, that they would manage that next time. The little girl was to be called Frances, after the mother he had never really known, and with that he departed to wet the baby's head and be stood several rounds in honour of his impending posting to some battlefield. Who could deny a man either?

Before the two boys went back to barracks, Sarah had left Gerry and Ruby alone together with their daughter to say their goodbyes, while Andy paced anxiously about the sitting room, waiting for a final glimpse of Iris that never came. In the bedroom, that something Ruby had noticed when Gerry arrived was still between them. He made an attempt at an embrace that died of embarrassment and ended up as a stiff, self-conscious hug. 'See and look after yourself,' he smiled, and looking at the sleeping child he added, 'and the wee one.' Then he left and, as she watched him from the bay windows of Sarah and Harry's bedroom, she laughed quietly to herself. The

HLI men, 'the Jimmies', were notorious. 'Never discuss religion or football with them,' ran one piece of advice about the HLI, 'never leave your kit unattended around them, and never loan them money.' Gerry was swaggering down the road beside Andy, kilt swinging, the Glasgow word for it was 'gallus' and Gerry was living up to every nuance of it, beside an altogether more sombre Andy. Maybe the army would be good for him, she thought, maybe he'll come back a man, if he comes back at all. She watched till she couldn't see them, but the only one who turned round for a last look was Andy, and she didn't know if the feeling she had was disappoint- ment that Gerry hadn't looked round or sadness that Andy had.

Years later she discovered that Gerry shouldn't have been wearing the kilt; apart from the territorials and bandsmen the HLI didn't wear the kilt then. Gerry had borrowed it to wear for effect. Said it all, really.

When Frances was christened in St Mungo's Flora refused to attend. It was just too much, she said, to expect her to witness the corruption of an innocent child's mind, even if she was ugly and looked like her father. Gerry's sister, Agnes, was the child's godmother, and George, who had turned religions to marry Marie, was her godfather, so Ruby knew Bea wouldn't turn up; knew, too, that once again there would be hell to pay later. Uncle Jakey wasn't there this time either, but they knew he had been. The church was full of huge statues of saints, Sacred Hearts, Virgin Marys and various others Ruby didn't recognise, all with their own racks of candles in front for the faithful to buy and light as a means of asking for help or a favour. But the statues had been turned round so that they faced away from the congregation and their candles. In fact, there were no candles, the racks were empty, and everyone who knew Jakey exchanged glances and tried to muffle their laughter. It could only have been Jakey, but how had he managed to move such heavy objects? The reason why he had done it was easy, Jakey didn't like faces, everyone knew that, and Ruby suddenly remembered him looking round the church so intently on her wedding day that he hadn't noticed her and Gerry passing him. He had been looking at the statues, she knew that now, and he had been chuckling quietly, if she wasn't mistaken. She glanced at Father O'Hanlon, the priest carrying out the baptism, and was astounded to see that he was pretending not to notice what had happened or to hear the laughter rippling then echoing round the congregation. She couldn't make up her mind which was the more bizarre behaviour: Jakey or the priest. Or the aunties, come to that.

'That's their Jakey, sure as God!' Dot boomed.

'You know me, Dot,' Cissie replied just as loudly.

'Aye, I know you, Cissie,'

'If you've nothing nice to say, say nothing, that's what I always say,'

'Aye, that's what you always say, Cissie,'

'But yon Jakey's not right in the head,' Cissie yelled. 'Daft bugger!'

'One of these days somebody'll sort him out, you mark my words,' Dot stated, warming to their shared theme, something both sisters excelled at with little need for encouragement.

'And that dog of his smells,' Cissie stated.

'Now how in hell do you know it's the dog? Sure their Jakey's always smelt. You could be maligning the poor wee dog there, Cissie.'

'Aye, right enough,' Cissie conceded.

'You should pay Jakey a wee visit, Cissie, see if you can't help him.'

'Why me?' Cissie demanded.

'Well everybody knows that laddie of yours isn't the full shilling either. Anybody but you would've put him away somewhere years ago, but you were a good mother, Cissie, and you manage him well with whatever pills you have him on.'

'My Sammy's not on any pills!' Cissie shouted, getting unsteadily to her feet.

'Is he off them now?' Dot smiled happily, popping a pear drop into her mouth. 'That's smashing, so it is. See what I mean, Cissie? You've managed your Sammy over his daft patch, and I never believed for a minute he was on the booze, by the way,' she patted her irate sister's arm. 'I've always stood up for him, Cissie,' she said piously. 'The number of times I've said to people 'Our Cissie's Sammy is not a drunk, he's just a bit soft in the head!' You could do wonders like that for their Jakey, whether it's drink with him or just plain daftness as well, so you could!'

Later, Ruby heard from her sister-in-law that Father O'Hanlon had muttered to her that he had no idea who could've done such a thing to the statues, though someone had mentioned seeing a little man in a bunnet with a wee dog in the vicinity earlier that morning.

Ruby nodded. 'Do you think he was hinting?' she asked innocently. 'Anyway, that's a description that could cover most men in Glasgow, bunnets and wee dogs.'

'Aye,' Agnes replied seriously, looking Ruby in the eye, 'that's what I thought. Could've been anybody. And how could one wee man and Wee D— and one wee dog, have managed that on their own?'

'Exactly,' Ruby said. 'The man's imagining things.'

Bea's performance was eagerly awaited back at Sarah and Harry's flat, or at least awaited, and in due course it was time for curtain up. The last stramash was caused, nominally at least, by George singing instead of Dainty Davy, but there was no preamble about this one, no pretence. At a certain point of her own choosing, Bea simply got up and screamed abuse at everyone within ear- or fist-shot. It was a sight to behold once again, Ruby thought, calmly watching Bea being held back, though everyone knew it was a sham. Bea could've taken on the whole crowd of them with one hand tied behind her back and hopping on one leg, had she wanted to, but she hadn't. As ever, all she wanted was to be the object of everyone's attention. If you didn't admire Bea – and Ruby didn't – you had to admire how she judged the level of noise and violence to get the balance just right. It was all so boringly familiar, the raucous screams, the arm-waving, the redness of her face matching the once whites of her eyes. Ruby shook her head at Agnes, who had taken the diplomatic decision to send her husband home after the church ceremony. He wasn't one of them, he had never witnessed a McLean family gathering and, Agnes had decided wisely, there was no reason to inflict this one on him. Ruby saw no reason to inflict it on herself either, so she got up to check on the baby sleeping in the bedroom. Then, from nowhere a bombshell was delivered.

'I'm expecting,' said a voice.

For an instant everyone stood still and silent before heads swung

81

as one to look in the direction of the voice, at Iris, who was sitting in a corner of the room. Everyone had their individual reactions and trains of thought. Sarah, who had been holding onto one of Bea's arms, let go, dropped into a chair and wept quietly. Instantly she knew that from her own and from the family's point of view, this was worse than Ruby being pregnant. With Ruby they were all sure that marriage to the father would follow swiftly, but where Iris was concerned there would be a list of suspects the length of numerous arms to choose from, none of whom would be in a position to marry her, none of whom Iris would have married either. Ruby carried on to the bedroom, her mind making several calculations based on her knowledge of her sister. Iris wouldn't be pregnant if she didn't want to be, of that she was sure, if she was stupid or unlucky enough to find herself in the club she knew various ways out. She had probably used them more than once already, come to think of it. And Bea, well, no one knew what was going on in her head, as she suddenly re-exploded with a rage magnified many times. 'Listen to her,' Ruby said to her innocently sleeping child. 'And just you keep in mind that this is the state your dear auntie gets into when someone upstages her!' And upstage her Iris had, as the old aunties spotted.

'What do you make of her?' Cissie yelled above the noise, without the slightest inkling or concern that she could be heard by everyone in the room.

'Which one?' Dot boomed back, equally innocently.

'Aye, you're right, they're both a disgrace, but I mean the slut,' Cissie yelled, 'their Iris. She must want to keep a hold of this guy or, knowing her, she'd have got rid of the wean long ago,' Dot replied, echoing Ruby thoughts.

'Aye, you're right there,' nodded her sister, 'and there's plenty she could point the finger at who couldn't deny it. There'll be more than a few taking sly looks into the pram to check up, I can tell you. I'll say this for their Iris, she believes in safety in numbers. Candy ball?'

'Oh, I can't resist candy balls, Dot!' Cissie cried, reaching into the proferred paper bag.

'Aye, their Iris has the same problem,' Dot said, 'only she can't tell the candy ones from the other kind and—'

'—and wouldn't care even if she could, all comers welcome!' Cissie yelled.

Sitting side-by-side they held onto each other as they heaved and shrieked with laughter.

'And look at Big Bea!' Cissie said delightedly, as Bea was finally hauled to the floor and pinned there by a posse of sweating neighbours. 'She's that angry at her moment being spoiled that she's spitting pure poison, so she is! Ha, ha! It's better than the Empire on a Saturday night, this. I wish we had some fruit to throw at her!' She put a hand to her mouth and shouted 'Bea! Bea, hen! Pull your skirt down, everybody can see your knickers!'

Then the two old sisters hugged each other for support again and wiped their eyes, breathless with fresh mirth.

'Well at least they're clean, I suppose,' said Dot. 'Thank God she put her Sunday best ones on.'

'Well, it is Sunday,' murmured Cissie, 'so you'll have *your* best ones on as well.'

'Och, you know perfectly well that in our house we don't have special best,' said Dot haughtily, 'we always have the best every day of the week.'

'Aye,' replied Cissie tartly, 'and it's the talk of the steamie that your lassies keep them like that by not wearing them too often.'

Ruby went back to the sitting room, glanced at the usual turmoil and, catching the eye of her daughter's godmother, motioned with her head to bring her out.

'I want you to sit with Frances while I go out for a few minutes,' she said. 'I don't really think the battle will spill out, but you never know.'

'Where are you going?' Agnes asked.

'Uncle Jakey's made himself scarce as usual,' Ruby grinned, 'haven't set eyes on him all day. I'm going to take him up something to eat, and a few scraps for Wee Dug. You know how he is, he forgets.'

Agnes nodded then put her hand over her mouth to cover a smile.

'What?' Ruby asked.

'I was just imagining it,' she laughed, 'them all piling from room-to-room like one of they bar room brawls you see at the pictures!'

'Don't laugh too soon,' Ruby replied wryly, 'it could happen yet,

83

just make sure you have your revolver ready to fire and hope the sheriff arrives quickly!'

She found Jakey in his flat as she had expected, and put his food on the table and Wee Dug's underneath. Jakey was painting by the light of a hundred or more candles, a delighted smile on his face.

'See the difference candlelight makes?' he beamed.

'Aye,' Ruby smiled. 'But were the statues not awful heavy, Uncle Jakey?' she asked gently.

A slightly pained look flitted across his face, then, 'A wee bit,' he replied quietly, 'but we managed.'

'But it must've taken you ages?' she persisted.

'A wee while, but we had to do it.'

Ruby had a mental image of Wee Dog up on his stumpy hind legs helping him. 'But why? And why did you take their candles?'

He tapped the side of his nose twice with his finger. 'A wee voice told me,' he said, and he winked.

With that he turned back to his painting and she knew there was no further enlightenment to be had. The 'wee voice' had closed the discussion and now he needed all his concentration for his art. But on her way out she suddenly stopped and remembered what he had said to her not long ago: 'Things change when wee people become big people.' Tonight she had asked him 'Why?' which meant she was no longer a child. Jakey had been right, with her marriage, such as it was, and motherhood, 'Wee' Ruby had become 'Big' Ruby. She closed her eyes and bit her lip. She no longer accepted Jakey as Jakey, she asked him 'Why?' and wanted explanations. Now his isolation was complete. She waited for a second outside the door and heard Jakey laughing inside. That made her feel better, she couldn't have offended him too much, then.

8

It was nearly three weeks before Ian Fraser, the housing association lad, called and asked if she would like to come back to Glasgow. On one hand she felt a fresh wave of apprehension, but on the other there was a kind of relief, because memories of her life and her family had been playing out in her mind so much that her sleep was more and more disturbed, and it was making her irritable.

'I've been doing a lot of research since the last time you were over,' he said, 'you wouldn't believe how it draws you in once you start. It's become an obsession.'

Ruby nodded. She did believe it. One memory, she had discovered, sparked off another, so she could imagine that learning each fresh piece of information would have the same effect.

'I thought we could have a bite to eat and I'll go over what I've found out, see if you can add anything. How does that sound?'

She had a sudden attack of cowardice and thought of casually suggesting he come to Largs, but he was busy, she knew he wouldn't fall for it, fond memories of the place or not. 'Aye, that would be fine, son,' she heard herself say.

'I was thinking of Café Gandolfi in Albion Street. It's in the Candleriggs, beside where the Fruit Market used to be, let you have a closer look at what's become of the place.'

'One of those fancy places we passed the last time?' she asked doubtfully.

He laughed. 'Aye, one of those, it's really trendy, no beans on toast these days! I thought it might amuse you to see the new Glasgow. Do you like fish?'

'I love fish, son,'

'Well this is the place for you,' he laughed. 'I'll pick you up from Central Station if you let me know what train you're getting.'

She smiled and breathed a sigh of relief and gratitude; this time she wouldn't have to battle through the traffic and pay over the odds for the privilege. Even so, she was slightly nervous. The boy was going out of his way to be pleasant, what if she felt out of place and hated this café place? When they arrived she recognised it as what had been part of the old Cheese Market in her day, a fine, solid, red sandstone building, big windows to the front with a shoal of stained-glass fish swimming from one to the other, caught in shades of blue. Inside, the furniture was just as solidly constructed of wood, simple but co-ordinated.

'A classy joint,' she remarked, as Ian took her coat.

'So you approve then?' he asked.

'Well, those windows!' she said. 'The colours! They take your breath away when you see them from the inside, don't they?'

He smiled and she was happy that he was pleased.

'Didn't this use to be McLellan's?' she asked, sitting down.

'Aye, it was the office part. McLellan's were still making cheese next door after the café opened, till about 1990 I think.'

'I can still see it as though it was yesterday,' she smiled. 'Who'd have thought one day I'd be sitting in McLellan's office having a fancy meal?'

'This was the first place in the Merchant City to be redeveloped, I still think it's the best, and you'll love the food.' He handed her a menu.

She put on her reading glasses and scanned it. 'Black pudding?' she asked. 'Is that legal any longer?'

'Do you want to try it?' he asked.

'It's years since I've had black pudding,' she sighed. 'And mackerel pâté, that sounds good.'

'Well, what if you have the black pudding and I have the pâté and we can share them? And what about after?'

Ruby glanced at the prices. 'We could just have the starters, son, everything's so dear.'

'I won't hear of it,' he said firmly, 'this is my treat. Now what would you like?'

She smiled, looking at the various dishes, feeling like a child being given the run of a sweet shop. 'Finnan Haddie then. I've always loved Finnan Haddie.'

'Good, and I'll have the Gravadlax. That's that settled. What would you like to drink?'

'I'll just have tea, if that's all right?'

'You wouldn't like a glass of wine?'

'Oh, I don't drink, son, never liked the taste or the effect,' she smiled, a diplomatic reply that covered a multitude of possibilities. 'But don't let that stop you.'

'No, I'm driving,' he grinned, handing the menus back to the waitress.

'Nice boy,' she thought.

'So, about the Bell o' the Brae tenements,' he said. 'We've decided to put together a wee history of the place, thought you might be able to tell us what it was like living there.'

He unfolded a large plan of the flats on the table while they waited and she was struck by the oddness of recognising rooms she had known so well.

'What surprised me,' he said, 'was that these flats had inside bathrooms way back in 1903. Some parts of the city were using shared outside toilets and had no baths right up to the 1960s or 1970s. Were you aware of that when you were living there?'

'Oh, aye,' she replied. 'Remember my pal Flora? The Communist lassie? Well her family, the McCreadie's, in George Street, had no bath and just a toilet on the landing for four families, and families were big then, remember. The whole McCreadie tribe came across to our house for a bath every week. They would just troop across the road.' She stopped and laughed at the memory. 'Her father, Big Ali, insisted on giving my mother a bag of coal every now and again for the hot water. She didn't want to take it and used to get all embarrassed. They had very little, not that it bothered them mind, and we seemed to have so much. I mean, my father had a good job and my sister worked, so we didn't need it, you see. Then Big Ali died of TB and after that my mother refused to take the coal, told

Mrs McCreadie we all had a duty to help each other according to our means, and of course that was clever, it played straight to the family's sympathies, didn't it?' She chuckled.

'TB seems to have carved a big hole in Glasgow,' he said.

'Oh, aye, in they days it was a bit better, but it was still everywhere,' she shook her head sadly. 'They called it the White Plague because people went very pale. Ali McCreadie was a great big strong man, but he withered away so fast, you wouldn't have believed it. Very few didn't have somebody in their family who'd died of it. We had it our family, too, everybody was scared of it. My man's mother and father died of it within months of each when he was a baby. His sister brought him up.'

'That's sad.'

'Och, son, there were sadder tales, believe me. He was lucky, Agnes did well by him.'

'And the flats, in your time were the people in them all from what they called the better working classes?' he smiled.

She looked at him, puzzled.

'Well they were intended for those with trades and businesses,' he explained, 'or good steady jobs at least. If you look at the census returns at the time, everybody was gainfully and well employed. You wouldn't find any unskilled labourers living there.'

She thought for a moment. 'Aye, it was pretty much the same when I was growing up. My grandfather had had his own carter's business. Uncle Jakey and my father worked with him up to the First War, then my father went to the railways and got Uncle Jakey in as well. Jakey lived with my grandfather then took over the flat when the old man died. Jakey never married, he lived alone all his life, apart from Wee Dug.' She looked upwards, thinking, and started counting off on her fingers. 'So my father was a train driver, and Agnes, my man's sister, was a seamstress. She had a job outside but she worked at home as well, there were always people looking for her even after she had moved out. And across the road was Betty Campbell, her that signed Jakey's will. A lovely woman she was, her man was a railway fireman, a big horror,' she grimaced, 'but the house had been Betty's parents'. her mother was a music teacher and her father a school headmaster. Betty was a music teacher, too, she gave piano lessons and played at dances, people always said she could've gone places with her music before she married. The sister I mentioned last time, the one who lived near the Barony?'

He nodded.

'Her and her man, Dainty Davy, ran ballroom dancing classes and Betty played for them.' She sighed, looking down. 'Lovely woman, she was,' she said again. 'I mean Betty, not my sister! Married to that big brute, poor woman.'

She looked up and saw him laughing.

'What?' she asked.

'I was just thinking about your description of your sister, not someone you'd want to run into on a dark night or even a bright day,' he chuckled. 'I'm trying to picture her teaching folk to dance!'

She laughed along with him. 'Aye, I know, but my, she could dance! A carthorse in the street, no, worse than that, carthorses had a kind of grace about them. A bulldozer!' she said triumphantly. 'But on the dance floor? Thistledown on the dance floor!' She shook her head, remembering. 'Honestly, you wouldn't believe the difference!'

'And Dainty Davy?'

She laughed again, seeing why he was amused, they sounded like a cast of characters in a play. 'That was her man, Davy White, he was a great dancer too, the two of them were champions of everything there was. Apparently their Charleston was something to behold. I could never watch it myself without laughing. It was such a daft dance, wasn't it? But people that knew said they were the best.'

'So that's why he was called Dainty Davy?'

'Well, kind of. Partly. He was the one I told you about, the one who drove passenger trains. A wee weasel of a man to look at, kind of deep-set eyes, "wee nippy, sleekit eyes," my old aunties used to call them,' she remembered with a chuckle, 'and he had crinkly hair that was always plastered in some stuff that smelt of lavender. I think it was to make it look less crinkly, but all it did was make it look it shiny and greasy *and* crinkly! He was a bit of a dandy, always well turned out, as they say. My brother George said he even had fresh creases in his overalls every day.'

Ian laughed out loud.

'I never knew if that was true, mind you, but George insisted it was. He said the railwaymen had another nickname for him apart from Dainty Davy.'

'I bet they had!' he chuckled. 'I just bet they had!'

They continued to talk over their starters.

'That black pudding is lovely!' Ruby grinned. 'And that wee pancake thing, it's just smashing. Who'd have thought of having a pancake with black pudding?'

'But it's not too sweet, is it?' he enthused. 'They really go together? Here, try a bit of pâté.'

'Och, I don't like,' she laughed, 'because I'm not giving you any of mine!'

'Did you know that the tenements were built as a competition?' Ruby shook her head.

'First the other side of the street, then yours. Apparently Charles Rennie Macintosh put in for it and only came third.'

'Really?' Ruby laughed. 'I think that's great!'

'Aye, I see that old Glasgow thing about bringing people down to size hasn't withered away in Largs! Think what the flats could've been like if he had won, though.'

'Museums for tourists?' she muttered with a shrug.

'Probably. And there were no pubs allowed.'

'I never saw the point of that,' she said. 'I mean, they were all around us, there was no escape.'

'I think it was supposed to encourage other housing projects not to put pubs near houses,' he explained. 'The Temperance lobby was strong then and they considered booze to be the root of all working-class evils.'

'So did the Communists,' Ruby said, 'and they were right, that and TB. It was nice not having to step over drunks where we lived. I always felt safe that way in my own street, but it was a different story when you put a foot outside.'

'It was that bad?'

'You've no idea,' she said with feeling. 'I was scared stiff when I had to walk down other streets near us. I used to work out in my mind how many pubs there were and kind of tick them off in my head as I passed them. Drunks terrified me. Living in High Street was a bit like being in a wagon train surrounded by marauding Apaches!'

He laughed. 'So there wasn't much trouble in the tenements?'

Ruby shook her head. 'Not that kind of trouble anyway. People brought booze in for parties and things, but we didn't get drunks lying about, I don't think the women would've stood for it, not being used to it.' She stopped. 'One woman didn't,' she thought to herself.

'And was it a very close community?'

'Oh, aye, but everywhere was back then, wasn't it? Everybody knew each other, we were always in and out of each other's houses, and the fact that there were so many railwaymen staying about there, that helped. You know what the railway family is like. But do you know the funny thing? I wouldn't like my life now to be like that, I like my own space. I wouldn't let everybody and his wife just walk in and out of my house. Isn't that strange? I mean, that's how I was brought up.'

'Maybe that's why,' he smiled.

'Aye, but why wouldn't it go the other way? It was a good thing, it held people together, nobody ever died alone and lay there for months back then.' She shook her head. 'I go on about nobody caring these days, just like all us old biddies, about how it's terrible we don't know our neighbours, but for all that, I like being able to shut my door and keep to myself.' She looked up at him and laughed. 'Contrary Mary!' she smiled.

'How about a dessert?' he asked.

'Oh, aye, I always have room for a wee bit pudding,' she said cheerfully. She looked at the waitress. 'Can I have rhubarb tart with ice cream?' she asked. 'No custard, no cream, but hot with ice cream?'

'Course you can,' the girl smiled.

'And Jakey,' Ian said, 'what happened to him?'

'Oh, he just died, son. It was so long ago I can barely remember when exactly.' She made it sound vague and casual, there was no need to go into detail, and she didn't think she could anyway.

'And Wee Dug?' he laughed.

She screwed up her face in concentration. 'Can't quite remember what happened to Wee Dug,' she said, adding a silent 'You liar!' to herself. 'So, have you decided what to do about his murals?' she asked, determinedly turning the conversation away from Jakey's demise.

'It's a difficult one,' he sighed. 'The smart thing to do would be to cover them over and forget them, but the more I find out about Jakey, the less I want to do that. He was a real wee man, it's all that's left of him, isn't it?'

'I can see your problem,' she smiled.

'What would you like done?' he asked.

'I don't know,' she replied, honestly. 'I hate the thought of them being destroyed, but on the other hand, I thought they had been years ago, so what would be the difference?'

He nodded. 'The plan at the moment is to strip all the wallpaper off so that we have a clear idea of what we've got, then finish the rest of the renovation before we make a decision. All the work stopped on Jakey's flat when we found the murals, we just concentrated on the ones round about, so everything has to be done, rewiring, plumbing, the floor will have to come up, the lot, that will all take a while, so we've got time.'

'Well,' she said with a grin, 'if you come across any bars of Fry's Five Boys, they're mine!'

After lunch they went back to her parents' old home, but it wasn't any longer. The last time she had been there the renovations had barely started and the place, though changed here and there, was still recognisable as the house where she had grown up, but now it had been transformed. The kitchen hadn't just been brought up to date, it had been relocated, so that she could no longer picture her mother at work, and that alone had altered the whole feel of the place. Outside was still beautiful, the proportions of the red sandstone building had always been pleasing, even to an eye untutored in the finer details of traditional architecture. But now, the inside could have been any modern home, and the remnants of familiar scenes visible through the new double glazing didn't disguise that. It wasn't her home any longer at any rate, and it no longer felt as though it ever had been. She looked at Ian, who was standing nervously in the middle of the sitting room.

'It's like a door has been closed,' she smiled, 'and not just closed, but locked, too.'

The only real reminder of her old life, she thought, was Jakey's flat a few closes up and, when the work there was finished, it would all be gone. She didn't know yet how she felt about that. Later, going back on the train, she kept thinking of her reply when she had been asked what had happened to Jakey. 'Oh, he just died, son,' she had said, a rehearsed reply to a question she had known was bound to be asked at some point. But he hadn't, had he? Ruby had no idea if the rest of the family ever had any suspicions, if they had they had never discussed them with her. There was no proof of anything, but even so, Ruby knew Jakey hadn't 'just died.' And neither had Wee Dug.

9

If anyone had expected Iris McLean to be weighed down with shame and guilt about producing an illegitimate child, they had another think coming. Iris had never cared a damn what anyone else thought of her and that hadn't changed just because her belly was growing. Not that she liked being pregnant, she found it boring, uncomfortable and unflattering and decided that this child would be her first and last, she would do whatever it took to make sure of that. No one had been told the name of the father, not that anyone asked, they knew Iris wouldn't tell them, even if she knew. Even a friendly inquiry about her future plans brought the same brittle, fixed smile. What Iris intended doing was Iris's business alone. Giving up her job on the cosmetic counter of Daly's was the biggest sacrifice she had to make. It had suited her. Iris had always loved the immediate and the superficial, and Daly's was sorry to see her go too, her nature had made her a perfect saleswoman. She left before the bump became obvious, telling them she was going to do something to help the War effort, and laughed to herself when they praised her for it.

As it was, Ruby had stayed on at Sarah and Harry's house after the birth of Frances, she was young and alone with a baby she had no idea what to do with, and it was natural she would need her mother's help. The flat up the road, Gerry's flat, took on a waiting quality, as did his civilian life, and she did no more than look after it. All that happened was that Frances became a member of the family and in due course it was assumed that Iris's child would do the same. He was born six months after Frances, and the two children, inevitably, were raised together. Looking back, things seemed to happen, to evolve, only they didn't of course, Iris had planned the whole thing. Two babies didn't need three women looking after them, she said, and Sarah and Ruby were there already, so she would return to work to earn her son's keep. She chose to become a tram conductress, the only area of wartime work that paid women and men equally. Typical of Iris, Ruby thought later, there would be no fighting for any cause where she was concerned. And, given that the flat on the corner was a bit cramped with four adults and two babies, and the Reilly flat wasn't really being used, it seemed only sensible that Iris should move in there, especially as she was working shifts and didn't want to disturb anyone or have her own sleep disturbed.

So when Ruby's first wedding anniversary came round in 1940, she was seventeen years old and the mother of a six-month-old baby girl and a newborn baby boy. She had married Gerry because she didn't want to raise a fatherless child, and now she was doing just that, and twice over, too, as Gerry wasn't around either. Frances and James, one brown-haired and hazel-eyed like her father, the other fair and blue-eyed like, well, like no one knew who. As Ruby settled into caring for both children, Iris went back to her pre-pregnancy lifestyle. Her new career, after all, brought her into contact with a whole new crop of men and, in a very short time, she was passing the door for days, then weeks, without stopping to ask how her son was doing. It had all been planned, Ruby realised that later, of course it had, but at the time, as it was happening, it had seemed to make a great deal of sense. As Iris had pointed out, Ruby was stuck at home with Frances anyway, and at least she had Gerry's army pay to live on, while Iris had to work to provide for James. Yes, when you thought about it from that angle it made solid sense, though pretty soon that proved a hollow promise. Whatever Iris earned, Iris kept.

And the strange thing was that far from resenting being used as a foster mother by Iris, Ruby loved the little boy she called Jamie and felt fiercely protective of him. She knew the entire area was speculating on who his father might be, as the old aunties had predicted. Many men and their wives wanted a quick look to eliminate or raise suspicions and possibilities, but they got very short shrift from Ruby. Betty Campbell was different though, Betty was a lady, and when she arrived to see the baby she was welcomed, it was just unfortunate her horrible husband was with her. Ruby glared at him. There he stood, looking, those eyes of his taking in everything as usual, slowly surveying as he listened to every word, picking up and storing information that might or might not become useful one day. She had always disliked him, and now she objected to him inspecting Jamie, looking at the wean as though he had 'bastard child' seared across his forehead. She could just picture him telling the other railwaymen – as long as those in the family weren't present, of course – that he had seen the boy, and giving his opinion on who he looked like. Maybe motherhood had given her confidence, but she knew she wasn't going to stand for it, so she got between Gus Campbell and the baby's cot, faced him and said pointedly, 'That's enough, we don't want strangers upsetting him.' They were so close together that she felt his breath on her face, making her feel queasy, and as usual he kept eye contact with her for slightly longer than was normal, but she held herself taut and resolved to hold her ground till he stepped back.

'Aye,' he smiled finally, through those strangely tight, in-turned lips, 'he's a fine wee laddie.'

'Aye, he is,' Ruby replied solemnly, still blocking his view of Jamie. Then he turned towards the sitting room and within seconds she heard him talking to Harry McLean by the fireside, as Sarah busied herself with the tea things in the kitchen. 'Bet he's filling his face with whatever's going as well!' she thought bitterly.

Betty stayed in the bedroom, gazing at the two sleeping babies.

'Don't mind Gus, hen,' she said gently, 'it's just his way, he doesn't mean anything by it.'

Ruby smiled but didn't reply; she'd been hearing that particular defence of Gus Campbell all her life and she still didn't believe it, even though it was Betty giving it this time.

'And I know things aren't just right,' the older woman continued softly, patting Ruby's arm, 'what with the War and everything, and you can't have an easy time looking after two of them, Ruby, you won't have a minute to yourself. I think it's great, what you're doing.'

'My mother's there, Mrs Campbell,' Ruby smiled in reply. 'I couldn't manage without her. Besides, it's not his fault, is it, and who else would look after the wee soul? His mother's no use to him, is she?'

'Och, don't be too hard on your Iris, Ruby, hen,' Betty chided her. 'I'm sure she has her good points.'

'Aye,' Ruby said wryly, 'there's her generosity. Pity it's confined to other women's men.'

Betty chuckled. 'I'm sure she'll settle down one of these days, Ruby, don't you worry. Some just take longer than others. I was wondering though,' she said tentatively, 'I don't have any wee ones to knit for, maybe you'd let me knit these two wee beauties the odd thing?'

'Oh, that would be awful nice of you!' Ruby said, struck by the graceful way Betty Campbell had put it: Ruby would be doing *her* a kindness, instead of the other way round.

'I never told you when you were expecting Frances,' Betty said softly, 'it wasn't the right time, but I was expecting when Gus and I got married.' She paused for a moment. 'It was a wee girl. She was stillborn. We never had any more. I aye wanted them, mind, it just never happened. I've always felt bad for Gus that I could never give him a wean, and it's too late now.'

Ruby reached over and hugged her.

'Now don't do that!' Betty laughed, wiping her eyes. 'You'll have me in tears here! That's why I was so happy that it all went well for you, though I know you had a hard time.'

Afterwards Ruby thought back on the conversation and was almost in tears herself, tears of pity for Betty. To have had to marry that horrible brute of a man because she was pregnant, and then to lose the child and never have another, well, it was so unfair. Now she was bound to him and without children to soften her life sentence. Poor Betty. Poor, poor Betty.

10

That she felt fiercely protective of Jamie there was no doubt, but sitting looking out over the sea all these years later, as the rain blurred the line between the water and the grey sky, she pondered a question that had haunted her all her life: What about Frances, what did she feel about Frances? It was one of those hindsight questions, though. Her thoughts on that issue were as blurred by time and experience as the scene outside was by the rain. She knew how things had been between them, but she could never make her mind up about why. There had been a distance between them right from the start; there was a detachment about Frances even as a baby, and she had been racked with guilt all her life wondering how much of it she had caused. Babies couldn't take a dislike to people, and surely not to their own mothers, she thought, but it had always seemed as though Frances had. Whose fault was that?

The little boy's arrival six months later made her wonder. He was what Ruby thought of as a normal baby, he loved been cuddled and cooed over, and all through his feeds he gazed into the eyes of the person holding the bottle and he would smile readily when he was spoken to. He had captivated the entire family, apart from Bea, who only ever looked at him askance, and his mother, who never looked at him at all. Ruby waited for some disparaging remark about him from Bea, ready to pounce if it ever came. Bea had no time for any child in the family. Though Jamie smiled and gurgled in every direction, including Bea's, she was the only one who never succumbed to his baby charms. Frances hadn't been like that with anyone, it hadn't just been Ruby, but had she caused it anyway? Over the years she had looked at it from every angle. Had she resented the child for trapping her into marriage and motherhood in a way that Frances had picked up on even in the womb? Yet she was just as trapped by having to care for Jamie and she accepted that was for life too, given that his own mother barely acknowledged his existence, but somehow Jamie was different from Frances.

If anyone had seen her with Jamie they would have assumed he was Ruby's child and Frances her niece and, sometimes, God forgive her, she had wished that was the case. Did Frances perhaps miss out on attention because the little boy had arrived so soon? That was another piece of torture she used against herself, but the truth was that both babies were fussed over and cared for, Frances missed out on nothing that Ruby could think of. And yet it was there, she knew that, there was no denying it, that distance. Frances had always set her own limits on how close she allowed people to her, and she had a strange way of making them feel unwelcome if they presumed to get too near. She wasn't joyless in the way of someone who was unhappy, rather she was a child devoid of joy, who seemed to have been missed when joy was given out, and that amounted to the same thing; a serious child who turned large, solemn eyes on you till you retreated.

Whatever she wanted, she took, and Ruby was forever ticking her off for taking things from Jamie, not really because she wanted or needed them, she came to realise, but simply because Jamie, or some other child, had them. 'Leave her alone,' her mother would chide her, 'all children do that, it's just a phase. Jamie will learn to stand up for himself soon enough and then she'll know all about it.' True, all true, she knew that, and yet there was an indefinable something that she couldn't quite put her finger on, like a red sign inside her head telling her that this was different, but not how. It was as though there was a little bit of Frances you couldn't get to, a certain level she had fenced off. Maybe her father not being there? But the country was full of children whose fathers were absent, and no one even knew who Jamie's father was. Besides, Frances had never known life with her father, so how could she miss him?

So she had carried on, looking after both children, making an extra effort to ensure Frances got as much attention and affection as Jamie, but aware that Frances didn't seem to want it or want to give it either. Every time she thought about it she recognised Frances was the same with everyone, not just Ruby, and Ruby wasn't the only one to notice it. Sometimes she would catch a look on the face of the child's godmother, her Aunt Agnes, as she watched Frances, a slight expression of puzzlement, of concern on her face, and all the guilt would rise to the surface again. She was the child's mother. It had to be her fault.

There was little news of Gerry and the few letters that arrived had so many sections blanked out by the censor to disguise where he was that all they did was confirm that he was still alive when they were sent, which was something all the same. After a time she found it difficult to recall his face, which unsettled her, even if he wasn't part of her life, she mused, he was her husband, the father of her child. She should be able to picture what he looked like.

At home, the blackout seemed to cause as many casualties as it was supposed to prevent, with people falling in the darkness and being hurt or even killed. There had been a suggestion that men should wear their shirt-tails outside their trousers in order to be visible, but where Ruby lived there was a name for men with unusual nether region arrangements and few, if any, risked it.

'I see Gus Campbell is an Air Raid Warden,' Ruby remarked to her mother.

'Well he could hardly fight as his age, could he?' Sarah replied.

'Bet he didn't try to find out,' Ruby sneered.

'Och, Ruby!' Sarah laughed, shaking her head. 'You never give that man a chance, do you? Sure, they wouldn't take him anyway, he's in a protected occupation, just like your Da.'

'Still,' Ruby muttered suspiciously, 'I wouldn't like to meet him in the dark, would you?'

'Now Ruby,' Sarah sighed, 'you have to give him credit. He works all those hours and then he goes out again as a warden when he's off-duty, though that's precious little these days. The man's always out and about.'

'That's my point,' Ruby said tartly. 'Why is he always out and about?'

'Because he wants to do something to help.'

'Help himself, more like.'

'Now you're not being fair,' Sarah chided her. 'Though I admit I don't know where he gets the energy, your poor Da and Jakey are exhausted, George too. Just as well there are only twenty-four hours in the day, that's all I can say.'

And it was true, Ruby knew that, the railwaymen were worked off their feet, especially since petrol had become scarce, which meant more pressure was put on the railways. The Goods Yard was kept open late on Saturdays and Sundays, and the workers, including booking clerks, signalmen, shunters and train drivers, were instructed to stay at their posts even when air-raid alerts had been issued. In daylight, passenger and freight services were to run as normally as possible during alerts and at not more than 30 m.p.h. during blackout. Only 'when danger was imminent' were they allowed to seek what cover they could, and they had to return to duty immediately the danger was judged to be over. For train drivers like Harry this meant that if an enemy plane was about to bomb or strafe his train, he had to stop the engine wherever he was and find somewhere to hide, advice that was far from practical as, by definition, being in the middle of nowhere guaranteed that there was no shelter to be had from the Luftwaffe's attentions. Train crews, therefore, made a tacit decision that if they came under fire they would just keep going, in the hope that a moving target might be that much harder to hit. Naturally Harry didn't tell his family this, but if he wasn't actually fighting, he was at risk of being killed everyday. And he was working all hours, as Sarah had said, as demarcation lines became blurred for the duration. Drivers who would normally step over a dropped lump of coal all day rather than pick it up, declaring it beneath their dignity to do the work of a fireman, especially a slovenly one, pitched in and did whatever was asked of them, as did everyone else. The only people who really complained were ordinary passengers, who regularly found their trains cancelled, delayed and diverted to stop at every out-of-the-way destination, as priority was always given to troop and munitions movements. There being little petrol for buses, they were faced with the official slogan 'Is your journey really necessary?' to discourage them from using any transport and, if they grizzled a bit about their lot, they received the usual reprimand of,

'There *is* a war on, you know!' So when July 1940 arrived, it was hard to imagine that people had been transported to the seaside just twelve short months before, even with a large, dark, Hitler-shaped cloud looming on the horizon. Everything had changed, every life was different, not just Ruby's, as she constantly reminded herself, she just had to look at the aunties to see that. As Flora had predicted, Cissie and Dot had been devastated when sweets were rationed, especially as sugar to make your own was also scarce. Even though Sarah had put away a good supply in the pre-war months and guarded it like gold dust, they knew she had it. Moreover, they knew she knew they knew.

'What the hell difference would it make to Hitler if we had a wee bag of Jap Delights?' Cissie demanded righteously, sitting in Sarah's front room, sipping tea.

'Or a wee bit of chocolate,' Dot suggested.

'You can still get sweets,' Sarah suggested meekly.

'What?' demanded Cissie, almost choking on her tea. 'A couple of ounces a week? Sure, how long do you think that lasts us?'

'And it's not as though we ever indulge ourselves,' Dot complained piously. 'We don't ask for much, do we, Cissie?'

'Not a bit of it!' Cissie replied staunchly. 'And what have we done to deserve this, that's what I'd like to know? We lived through the last show and we won that, now they're at it again and we're having to put up without honest-to-god necessities.'

'I don't think sweets are really necessities,' Sarah suggested quietly.

'Would you listen to her, Dot?' Cissie shouted, stabbing an accusing finger in the direction of her younger sister, her cup and saucer rattling in her other hand. 'Have you ever heard the likes?'

Dot nodded, her eyes narrowing as she stared at Sarah. 'Me and Cissie have no vices,' she seethed. 'We don't drink and we don't smoke, we've brought up our families to be decent people, and you're denying us a wee sweetie now and again?'

'I'm not denying you anything,' Sarah said, her voice already conceding defeat, 'I'm just saying sweets aren't food, that's all.'

'Man does not live by food alone!' Dot said accusingly. 'Man needs a wee sweetie now and again, Sarah!'

'I've said it before and I'll say it again, all they have to do is shoot that Hitler,' Cissie continued enthusiastically, 'and all this would be over. You wouldn't think it would be beyond them, would you? All these men, they just want to play at soldiers, travelling the world at our expense and running around with guns, that's the truth of it!'

'Och, that's not really fair, Cissie,' Sarah replied, sipping gently at her tea. 'I don't think anybody would be getting shot at unless they had to be.'

'I'll do it myself!' Cissie announced, nodding her head. 'Just give me a gun and I'll shoot that Hitler myself!'

Ruby looked across at her mother and smiled. Sugar deprivation was indeed a terrible thing for those who were addicted and, true to her nature, just as the aunties had fully expected, Sarah relented under their combined pressure and handed over a bag of sugar as her sisters got up to go, receiving beaming smiles in return.

'Oh Sarah! That's awfy kind! Are you sure you can spare it?' Cissie exclaimed, all innocent delight. 'Oh, I never expected that, did you, Dot?'

'No, I did not!' Dot lied in her teeth.

'We can make candy balls, and maybe a bit of tablet,' Hitler's would-be assassin suggested in a girlish tone.

'Well, I'll make them, Cissie,' Dot responded, 'I don't want you having to do all that by yourself, especially when you've got Hitler to shoot as well.'

'No, no, not at all, Dot, I'd be happy to do it.'

'Well, I'll help you,' Dot insisted, brightly, as they left.

As they made their way downstairs their voices could still be heard determinedly offering and refusing help in the art of sweetmaking. Ruby and Sarah exchanged smiles. 'They don't trust each other an inch, do they?' Ruby asked.

'Nor an ounce!' Sarah replied.

11

In July, Sarah suggested having a small party to mark Jamie's first birthday and Ruby's wedding anniversary. She and Ruby were laying the table for dinner, with Harry due in any time soon, hopefully, though these days you never could tell. Ruby stopped and looked at her mother, wondering aloud if she had gone mad. Both events lacked the same essential element: the all-important male. Gerry Reilly, the erstwhile groom, was in some unknown destination, while Jamie's unknown father was, possibly, nearby, but still no more available.

'I suppose you could invite every married man for miles around and maybe you'd find him,' Ruby remarked acidly, 'though it's possible he could be far away too. If I remember rightly, the fairground was in full swing about that time. Maybe it was the lad who ran the waltzers or the dodgems on Glasgow Green.'

'Ruby, there's no need for that!' Sarah reprimanded her. 'I just thought a nice wee tea would be good for everybody, cheer us all up, that's all, bring us all together.'

'You know what happens when something brings us all together,' Ruby snapped. 'Her up the road, Big Bea.'

'Och, she won't do anything this time,' Sarah said soothingly. 'Sure it's just a wee party for a wee wean and for you, Ruby, she'd have no reason to go mad.'

Ruby laughed out loud. 'You say that as though she had a reason all the other times!' she giggled, putting an arm around her mother's shoulders and shaking her affectionately. 'Isn't she the woman who's practically had to be carried out of every family do in a straightjacket since the beginning of time? Ma, are you listening to yourself?'

'Well,' Sarah said uncomfortably, 'maybe Bea has her reasons.'
'Like what?'

'Och, I don't know.' She looked up at Ruby and laughed quietly. 'I've never understood her either, and she's my daughter. How do you think that makes me feel?'

'It makes you feel the way she wants you to feel, the way she wants us all to feel: guilty. She wants us to think we're all to blame for the way she is, and we're not, Ma, you're not.'

'I keep thinking she can't be happy,' Sarah sighed. She stopped setting the table and sat down. 'I mean, why would anyone get themselves into that state if they were happy?'

'Because she's evil!' Ruby replied brightly.

'Och Ruby,' Sarah smiled weakly, 'you are terrible sometimes! I wonder if there was something I could've done. I suppose, if it's my fault.'

'How could it be your fault?' Ruby laughed.

Sarah shrugged her shoulders. 'Who knows?' she whispered.

So the ingredients for a small cake were brought forth from under a bed and the date was arranged. The usual guests were invited and some were otherwise engaged, even though it did take place in the early evening before the blackout. Betty Campbell arrived, welcome as ever, and immediately gathered the children up in her arms. Ruby watched carefully and tried not to notice that Jamie laughed and clapped his hands while Frances did nothing in particular, she was just there, engaged in her own thoughts. Gus and Harry were working, and it was almost worth the absence of her father not to have *him* nearby, she mused. Uncle Jakey sat in the corner with his usual blank expression, while Wee Dug took up position under the chair, shaking slightly, his strange big head turned to the wall, as though pretending none of this was happening or, if it was, he wasn't actually present. Looking at the two of them, Ruby suddenly remembered how little of them she saw these days and felt a stab of guilt. Agnes, Gerry's sister arrived and Cissie and Dot brought their sweet tooth, as did Bea.

'Do you think they ever wonder if she's inherited it from them?' Ruby asked her mother.

105

Sarah laughed in reply. 'They'd be horrified if they thought she was like them in any way, and I don't think she'd be too pleased either.'

'Strange isn't it, all of them with those bitter-sweet streaks and they don't see it in themselves!'

All the women laughed.

'Do you fancy telling them?' Agnes asked playfully.

'Or her?' Ruby suggested.

George was at work too, but Marie came with their two children and though they waited for a while, Jamie's mother didn't arrive either.

'I could've put money on that,' Ruby said sourly.

'Now, now,' Betty laughed, patting her arm, 'Iris is working just as the men are, and you're not blaming them for missing it, are you?'

The cake was cut, tea and gossip handed round and George and Marie's little ones sang 'Happy Birthday' off-key to Jamie and were praised as though they had performed like angels. The two smaller children, so exhausted that they had to be put down for a nap, were passed around the women for kisses. And that's when it happened, of course, when it seemed that they were almost home free. Bea. Once again there was no preamble, she just erupted.

'Look at you,' she sneered at the assembled company, 'with your comfortable wee lives and your boring families.'

'I think that's enough, Bea,' Sarah said gently. 'Our guests came here today to have a nice time, now you're embarrassing them.'

'Again,' Ruby said bluntly.

'And you can keep quiet!' Bea advanced on her, that awful voice rising in pitch and harshness. 'You think everybody admires you for looking after two weans. Wee Saint Ruby, who got herself knocked up by the first lad who came along!'

Ruby sat where she was, her cup and saucer in her hand. 'At least,' she said with icy calm, 'somebody wanted to knock me up, Bea.'

It really was like slow motion, she thought afterwards. Bea's hands shot out and grabbed Ruby by the hair and at the same moment Ruby raised her hand instinctively to throw her hot tea in Bea's face. Then all was tumult and chaos, with women's voices filling the room along with the frightened cries of the children, and all Ruby could think was that Bea had never cared about anyone and the selfish bitch didn't care about the children either. Above all the noise was the sound of Bea, as she was held down and attempts were made to subdue her. Ruby couldn't help herself. She was perfectly calm as she rose slowly, advancing on the crowd with the screaming Bea at its centre.

'You think we're all so contented?' she asked. She raised her voice but without anger, and the other voices were suddenly still. 'There isn't a woman here who doesn't have at least one man fighting somewhere, who doesn't lie awake at night wondering if she'll see him again, whereas you have that thing you call a man coming home to you every night. You live more comfortably than any of us, and we have never grudged you that, because you've earned every penny with a talent none of us have. We have never wished you any ill, but this is what we get in return every time we try to have a happy family time. You are a disgrace.'

'And why are we having this party anyway?' Bea screamed.

'Why shouldn't we?' Ruby asked with studied calm.

'Your man's a useless sod and that wean's just a bastard!' Bea screeched. 'You think that's something to be proud of, do you?'

With that Ruby raised her hand and slapped Bea hard across the face. Nothing happened, they were becalmed, all of them caught like one of George's insects in a web, until the spider got her bearings and Bea roared louder than the steam trains in the Goods Yard outside the window. And Ruby, still perfectly calm, looked down at her and noticed that for the first time ever, Bea's eyes didn't have their usual, triumphant expression that said 'Mission accomplished.' She still looked angry but she also looked defeated, and it only took three or four of the women to bundle her out of the house, downstairs and up the brae to her own home.

Inside the McLean home she had just been dragged from, the stunned silence continued. No one had ever deliberately hit Bea before. There were plenty of times when it was threatened, even more times when she was bruised all over from desperate attempts to control her during one of her insane tirades, but no actual blow had ever been aimed at her. Till now. It was Sarah who broke the spell.

'Ruby, that was a terrible thing to do to your sister,' she whispered, from her seat by fire, looking into the flames.

Ruby didn't reply.

'Away to hell!' came Cissie's voice. 'She's had it coming for years.'

'Aye,' said Dot, 'good for you, Ruby hen, I wish I'd done it myself.'

'Will you two keep out of this?' Sarah said.

'No, we bloody well won't,' Cissie told her staunchly. 'You can maybe tell your daughter off, Sarah, but we're your older sisters, we have privileges, and we say somebody should've slapped Bea long ago.'

'Aye, good for wee Ruby!' Dot said again.

'You've let her away with murder all her life, Sarah, and you made a rod for your own back and for everybody else's. We told you that often enough even when she was wee. You gave her a good life, you and Harry, same as you gave the others, but you let her run riot, same as you did with Iris. Iris was aye a slut and you did nothing about that either, as though it was your fault, when all the time it was hers. She's caused nothing but trouble to everybody all her life.'

'Just the same as Bea,' Dot added.

Sarah was by now weeping quietly. 'So it's my fault, then it is!' she sobbed. 'Thanks very much!'

'It's your fault for letting them behave the way they do, Sarah, instead of letting them know early on that you wouldn't stand for it. We've been there all their lives and how many times have we told you that?' Cissie demanded.

'I know, I know,' Sarah cried, 'but it's not as easy as that, is it?'

Betty Campbell knelt beside her and put her arms round her. 'Sarah, they're right in a way,' she said softly. 'You've done nothing to make Bea behave the way she does.'

'Aye, but she's done nothing to stop her either,' Dot insisted, rummaging around in her bag of sweets, 'that's the point we're making.'

Betty shot her a pained look then turned back to Sarah. 'Maybe Ruby's done everybody a favour by stopping her in her tracks for once. It wasn't a nice thing to do,' she looked at Ruby to make sure she knew Betty only slightly disapproved, 'but I think something positive could come out of this, I really do.'

Ruby, returned from putting the children down and calming them, stood at the window, her back to the room, her crossed arms wrapped around her waist. She felt liberated, free of the tyranny of her sister for the first time in her life. Whatever criticism might come her way, regardless of the repercussions, she knew no one and nothing could take that feeling away from her. Unseen by the others, she smiled. Then she felt a tap on her shoulder.

'Fancy a hazelnut swirl?' Cissie asked.

'Can you spare it?' Ruby grinned at her.

'For you, Ruby hen,' Cissie said, proffering the paper bag, 'only for you.'

Ruby dipped her hand in the bag. 'Thanks, Auntie Cissie,' she said quietly. She looked around. 'Where's Uncle Jakey and Wee Dug?' she asked.

'Och, they got out just as Bea was starting her nonsense,' Cissie said matter-of-factly. 'He's as daft as a brush that one, but he has an instinct where Bea's concerned, he gets to hell out of the firing line even before the rest of us know she's about to blow.'

'Maybe he's not that daft then, Auntie Cissie,' Ruby said gently. 'I think he's seen the performances often enough to know the signs.' She held the sweet to her mouth. 'So he didn't see me slapping her?'

'No, hen,' Dot told her, 'him and that stupid-looking dog of his were long gone by then.'

Ruby nodded. For no reason that she could pinpoint, she was glad about that.

There was a strange atmosphere in the house for a while after the great slapping, so for the sake of her mother, Ruby decided to try to make amends with Bea by taking her a slice of the birthday cake that evening. Bea could never remain cold to something sweet and sugary. She decided to take a few things to Uncle Jakey and Wee Dug on the way, but even though she would pass Gerry's flat, where Iris now lived, she took nothing for her. Jakey was sitting in his armchair with her mother's crochet thing across his knees when she went in.

'Everything all right, Uncle Jakey?' she asked.

'With me, hen? Och, aye, sure I'm fine. Just sitting here thinking on what to do next. Haven't had much time for the painting with work, you know.'

'Aye,' she smiled, 'I was surprised you could make it earlier, I thought you'd still be at the yard.'

'I'd been on all night,' he said wearily, 'and I'd just finished for the day. I left your Ma's tea a wee bit early, felt a bit tired.'

With anyone else she would have taken this as diplomacy, but not with Jakey, he had no side to him. 'I brought you a slice of cake,' she said, 'and Ma's sent you up some soup and there are some scraps for Wee Dug. Where is he?'

He waved his hand airily. 'Och, somewhere about.'

'I'm sorry I've not been to see you very much lately,' she said, 'but the weans keep me busy.'

'Have you not, hen?' he smiled vaguely. He fell silent for a moment before adding. 'What weans?'

Ruby laughed quietly. 'Frances and Jamie.'

'Oh, aye, they weans,' he said, nodding, then he lapsed into silence once again.

'I'm a wee bit tired,' he said again.

'I'll leave you then, Uncle Jakey, but mind and have your soup. And if you need anything you'll ask, won't you?'

'Oh, aye, aye,' he smiled absently, 'but I'm fine, hen.' He got up from his chair and she just glimpsed the bundle that was Wee Dug underneath.

'Don't get up, Uncle Jakey, you get some rest, okay?'

He looked around the walls sadly. 'But my paintings,' he said again in a worried voice, 'I'm hardly getting any time to paint.'

'Well, there *is* a war on, you know,' she joked, repeating the excuse for everyday annoyances that drove everyone mad, but the humour passed Jakey by. 'It'll soon be over, Uncle Jakey,' she said reassuringly, 'and you can get back to painting as much as you like.'

'Aye, aye,' he murmured absently, 'I suppose that's right. When do you think that will be?'

She felt tears pricking behind her eyes though she couldn't quite understand why. 'Soon, Uncle Jakey,' she said gently, as though soothing a child. 'I don't know just when, but I'm sure it will be soon.'

He nodded. 'Aye, well, that's good then,' he replied. He settled back into his chair and pulled Sarah's crochet thing around him, creating a hiding place once again for Wee Dug underneath it.

As she made her way downstairs she reflected, not for the first time, on the gulf between them since she had become an adult with adult responsibilities and cares. All her life she had used simple language with Uncle Jakey, he had never dealt in jokes or abstractions. A year or so ago she would have remembered that.

Bea was the only person she knew who kept her door locked; she had never understood it, no one would have dared steal from Big Bea. And you never knew if she would answer her door either. According to Sarah it depended on how she was feeling. This time Bea opened the door when Ruby knocked, looked at her with no particular expression on her face, then turned and walked back inside, leaving the door ajar. It was the nearest anyone ever got to an invitation to enter, but as Bea didn't have any friends that Ruby knew about, she supposed she had never had a reason to perfect a welcoming approach.

'And what are you after?' Bea asked wearily, sitting down at the table by the front window.

'All grace!' Ruby thought, still standing, there had been no invitation to sit with her sister. 'I thought you might like a bit of the cake,' she said.

Bea shrugged, trying to indicate that she didn't care one way or the other, but when Ruby put the plate on the table, Bea's eyes settled on the offering as Ruby silently dared her to reach out and bring it closer to her.

'Who am I kidding?' Ruby thought. 'If I tried to take it back she'd bite my hand off at the elbow.'

'Davy at work?' she asked brightly.

'Aye, he's never in these days,' Bea replied.

'Da's the same,' Ruby said, 'I think they all are. Uncle Jakey's tired out, he's been working all night, I've just left him tucked up in his chair.'

111

Bea nodded in reply and Ruby sensed a change in the atmosphere, a softening, if anything connected to Bea could be described as soft.

'I thought you might have come to say you were sorry,' Bea finally said, a touch of belligerence returning.

'What?' Ruby asked slyly. 'Because the men on the railways are working all hours and are tired out?'

'You know fine what I mean,' Bea replied, looking casually out of the window to the street below, but there it was, the beginnings of her horrible screeching whine.

Ruby waited deliberately until Bea had to look at her. 'Don't start, Bea,' she said firmly, looking her in the eye, 'just don't start. You're the one who should be sorry, and you know it.'

'Me?' Bea screeched in amazement.

'Oh, not for the usual screaming hysterics,' Ruby told her, 'we're all so used to them that we barely notice them these days, but for what you said about Jamie. That was unforgivable.'

'I said only the truth,' Bea replied coldly.

'The fact that his mother is trash is hardly his fault,' Ruby told her, 'but that's by the by. It's bad enough that other people whisper about him, but he's family, we look after our own.'

'A lot *you* know!' Bea shouted. 'You think this family is perfect, but let me tell you—'

'Perfect?' Ruby shouted back at her. 'Perfect? With Iris in it? And you? How can we be perfect with you two exhibits in it? We do our best, Bea, given what we have, we try. Or the rest of us do, but you, you just try *us*!'

Ruby could see the gathering storm in Bea, before her eyes she seemed to be expanding into the caricature everyone knew as Big Bea, and for a moment it looked like Bea was thinking about standing and fighting.

'Och, sit where you are, Bea!' Ruby said harshly, turning to go. 'Or I swear to God I'll lift that vase off your mantelpiece and fell you with it!'

'You think you could?' Bea asked, her voice still rising up the scale.

'Any minute now,' Ruby thought, 'only Wee Dug will be able to hear her!' She turned round again and faced Bea. 'Do you think I couldn't?' she demanded, reaching a hand out as though she was going for the vase. 'Or do you just hope that? Go on, chance it if you do, there's no court in the land would convict me, everybody knows what you're like.'

The two sisters stared at each other for what seemed a long time, then Bea seemed to subside back into herself. Ruby took a deep breath as quietly as she could. 'I don't know why you do it, Bea,' she said. 'All that nonsense of yours upsets everybody else, and that's what you want, but it never does *you* any good. That's what I don't understand.'

'Aye, well,' Bea muttered darkly, returning her gaze to the street below, 'you wouldn't understand, would you? You're just like the rest, you know nothing, with your cosy wee life.'

For a moment Ruby eyed the vase on the mantelpiece once again and her hand itched to pick it up. 'This again?' she asked wearily. 'You know what you are, Bea? You're daft as a bloody brush! We all have cosy wee lives? Have you looked around you?'

Bea looked back at her and opened her mouth.

'No, no, don't say anything,' Ruby told her dismissively, putting out a hand to stave off whatever Bea was thinking of telling her. She stood looking at Bea, the self-appointed victim of some mysterious crime, wallowing in her misery, and she thought of a million things more to tell her of the cosy lives everyone, apart from Bea, supposedly enjoyed. Then she thought better of it. Why waste her breath? 'Eat your cake, Bea,' she said sourly, 'just eat your cake.' She turned to go again. 'At least,' she said over her shoulder, 'while you're stuffing your face we won't have to put up with the shite you talk!'

12

Everyone dreaded New Year 1940–1, the first year of the War that
their menfolk would be in far-off lands. The McCreadies sang and
the women cleaned their houses and called to each other from
their windows as always, though with less enthusiasm, Ruby felt,
as though they were going through the motions because they didn't
know what else to do. There were no celebrations, no gathering at
the Tolbooth or parties and George was relieved of his first-footing
duties for the first time since he had grown tall and dark. He was
too busy in the Goods Yard to go round the neighbours when
daylight arrived on 1st January, so New Year, always an emotional
time, had a new edge to it, and even a simple 'Happy New Year!'
when neighbours met in the street seemed to stick in apprehensive throats.

Shelters had gone up in back courts for air-raid alerts, though
after the false alarms during the dummy War many people tended
to stay put in their beds rather than risk the cold, dark and damp
for nothing. Harry had started a communal vegetable plot that all
the neighbours took turns to care for, and his chicken coop produced
a limited number of eggs for everyone, and the occasional chicken.
Queues for rations became a fixed part of life and people learned
to make do with what they had, all of them hoping, because there
was nothing else for it, that it would soon be over and life would
return to normal, even if in their hearts they didn't believe it. The
sight of a post office boy on a bike with a telegram in his pouch
had struck terror into the hearts of those who lived through WWI
and still reduced Sarah to tears in WWII. The word would spread
that he was heading in any direction long before he arrived and,

when he came close to his destination, the hapless boy would pass fearful women who would cry with relief as he passed their doors, knowing that he would meet a different kind of tears at the one he was about to knock on.

Then, one day at the beginning of March, Betty Campbell arrived on the McLean doorstep to see the babies, as she often did. Ruby showed her into the bedroom where they were asleep, vaguely aware that Betty didn't seem herself, that there was something wrong.

'Sit down, Ruby,' she whispered, 'I don't want your mother to hear this.'

'What is it?' Ruby asked, suddenly afraid, but unsure why. This wasn't how bad news about fighting men was broken, she knew that, but still.

'Ruby,' Betty said, her voice pained, 'I've come to tell you that I'm going away.'

Ruby stared at her, confused. 'Where?' she asked. 'Why? When?'

Betty, sitting beside her by the big bay window, took Ruby's hands in hers and looked down in silence for a long time.

Ruby felt her heart thudding in her chest and her mouth was dry.

'I found out something last night,' Betty said quietly, 'something terrible, Ruby. I saw Gus going into your close, Gerry's close I mean, and I thought it was about the blackout, somebody showing a light, you know?'

Ruby nodded.

'But when he didn't come out again I ran across in case something was wrong, somebody ill or had taken a tumble maybe.' There was another silence. 'Your door was open a wee bit, so I just pushed it and looked in. And that's when I saw them. It was dark, but I saw them.' She looked up at Ruby, her eyes heavy with tears. 'Gus and Iris.'

Ruby was bewildered, her mind a blank.

'They were in bed together!' Betty let go of Ruby's hands and covered her mouth to stifle a sob. 'They didn't hear me or see me, they were too busy, if you get my drift, so I just crept out and went home.'

'That bitch!' Ruby whispered furiously, jumping up.

'Ssh, Ruby,' Betty said, looking back at the babies, 'don't wake the wee ones! And it's all right.'

'How can it be all right?' Ruby demanded furiously.

'Because I've decided what I'm going to do. He didn't come back all night, just this morning to get changed for work. I stayed in bed with my back to him as though I was asleep so that I didn't have to see him or talk to him, and when I heard him go out again I packed a case. By the time he comes back I'll be well away.'

'And you're just going to go? You're not going to do anything?' Ruby asked, aghast. 'About them, I mean?'

'What is there to do, Ruby?' Betty asked sadly. 'I can't not see what I saw, there's no way back from that, and what good would it do to scream and shout? I've been thinking about it all night, but I still haven't made up my mind where I'm going yet. I've got relatives and old friends all over though, and as soon as I get settled I'll get in touch with you.' She gave a strange little laugh that sounded like a buffer against a sob. 'I'll want all the news about these ones. Frances will be walking by herself any day now, I'll want to know all about them, but just promise me one thing?'

'Anything,' Ruby nodded.

'That when Gus finds I'm missing you don't tell him I know what he's done, you don't tell anybody anything. And when I write to you, promise me you won't tell him we're in touch or that you know where I am. There's nothing he can say, nothing to talk about. I'm finished with him.'

Ruby nodded helplessly, her mind still whirling with confusion.

'I was thinking of some grand gesture,' Betty laughed in a small voice. 'I was thinking of dropping my wedding ring out of the train window, but he never bought it.' Holding her hand up and gazing at the thick band of rose gold, she gave a shrill little laugh. 'It's my grandmother's wedding ring. It has an inscription inside, "Rose, my one true love, Alex." And she was, my grandparents were the happiest couple I ever knew.'

'It's a lovely ring, I've always admired it,' Ruby said, blindly trying to make conversation, looking for a place in her mind to make sense of what she had heard. 'I've never seen one as broad, it must've cost a lot.'

'My grandfather was a goldsmith,' Betty smiled, 'he made the ring and even inscribed it himself, rose gold for his Rose. So you can understand why I won't be throwing it away for the sake of Gus Campbell! I've got her engagement ring too but I never wear it. I'm always scared that I might damage it cleaning out the fire or something, or maybe lose a diamond, so I've just kept it safe. Granny Rose had lots of bits and pieces my grandfather made for her over the years: there's a lovely brooch with a watch on it, a fob watch it's called, but you can take the watch off and just wear it as a brooch. And there's a bangle with some wee rubies, a beautiful thing it is, I'll show it to you one day, Ruby, covered in engravings and scroll work. Must've taken him ages to make. I've got her locket, too, with a big emerald in the middle, a really clear green one, not milky. Emerald was her birthstone but he waited till he found a really big, fine quality one before he made the locket. She used to say it cost a lot of money. I've got them all packed in my suitcase. I'll take her wedding ring off and put it with the other things. I don't feel like a married woman any longer. Gus used to say I should sell the jewellery and make use of the money. It was just sitting there in a box. He never understood.'

Ruby's eyes instantly narrowed with distaste and Betty smiled at her and patted her hand.

'I know, I know. My mother and my sister, Irene, didn't like him either, Ruby, hen, not from the minute they set eyes on him. I fell out with Irene over Gus, I've hardly set eyes on her since. I've only had a couple of letters from her, but a birthday card and a Christmas card every year, mind.' She smiled sadly. 'Irene told Gus exactly what she thought of him, what they all thought of him. He just said they were snobs and to this day he won't hear her name mentioned.'

'So you lost your family for him?' Ruby asked.

Betty nodded. 'I lost Irene, and we had always been close, so that hurt. My mother was upset, but she was still my mother. She even offered to help me bring the baby up between us rather than see me marry him. She was so right.' She sighed. 'Why do the young never listen? She said I needed all the luck I could get, so she gave me her own mother's ring. Didn't do me much good, did it?' Betty laughed bleakly again. 'I thought about that last night, lying in bed.

I lost the baby anyway, so if I'd listened to my mother and Irene I would've been free of him after that. I've often wondered how my life would've turned out if I hadn't married him.'

Ruby, who was having similar thoughts about her own marriage that she hadn't shared with anyone, wondered if Betty had guessed, if she knew they were two souls with a shared experience beyond their shotgun weddings. 'Why did you marry him?' Ruby asked quietly. 'I never understood that, you're so different.'

'I thought I was doing the right thing. You make your bed so you have to lie in it, that kind of thing, I suppose. And I thought it would be all right, we'd be a family and live happily ever after. All of that. I refused him nothing, Ruby, I could swear to that on a stack of bibles, I gave him everything he could've wanted,' she sighed. 'Except a family, of course, I never gave him that. But now I never want to see him or hear from him again, that's for sure, just the thought of him disgusts me.'

'I've always been with your mother and Irene,' Ruby murmured, 'and he's always disgusted me.'

Betty almost laughed. 'I know that, lass,' she said quietly, 'and every-body tried to tell you were wrong. But listen now,' she continued in a determinedly business-like tone, 'this is important. I don't want your mother to know. She'd be upset because of Iris and it's not Sarah's fault, your mother's a good woman. The word will get around in time, it always does, but can you keep it quiet for as long as possible?'

Ruby threw her arms round her and hugged her. 'My sister's is a slut, an evil slut, I'm so sorry Betty,' she said.

'Now don't blame Iris,' she said, blowing her nose. 'He's more than twenty years older than she is and he's a married man. It's his fault.'

'Don't let her off the hook, she always goes after married men, sure she even carried on with her cousin's man! That was Andy Morris's problem, he was single. I've often thought of telling him to go out and marry the first lassie he met, then Iris would be inter-ested in him.'

'I know, I know,' Betty said quietly, 'but she's still young.'

'She won't get any older once I get my hands on her!' Ruby said angrily.

'No, no, Ruby, hen, you've not to do anything. I'm trusting you not to tell anyone, I would feel black affronted.'

'But why? None of this is your fault!'

Betty shrugged her shoulders helplessly. 'I just feel such a fool,' she said. 'I always felt people here looked up to me a bit, you know?'

'Everybody does!' Ruby said with feeling.

'Well maybe they knew what I didn't, that's what I'm thinking. They say the wife is always last to know, don't they? It would make me look stupid, or feel stupid at any rate. I couldn't hold my head up thinking that other people had known all along.' She sighed shakily, holding back tears, twisting a handkerchief in her hands. 'I never slept a wink last night, trying not to think about what I saw, and I can't help wondering how long it's been going on, and if it's the first time he's done something like this, you know? But I'll have to go now. I want to be well away before he gets back from work. I've always been fond of you, Ruby, I always felt we were close and I didn't want to go without telling you in case you worried. I can't say when I'll write to you, Ruby, it could be a while, but we'll keep in touch, won't we?'

'Of course,' Ruby said, hugging her again, 'of course.'

Betty turned as she reached the front door. 'Oh, I forgot a couple of things.' She put her hand in one coat pocket then the other, brought out an envelope and held it out to Ruby. 'Your Uncle Jakey gave me this to keep for you,' she smiled absently. 'He made out a will leaving everything to you and got Tam McVicar and me to sign.'

'You're kidding!'

'Och, it was ages ago,' Betty laughed, 'about the time you were getting married. You know what Jakey's like, he gets these notions, doesn't he? I don't think he was intending dying or anything. One of his wee voices would likely have told him to do it. I promised him I'd keep it safe. He's never mentioned it since, probably forgotten about it by now, but I thought you should have it since I won't be around.' She paused for a moment, looking down, then 'And I feel bad about Bea,' she said, frowning.

'We all feel bad about Bea!' Ruby replied with feeling.

Betty laughed. 'I still play the piano for her dance classes, who will she get now? I haven't told her I'm going.'

'Oh, I wouldn't worry about that,' Ruby muttered. 'It'll only make her feel hard done by and give her more ammunition for her next screaming match. Not that she needs it.'

'Well, one of these days, later like, could you give her my apologies anyway for leaving her in the lurch?'

When Betty had gone Ruby sat and thought. That her sister had no morals, felt no loyalty and had no standards, well, all of that was well-known, but Gus Campbell was so much older than her, as Betty had said. Ruby squirmed. How could she? And more than his age, he was Gus Campbell – *Gus Campbell!* – so once again, how could she? There was a shortage of young men, to be sure, but *Gus Campbell?* She was so shocked and angry she could hardly sit still. She wanted to do something, but Betty was right, there was nothing to do. Betty was handling this like the lady she had always been, but even so, her dignity was amazing. If Ruby had her way Gus Campbell would have a knife in his back and Iris would be paraded through the streets, tarred and feathered. She would have gladly done both herself. But she had to calm down and think. Betty had trusted her with this information and she had to control every urge in her body that told her to scream it from the rooftops to shame the two of them. Wait, just wait. Take a deep breath. See what happens, nothing to be gained from rushing things. There would be time enough once Betty was settled and knew what action she wanted to take. The hurt was on Betty's side, only she had the right to decide what anyone should do, including Ruby.

Sitting by the bay window, Uncle Jakey's secret will in her hands, Ruby looked up and spotted the figure of Betty, suitcase in hand, walking towards the bottom of High Street. As she reached the corner she stopped, glanced up at the window and waved, then she turned right into George Street and disappeared from view.

13

When Betty Campbell was speaking to Ruby she had no clear idea of where she intended going, only that she wanted to be as far from Gus as possible, somewhere he would never find her. Not from any danger of being persuaded back to him if he did, but because, as she said to Ruby, she couldn't stand the thought of seeing him ever again. She went over her options. If she sought out a friend from years ago she would have to explain why she had arrived on their doorstep, suitcase in hand. She would look pathetic, she thought, and she didn't feel like losing the tiny shred of self-respect she was desperately trying to hold onto. Talking to Ruby about her family had put them in the forefront of her mind again. Her parents were long dead, she and Gus had moved into their flat above the Co-op when her widowed mother died, but Irene was very much alive. Every year she hid Irene's birthday and Christmas cards from Gus, and every year, again without his knowledge, Betty had sent one to Irene. Somewhere, in the recesses of her mind, and probably her sister's too, this tentative contact held the hope of meeting and being a family again at some time in the vague future. From the cards and the odd letter they had exchanged, she knew Irene and her husband, Tommy, lived in Clydebank with their two children, where Irene taught music at the local school and Tommy worked in the shipyards. Better, she thought, seek out family, if Irene would have her that was. Given her feelings about Gus, Irene would understand, even if, Betty thought wryly, she said 'I told you so!' Well, she had earned the right and she felt, or hoped, she could count on her sister. In her suitcase she had packed little. There were a few clothes, somehow they weren't important, all she wanted to take with her were things that mattered to her. All Irene's letters and cards, Granny Rose's jewellery, pictures of her family, of herself with her parents and grandparents, with her sister when they were children, and her gas mask, of course, with her identity card and her ration book safely tucked away underneath in the box. Funny how you felt underdressed without your gas mask, and it was second nature to carry your identity card too, and as for her ration book, well, she didn't want to be a burden to Irene and her family, like everyone else they would be struggling with rations. She took with her no snaps of Gus or with Gus when she left High Street, not even their few wedding pictures. Everything that signified her life as Gus Campbell's wife had been left behind, she had no need or wish to be reminded of a life now firmly in the past, even if her heart lay like a dead weight in her chest with the misery of it all.

She arrived in Clydebank just after one o'clock. There was a certain mythology about Clydebank, the home of shipbuilding on the River Clyde, a place built for workers who put the Red into Red Clydeside. She had never been there before and was struck by how busy it was, a bustling, alive little town, and she stopped a woman of her own age in Glasgow Road and asked for directions to Radnor Street.

'Och, it's up at the top of the hill on Kilbowie Road, lass, you can't be walking up there,' she was told, 'it's steeper than it looks.'

With that she was bundled onto a single-decker tram, and the conductor given instructions to put her off at the right stop. Betty smiled at the assumption that she was a very old biddy who couldn't climb the hill with a suitcase, then, catching her reflection in the window as she sat down, she realised it had been a fair assumption. She adjusted her gaze to look through her reflection and out of the window to distract herself from that thought. Passing under a low railway bridge she understood why the tram had to be a single-decker. Past the canal and rows of tenements and there, on the left, was the Singer's Sewing Machine factory with its enormous clock tower, the tiers of flat-roofed tenements called the Holy City beyond that, built into the hill, and a row of shops on Kilbowie Road, their canopies unfolded against the bright spring sunshine. When the tram reached the crest of the hill she was put off and her case handed down to her after a journey that had only taken minutes, and pointed in the direction of Radnor Street just behind her. She hadn't expected to be there so quickly, so she put her suitcase down on the pavement to stop and think, going through a hundred different scenarios and 'what ifs?' in her mind, before picking up her suitcase again and walking down the short street. At Irene's door she hesitated and ran through her situation once more, before knocking on the door. There was no reply. She didn't know whether to laugh with relief or cry with disappointment, but before she could do either she heard voices and footsteps coming up the stairs behind her and turned to see two women struggling with armfuls of school jotters. One was Irene. The two sisters looked at each other, too shocked to examine the differences brought by the years since they had last met, then Irene hurriedly put down the bundle she was carrying, rushed forward and threw her arms around Betty.

'Jessie,' Irene said to the other woman, 'this is my sister, Betty, I haven't seen her in years. Betty, this is one of the teachers at my school, I was going to help her with some marking.'

'Nice to meet you, Betty,' the younger woman smiled. 'Look, I'll leave you two to catch up. I'll see you later about the marking, Irene.'

Irene was still staring at her sister, smiling, eyes bright. 'Aye, right, fine,' she said absently, then she turned around again and said with a little laugh, 'I'm sorry, Jessie. I'm just surprised at seeing Betty here. How about coming up at three o'clock? We can have a cuppa while we break the back of this pile.'

'If you're sure you can be bothered?' the younger woman said, looking from Irene to Betty and back again.

Irene nodded firmly. 'She's a student,' she whispered to Betty, 'she still panics a bit, but she's a lovely wee lassie, lives down on the bottom floor.' She waited as Jessie's footsteps retreated downstairs before turning back to Betty.

'Is he dead then?' she asked excitedly.

Now Betty got to laugh and cry at the same time. 'No, he's not dead,' she whispered, 'but he is to me.'

'What has he done?' Irene asked, trying frantically to unlock her front door with shaking fingers, so that the key chattered against the metal for a long time before finding its mark. 'Come in, come in,' she said, taking Betty's suitcase. 'Here, sit down.' She spun Betty out of her coat and pushed her into a chair at the kitchen table. Then she hurriedly took off her own coat, filled the kettle at the sink and lit the gas under it, all in the same movement. 'What has he done?' she asked again, settling herself in a chair facing Betty and holding her hands across the table. Betty lowered her head and cried till the whistle of the kettle interrupted her. 'You just sit there and I'll make the tea,' Irene said, jumping up. Betty nodded wordlessly and watched her. She had quite forgotten that her sister did everything at breakneck speed, usually, as now, several things at once. As one hand was pouring boiling water from the kettle into the teapot to warm it, another was reaching for the tea caddy and emptying the warming water into the sink. At the same time, it seemed, as scoops of precious tea were dropped into the teapot, a bowl of even more precious sugar was being brought forth from a cupboard. A pirouette followed to locate a jug, into which milk was poured from a bottle and, finally, fingers of homemade sponge cake were removed from a biscuit tin and deposited on a little plate. Even at speed, everything was done with rhythm and grace, too, she thought, a lass governed by music.

'I forgot how quickly you move,' Betty smiled weakly. 'What was it Dad used to say? "She'll bump into herself coming in the opposite direction one of these days."'

'Mum put it in musical terms, she used to say I ran from *vivace*, through *presto* to *accelerando* without a pause!' Irene laughed at the memory. 'Och, but I was always sure it wasn't me, it was you other people, you're all so slow!' She watched Betty sipping her tea for a few minutes, glancing at her left hand and noting the missing wedding ring. 'So tell me,' she said.

So Betty told her all, and not just about Gus and Iris, but about her less than fulfilling marriage, saying things she had only thought in her darkest moments over the years, while she was putting on a show of being the happy, contented wife she had never been. She had felt stifled by Gus all those years, that was the truth of it, and admitting it was like letting out a breath she had held too long. All the things she had been brought up to admire and enjoy, like music and reading, were wastes of time to him, but in the absence of children, time was all she had. She still read and listened to music, but only when he wasn't at home and never with the natural joy she had been used to all her life before she met him. Even listening to the wireless when he was at work had become a guilty pleasure, there had to be something she should be doing for him instead. Sometimes, if she was listening to music or a play on the wireless when he came in from work, he would just lean over and switch it off before settling into his armchair with his newspaper. He didn't do it, she felt, to upset her, but because he didn't, couldn't understand that she was listening to it from choice, that it meant something to her. To him it was just a background noise he didn't want as he read his paper at the end of his working day. They were, as Ruby had said, very different, but it was his house, even if it had been her family home, and a man had the right to some peace to do his crossword after a hard day's work. Everything she loved was an irritation to him, it simply never occurred to him that she should actually enjoy them, and he wasn't the kind of man she could explain these things to. She had made the best of it and never answered back or picked him up on anything, because, well, because she felt guilty about letting him down by losing the child and never falling with another. Truth be told, she had short-changed Gus, she had failed in the most basic requirement of any wife and felt she had to make that up to him in any and every way she could thereafter. But him and Iris, that was something she couldn't indulge him in, that was too much, and so, she told her sister, she had left.

'Well you'll be staying here,' Irene stated.

'Have you got room?' Betty asked.

'We'll make room,' Irene said. 'Tommy's mother lives next door, our Jenny can stay with her till we sort things out, you can have her room. The old woman's a bit of a trial at times,' she smiled tightly. 'She had him late in life and she's a widow now, he'll always be her one and only adored baby. She was disappointed he didn't marry "a real teacher." Teaching music is on the same level as milk monitor in her book!'

'She doesn't have anyone else at all?'

'No,' Irene grimaced, 'or I'd have her living next door to *them!* She's just old,' she shrugged, 'and who knows what we'll be like when we're her age, eh? But she's fond of Jenny and Jenny's fond of her, so neither will mind.' She looked at Betty. 'And that big beast doesn't know where you are?'

Betty shook her head. 'He doesn't know where you live, hasn't the slightest clue. I never told him I'd had any word from you in all these years.'

'Good. We'll keep it that way. Did you tell anyone where you were going?'

'The lass who lives across the street, Ruby, I told her I was going and why – this Iris is her sister.'

Irene frowned.

'No, no, Ruby has no time for her sister, she was so angry I had to stop her going out and looking for her. Ruby's a good lass, the kind of daughter I'd like to have had. I told her I'd be in touch when I was settled, but I didn't know for sure myself where I was going till I started walking down the street. She wouldn't say a word even if she knew, she's known Gus all her life and she's hated him as long.'

'Sounds like a lass I could get to like!' Irene laughed.

'Are you sure your family won't mind?' Betty asked tentatively.

'What are talking about? *You're* my family!' Irene replied. 'They're *your* family! Besides, they'll be fascinated to meet you, their secret Auntie Betty.' Irene got up and rifled through a drawer on her dresser and came back with some photos. 'This is Jenny, she's fifteen, and Ronnie's thirteen. They're going down to the La Scala tonight to see Shirley Temple in some film, so you won't see much of them. Hideous wee beast, but some seem to like her. I don't think Ronnie's bothered, it's a night out to him.' She looked at Betty. 'You look all in,' she said gently.

'I know. I didn't sleep a wink last night, just waited for him to come back and get ready for his work this morning so that I could leave.'

Irene got up. 'I'll get a couple of things from Jenny's room and you can lie down there.' She put a hand out. 'Come on, you need to get some rest, Betty.'

Betty rose and linked arms with her sister as Irene picked up the suitcase.

'You haven't got much in this,' Irene smiled.

'Family things,' Betty smiled sadly. 'Pictures, letters and Granny Rose's jewellery. We can have a look later if you like.'

Irene nodded. 'The weans will enjoy that, especially Jenny.' She put the case on the floor and looked through a chest of drawers, collecting clothes Jenny would need. 'Now you lie down,' she smiled as she shut the door, 'take as long as you need, we'll be quiet to let you sleep.'

Alone in the bedroom, Betty sat on the bed and looked out of the window. Suddenly she was felt overwhelmed with weariness. She folded back the quilt and lay down, fully clothed, on her niece's bed, pulling the quilt back over her, her eyes still fixed on the scene beyond the window. The weather had been unusually dry and warm these last few days, and the afternoon sun was climbing high in a sky that was exceptionally bright and blue. Maybe, she thought, that was an omen of better things to come.

14

The War was still there to occupy every mind, which in Ruby's case was a good thing, it stopped her leaping on Gus Campbell or Iris – though not the two at the same time, that thought disgusted her – and giving them a sound slapping. The evening of the day Betty left High Street the Germans bombed Clydebank for the first time. On her way to the shelter in the back court with the children on the night of the first raid, Ruby watched the German aircraft overhead. It was a still, clear, moonlit night – a Bomber's Moon, they called it – and the sheer volume and noisy menace of the planes overhead was frightening. She stood watching them, trembling slightly, when Gus Campbell arrived and put his arms around her to usher her more quickly into the shelter.

'Get your hands off me!' she told him coldly.

'Get into the shelter then,' he ordered, looking down at her from under his official ARP helmet. 'You don't want to be standing out here with two wee weans if a bomb falls, do you? Let me have the wee boy.'

'Get your hands off him, too!' she spat at him, twisting round so that he couldn't touch Jamie. 'I look after him all the time. I can look after him now without any help from you.'

'My God, but you're a sweet wee thing, aren't you?' he remarked. 'You've always been the same, give a kick easier than a kiss.'

'That's true as far as you're concerned,' Ruby scowled at him, shrugging him off.

As she moved away from him, from the corner of her eye she caught sight of Iris exchanging a glance with Campbell. It almost took her breath away and she had the feeling that time had stood still for a long moment as she watched them. If she hadn't known what she already knew she wouldn't have noticed anything special about that look, nor the fact that they had arrived together. But now she did know. She felt angry and wanted to hit back at them, she wanted to say 'Wonder where your wife is tonight, Gus? Do you wonder that, too, Iris?' and just managed to bite her tongue.

Betty Campbell, asleep in her niece's bed, heard only the occasional noise in background. Distant voices, doors opening and closing, the now familiar sound of a siren mixed up with her dreams, until Irene came in and shook her fully awake.

'Betty, you'll have to get up, I think we're going to be bombed,' Irene said in an entirely calm voice.

Betty looked around her. 'Really?'

'Looks like it,' Irene said, indicating with her head towards the window as she rushed around. 'Come on, Betty, hurry!'

'What time is it?'

'Just after nine o'clock, now move, Betty!'

Betty jumped up. 'Oh, my God!' she breathed. Earlier she had looked out of the window to see sunshine and blue sky that seemed like heaven on earth, but now she was looking through the same window at an earth that had descended into hell. Clydebank was ablaze, the landscape consumed by orange flames and loud explosions. While Betty slept the German Pathfinders had lit up the night by dropping incendiaries to guide the bombers that were now upon the town. A door opened and voices called out. Irene looked up. 'That's Tommy back in with the weans,' she said. 'I sent him down to the La Scala to get them while I got his mother organised for the shelter at the school. Now grab whatever you need, and we'll get out of here. Quick now, Betty, you'll have to move!'

Betty followed her sister out of the bedroom and, in her panic, only vaguely noticed Tommy and the two children. An old lady, his mother, she realised, was clinging to Tommy and weeping, as Irene tried to hurry everyone out and downstairs.

'Here, Betty, take your coat,' she said, throwing it at her. 'We've no idea how long this will last, it's never happened in earnest before. You'll likely need it.'

Betty pushed her arms into her coat sleeves and looked at the clock on the mantelpiece. She recognised it as the one that had stood on her mother's mantelpiece throughout her childhood, and it reminded her about the contents of the suitcase she had left in the bedroom. Instinctively she turned back. All the worldly possessions she cared about were in the case, she wasn't, she decided, about to leave it behind. It took her seconds to collect it and join the tail-end of the family as they all rushed downstairs together.

'The school's just across the road,' Irene said encouragingly, 'it'll only take us a minute to get there.'

Ahead of them they saw Jessie, the student teacher, but she was going in the wrong direction and back to the tenement.

'Where do you think you're you going?' Irene demanded in her best schoolmistress voice.

'The jotters!' Irene shouted, above the noise of the planes and the bombs exploding around her. 'I've left them in the house!'

'Away for God's sake!' Irene yelled angrily. 'To hell with the jotters, just you turn round and run for your life, lassie!'

Jessie stopped, looked thoughtful, then almost laughed as she turned around again and ran for the shelter in the school. Irene shook her head at her. 'Would you credit it?' she asked no one in particular. Then she gathered her family around her, checked that everyone was there and said, 'We'll be all right. We're all together so nothing bad will happen to us, okay? Right now everybody, run!'

In the weeks after the Clydebank raid the survivors were evacuated to places all over the country but the work of digging the dead out of the ruins would continue for many months. The industries the little town specialised in were largely untouched in what had been a terror bombing. The Germans had gathered countless reconnaissance photographs of the area over the years, plus they had that Bomber's Moon. They hit the targets they intended hitting and came back the following night and did it all again; if the first raid had been a mistake, why repeat it after reviewing the photos the next night? Their aim had been simply to terrorise the people, any damage to the industrial heart of Clydebank had been incidental and relatively light. Street after street of houses was flattened, with only six homes in the town left undamaged. The official line was that there had been little destruction and only 500 deaths had occurred; a deliberate underestimate for reasons of morale apparently, and that number didn't take into account those who had simply been obliterated and would never be found. Beyond the official declaration, the scale of the damage inflicted on the town was kept under wraps. 'Bankies guarded their independence fiercely and would not tolerate being labelled as part of Glasgow, but even so, in many ways Glasgow begat Clydebank and most 'Bankies had friends and relatives in the city, so the news of the carnage spread quickly by word of mouth. One ARP Warden, who had been digging bodies out of rubble for weeks, looked up when told the official death toll and asked wearily, 'In which street?'

From their temporary homes Clydebank's hastily evacuated workers returned the next day and the next, picking their way through the debris of their town to keep producing ships and munitions for the War effort, hopeful that their homes and their lives would be quickly rebuilt. Glasgow, too, suffered bombing that March, it was intended as a raid on Clydeside, and other bombs fell on the city during the War, but the small burgh of Clydebank took the hardest hits. Clydebank was all but destroyed.

It soon became obvious that the usual laws and niceties would have to be re-thought, as the decimated community struggled to cope with its devastation. There was no fresh water because a water main had been fractured and a huge crater had formed around it, so the first thought was to repair it. It was then discovered that the water had been contaminated with sewage, and there would be no drinking water for weeks. And, as in all emergencies, the plight of Clydebank brought out the best and the worst in humanity. As the dead were still being recovered, anything with wheels arrived from Glasgow to steal their belongings, while others came to do anything they could to help. Meals were provided by Glasgow's Education Department, and the workers had one bright spot in their lives – food galore with all the sugar they could consume. Until, that was, the Ministry of Food ordered the town council to take over and they were back to half a teaspoon of sugar per cuppa.

The bureaucrats of the Civil Service were of no help, they simply sat at their desks waiting for something to happen, so a committee was set up to try to bring some order to the chaos. The dead were laid on church hall floors in the hope that relatives would identify them. Some had died from bomb blast and hadn't a mark on their bodies, while others were unrecognisable. What made the search for missing family harder was that often they had no idea where they would be found, with many recovered long distances from where they had died. Then it was discovered that if someone died in an ambulance taking them to hospital they would be left at the side of the road so that someone living could be taken for help. Unceremonious and undignified, to be sure, but practical.

An unofficial little group was set up by the Town Clerk Depute, Mr Hastings, to help identify the dead. They took photos, wrote down descriptions and removed trinkets and put them in envelopes, but even so, on health grounds alone, it became clear that something would have to be done with the unclaimed and unknown dead. On 17th March, four days after the first wave of bombing, sixty-six bodies went into a mass grave in nearby Dalnottar Cemetery, forty-eight of whom were unidentified and eighteen identified but unclaimed by family. The following day another twenty were buried in the same way. Because the town officials had been refused even cardboard coffins, the victims went to their graves covered in white sheets tied at the neck and waist. 'They looked like ghosts,' the Town Clerk Depute remarked, 'it was a horrible sight.'

But even those who had been claimed and their funerals arranged by family, soon found more problems. As no doctor had provided a death certificate, the Registrar in the town was refusing to register the death, and without registration there could be no burial. Once again Hastings stepped in, pronouncing the situation with the town's Registrar 'untenable' and accepting that there was no possibility of anyone registering a death in Cydebank. Instead of wasting time arguing, Hastings promptly brought in another Registrar from nearby Old Kilpatrick and on his authority the necessary paperwork was issued to allow people to bury their dead.

In all, 180 were buried as unidentified, but because of Hastings' work, only five or six remained unidentified after six months. This, however, didn't take account of 'the disappeared', whose bodies would never be found or were in so many pieces they could not be identified.

And yet, in the all the horror of the landscape there were lasting memories of beauty. Caged birds had escaped and were flying in flocks around the town, and many workers engaged in their grim tasks would recall years later how they had stopped to watch bright yellow canaries and listen to them singing among the rubble and the carnage. Somehow it brought a little hope.

But for Ruby, the Blitz became personal. For the rest of her life the images of those dark shapes in the moonlight overhead, on their way to destroy the little town up the river, would remain clear in her memory and, years later, still made her tremble.

15

The Christmases and New Years of her childhood had changed out of all recognition now that Ruby was an ancient. When she moved to Largs and finally accepted that she would never shake Paddy off, she resigned herself to spending what the TV people liked to call 'The Festive Season' with her neighbour. As it was Christmas Eve he had come over to place her usual present of bath salts under the tiny tree in the corner of the room. He must have bought a job lot, she often thought. He had then taken advantage of the situation by planting his large frame in a chair in the other corner where he sat glumly going over the newspapers for the feast of entertainment planned by the TV companies.

'Nothing but repeats,' he muttered. 'Have you seen this, Ruby? Nothing but bloody repeats, it's scandalous!'

Ruby was preparing as much of Christmas dinner in advance as she could. 'Aye,' she sighed, 'and repeats of things you didn't want to watch the first and second times round at that.'

'Ne'erday's no better,' he complained, ferreting through more pages. 'I suppose it'll be another of they terrible tartan programmes at the Bells and they're not a patch on Andy Stewart and the *White Heather Club*.'

'Aye,' Ruby laughed, 'the wee teuchter from Arbroath, complete with Highland accent!'

'Well Arbroath is the Highlands as far as I'm concerned,' Paddy protested primly.

'Away with you! You can get there faster than you can get to Glasgow!'

'Aye, well, still, Wee Andy was better than this muck, it makes you want to put your foot through the screen, so it does.'

Ruby looked at his feet. 'Well I wouldn't do that,' she said wryly, 'given that your feet are sticking out of what you call slippers, you'd end up in casualty getting those big ugly toes stitched together while they picked out bits of faded checked rubbish.'

'You still on about my slippers?' he demanded absently, scattering newspaper pages everywhere.

'My God, but you're such an untidy creature!' she said, watching him.

'It's not me!' he protested. 'It's the way they do these papers nowadays.'

'Well everybody else manages,' Ruby replied, '*I* manage.'

'Aye, but you would,' he scowled, 'you're perfect, we all know that.'

'Any more of that and you'll get this turkey about your ears,' she said conversationally.

Paddy looked up at her and smiled, watching her work. 'When was the first time you had turkey at Christmas, Ruby?' he asked.

'You mean made it myself?' she asked. 'Because I had it in hospital canteens before that. I think it was the first year I made it for you,' she said thoughtfully, 'before that it was chicken.'

He chuckled. 'Aye, thon chicken in a tin, that's what we had. My wife used to boil it up to make soup out of it. You thought you'd won a watch if you found a sliver of chicken in it! Then we had it sliced with roast tatties and Russell Spouts.'

She looked across at him and laughed, he could never say 'Brussel Sprouts,' but if she picked him up on it he insisted that's what he had said.

'And plum duff and custard afterwards,' he said mistily. 'I never liked the plum duff, mind,' he recalled, 'but I ate it all the same.'

'Why?' Ruby asked.

'Well, it was Christmas, you had to,' he replied.

'Daft bugger!' she smiled. 'And wasn't it was amazing how far those tinned chickens stretched? Talk about the loaves and fishes!'

'Well, they had to!'

'Did they ever taste of anything once they'd had the hell boiled out of them for soup?' she laughed.

'I don't think they did,' Paddy smiled, 'it was just the idea, wasn't

135

it? We never had chicken any other time, did we? It was only the rich folk who could afford to buy a whole chicken back then.'

'We had it once or twice during the War,' Ruby remembered. 'My father built a chicken coop in the back court. Everybody, all the neighbours, took their turn at looking after the hens.'

'Stinking bloody things, hens,' Paddy commented. 'Helluva stupid as well.'

'Aye, but they gave us eggs when everybody else only had dried egg and we got the odd bit of chicken as well and at least they tasted of chicken then. There are weans born the day who think that muck we get in the supermarket is what chicken's supposed to taste like.' She thought in silence for a moment. 'Y'know, I've often wondered since why nobody back then stole the eggs or the chickens.'

'Different days,' Paddy said sadly. 'People had more respect back then.'

'Now you're not going to give me all that old twaddle about everybody pulling together during the War, are you?' Ruby demanded.

'Well they did!'

'Och, Paddy, you're a sentimental old wife!' she mocked him. 'Remember the Clydebank Blitz in 1941? All those nice Glaswegians who went down there in droves and picked through the rubble to steal anything they could lay hands on from the poor folk who had been bombed?'

'I don't believe that,' Paddy said staunchly. 'Glaswegians aren't like that. You shouldn't believe everything you hear, Ruby.'

'Well that's just proof that you're a sentimental old wife,' Ruby repeated. 'The bodies were still being dug out and their stuff was already being hawked around Glasgow. Sure, lots of people helped each other out during the War, but lots more helped themselves, and you know that fine. My mother had stockpiled everything she could for ages before the War, and she shared what she had with other people – shared it mind, *gave* it away, she never took a penny for it. Then she discovered some of them were selling it on the Black Market.'

'You're such a … a … what's the word?' he asked.

'A realist,' Ruby replied.

'No, that's not it,' he said. 'A ... a ...'

'I would say you're looking for the word cynic,' Ruby suggested, 'but you've not got the brains for that.'

'A misery guts!' he said triumphantly, banging his hand down and putting it through several pages of the newspaper he was holding. 'That's what you are, Ruby, a misery guts!'

'And you're the messiest human being I've ever laid eyes on,' she replied, shaking her head at the shreds of newspaper now strewn all over the carpet. She went back to her cooking. 'Will your son be calling you on Christmas Day?' she asked.

'I suppose so,' Paddy muttered.

'You don't sound very pleased about it, you miserable old bugger. At least he makes the effort.'

'And that's just how it feels, as though he's making an effort,' Paddy said quietly.

'Huh!' Ruby replied. 'And you call me a misery guts! What do you want of the boy? He asked you to go to Canada with him and you turned him down. He calls you regularly and he asks you to come out on holiday, and still you complain.'

'I'm not complaining,' he said, shifting restlessly in his seat.

'Canada's a nice place,' she said. 'You'd think you'd at least be curious.'

'What do you know about Canada?' he murmured. 'Sure, you've never been there.'

'I've seen it on the TV,' she replied tartly, 'and I know people who emigrated.' She looked up at him. 'What? Do you think you're the only one who's had somebody emigrate? This is Scotland, in case you haven't noticed, we breed emigrants here.'

'Anyway, I can't afford to go all the way over there.'

'You know fine you don't have to!' she said scornfully. 'Hasn't he offered to pay over and over again, and you've always refused him?'

'I don't want charity,' he muttered, 'I'd feel I was there under sufferance, as though I'd inflicted myself on them.'

'Huh,' Ruby replied, 'but you don't mind inflicting yourself on me!'

'Besides,' he said, ignoring her jibe, 'we don't have very much in common. We've nothing really to talk about.'

'Well what do you expect? You're living different lives in different parts of the world, but you could try a bit harder.'

'What do you mean by that?' he demanded petulantly.

'I've heard you on the phone,' she accused him, pointing a spoon at him. 'You sound like the speaking clock.'

'Well I'm just conscious that I'm speaking into a bit of plastic,' he whined.

'So what?' she demanded. 'We all speak into a bit of plastic when we're on the phone, doesn't mean you shouldn't talk like a human being. The poor lad's probably saying to his wife at this very moment "I've got to talk to my miserable old man tomorrow, but he always sounds so bored, as though he doesn't want to speak to me." You've got somebody, Paddy, you should be grateful,' she said quietly.

'So have you!' he accused her. 'You've got a daughter!'

'A low blow!' she thought. 'No I haven't Paddy,' she replied firmly. 'I gave birth to her, but I never had her, not for an instant.'

'Well I just don't understand that,' he said, his tone betraying his guilt at mentioning her daughter.

'That's because you did have your son. You still do, Paddy Keenan,' she said, poking the spoon in his direction again. 'He's making the effort, so you do the same when you're talking to him tomorrow. Okay?'

And she never did have Frances, it was true. She walked before the age of a year old, Ruby remembered, a reasonable time, but she showed no real joy at being upright and independent, unlike Jamie, who had been so overcome with his new skill when the time came that he had laughed so hard he kept falling down again. It kept coming back to that, she thought, Frances had no joy, no ups or downs, she just was. Sarah kept reassuring Ruby that no two babies were alike, that Frances had her own personality and she was just aware of it because Jamie was so different. Jamie was an affectionate little boy, he hugged and kissed everyone and everything, even pictures in magazines, he was a happy child. Sometimes she felt bad about what lay ahead for him, she was the only mother he had ever known, but there would come a time when he would have to absorb that Iris was his mother and come to terms with her complete indifference to him. But there was nothing she could do about that, she reasoned. While she had him she would make sure he was cared for, happy and protected, she couldn't do more than that.

16

It was sad that Betty Campbell left before Frances took her first independent steps, Betty was so interested in everything to do with the babies, and the two events would forever be linked in Ruby's mind. The reason for Betty's departure also took Ruby's mind off her daughter's achievement, of course, as she found herself constantly watching for more signs that Gus Campbell and Iris were still involved. From Harry and Sarah's flat, her married home, Gerry's place, was further up the brae, where it curved to the right, and so was out of her immediate view, as was the Campbell home directly across the road from it. Stoking her wrath, she conjured up pictures of them signalling to each other from their windows when Betty's back had been turned. It was probably just as well she couldn't see them, she mused, or she'd have watched too closely and maybe given the game away.

Over the following weeks Ruby waited every day for news of Betty's disappearance to filter through. It was her mother who mentioned it first.

'Isn't it odd without Betty?' she asked, conversationally, as she sat by the fire, crocheting. 'She'll notice a big difference in the wee ones when she comes back.'

Ruby glanced at Sarah's latest 'thing' and hoped she or the weans wouldn't be the unfortunate recipients. 'Oh?' she said, aiming for no more than casual interest. 'Come to think of it, I haven't seen her recently right enough. Where has she gone?'

'Gus told your Da her sister's ill, so Betty's gone to stay with her for a while.' Sarah beamed over her crochet hook. 'There are weans to be looked after, and you know what Betty's like with weans.'

'Mm,' Ruby replied, wiping Jamie's nose as he turned his head from side-to-side. 'He never said a word before. Did he know she was going?'

'Oh, aye, he took her down to the station and put her on the train.'

Ruby swallowed hard. 'So where does her sister live then?'

'In Yorkshire somewhere apparently. I never met her, but Betty's mentioned her a couple of times. Irene her name is, if I mind rightly, she doesn't come near because she doesn't get on with Gus,' Sarah said.

'Sounds like somebody I'd like,' Ruby said.

Sarah laughed. 'Gus says Betty keeps in touch with him, though, even with the War, sends her best to everyone and says she'll be home as soon as her sister's better.'

Ruby gritted her teeth. *The lying hound!* 'Aye, well, we miss her,' she smiled back at her mother, 'but as long as she's all right.'

'Oh, aye, she seems to be, Gus says she's in her element looking after Irene and the wee ones, as I say, you know what Betty's like. I've told him to tell her everybody here's asking for her.'

'I'm sure he will,' Ruby said sourly. 'Him being such a caring big beast.'

'Ruby!' Sarah laughed, shaking her head. 'He can't do anything right in your eyes, can he?'

'No,' Ruby thought angrily, 'he can't.'

17

She hardly saw Flora during those days. While she looked after the children, her old pal spent all her time at the Rolls Royce factory in Hillington, working all hours to produce plane engines. The most contact they had was a quick wave to each other in passing, but as the silence from Betty Campbell continued, burning holes in Ruby's patience, the next time she saw Flora she motioned her to come up to the house. Flora had a safe, sensible pair of ears.

'Have you got time?' she asked, holding Flora by the arm and propelling her inside.

'Looks as though I don't have a choice!' Flora laughed.

'I need to talk to you,' Ruby explained, 'and my mother's out queuing up for something, so I've got the house to myself.'

'Sounds interesting,' Flora grinned, settling by the fire and warming her hands.

'Well, not interesting,' Ruby frowned, 'more horrible.' And with that she told her Betty's story. 'I promised her I wouldn't say or do anything,' she explained, 'but I had to tell someone.'

'And you decided it should be me,' Flora said, blowing out a long breath. 'Well, thanks very much for that, Ruby!' She was quiet for a moment. 'And you haven't heard from her since she left?'

Ruby shook her head.

'Does she have a sister?'

Ruby nodded. 'Irene,' she said. 'She hated Gus and tried to stop Betty marrying him. Betty fell out with her and they haven't had much contact since then.'

'So it is possible that she did go to stay with this sister, Irene, in Yorkshire?'

'I suppose so. She didn't tell me where Irene lived. She said she would stay with friends or relatives. She hadn't made up her mind.'

'Well maybe she did go to her sister's, then calmed down, thought about things and decided she'd try to make a go of it with Gus. For all you know she has been in touch with him, just as he says, and all he's doing is coming up with a story to stop people gossiping until Betty comes home.'

'I don't think so,' Ruby replied firmly, 'she was absolutely sure of what she was doing. Besides, I'm not worried at her not being in touch, it hasn't been that long, and I'm sure she'll write once she's settled, just as she said. There *is* a war on you know.'

They both chuckled quietly.

'Well what are you worried about then?'

'Them!' Ruby said furiously. 'Gus and Iris! What am I to do about them?'

'Is that all?' Flora laughed. 'Nothing, of course! Isn't that what Betty asked you to do?'

'But they can't get away with it!' Ruby said.

'They won't, will they? Not in the long run, it will all come out, these things always do. What you're really asking, Ruby McLean,' she said sternly, 'is my permission to wade in there and do battle on Betty's behalf, when she has specifically asked you to let her deal with it in her own time and in her own way. Isn't that right?'

'I suppose so,' Ruby admitted sheepishly.

'And you're scared that Betty *has* changed her mind and you won't get to see Gus and Iris face the music, isn't that right too? So it's about what *you* want, isn't it, it's not really on Betty's behalf?'

'Well, I'd like to give them a slap or two, and in public, that's true ….'

Flora laughed out loud.

'But they shouldn't get away with it, should they?' Ruby persisted. 'What they've done is terrible.'

'Oh, I'll grant you that,' Flora said. 'Of all the low blows your sister has handed out to countless other females, this is probably the lowest. And Betty has always defended her, hasn't she? I can remember her speaking up for her when everyone else was running her down. But there's nothing you can do, Ruby. It's Betty's problem.'

She looked across at Ruby and smiled. 'You know, I'm finding this violent streak in you a bit worrying,' she said. 'You know who it reminds me of?'

Ruby looked back of her.

'A red-haired harridan not a million miles from here who explodes on a regular basis?' Flora suggested.

'Don't you dare say that!' Ruby said, horrified. 'I'm nothing like Bea!'

Flora shrugged her shoulders. 'Well, I have heard that you've taken to slapping her too,' she said, pursing her lips to stop herself laughing. 'Seems to me you've taken to it like a duck, or a sister duck, to water!'

Ruby, realising that Flora was joking with her, raised a hand in a fake attempt to hit out at her.

'You see!' Flora giggled. 'You've just proved my point!'

As they settled down to catch up on other matters, Flora asked 'And how's Uncle Jakey?'

'Exhausted,' Ruby frowned, 'completely worn out.'

'Aye, well, we're all that way,' Flora sighed.

'I don't know,' Ruby said quietly, 'it seems more than that with him. He can't get time to do his painting and that's upsetting him. It's almost like he needs to do it.'

'Well why shouldn't he?' Flora asked sternly. 'Your mother does her hellish crochets that are no good to man nor beast, even if man or beast knew what they were supposed to be. That's what she needs to relax, why shouldn't Uncle Jakey need to paint just as much?'

Ruby laughed. 'Aye, you're right. Uncle Jakey's paintings are better than my mother's crochets! He keeps one as a blanket, my mother's crochets, I mean. He sleeps in his chair more often than in his bed, and he covers himself with it. Takes it with him when he goes off wandering, too. If he isn't in you always check to see if it's there. If it isn't you know you might not see him for a while.'

'It would be interesting to know what your mother intended it to be,' Flora laughed affectionately.

'Probably a tea cosy,' Ruby giggled, 'that just grew and grew into a big thing, there's no other description that fits. It's a big thing!'

'He's one of life's sensitive souls, Uncle Jakey,' Flora said thoughtfully, 'I think things matter more to him than to the rest of us.'

'He gets easily upset, that's for sure,' Ruby replied, 'though you have to know him to see that. Anything going wrong in the family and he just takes off. He recognises Bea getting ready to explode even before the rest of us and disappears, the aunties say it's because he's sleekit!'

'Well that proves it,' Flora almost snorted. 'Those two nasty old biddies wouldn't recognise sensitive if it sent them a telegram first, the nearest they could get to finer feelings would be sleekit right enough!'

The two friends laughed together.

'So,' Flora finally asked, 'any news from your lord and master?'

Ruby shrugged. 'The odd letter. Nothing much in them, but I suppose it shows he's still alive.'

'Or he was when he wrote them,' Flora replied.

'Trust you to always look on the bright side!' Ruby laughed. 'Andy Morris is due home, did you hear?'

Flora shook her head.

'He was wounded. He stepped on a mine, lost a leg.'

'What a shame!' Flora said in a shocked voice.

'I know, terrible, isn't it? They had him at some hospital down south for a while, now he's coming back home. His mother's in a terrible state.'

'Who can blame her?' Flora shook her head sadly. 'We'll have to see what we can do to help him.' She sighed. 'And you know what?' she asked. 'I bet he's hoping it will impress Iris in some way. I think he'd take her pity if nothing else was forthcoming. That's such a shame, too, isn't it?'

Ruby nodded. 'That's what I think. I always felt like telling him that if he really wanted that slut, and I have never understood why he would, he should've married someone else, anyone would do, and he'd be back in business with Iris.'

'Can't see her wanting much to do with him now, can you?'

'No,' Ruby murmured. 'He couldn't compete against her usual band of followers with two legs, can't see him doing it with one.

Besides,' she sighed, 'Iris has forgotten all about him, I mean *really* forgotten, I don't think she even remembers his name, never mind that she once said she'd marry him.'

'I suppose when he comes back he'll be able to give you some news of your one true love,' Flora said. 'Are you missing him? Come on now, the truth!'

'We weren't married long enough for me to miss `him,' Ruby replied. She thought for a moment. 'It sounds terrible, but it's like he's someone I used to know.'

'You should've left it that way, too,' Flora said wryly, 'but now that you've got his wean, well, what more is there to say? You were really stupid there, Ruby.'

'This again?' Ruby sighed. 'There might well be no more to say but you always come up with something – *this!'*

'Well, I expected better of you, Ruby, or maybe it's that I wanted better for you, that's all I'm saying.'

'Flora, *I* expected more of me,' Ruby said with feeling, 'but what's done is done.' She shrugged helplessly, remembering what their short married life had been like, and how unhappy, come to that, before Gerry went away. 'He's just a boy, maybe the War will make him grow up a bit. Who knows?'

'Well they say what doesn't kill you makes you stronger,' Flora smiled. 'I suppose he's the perfect experiment.'

Ruby looked at her friend and shook her head, then went on the attack. 'There's something different about you, though,' she said suspiciously.

'I've no idea what you mean,' Flora replied innocently.

'I'd swear that hair of yours has an actual style,' Ruby said, examining Flora, 'a brush has gone through it instead of the usual fingers pushing it behind you ears, and there's something about your eyes, something shifty.'

'They're just the same eyes I've always had!' Flora scoffed, looking away. 'Apart from dark circles, of course. They're the height of fashion at Hillington.'

'I've never known you to laugh so much either, usually I have to listen to a political lecture before you even sit down. What's going on?'

'Oh, just happy in my work,' Flora smiled, sipping her tea and looking into the distance. 'I've got all the women away from that old sod in Paisley, did I tell you?'

'No!'

Flora nodded vigorously. 'Every last one! They're all at Hillington now and he's on his beam end.'

'Serves him right!' Ruby said. 'But how did you manage it?'

'Well, I knew they wouldn't just listen to me, as all the gods I don't believe in know, I've tried everything over the years. So I got one of the lads from Hillington to go with me to talk to them.' She sighed. 'Do you think the day will ever come when women don't have to hear it from the lips of men before they'll believe something?'

'Who was it?'

'Who was what?' Flora asked absently.

'The lad from Hillington who went with you.'

'Oh, a lad called Denis,' Flora replied, in a casual tone that didn't fool Ruby for an instant. 'He's been really great, talking to the women in the factory about joining the union, explaining tactics to them. They don't want to join because they're classed at temporary workers and because the union does nothing for women anyway, but as Denis says, if they want things to change they have to get involved.'

'Well that's okay for him!' Ruby said scathingly. 'Does he realise that those same women have to look after families and a house and stand in queues for everything as well as travelling back and forth for their shifts at Hillington?'

'But no one is going to hand us fairer wages, are they, Ruby?' Flora asked. 'Do you know there are three grades, skilled men, unskilled men and others, and even skilled women are classed as the others? We train boys and then see those boys being paid more than us. Is that right?'

'Of course it's not!' Ruby replied. 'But there are only so many hours in the day, Flora, you can't expect women to take on everything can you?'

'Women in the factory earn – no, they get paid – forty-three shillings a week, while men get seventy-three shillings. And it's our fault, us women, because we let them get away with it, and the union isn't interested because it's run by men, for men. Denis is right, it may be hard, but we've got to fight back.'

Ruby laughed. 'I wondered when the political speech would come, I've really missed you! And Denis who?' she asked.

'Denis Kelly, just one of the lads.'

Ruby glared at Flora, who was determinedly looking away from her. 'Flora, you sly dog!'

'What?' Flora asked, wide-eyed.

'This "one of the lads," is that all he is?'

'Well he is a Communist Party member, of course,'

'Of course,' Ruby nodded solemnly. 'And?'

'His family comes from Clydebank. His father works in Brown's.'

'Did his house get hit?' Ruby asked.

Flora shook her head. 'Theirs was one of the few that wasn't damaged at all. I think they feel guilty about that. He wanted to join up, he still does, but because he's working at the factory they won't take him.'

'What does he do?'

'He's an engineer, an apprentice still, really very highly skilled, though, but when the War is over he wants to become a solicitor. He's very, very bright, you know.'

Ruby waited, smiling, as she watched the colour rise and spread over Flora's cheeks. 'And that's all you want to tell me, is it?' Ruby asked, raising her eyebrows.

'Now I'm disappointed in you, Ruby!' Flora said archly. 'You know perfectly well that I don't subscribe to your love and marriage nonsense. All that romantic hoo-ha women fall for is just a means of enslaving them. Denis and I are comrades, that's all.'

'What a liar you are!' Ruby clapped her hands. 'Miss Honest-at-all-costs, and you're sitting there lying in your teeth!'

Flora looked up at her and laughed. 'Why don't you understand that we're far too busy for what you're implying?' she protested unconvincingly. 'The struggle is too important for all that—' she waved a hand in the air '—that rubbish! We have to defeat the Fascists and then carry on with the Cause.'

Ruby laughed so hard that she had to put her cup down. 'You

are such a fraud!' she giggled. 'If you could only sit where I am and see yourself, Flora McCreadie!'

'I can't believe you have such a small, suburban mind, Ruby!' Flora said haughtily, which made Ruby laugh even more.

'So tell me about him,' Ruby demanded.

'There's not much more to tell.' Flora was pursing her lips, trying to appear totally objective to the point of disinterest.

'Dammit, woman, what does he look like?'

'Oh, that,' she said in a determinedly vague voice. 'Dark hair, lots of it, brown eyes, full of energy, very committed. Knows where he's going, very focused, if you know what I mean.'

'I should do, I've had to put up with someone quite like that since before I went to school! Sounds like you're two peas from the same pod.'

'Only he's got so much more ability than I have,' Flora smiled.

'Will you listen to her!' Ruby said to no one in particular. 'This is the woman who has campaigned all her life on the belief that women and men are equal, who has fought for equal wages-'

'Is *still* fighting for equal wages,' Flora reminded her, blue eyes dancing.

'—and just because she fancies this bloke she's decided that he's superior to her! What is the world coming to?'

'He's *not* superior, Ruby,' Flora said primly, 'but he has all the right qualities to go far and to take the struggle forward. I can help him, but I know my own strengths and weaknesses and I know the future of the Cause lies with him.'

'Oh my God!' Ruby cried, slapping her hand to her forehead. 'You're hooked, Flora, anyone can see that, and you can't even admit it!'

'There's no denying that I do admire him,' Flora murmured, pushing a stray lock of curly blonde hair behind her ear in a familiar gesture, 'but that's all. I just don't understand why you're implying anything else, you should know me better than that, Ruby McLean.'

Ruby waved her protests away as she giggled. 'And I thought I hadn't seen you for a while because you were working your fingers to the bone building planes!'

'I am!'

149

'And all the time you've given me the bum's rush because of some bloke!'

'He's not "some bloke!"' Flora protested.

'No, Flora,' Ruby grinned, hugging her, 'they never are. Take my word for it, they never are, even when that's exactly what they are!'

18

When Andy Morris came home he was no longer in uniform, nor did he look like the hero he wanted Iris to see. In fact, he looked diminished in ways that went beyond his obvious handicap. He looked tanned and fit, but there was a quietness, a sorrow about him now that was only partly to do with his longing for Iris. Walking with a discernible limp, thanks to the newly fitted artificial leg, Andy felt less than masculine, when the society he had grown up in and must still inhabit was all about manly men. The fact that he had lost his leg in battle could not change how he felt about himself or how he thought other men would regard him. His mother reported that he refused to let her see him without the leg, indeed he refused to let her help him in any way, leaving her bereft, for what else was a mother for if not to look after her son, especially when he was ailing? The people he had known all his life in High Street tried to be welcoming and supportive without appearing overly curious, they didn't want the boy – the young man – to feel like a freak, sensing that this was how he felt. His mother had warned anyone he was likely to come into contact with not to ask for details, not, in fact, to mention the leg, or the lack of it, the entire subject was to be totally ignored.

George McLean though, whose love of nature extended to all living creatures, apart from his sister, Big Bea, went to see Andy to tell him that his job in the Goods Yard Office was waiting for him when he felt like returning. Indeed, he told him, the railway had suffered without him. George reported back that the lad seemed in reasonably good spirits, people just had to be sensitive and let him take his own time. Andy had brought George a tale of an Egyptian scorpion being tortured by soldiers who had enclosed it within ring of burning fuel in hopes, apparently, of seeing it sting itself to death rather than burn. Andy had stepped in to rescue it and had been stung on the thumb for his trouble, which made the tormenting soldiers just as happy as watching the scorpion die, but one of them had kindly opened up the sting site with the tip of a knife and sucked out the poison.

'Was it a big scorpion or a little one?' George asked, his face screwed up with concentration.

'A big black thing,' Andy replied helpfully.

'Oh well, that's okay, then,' George blew his cheeks out and pronounced with authority, 'it wouldn't have had a sting any worse than a bee. It's the wee ones that are the most dangerous. And it's not really poison,' he explained, warming to his theme, 'it's a toxin that causes such agonising pain that your nervous system can't cope with it, you die from shock more than anything.'

'So I got my thumb slit for nothing?' Andy asked, surveying the v-shaped scar on the ball of his thumb.

'Well, you did a good thing,' George smiled approvingly. 'You saved the scorpion from those morons!'

'Thanks a lot, George,' Andy winced, 'I'm glad I told you now!'

Andy had a package for Ruby he had promised Gerry he would deliver as soon as he could, and so she found him at the door of the McLean home a week or so after he arrived home. Seeing him standing there she wondered briefly if he had gone to her married home first and found Iris there, but she decided not to ask. Inside he greeted Sarah politely and looked at the two children to show willing, while Sarah and Ruby tried not to stare at his new look or ask after his health, as his mother had already advised if they met him. Sarah, thrown by the dictum about respecting the forbidden topics, mentioned how tanned he was and that he must've had a lot of time for sunbathing, then bit her lip and looked away, stricken with remorse and embarrassment. To divert attention from the faux pas, Ruby opened the parcel and was bemused to find herself unfolding a full Arab outfit. Andy took it from her.

'This black-checked material is a keffiyeh, it's worn around the head and this,' he explained, picking up a thick band of black coils, 'is an akal, it goes around the head as well. It keeps the keffiyeh in place.'

Ruby nodded. She didn't understand a word.

Andy held up a long dress with a deep v-neck edged in gold embroidery. 'This one's a jellaba, they wear silk shirts underneath, called brussas, and somewhere,' he searched inside the parcel, 'there's a burnoose, a long cape with a hood for travelling, and a curved sword. Oh, and black leather sandals.'

Ruby was none the wiser but Sarah was enchanted, especially with the embroidery.

'Is that it?' Ruby asked.

'Looks like it,' Andy smiled shyly.

'What am I meant to do with it?' she asked. 'I mean, is it *for* somebody?'

Andy shrugged self-consciously. 'I don't think it's a present if that's what you mean, Ruby. I think he wants you to keep it for him for when he comes home.' He paused. 'You know what Gerry's like.'

'No note or anything?' she said, searching in the wrapping paper.

'Maybe he didn't have time,' Andy offered. 'He gave it to me as soon as word came through that I was being shipped home.'

Ruby looked at him blankly. She didn't feel disappointed exactly, just bewildered. She couldn't imagine why anyone living in a life-or-death situation and, having the opportunity to send something home to his nearest and dearest, would choose a parcel containing a fancy dress outfit, and a man's fancy dress outfit at that. 'So,' she managed to say in a small voice, 'is he okay?'

Andy nodded. 'Last time I saw him,' he replied quietly. 'It's been pretty hard, the fighting, but they keep each other going.' He laughed self-consciously. 'In fact, I think Gerry enjoys it, he's in his element.' He shrugged again.

'Good,' she nodded, 'I'm glad somebody's enjoying the War,' then couldn't think of anything more to say.

Andy, seeing how things were going, decided to leave, but as Ruby saw him to the door he was pushed aside by the two aunties intent on coming in at all costs.

'Hello, Andy, son,' puffed Cissie, an arm out to clear her way, 'I hear you've only got the one leg now?' and then was gone.

Ruby raised her eyes to the ceiling. 'Sorry about that, Andy,' she apologised, 'my Auntie Cissie is blessed with a sweet tooth but not a sweet nature.'

Just then Dot arrived, wheezing from running up the stairs, and dashed past them. 'If she's in that lavatory I'll swing for her!' she screeched, and ran on raggedly, before her voice sounded plaintively as she hammered on the bathroom door. 'Cissie! Cissie! Come out of there! I'm worse than you, and don't use all the paper!'

'Away you to buggery!' Cissie's muffled voice could be heard replying with feeling. 'You're not as bad as me, never mind worse, nobody's near as bad as me!'

'I'd better go,' Andy smiled.

'Aye, it might be better, Andy,' Ruby told him. 'I don't know what's up with them, but I'm involved, I'm family, God help me. There's no reason you should be subjected to whatever it is. And thanks for bringing Gerry's parcel,' she said, then, as she closed the door, she added dubiously 'I think ...'

As the door closed the shouting, threats and hammering on the bathroom door continued. Eventually it opened and Cissie could be heard yelling 'Don't you be long now, Dot, I'm still desperate, I'm only letting you in for a minute.'

The bathroom door slammed with a ferocity born of relief and Cissie joined Sarah and Ruby in the sitting room.

'Now, don't start any long conversations,' she warned them, panting and holding her stomach with a pained expression on her face. 'I won't be here long enough, the minute Dot comes out of the lavvy I'll be back in again.' Her gaze fell on the parcel Andy had left and she straightened up as though suddenly cured of whatever her affliction had been. 'What in hell's that?' she asked, curiously, lifting the keffiyeh and inspecting it. 'It's a nice checked pattern that. Whose is it?'

'It's a thing you put on your head,' Ruby replied.

'Like a headscarf kind of a thing?' Cissie asked.

'No, like an Arab kind of a thing,' Ruby said flatly, 'and it's Gerry's.'

'Did you buy it for him, like?' Cissie smiled.

Ruby shook her head. 'Of course I didn't! Now why in hell would you ask such a daft question? He got Andy Morris to bring it back.'

'What for?' Cissie was rummaging about inside the parcel, inspecting all the bits and pieces.

'Search me,' Ruby shrugged.

'Oh, but that's an awfy nice coat!' Cissie breathed. 'Have you seen this, Sarah? Look at the colours in the weave. Is that not lovely? It's a wee bit long but you could aye take it up.'

'And look at the embroidery on this dress thing,' Sarah enthused.

Suddenly Cissie dropped the nice coat, clutched her stomach and ran, screaming, in the direction of the bathroom. 'Get out of there!' she yelled. 'Dot, I need to get in, I need to get in *now!*'

A heated discussion ensued before Dot appeared in the sitting room in much the same state as Cissie had before her.

'What the hell's going on with you two?' Ruby demanded.

'It was her fault,' Dot said, jerking her head towards the door and beyond to her sister, now ensconced in the bathroom. '"I know where we can get chocolate," she said, 'They keep it for weans, but we can buy it as well, as much as you like. So we did.'

Sarah and Ruby looked at her, confused.

'Only it was laxative chocolate, wasn't it?' Dot stated bitterly.

Sarah managed to look away as she smiled, but Ruby laughed out loud and clapped her hands.

'Well may you laugh, madam,' Dot rebuked her, 'it's not you that's been running to the lavvy every two minutes, is it?'

Just then Cissie joined them. 'What have I ever done to deserve this?' she groaned, wincing as she sat down. 'Me, that's never done any harm to any being, living or dead, in my entire life!'

'You've done *me* harm!' Dot accused her. 'I've just been telling them it's all your fault.'

'Well how was I to know?' Cissie demanded plaintively. 'And you were the one that got us to eat they horrible Horlicks tablets, then they damned cough sweeties, near took the roof off my mouth, and they tasted hellish as well. Anyway, there was nice wee animals on that chocolate. Why would they put nice wee animals on a thing that turns your insides out?'

155

'Of course there was wee animals on it, Auntie Cissie,' Ruby giggled, 'laxative chocolate's for weans. It's to encourage them to eat it!'

'It's *chocolate!*' Cissie screeched. 'How does anybody have to be encouraged to eat chocolate?' but the effort of yelling had brought on another desperate need to head for the bathroom and she ran out, one hand on her stomach, the other clamped to her nether regions.

'And it tasted just like chocolate!' Dot took up her case plaintively. 'Something that does this to you should taste like it does this to you, it's only fair!'

'But if it tasted like that weans wouldn't eat it,' Ruby said reasonably, 'whether it had nice wee animals on it or not. You must've come across it before. Didn't you have to give it to your own weans sometimes?'

'Are you suggesting that I needed anything to keep my weans regular?' Dot demanded haughtily.

'I'm just saying,' Ruby giggled again, 'that's all. Surely it said something on the wrapper to tip you off?'

'Oh, aye, that's right,' Dot said accusingly, 'just you make smart-arse remarks when we're dying here.'

'Who reads wrappers on chocolate?' Cissie demanded, returning to the company and lowering herself into a chair with a pained expression. 'Chocolate's chocolate, for God's sake, what did we need to know apart from that?'

'You can still get ration chocolate,' Sarah suggested.

Cissie leaned forward in her chair and stared into her sister's eyes. 'Look, Sarah, hen,' she intoned, 'if we wanted to eat cardboard then cardboard we would eat, but we don't. Now, is that okay with you?'

'I'll tell you this, Cissie,' Dot announced solemnly, 'since this War started life has gone to hell in a wheelbarrow. When it comes to two decent women unable to eat a harmless bit of chocolate without being killed, well, I don't know.' She shook her head mournfully, eyes closed. 'No wonder they call it the dire-rears,' she protested, 'I'll tell you this, I don't think mine will ever be the same again, red raw it is.'

'I'll take your word for it,' Ruby sniggered, 'you don't have to let me see it!'

Cissie looked at Dot and nodded towards Ruby. 'Mind the time she was a nice wee lassie?' she said pointedly.

'Well, it could be worse,' Ruby said quietly. 'Some people have died. Look at Clydebank, and some people have come home with only one leg.'

Cissie and Dot exchanged puzzled looks. 'Oh, aye, the Morris boy, you mean?' Cissie asked.

'Aye, but be fair, Ruby, hen,' Dot remarked in an aggrieved tone. 'He's not as bad off as us, is he? He's still got one good leg, if the worst comes to the worst he can aye hop about a bit, but me and Cissie here haven't got an inch of decent innards left between us.'

Beside, her, Cissie nodded, glaring at Ruby, then her face suddenly crumpled and with an anguished cry she raced towards the bathroom again. When she returned after a few minutes she slowly lowered herself into the chair beside Dot, clutching her arm for support, eyes closed, her face with the mournful expression of a hapless victim.

'I mean,' she whined, 'where is it all coming from, that's what I'd like to know.'

Ruby sniggered and Cissie shot her a pained look.

'I'll tell you this, Sarah,' she said, returning to her thoughts with feeling, 'I've never liked the notion of having a lavvy in the house, but if I'd had to run up and down the stairs to one on the landing like we have, I'd never have made it. Yours has saved my life the day, so it has!'

'Aye, but she always keeps it nice, Cissie,' Dot reminded her, 'she keeps it spotless.'

Cissie glared at Dot then threw her arms wide and addressed an invisible multitude. 'Has anybody here,' she demanded, 'heard me saying my sister Sarah doesn't keep her lavvy spotless?'

The multitude gave no reply.

'I was only remarking,' Dot protested.

'Aye, that's your trouble you're far too bloody pass-remarkable for your own good, you should learn to shut your yap once in a while! I was only saying that I've always thought the one on the

157

landing was better,' she wrinkled her nose, 'what with all they whiffs and that.'

Dot immediately took offence. 'Are you aiming that at me?' she demanded. 'Because let me tell you, lady, at least half of they whiffs in Sarah's lavvy the day are yours, probably more!'

'And what do you mean by that?'

'You know damned fine what I mean!' Dot sneered. 'They say it's better up than down, but as I've often remarked, and as sure as God's my witness, with you there's never a guarantee that the first one will cancel out the other one!'

'There she goes with the remarking again!' Cissie screeched.

'Anybody for a cuppa tea?' Ruby cut in brightly. 'And maybe a wee biscuit?'

Both aunties promptly forgot about their tortured innards and their battle about who whiffed the most and turned the sweetest of smiles on their niece.

'Oh, well, we wouldn't say no, would we Dot?' Cissie asked with girlish delight.

'We never turn down a cuppa tea,' Dot beamed then, 'it's only polite after all, isn't it?' Then, to make sure there was no misunderstanding of what had been offered, she said, stressing every word, 'or a wee biscuit neither.'

When Cissie and Dot felt safe enough to leave the proximity of the bathroom and go home, Ruby took Gerry's parcel to Uncle Jakey's house. He had found a moment to paint again and so seemed reasonably happy.

'See what Gerry's sent home,' she said, as though the parcel contained something precious and personal that she had always longed for. To her joy, Jakey was captivated, holding the robes up and turning them in every direction to get a better look. 'What are they for?' he asked.

'I don't really know,' she laughed. 'Andy Morris brought them back, I think Gerry just liked them and wanted them to get back safely.'

Jakey continued his examination by swishing the curved sword in the air a few times, a delighted smile on his face. 'Can I keep them for a wee while?' he asked at last.

Ruby shrugged. 'I don't see why not,' she said. 'Maybe you could keep them till Gerry comes home? They'd likely be as safe here than anywhere, wouldn't they?'

'I was thinking of maybe putting them in a painting,' he grinned, now lost in his vision. He looked at her. 'There's not many will have a real Arab in their paintings, is there?' he said, as though the walls of all Glasgow homes were covered in fantastical murals. 'It would be kind of different, wouldn't it? Special like?'

'Aye,' Ruby nodded, smiling, 'it would, Uncle Jakey. That's a good idea.'

By then Jakey was had re-entered his own little world though, he no longer heard her or noticed as she let herself out.

The following night there was a gas supply failure to coincide with the blackout. Everyone was used to gas or electricity failures, they had long ago learned that there was no point complaining, they were just part of what had now become normal life. For Ruby it was a minor inconvenience because she had to heat water for the babies' bottles, but even so, the house had a coal-fired range. It might take more time, but it worked. Later, all she remembered was that Uncle Jakey, with Wee Dug in tow, had turned up for a meal, which usually meant he was all right, and she had remarked that the gas being off was a nuisance. It was still off when Jakey and companion left, and he was warned to be careful going up the brae in the dark, even if it was the start of June and night was taking longer to fall. The next day, though, the entire neighbourhood was buzzing with a strange tale. Apparently an Arab in full regalia had walked the streets in the blackout, with his face tinged dark with what looked like some kind of powder, powder paint, perhaps, and a less than convincing black beard and moustache of some material. After midnight he had appeared at the substation at the top of the brae and remonstrated with the workers about the gas failure, saying children were dying for want of a bottle of warm milk and to get their fingers out immediately. He had, they said, the biggest, meanest dog anyone had ever seen, with red eyes and slavering jowls. To emphasise the point, the Arab had unsheathed a long, curved sword, waved it at them in a threatening manner and, in a distinc-

159

tively Arab-sounding voice, told them they were all child killers and were worse than the Germans. The workers, none of them local men, had called the police who, having more pressing matters to attend to than reports of a lone Arab in High Street, didn't arrive till long after the intimidating figure, and his enormous red-eyed, slavering hound, had disappeared.

'I told them,' the local bobby, Tam McVicar, told Ruby later, 'that they had been seeing things, and if they weren't careful I'd report them to their bosses for making and drinking illicit hooch during working hours.'

'Are they making illicit hooch up there?' Ruby asked incredulously.

'Of course they are,' he said, 'everybody's at it, but they don't all bother me with their hallucinations. I mean, Ruby, as I told them, where would you find an Arab around here?'

Ruby looked away, smiling. 'Search me, Tam,' she said.

'But for God's sake,' he said in a low voice, 'tell the Sheik of High Street not to wave that bloody big sword at folk that don't know him, or he's sure to get lifted one of these days if we're in the right place at the wrong time.'

'I'll tell him, Tam,' she whispered, 'and thanks,' though she knew there was absolutely no point in even mentioning it, far less warning whoever Tam was talking about.

'And tell him to get that big dangerous dog with the red eyes under control while he's at it. Okay, Ruby?'

Ruby laughed quietly. 'Aye, I'll pass it on Tam.'

19

A few evenings later there was a knock at Gus Campbell's door. When he opened it he found two policemen on his doorstep. One he recognised as Tam McVicar, but the other, much younger, was a stranger. The first thought that went through his mind was that he was under suspicion for something to do with Betty's disappearance. He had done his best to defuse all inquiries by appearing nonchalant and passing on fictitious messages to and from his wife down in Yorkshire, but that wee bitch, Ruby McLean, always glared at him suspiciously. Mind you, she always had, right from when she was a child, so maybe, he thought, he was being overly-sensitive. Even so, the sight of the two policemen made him breathe in a bit sharply.

'I wanted to speak to your wife, Mr Campbell,' the unknown officer said.

Gus Campbell breathed even deeper. It *was* that wee bitch, Ruby McLean, then, she was the only one who seemed as though she doubted him, he saw it in her eyes, everyone else had swallowed his explanation without a second thought. He had seen her talking and laughing with Tam McVicar only days ago, she must have told Tam he had done something to Betty. He looked at Tam McVicar. 'My wife isn't here,' he said.

Tam McVicar nodded.

'Can I ask where she is and when she might be back?' the younger officer asked.

Gus sighed uncomfortably and looked over their heads.

'Gus,' Tam said quietly, 'it might be better if we came in.'

Gus stood back to let them pass him in the hallway, before closing the door and following them into his living room. His mouth was suddenly dry, not that it mattered, as his mind had gone blank and he had nothing to say.

'Gus, this is PC Connelly. We need to know where Betty is,' Tam said gently.

Gus was defeated. 'I don't have any idea, Tam,' he said. 'I came home from work one day a couple of months ago and she had gone, that's all I know.'

'No argument or anything?' Tam prompted.

Gus decided instantly to take the offering. 'Tam, I know everybody thinks Betty is a nice polite woman, but they don't know the Betty I know.' He paused for a moment to give himself time, but it made him appear suitably sad, a dutiful husband having the secrets of his marriage drawn out of him. 'She could be very difficult at times and we had a few wee tiffs. Recently it's been about the time I spend out at work then at my ARP duties. And there's her age, of course,' he suggested with a shrug. 'Women of her age can be a wee bit, well, difficult. Usually the disagreements blew over as though they had never happened, and I thought that's what would happen this time. I knew there would be gossip, and I made up a story that she had gone to her sister's in Yorkshire so that people wouldn't talk and make her feel embarrassed when she came back.' He sighed heavily.

'Does she have a sister in Yorkshire?' Tam asked.

'She has a sister, or had one, I've no idea where she is. We never got on so it's years since we saw her.'

The two policemen exchanged a look, then PC Connelly spoke. 'Mr Campbell, I'm from Clydebank. I'm here to tell your wife that her sister, her sister's husband, their two children and her mother-in-law all died in the bombings there in March, in Radnor Street. There was no way of tracing any family fast enough. They're all in a mass grave in Dalnottar Cemetery. That's what I came to let Mrs Campbell know.'

'But Betty's not here ….'

'I know that,' he said. 'When did your wife leave you?'

Gus was too stunned to think for a few moments. 'In March,' he finally said. 'I'd been out all night on ARP duties and when I came home and got changed for work, she was still asleep. That night I didn't even get back home, I went straight from work to ARP duties. To be honest, I thought she'd made her way to the shelter as usual. When I got back after the all-clear I realised she wasn't there.' He sighed heavily. 'It was the night the Germans bombed Clydebank right enough,' he said.

Another look between the policemen. 'I've got some personal possessions that were dug out of the ruins of her sister's house,' the younger one said, 'I was going to give them to your wife. We got your address from some letters we found. Some were addressed to your wife here, at this address, that's how we found you, but we wondered why letters addressed to Mrs Campbell would be found in Clydebank.' He was speaking very quietly and slowly, waiting for Gus to catch up.

'Where are they?' Gus asked. 'The things you've got for Betty?'

'They're up at the station, Gus,' Tam McVicar said. 'You can come up any time and collect them, but I think it would be better if you came up now. It would be better to clear things up as soon as we can. They're in a suitcase. We didn't want to bring it with us in case there was no one at home. As far as the lad here knows there are no other relatives, is that right?'

Gus nodded. 'Not on Betty's side anyway.' He sighed. 'I'll come up just now.'

'That would be a good idea, Gus,' Tam told him. 'There's likely a simple explanation.'

Nothing fazed Gus Campbell, not normally. He had always been powerfully built and realised when he was young that it gave him a certain power that could be used to intimidate people, females especially. The slight fear they had of him meant that all his life he had been able to keep one step ahead of any trouble, but now he found that his legs were stiff and, when he got them going, curiously unsteady. All the way up to the police station he felt as though he had forgotten how to walk and had to keep reminding himself to put one numb foot in front of the other. Finally, he was shown into a side room and a battered suitcase was produced and put on a table in front of him.

'It's been bashed about a bit,' PC Connelly said, 'there are holes here and there, so be careful.'

Gus nodded. It was too damaged to recognise.

'We had to open it earlier to see if there was anything identifying inside,' PC Connelly explained, 'but we put them back and sealed it again.'

'Do you want to open it?' Tam McVicar asked quietly.

Gus shook his head. 'Can you do it, Tam?' he asked.

It was done in silence apart from cracks and creaks because it was being opened against its nature. Dust flew up and, when it was opened, even more dust filled the air. The three men sifted through the contents. A pile of family photos. The letters and cards the younger policeman had mentioned. A box with a gas mask inside, and another, smaller one that rattled. Tam opened it and there was a glint of gold jewellery inside a cloth bag. Tam emptied the pieces out. A bangle with red stones of some description. A fob watch with white stones. A locket with a green stone. An old engagement ring and a broad wedding ring of rose gold. Gus lifted the wedding ring and turned it in his fingers.

'I can't see,' he said. 'Is there something inside it? An inscription?'

Tam took out a spyglass and looked at the inside of the ring. 'I think it says "Rose, my one true love, Alex," he said, handing it back to Gus. 'Do you recognise it, Gus?'

'It's Betty's wedding ring, Tam,' he said quietly. 'It belonged to her grandmother, Rose.' He put his hands up and covered his face.

Tam McVicar took his arm and guided him into a chair. 'The thing is, Gus,' he said gently, 'that the letters in the case are addressed to Betty at your address, as we said.'

Gus said nothing.

The younger policeman had opened the other box and taken the gas mask out, then he put his hand deep inside and brought out an identity card and a ration book and handed them to Tam.

'These belonged to Betty, Gus,' he explained. 'Do you see what I'm saying, Gus. Do you see what we're thinking?'

Gus nodded dumbly, then he looked at the two policemen and realised they had both suspected as much from the start. Betty had walked out on 13th March and hadn't been seen or heard of since, now her belongings had turned up in the ruins of her sister's home in Clydebank that had been bombed that same night.

'There wasn't a lot left to identify,' Connelly said, 'they've all been in that mass grave since 17th March.'

Tam McVicar shook his head at the young man to stop him saying anything more about the mass burial at Dalnottar or the reasons for it. Gus had enough to deal with at the moment without that image in his head.

The younger man nodded, but he still had a job to do. 'Mr Campbell,' he said in a quiet, pained voice, 'I'm going to go back and report to the Fiscal that it looks like we have enough evidence to identify another victim. Do you understand?'

Gus nodded wordlessly again.

'I'll get Tam to report to you on progress, on what happens next.'

'What do you want to do, Gus?' Tam asked sympathetically.

'I'd like to go home, now,' he replied.

'I'll go with you,' Tam said.

'No, it's okay.'

'I'm going to see you home, Gus,' Tam said firmly, 'you're in no fit state to walk there alone, and you can think of anyone you want me to let know.'

'I don't want to tell anybody just now,' he said quietly. 'I need a bit of time to myself first. I'd be grateful, Tam, if you didn't say anything to the neighbours.' He shook his head as though dazed. 'I don't think I could cope with them yet.'

Tam McVicar nodded. It was understandable. 'Not a word, Gus, not a word till you're ready.'

At the front door Tam parted with Gus Campbell. The man seemed creased, he thought. As the local bobby he didn't miss much and he had been aware of the Iris McLean connection for a while, but you couldn't blame any man for taking it when she handed it around on a plate. It didn't mean the man was about to leave his wife for her, and everyone knew that wasn't what Iris ever wanted anyway. And who could blame Gus for looking for a bit of diversion in times like these, when he was working all hours and the hours he wasn't his wife was complaining? Besides, Iris had a high turnover of married men, Gus was just the latest. In fact, it was doubtful that he was the only one in the frame at the time, or had even thought he was. Walking back to the station in the dark, Tam wondered if maybe Betty had found out and that was why she had taken off that day in March. If it was, Gus was hardly likely to admit to that now, was he? Didn't matter. Whatever had happened between him and his wife, he'd paid the price now, all right, poor sod.

Back inside his house, Gus Campbell took out a half bottle of whisky he had stashed away, poured a large glass that he set down on the table beside the fire and sat down. Then he put his head in his hands and sobbed noisily. It had been a close shave. He had turned it over in his mind often these last months. If he had been accused of doing Betty in, how could he have proved he hadn't? Her clothes were still hanging in the wardrobe or folded in the chest of drawers. He had thought that odd at the time, and other bits and pieces had been left in the laundry basket as though she had been just about to wash them. When he came home that night in March he hadn't understood at first that she had gone, that had been true. He had been later than usual because he'd been with Iris under cover of the blackout, and when he was late Betty never questioned that he had been working. There was no note and the house looked like it always did, as though she had stepped out for a chat with one of the neighbours. He had been mildly irritated at that thought. She knew fine he expected his tea on the table within seconds of coming home from work, so she had no business gossiping somewhere, she had all day to do that. Then he noticed there was no smell of cooking and looked in the kitchen and everything there seemed as it always was. Maybe, he thought, she was in bed, though he couldn't under-stand why she should be, and somewhere in the depths of his mind the thought occurred that she might be *really* ill ... or even worse. But she hadn't been there either. The bed had been made and every-thing was as usual. It was only later that he noticed the missing photos, but he paid them no heed, they were nothing to do with him, they were all snaps of her family and her family hated him as much as he hated them. They thought they were something special, that he was some uneducated oaf who had besmirched their princess daughter, snobs the lot of them. The only photos left behind were taken on their wedding day, such as it was. That struck him as odd too, but he didn't read anything more than that into it. She had gone, that was all, and he had no idea where, why or for how long.

On those weary nights on ARP duty he had often fantasised about her not being there, not dead, exactly, he had never thought it through that far, just not there, and about the life he could have if she didn't exist. There were lots of accidents during the blackout, perfectly healthy people tripped, fell and just died. He had often thought that a push in the dark would've done it, but what if she survived and he then had to look after her or, worse still, what if she accused him of pushing her? Not that she was a bad wife, she did what was expected of her and did it well. He wouldn't have done anything to her, of course, it was just the idle thoughts of a man in a sterile marriage who had no way out. Sterile in more ways than one. But a case could be made against him, he had thought that often. The longer she was away with no sign of coming back, the more his dread increased.

Then to find Tam McVicar and that other one on his doorstep, well, his heart had pounded so hard he thought they must've heard it too. He went over in his mind what he had said, what they had said, and regretted suggesting he and Betty had had a tiff. He should just have said she had gone and he didn't know where or why. It would have been perfectly believable that after he had left for work that day she had simply gone to see her sister, that would've explained why she took so little and all of it family stuff. Given that he didn't get on with her family and they never spoke of her sister, it was reasonable that Betty wouldn't tell him she was going on a visit, intending getting home before he did. No, maybe he shouldn't have mentioned a tiff, but he had been caught off-guard by the two policemen standing there. On the other hand, admitting to a falling out could have made him seem honest, especially with her wedding ring being found inside the case and not on her finger. Nothing to worry about then, everything had worked out, and not even that wee bitch Ruby McLean could suggest he had deliberately taken Betty to Clydebank to have her killed by the Germans, so he was home free.

He drank his whisky in one gulp to steady himself. It was done now. She was gone for good and no one could blame him, even if he didn't know why she had left in the first place. Maybe she *had* just gone on a secret visit, and hadn't actually left him after all. For all he knew she could have been seeing her sister regularly without telling him. He had told her often enough to sell all that family junk, maybe she decided to give it to her sister or her sister's weans rather than sell it. She could've taken the ring off to show them the inscription inside then had to quickly push it all in the bag and make for a shelter when the alert sounded – anything was possible. He ran his hand over his hair. He had to stop thinking up different scenarios, best to keep it simple, it had all worked out and the tiff explanation had actually worked out well. Even so, he couldn't stop his mind from working, seeking cracks in his story, plugging loopholes in case and before anyone else found them.

She knew nothing about him and Iris, he was sure of that, nobody did. But he wasn't fool enough to think Betty was any happier than he was, so it was equally possible she could have got up that day and just decided to go. They had been stuck together by circumstances all those years ago, that was all there had been to it. There had once been lust, he remembered that, she was so different from him and from the usual sort he went for, she had class and a calmness that he found attractive at the time, though it came to grate on him after a time before boredom set in. After boredom there was nothing really, just habit. Certainly there was no love between them, no affection, on his part at least, though give Betty her due, she had doted on him and looked after him and the house well. Better than well, if he was being honest. And now it was over, and he didn't even have to pay for a funeral. There would be insurance money, he suddenly realised, all those policies her parents had paid into from when she was born, and others he and Betty had taken out since they got married. He got up to search through the sideboard, wondering if there might be anyone left, her sister's in-laws maybe and, if there proved not to be, he might be able to claim on their insurance too. Even if he only had Betty's policies, he would still have some cash, and his freedom.

20

The news of Betty Campbell's death spread slowly at first, because Gus was reluctant to tell anyone. He had no idea why this was, but it certainly wasn't through any feelings of guilt, he had done nothing wrong, after all. He told Iris McLean the following morning, with instructions to keep it to herself till he had worked out what to do next, then he told Harry McLean a few hours later while they were working together. He knew Harry wouldn't be home till very late that night, so that would gain him another day and, hopefully, night. With luck it could be into the following day again before the word spread round High Street and he had to face the inevitable questions.

'I was hearing that the police were at Gus Campbell's door last night,' Sarah told Ruby that lunchtime. It had become their habit to feed the babies together then to sit down for a chat while they slept, unless there was a queue somewhere, of course. Queues had to be joined, even if you didn't know what you were queuing for.

'Really?' Ruby replied. 'About time too.'

'Now Ruby, nobody said he'd been arrested,' Sarah laughed, 'it could've been about anything! Probably to do with the railway.'

'I can dream, can't I?' Ruby retorted.

'Seems there were two of them, Tam McVicar and another one nobody recognised, and he went up to the station with them then Tam saw him home.'

'But no handcuffs?' Ruby joked.

'No, no handcuffs!' Sarah continued feeding Jamie. 'Wonder what it was about though?' she said distantly.

'I'm sure we'll hear,' Ruby replied, 'but if they're not going to lock the horrible big brute up they have no right raising decent folk's hopes.'

In fact Gus didn't get much more time to keep the news to himself. Harry told George at the Goods Yard and he sprinted up to tell his mother. Ruby was putting the babies down for their sleep while Sarah cleaned up the debris of their lunch feeds. From the bedroom she couldn't hear what was being said, but she registered the shocked tone of her mother's voice and went back to the sitting room to find out what was going on.

'It's Betty,' Sarah said in a hushed voice. 'It's Betty, Ruby.' She had a hand at her throat, a characteristic gesture from Sarah when words were being forced out of her. She looked at George. 'You tell her, George,' she pleaded.

'Gus has just told Da that Betty was killed in the Clydebank Blitz,' he said evenly.

'Betty?' Ruby asked dumbly. 'Betty? *Our* Betty?'

George nodded.

'The police were at his door last night,' Sarah whispered.

'But how ...?' Ruby asked helplessly.

'Seems she had a sister there,' George said.

'Irene,' Ruby whispered, feeling for a chair and sitting down.

'And Betty and Gus had fallen out and she'd gone to her sister's, this Irene's, and then the Blitz happened that night.'

'He said she had gone to Yorkshire,' Sarah whispered. 'Why did he say she had gone to Yorkshire, George?'

George shrugged. 'No idea,' he replied.

'So she was lying dead in Clydebank all that time he was giving us messages from her in Yorkshire? Why would he do that?' Sarah wondered aloud.

George looked from Sarah to Ruby. 'Looks like she was going to stay with her sister but the whole family was wiped out and Betty with them,' he continued. 'Her sister—'

'Irene,' Ruby breathed, gazing at the floor.

'Aye, Irene,' George continued, 'and her man and two kids, and her man's mother, and Betty as well.'

'Oh my God!' Sarah cried.

'Looks like they were on their way to the shelter together but a bomb got them at the close mouth, a direct hit.'

'So how are we just hearing now?' Ruby asked.

'They had to be buried quickly in a mass grave, there was nobody left to identify them, and it's taken time to find out who was there. Apparently it wasn't till they dug out a suitcase with Betty's stuff in it that they wondered if she had been there. So Tam McVicar and a lad from Clydebank came for Gus last night and he identified it as Betty's. With that and nobody hearing from Betty since 13th March, well, it's obvious.'

'But he said she was in Yorkshire!' Sarah said again. 'He said he had heard from her, that she was asking for everybody!' She subsided into tears.

George shrugged. 'He had his reasons, I suppose, Ma, no doubt he'll tell us when he feels up to it. I think he's only at his work because he didn't know what else to do. He's needed and there's nothing he can do at home, no point in sitting by himself, is there?'

Ruby thought Gus Campbell was being given far too much understanding and was about to say so, but then she remembered that George didn't know what she knew, and kept her silence. Gus Campbell was the least of her concerns, all she could think about was Betty's death, though her mind refused to take it in. It couldn't be. How could it be? It had to be nonsense. Betty gone for good? No, don't say that, don't even think it. If she did it would make it true. In the background of her thoughts she could hear her mother's stunned voice and George's reassuring one, but their words didn't register, she was lost in her own thoughts. She went back to the bedroom and sat on the bed. Betty had sat right beside her, just there, and told her of Gus and Iris's treachery. She could still conjure up her voice, almost see her sitting there, feel Betty's hands grasping her own. She twisted one wrist between the thumb and finger of her other hand, where Betty had held it as she pleaded with her to keep her secret. So the last time she saw Betty was the last time she would ever see her? She shook her head as though throwing off the thought. Shouldn't there have been a sign that she only had hours to live? Something, anything? Ruby got up and took the few steps to the window and stood on the same spot where she had watched Betty walking down High Street that bright March day. She had stopped at the corner there, turned and waved, and was off down George Street, case in hand. Ruby had watched her till

171

she was no longer visible before turning away and returning to her normal life, though it had been made abnormal by the knowledge of Gus and Iris that Betty had made her swear she would keep to herself. Suddenly she remembered Gus Campbell manhandling her into the shelter that night, with the dark, threatening shapes of the planes overhead and the awful noise of their engines burrowing through your ears and into your head. They had been on their way to kill Betty. Gus and Iris had arrived together and Ruby had wanted to say 'Wonder where you're wife is tonight? Do you wonder where his wife is tonight, too, Iris?' Little did she know, little did anyone know.

She felt her eyes fill with tears and was seized with fury and headed quickly for the bedroom door. She would go out now and tell the world, shame those two and – her hand was on the door-knob, all she had to do was turn it and storm out, but she stopped and thought instead. Knowledge was power. She couldn't remember where she had heard that or when, probably from Flora, though, it sounded like one of hers, but now she understood for the first time what it meant. She would wait, hard though it was, choose her time. Betty wasn't there any more, she was released from her promise, but she deserved better that a sudden hysterical outburst. Calm down. Take a deep breath, Ruby. She threw her head back, her eyes closed, holding the doorknob almost as a support. Now another deep breath. Then she opened her eyes, stood perfectly still and steady for a few moments, and went back to the sitting room.

In the next few days the people of High Street coped with the news as best they could, with neighbours convening in little huddles in closes, shops and on street corners, all whispering the same details in hushed, shocked tones. Gus just thought she was in a huff and would be back in no time, he just made up the Yorkshire story so that Betty wouldn't come back to any gossip. Heads nodded. She would be black-affronted at folk talking about her business, right enough. She was a decent body, she wouldn't want anyone to know they'd had a fight. He had done the right thing. But why Yorkshire? Well, why not? He probably just picked a place, poor man. If he'd known her sister was in Clydebank he would've said that, but he didn't know, did he? My, he must've suffered, but he just carried on and he's doing the same now, though it must be terrible having no body to bury. Aye, poor man. My, but she'll be missed, she was such a gentle soul, never a bad word to say about anybody, would help anyone. Life is an odd thing, isn't it? You just never know the minute, do you?

Over the next few days Ruby retreated into a world that contained herself and the babies. She found the constant talk and tears threatened her composure so much that she couldn't bear it, so she attended to tasks and chores, routine things that brought a bit of calm distance, a breathing space. She slipped a note under the door of Flora's home in George Street, asking her to come over when she had time, and that evening she arrived.

'I know,' Flora said. 'It's terrible, isn't it? I wish there was something else I could say, but there isn't, is there?'

Ruby shook her head.

'How are you? I know you were fond of her.'

Ruby shrugged.

'How's your mother?'

'Like everybody else, I suppose, shocked. And Uncle Jakey's disappeared again, he always does when there's trouble.'

'He's a sensitive soul, but he'll be back,' Flora said soothingly. 'He always comes back, doesn't he?'

'I know he will, but you can't help worrying a bit when he takes off like this,' Ruby said. 'And I keep thinking about Betty, maybe she wasn't there at all, you know?'

'Ruby ...'

'No, no, think about it, Flora,' she protested. 'When she left me that day she still didn't know where she was going. What if she just left her suitcase at her sister's and went somewhere else? I mean, it was all family stuff, there were no clothes in the case, so maybe she went somewhere else and she's still alive, maybe she doesn't know we all think she's, you know ...'

'Dead,' Flora said firmly, looking at her. 'Didn't they find her identity card and her ration book with her gas mask? Why would she have left them behind, Ruby? Now you think about it.' There was a long silence. 'Have you said anything, Ruby?'

'About him and Iris? About Betty coming to see me?'

'Either,' Flora said.

Ruby shook her head again.

'Maybe that's for the best, Ruby,' Flora suggested.

Ruby didn't reply. 'I was thinking,' she said. 'You know your pal, the lad from Clydebank?'

Flora nodded. 'Denis.'

'Aye, Denis,' Ruby said impatiently. 'Well, I was wondering if he could maybe ask around, see if anybody saw Betty there.'

Flora looked at her friend, at her pleading eyes and gave in with a sigh. 'I'll ask him, Ruby,' she said gently. 'But you have to remember that most people are still evacuated. There aren't many folk living in Clydebank.'

'But his tenement wasn't hit, was it? So they're still there, and I heard people were coming in every day to work and his father works in Brown's, doesn't he? Maybe he's heard something, maybe he could ask. It does no harm to ask, does it?'

'Aye, that's a thought,' Flora said kindly, almost as if she believed it. 'Where did Betty's sister live?'

'Radnor Street,' Ruby said. 'She was called Irene and her man was Tommy. Don't know the names of the two weans.'

'Okay, Ruby, I'll get Denis to ask around.' She hugged Ruby as she got up to go. 'But don't get your hopes up, okay? Remember what I said – who goes anywhere and leaves their gas mask, their identity card and their ration book behind these days?'

'But it's still possible,' Ruby persisted, 'isn't it?'

Flora could think of no words, so she hugged Ruby again and was gone.

21

'So did you lose anybody in the War, Paddy?'

Paddy looked up at her suspiciously. They were sitting on the bench they had made their own on the Largs seafront, eating ice creams. 'This you thinking again?' he demanded.

'Aye, well, people do it from time to time,' she replied, 'people apart from you, that is. When you get to our age you're allowed to think back on the past, nobody can lock you up for it.'

'I wish to God they could!' he protested. 'You're a helluva wifie for the thinking, Ruby, you should see somebody about it.'

'The trouble with you ...' she said, licking a rivulet of liquid ice cream as it ran down the cone.

'Here we go,' he muttered, 'you take all the good out of a pokey-hat, so you do. If you're not at the thinking you're at the lecturing.'

'The trouble with you,' she repeated, 'is that you've let your mind contract to the size of the *Daily Record* and the *Evening Times*.'

'What makes you think my mind was ever any bigger than that to start with?' he demanded. 'And what makes you think it should be?'

'Answer the question.'

'What question?'

She stopped chasing melting ice cream and glared at him.

'No, Ruby,' he replied, as if he was declining the ten times table, 'I never lost anybody in the War.' He went back to his cone. 'Saw a few killed, of course,' he said thoughtfully. 'In the army, like.'

'Anybody you were close to?'

'Oh, pals, you know, you got close when you were living like that. It happened, Ruby, folk were firing guns at us, bloody big cannons

175

as well, they were bound to hit their mark sometimes. What made you ask that anyway? Did you lose family?'

'No,' Ruby replied, looking out to sea, 'I didn't lose family in the War, Paddy. Nobody was shot, though I did know a laddie who lost a leg. I was just thinking, that's all.'

'You see? I was right, all that thinking of yours does nobody any good. It's probably your dying people put it into your head, Ruby. I've told you before, it's morbid.'

'Don't be daft!' she laughed at him. 'Just because someone's dying doesn't mean it has to be morbid!'

'You see? Daft as a brush!' Paddy retorted. He watched her for a moment from the corner of his eye. 'You're doing it again, aren't you?'

'What?'

'Thinking,' he said, grimacing.

'Och, eat your pokey-hat, you silly old bugger,' she said dismissively, 'you look like you're chewing on a wasp's nest!'

It had been a week before she heard again from Flora. She brought the much-talked about Denis to meet her. Ruby was surprised. She hadn't expected Flora to introduce him. He wasn't tall, about average for men of his time – George being the exception – about twenty years old, she guessed, and he was a handsome chap, no denying that. Dark brown hair, the kind that curled fiercely unless brutally cut back, and extraordinary dark brown eyes too, with the most amazing expression of fire and confidence.

'I thought I'd get Denis to tell you what he's found out,' Flora smiled, and from the smile Ruby's suspicions about Flora's feelings were completely confirmed.

He shook hands with Ruby, his eyes meeting hers and she was struck once again by how expressive they were. He was looking at her with a warmth and friendliness that was almost mesmerising. She could see why Flora was entranced.

'Flora's told me what you've been hoping,' he said, sitting down. 'I'm not sure you'll want to know what I've found out.'

Ruby's heart sank, but she smiled back at him. 'I just want to be sure,' she assured him.

'My family lives in Crown Avenue,' he explained. 'That's just round the corner from Radnor Street. I knew Irene and Tommy McCulloch, not well, you understand, just to say hello to, but a friend of mine lived in the same tenement, Jessie Gordon, she's a student teacher.' He looked at Flora, who nodded slightly. 'Jessie was hurt that night, too, she was thrown a fair distance by the force of the blast and was pretty bashed about. She's still in the Western Infirmary, but she's getting better now, so when Flora mentioned your friend I went to see her.'

As Ruby was listening to him she concentrated on the soft, gentle tone of his voice, conscious that she was doing so to keep her mind off what he was going to tell her, even though there was no way of avoiding the inevitable.

'Jessie got out of the building before the McCullochs and was running for the shelter across the road at the school, then she turned back because she'd left some school jotters in her house. Irene McCulloch gave her a helluva bawling out, yelled at her to turn round again and get to the shelter, so she did, then there was a big blast and the next thing she remembers is waking up in an ambulance.'

'So she doesn't know if Betty was actually there?' Ruby asked, brightening.

'Well, actually, she does,' Denis said quietly. 'She remembers all the McCullochs being together, and this other woman.'

'Doesn't mean it was Betty,' Ruby said defensively.

Denis looked at Flora again. 'It was though,' he said gently. 'Earlier that day Jessie was going up to Irene's flat with her, Irene was going to go through some marking with her – the jotters Jessie was going back for that night—'

Ruby nodded.

'—and this same woman was on the doorstep with a suitcase. Irene introduced her as her sister, Betty, said they hadn't seen each other in years and Irene was really surprised. Jessie said as she was running back to the shelter after Irene bawled her out, Betty was with the McCullochs behind her, her and the two weans and Tommy's old mother. The bomb that blasted Jessie must've been the same one that got the McCullochs and your friend. Jessie was badly hurt, but the McCullochs got a direct hit, there wasn't anything recognisable left. She didn't hear about it till she was out of the woods. Nobody wanted to tell her while she was so ill.' He stopped. 'I'm sorry,' he said, 'I wish I could've found out what you wanted to hear.'

'No, no,' Ruby replied, trying to form her mouth into a smile, 'I just needed to be sure, that was all.'

'Look, Denis,' Flora said, 'I'll stay here with Ruby for a wee while. You can take the books up to Andy.'

'Are you sure?' he asked.

Flora touched his hand. 'Aye, that's fine, on you go.'

Ruby looked up. 'I'm really grateful to you for going to all that trouble, Denis,' she said quietly. 'It was good of you.'

'No bother, Ruby,' he smiled as he left. 'If there's anything else I can do to help, just let me know.'

'Thanks,' she nodded.

Flora and Ruby sat in silence for a while, then Flora asked, 'What are you going to do now?'

'Do now? Nothing of course. What is there to do?'

'I wondered if you were going to tell Gus Campbell that somebody had actually seen Betty there,' Flora suggested.

Ruby snorted. 'As if he'd be bothered!'

'Well, Ruby, he must be wondering what you were wondering, if there was the slightest chance she might still be alive, you know?'

'Why should I care about that?' Ruby demanded.

'Ruby, maybe it would be a nice gesture if you told him.'

'I don't want to give him a nice gesture!' Ruby said incredulously. 'You know fine the kind of gesture I've always wanted to give *him!*'

'Well, maybe you could tell Tam McVicar and he could tell him, it would make things easier for Gus if he knew for sure.'

'Will you listen to yourself?' Ruby demanded angrily. 'Why would I want to make anything easier for that big brute? Why would you? You know what he did. You know what Betty saw! If she hadn't caught him and my slut of a sister together she wouldn't have gone to Clydebank that day, and if she hadn't gone to Clydebank she wouldn't have died that night! And you're asking me to help *him,*

178

Flora? And don't you dare say a word to him, if you do I'll never forgive you!'

Flora put her arms around Ruby, who immediately broke down in deep, painful sobs. 'I promise I won't say anything if it means that much to you,' she told her, and stood holding her friend till the sobbing stopped.

In due course the shock of High Street at losing one of their own in such odd circumstances began to fade and Jakey and Wee Dug came home, as they always did. Normal life, or as normal as life could be in wartime, resumed, but still Ruby waited. She didn't really know what she was waiting for, but as she did so she continued to watch Gus Campbell and Iris as closely as she could. Though she had never liked Gus it had always been a matter of pride that she met his eyes, it was her way of telling him he didn't frighten her, that she wasn't coerced by his gaze. Now, though, she found that she couldn't glance in his direction, couldn't even say his name, without feeling disgust so strong that she felt she would vomit on the spot, and even though she sensed he was taking this as some sort of surrender on her part, there was nothing she could do about her reaction. Iris was no different, but Iris at least could be avoided easier than he could, she was working all sorts of shifts on the trams and was rarely about. Gus Campbell, though, seemed to be in her parents' home more often than necessary, receiving sympathy with that odd, tight-lipped half-smile that turned her stomach, and he appeared the instant there was a raid alert.

'It's always him,' Ruby complained to Sarah as they settled down in the shelter again, the air raid sirens howling outside. 'I'd rather come face-to-face with Hitler than have to look at his ugly mug. Is he the only warden they've got?'

'Och, Ruby,' Sarah said sadly, 'we're neighbours, almost family. Gus is looking after us.'

'He's not family of mine!' Ruby almost shouted.

'Ssh, Ruby, you'll waken the wee ones! They can sleep through the siren but not through you yelling in their ears! The less they remember about being in here the better, let them sleep.'

'Well don't say that about *him*,' Ruby spat viciously. 'I hate his guts!'

'Ruby, that's a terrible thing to say!' Sarah whispered fiercely. 'The poor man's been through so much, for heaven's sake ease up on him.'

'Why?' Ruby asked just as fiercely. 'Did *he* die in Clydebank?'

'The man has been widowed, Ruby,' Sarah replied severely, 'and he was looking after us, here, while his own wife was dying in a raid. Think how that must make him feel?'

'Aye,' Ruby muttered sarcastically, 'if only she'd been in Yorkshire instead of Clydebank, eh? Besides, he doesn't feel, he's like a shark, he just reacts.'

Beside her, in the dark, she felt Sarah shake her head disapprovingly.

In Clydebank, attempts to positively identify the unclaimed dead in the mass grave at Dalnottar continued. PC Connelly had already reported to his inspector that there would seem to be another victim of the first raid, a Glasgow woman visiting relatives in Clydebank. The evidence was pretty conclusive, but he was a conscientious young man and Gus Campbell's shock at the news had touched him. As Tam McVicar had said at the time, the man had been creased, gutted. He didn't have time to go out of his way, he decided, but if his investigations brought him into contact with anyone who could throw more light on the case, he would ask questions. And that was how he found Jessie, the student teacher who had survived the bomb that killed so many in Radnor Street. She had broken her skull as well as various other bones in her body, and she had drifted in and out of consciousness for many weeks, missing entirely the second two nights of raids in May. Once she was well enough PC Connelly talked to her, to see if she could remember anyone who was there and help with the task of identifying the dead and buried. Jessie once again recounted her memories of that day and night, placing Betty Campbell in the fatal path of the bomb that had caused her so much pain. PC Connelly then reported the details to his superiors, who in turn placed Jessie's signed statement before Hastings, the industrious Town Clerk Depute and the Procurator

Fiscal, John Binnie, who instructed the Old Kilpatrick Registrar to officially register the death of Elizabeth Campbell, wife of Angus Campbell of High Street, Glasgow. The information was passed to Tam McVicar and then to Betty's grieving widower. Gus hadn't had to do a thing, it had all fallen into his lap and he was indeed home free in every possible way he could have hoped for.

When Ruby heard the news she went into the bedroom she shared with the babies and sobbed into her pillow with rage and disappointment. It wasn't fair, more than that, it wasn't *right*. It was as though Betty didn't matter, she had lost everything and *he* had won everything. Moreover, he had come out of it with the sympathy and support of all the people who had counted Betty as a friend. It wasn't *right!*

22

As Ruby was anguishing over the rights and wrongs of the events before and after Betty's death, Gus was getting on with his life, his eyes firmly fixed on the future. Less than two months after receiving confirmation of his widower status he had claimed his late wife's insurance and inherited everything of value left to her by her parents, including a tidy lump sum in the bank that she hadn't told him about. Despite this new found wealth he had also asked about any policies on the lives of his sister-in-law's family, but, he had been told, he could not make any claim, such payouts were intended for dependents, not in-laws. Gus was disappointed and it irked him that the money would simply die with the McCullochs. But even without it, thanks to Betty's snobby parents who had so disliked him, Gus Campbell was now a man of decent means for the first time in his life. He decided to keep this to himself, it was no one's business but his own. His and Iris's, that was, and he still wasn't sure how much he would tell even her.

That he was also openly courting Iris McLean caused a mixture of thoughts and emotions among family and neighbours. Ruby was outraged but silent with fury, while the rest of the McLean family worried that it was too soon after Betty's death, and the age gap between him and Iris was also a concern. Similar comments came from the wider community, and there was another strand of disapproval, one not shared with the family because it centred on Iris.

In the last few months something had happened to Gus Campbell's standing. It was as though becoming a widower had bestowed upon him an invisible cloak of respectability, of nobility almost. Suddenly he could do no wrong and his every thought was pure as the driven snow, with everyone inclined, if not to grant his every wish, then to overlook certain doubts they might have about him. Even women who had felt instinctively uneasy around him, and there were many, now seemed to gift him a blank sheet, a blank sheet of a rosy hue at that. The goodwill they had for him, the esteem they now held him in, was in direct reverse ratio to the discomfort they had felt about him in the past, and in this new vision of the widower Campbell, they asked one question among themselves: why Iris McLean? She was the town bike, the city bike, come to that. She was a slut, she was anybody's and everybody's and had been since her first dalliance – the first they knew about at any rate – with the Co-op manager at the age of fourteen. Gus, poor Gus, poor heartbroken, recently bereaved, almost saintly Gus, had been blinded by her youth and her availability when what he needed, when the time was right of course – and everyone agreed it was not – was a good, sensible wife in his own age group to take care of him. Yes, that was what Gus needed, to be taken care of, not taken for a fool. The aunties though, unlike the neighbourhood, did not hold back in the presence of family.

'I don't know what he's thinking!' Dot exclaimed, sitting in her chair like a Glaswegian Buddha, her fingers linked in a tight clasp across her belly, her lips clenched together in a barely visible line of tight righteousness. 'He can do better than her, so he can!'

Sarah poured the tea in silence, treating her sisters like a couple of wasps it was best not to irritate by trying to swat them.

'Wee Betty dying like that must've left him weak in the head,' Cissie opined, 'that's all I can say.'

Ruby felt her mother's distress and, knowing she had nothing to offer in defence of her sister, wished that was all Cissie could say, and Dot too, but knew it wasn't to be.

'She'll take him for every penny and then dump him,' Cissie nodded, 'she's aye been the same. As long as there's some man daft enough to be taken for a sucker, there you'll find Iris.'

'As long as he's *married!*' Dot put in, nodding her head till it looked like it might fall off her shoulders.

'Aye, you're right there,' Cissie agreed, 'as long as he's married, and that was bad enough. But to take advantage of a poor man who's just lost his wife, well, I just don't know, I really don't! She should be tarred and feathered and run to Hell in a wheelbarrow.'

'Not just out of town, but to Hell,' Ruby thought, smirking, 'in a wheelbarrow? Well *he* can join her as far as I'm concerned.'

'I tell you this,' Dot stabbed a podgy finger in mid-air, 'if there was any justice she would be struck down dead this instant!'

'It would,' Ruby thought flippantly, 'save on the tar and on plucking all those birds. Besides, you'd probably have to queue up for them. We need all the ones in the back court for eggs.'

But Dot's death sentence on Iris was too much for Sarah. 'That's a terrible thing to say about your own niece,' she protested, 'and remember she has a son.'

'Remember she has a son?' Dot laughed, nudging Cissie in the ribs. 'Did you hear that, Cissie?'

'I certainly did,' Cissie laughed back. 'I tell you, Sarah, you should be on that new thing on the wireless, what's it called, Dot?' She screwed up her face and executed a flapping motion with one hand.

'Worker's Playtime,' Dot supplied. 'It's awfy good, Sarah. Have you heard it?' she asked conversationally.

Cissie glared at her and, suitably chastised, Dot resumed her disapproving, matronly pose. 'Why would we remember that bitch has a son when *she* doesn't remember herself? Isn't that what you meant, Dot?'

'That's what I meant to the letter,' Dot replied, in her previous stern tone. 'Remember she has a son? That's a laugh, Sarah!'

'And what you have to remember, Sarah, is that she even took on with her own cousin's man!' Cissie pointed out. 'That's the kind of slut she is.'

'I seem to recall,' Sarah said, with as much dignity as she could muster, 'that he went with her of his own free will, so why should Iris take all the blame?'

'Are you listening to yourself?' Cissie demanded incredulously. 'She's gone through her entire life throwing herself at every married man like the whore she is, and you're blaming my lassie's man?'

'I'm not saying Iris is blameless,' Sarah conceded in a small voice, shifting uncomfortably in her seat as the two sisters cackled out loud.

'Well it's not all Iris's fault, Sarah, that's the truth of it. It's *your* fault,' Cissie told her firmly. 'We've told you that umpteen times. You let her away with far too much when she was young, when she should've been slapping the arse off her. It's up to you to stop her ruining a good decent man now.' She held out a paper bag. 'Acid drop, Dot?' she asked sweetly.

They had obviously just collected their sweet ration from McLellan's in George Street and Ruby, watching them from the other side of the range, mused with a wry grin that this performance, therefore, was them in a good mood. She hadn't said a word during the diatribe because she knew they were only repeating what everyone outside the family was saying and, besides, there wasn't a word to be said even by her own family in Iris's defence. Her sister was everything the old aunties said, but she bridled at Gus Campbell being described as 'a good, decent man.' She had watched and listened these last weeks with growing incredulity and nausea as his position in the community had been gradually elevated. Any day now he would sprout wings and a halo. But good and decent? That took some beating. There would be candles lit for him in St Mungo's next, even if he wasn't a Catholic. Still she said nothing, unsure why, unaware that she was instinctively nursing her wrath to keep it warm.

At the end of 1941, Gus and Iris announced their engagement. It was little more than six months since he had been told of his wife's death, so the news was greeted with the same mixture of reactions, from rather forced congratulations to shock. The McLeans tried their best to seem pleased, but gave a muted response because throughout the few months of the open courtship they had fully expected, hoped even, it would fold at any moment and so they were genuinely unsure what to think or what was expected of them. Ruby's mind was thrown into total turmoil, the unlikely, *unholy* partnership was unthinkable, it was disgraceful, and she couldn't stop thinking about it, even though she didn't want to. Since Betty had come to see her, nine months ago, her brain had been fermenting with rage and disgust, so, after the grand announcement, she decided to go up the brae to her and Gerry's marital home and pay her sister a rare visit. She found Iris getting ready for a tram shift and full of herself, but then Iris always was.

'Did you come to see the ring?' she asked smugly. She held up her left hand and waved it extravagantly, inviting admiration for the display of three diamonds on a gold band.

'No,' Ruby replied calmly, 'I came to ask you if you'd gone mad.'

Iris laughed at her. 'Aye, we took everybody by surprise, didn't we?'

Ruby ignored the question. 'Are you really going through with it?' she asked.

'Why wouldn't I?' Iris asked, applying her make-up.

'Well for starters, it's not the first time you've been engaged, is it??'

Iris looked up at her, a puzzled look on her face.

'Andy?' Ruby suggested angrily.

'Oh!' she said after a few moments. 'You mean the Morris boy?'

'Aye, Andy Morris,' Ruby said, emphasising each syllable. 'You even bought a wedding dress to marry him.'

'Och, he was just a boy!' Iris said, waving her left hand again, showing off the ring and dismissing Andy with the same gesture.

'But you still said you'd marry him,' Ruby persisted.

'It was just one of those daft notions you get when you're young,' Iris laughed. 'I never had any intention of actually doing it, you know!'

'Well it wasn't a daft notion to Andy, he thought you were serious.'

'Aye, well,' Iris sighed, 'that's his problem, he should've known better.'

Ruby shook her head. 'Let's hope to God you back out of marrying *him* the same way,' she said. 'He's the daftest notion you've ever had.'

Iris looked at her solemnly. 'You've never liked Gus, have you?' she asked curiously.

'Liked him?' Ruby cried. 'Liked him? Are you stupid? He's bloody horrible, how could anybody like him?'

'Well, I do,' Iris replied with a bright smile.

'But why?' Ruby demanded. 'Apart from the fact that he's bloody horrible, he's more than twenty years older than you! How can you let that touch you?'

'Maybe I just like older men.'

'Iris, this is me, your younger sister. I've watched the parade over the years. Older men? Since when has it mattered what age they were? They only had to be married to some other poor lassie for you to get your mitts on them, for a while at least.'

Iris ignored the charge. 'Well, Gus isn't married, so that's okay then, isn't it? And he'd do anything for me. He knows when he's lucky so he'll treat me better than any of those young lads.'

Ruby bit her tongue. She had been about to say 'But he *was* married, wasn't he? You were carrying on with him while he was still a married man,' but she checked herself and took a deep breath instead. 'Are you telling me that this is a case of true love?' she asked, laughing bitterly. 'You and *him*?'

'That's exactly what it is,' Iris smiled sweetly.

'Now I've heard everything!' Ruby said sarcastically. 'Your taste can't be that bad, Iris. After all, you must've sampled most of the men around here, and this is the best you can come up with?'

'Well I've done better than you, that's for sure,' Iris shot at her. 'You've no room to talk, have you? Look at the thing you stuck yourself with.'

She wanted to slap her, really slap her, not because she felt Iris was insulting Gerry, but because Iris was right. Instead she turned and walked out, with Iris shouting a derisive 'Bye now!' as she retreated from what was supposed to be her marital home, and almost ran back down the stairs. The first thing she'd do when Gerry came home and they moved in was buy a new bed, she decided. The thought of Gus Campbell and Iris rolling around on the present one was enough to make her sick. She stopped outside the close and leaned against the building, trying to calm down. Look what Ruby had stuck herself with indeed. There was no answer to that one. Just then Flora came running up the brae.

'Your mother told me you were going up to see Iris,' she panted. 'You didn't, did you Ruby?'

Ruby was standing with her back pressed against the red sandstone, her feet slightly spread on the pavement and her arms wrapped round herself. She laughed bitterly. 'Depends what you mean,' she said quietly.

187

'You know what I mean,' Flora retorted, 'stop messing about.'

'No,' Ruby sighed, smiling at her, 'if you mean what I think you mean, I didn't, Flora. I just asked her why she was marrying that horrible big reptile, that insect, that—' she looked up. 'What's so funny?'

'I was just thinking,' Flora giggled, 'that your George would see those descriptions as compliments to Gus and insults to the reptiles and insects, and here you are, trying to insult Gus Campbell with them!'

'It's all very well you laughing,' Ruby protested, trying not to smile, 'but do you realise that when they get married – if they get married – he'll be my brother-in-law?'

At that Flora laughed even more.

'I was going to slap that slut up the stairs there,' Ruby said, 'but I think I'll just slap you instead!'

'You see what I mean? You're getting slap happy, Ruby McLean! You'll have to watch your step or Tam McVicar will be dragging you away in handcuffs!' She linked arms with Ruby and began walking her back down the brae to the McLean home. 'But seriously, Ruby, what good would it do to make a scene about Betty now?'

'Oh, I don't know,' Ruby mused, 'it would do me good, you said that yourself a while ago.'

'But only you, Ruby. Think of the trouble it would cause in the family. Your mother would be upset, the whole of High Street would be up in arms, and for what? Nothing, that's what for.'

'Well I didn't do it anyway,' Ruby said, 'so stop going on about it or I'll run back up there and just do it to spite you.' She sighed heavily. 'Do you know, she could barely remember the whole Andy Morris escapade?'

'Well you couldn't have been surprised by that, that's Iris for you,' Flora replied.

'She said he was just a boy and the whole thing had been a daft notion, and if he didn't see it that way it was his problem.'

Flora shrugged and smiled lopsidedly.

'The boy was really upset,' Ruby persisted. 'He still looks at her as though she was some great prize he won in a raffle but then found he'd lost the ticket.'

'He'll grow out of it,' Flora said. 'She was right, he was just a boy, he's older now, life goes on. Why do you always have to take on other peoples' troubles?'

Ruby laughed. 'I wish I knew.'

'Andy Morris is fine, I've seen him a few times since he got back,' Flora smiled at her. 'Stop worrying about him, and everybody else.'

'You didn't mention his leg, did you?' Ruby asked. 'His mother has us all so well warned not to mention the leg that I can't look anywhere else when I meet him, I'm terrified I'll just burst out and yell "Leg! Leg! Leg!" each time I see him.'

'Och, she told me the same thing,' Flora said, 'I just ignored her. I talked to him as though he was a normal, thinking human being.'

'But you didn't really ask him about the leg, though, did you?'

'Aye, I mentioned it,' Flora said, 'seemed really silly not to, I asked how it happened and how he's coping.'

'You did not!' Ruby exclaimed.

'Of course I did and he was fine about it. I told you he was fine, didn't I? He talked about what he wants to do. He doesn't fancy staying in the Goods Yard all his life, says the War had wakened him up a bit and he wants to know things now. Denis and I take him a few books every now and again. He's very keen to learn.'

'Oh, Flora! You're not going to have him manning the barricades with the comrades, are you?' Ruby exclaimed.

'Only if he wants to,' Flora giggled. 'All we've done is point him the direction of reading, the rest is up to him. He's actually pretty clever, the Iris situation apart, of course. As Denis says, he doesn't need two legs to read and educate himself.'

Ruby glanced at her. 'I like your Denis,' she grinned.

'I've told you before, he's not *my* Denis,' Flora replied primly. 'He's just Denis.'

'Away with you! I saw the two of you together, he's your Denis!'

'Ruby, he is not!'

Ruby nudged her. 'It was good of him to go to all that trouble for me,' she said. 'I hope he knew I was grateful.'

'He's like that,' Flora said gently, eyes shining, 'he does things for people. He's very kind and very considerate, you've no idea.'

'And he's very good looking as well,' Ruby said slyly. 'Or are you

189

claiming you didn't notice that, what with all your pure intentions and your ideals? And those eyes! No wonder you fancy him.'

'Ruby!'

Ruby giggled. 'I know, I know, he's just a comrade, I believe you. Thousands wouldn't!'

23

With breathtaking insensitivity, Iris and Gus Campbell set their wedding date for March 1942, almost a year to the day after Betty's death. If anyone else noticed the crassness of the timing they didn't mention it. Despite the many misgivings of family and friends, everyone wanted a happy as well as a quick outcome for Gus after all he had suffered, an attitude that incensed Ruby even more. It seemed to her that everything was being organised to add to her rage. Though in her more rational moments she knew it was all down to a series of ghastly coincidences, somehow that didn't help improve her mood. She was disappointed the ceremony wouldn't be taking place in the Barony Church at the top of the brae, thereby ruining enjoyable visions of the old place collapsing on top of the bride and groom as they took their vows, a wedding present from a rightfully vengeful God. Instead, with the introduction of civil marriages for the first time in 1940, the happy couple would be united at Martha Street Register Office, within walking distance of High Street.

'I don't suppose you'd be interested in being bridesmaid?' Iris asked Ruby, out of mischief.

Ruby didn't reply but gave her sister a look of heartfelt disgust.

Iris laughed delightedly. 'We've asked Bea and Davy to be witnesses,' she chortled, 'but I thought I'd give you the option anyway.' She glanced at Ruby. 'You'll be coming though?' she asked.

'Do they search you for weapons at the door?' Ruby asked glumly, and Iris laughed again.

The bride decided against wearing the dress she had bought to marry Andy Morris, the dress Ruby had worn to wed Gerry, and opted instead to use her clothing coupons for the grey suit that had become the norm for brides during the wartime austerity. The decision, Ruby was sure, had nothing to do with keeping a low profile in the circumstances. Iris was completely ignorant of the mores of decency. After the marriage there would be a reception at the McLean home, as was the custom, with Gus using some of his recent inheritance to buy whatever was available on the black market to top up the combined rations of the family, though he resolved to wait till he could see what was being provided before dipping into his pocket. Everyone gave, except Ruby, which added to Iris's merriment, she had taken a great deal of delight in goading Ruby over the wedding, even asking her to bring Jamie to Martha Street to see his mother marry.

Ruby had almost choked. 'He doesn't even know you!' she protested, 'and I won't be there, so how can I bring Jamie?'

'Oh, well,' Iris sighed happily, 'Ma can bring him. Just make sure he's dressed for the wedding, his best togs, you know.'

And Ruby had almost choked again.

After the family reception Iris would move into Gus's house across the street, Betty's family home, where they would live happily ever after. There would be a seamless transition between the first Mrs Campbell and the next, treachery had won the day. But before that there was the wedding itself and, for some peculiar reason, the blushing bride decided to conform to tradition and spend the evening before at the home of her parents. On the morning of the big event Iris exulted in being the centre of attention and flapped around unconvincingly, acting out the role she had assigned herself, as a virginal young bride, neither of which was true. Her hair was forcibly skewered into a high edifice of tight curls on top of her head, so that a pink creation of lace and straw could perch perilously aloft, from which a veil descended over her eyes in demure fashion. The grey utility suit had been fitted to her impressive contours within an inch of its life, and a little froth of pink lace frilled at the neckline. Complimenting the ensemble was a gift from the groom, a small brooch pinned to the lapel.

'They're real diamonds!' Iris told everyone, her eyes bright with excitement. 'There's a wee fob watch you can hang on it,' she continued, giggling, 'but I think it's a bit old-fashioned. Maybe when I'm fifty, eh?'

Ruby, who had been ignoring the entire charade by thinking herself somewhere else, was jolted back to reality by Iris's description. Suddenly she froze, going over Iris's words in her mind. 'A wee fob watch you can hang on it.' It couldn't be, could it?

'It's made of rose gold,' Iris boasted, 'and it's very heavy. Real quality.'

Ruby swallowed hard and returned to her secret calm place, determined to stay there till the day was over. They would all be gone from the house soon, she told herself, all would be quiet once again. While the marriage was taking place, she would just have to draw strength from that short spell and hope it would carry her through the awful prospect of the reception party. When the time came Jamie was taken from her, screaming and holding his arms out to her, as he was placed into the awkward possession of his mother who laughed as he cried because she knew no better. Sarah approached Ruby at the last minute.

'Are you sure you won't come?' she pleaded.

Ruby turned her head, looked at her mother in the eye and turned away again without a word.

'Well, maybe you could—' Sarah said, about to suggest Ruby might perform some last minute domestic task while the family was away, then she thought better of it and murmured, 'It doesn't matter, it'll keep.'

George wouldn't be at the ceremony either. There was a war on, he said, he had to work, though he would try to get to the reception, and Uncle Jakey jumped on that handy bandwagon to excuse himself too. Even Harry would have to return to duty and take a troop train south later in the day, though the groom would be allowed his wedding night with his bride. Ruby decided not to dwell on that thought for fear of being sick. The aunties, with typical candour, declared the idea of actually going to Martha Street 'Not worth it,' but let it be known they would be prepared to grace the celebrations with their presence later, so there would only be Harry, Sarah, Bea and Dainty Davy from the bride's side and no one from the groom's, though a handful of curious neighbours would be sure to show up. The general feeling of unease about the nuptials persisted. It was as though everyone had decided it was going to happen and, however uncomfortable they felt, they had to go through the motions and get it finished as quickly as possible. They would see this thing through, over and done with the minimum of fuss and, when it hit rocks in due course, as everyone expected it to, they would shake their heads and say 'I knew at the time it would never last, but you had to show willing, didn't you?'

Ruby breathed a sigh of relief when the noise and bustle faded downstairs and into the street and didn't look out of the window to see the parade off. Instead she took her daughter for a walk in the sunshine, pointing out things to her as mothers do. A horse and cart clip-clopped past on the cobbles and Frances ignored it though the carter waved at her, and a passing tram was greeted with the same level of enthusiasm. Frances was just that kind of child, she decided. She was self-contained and preferred to be left that way. She pushed the pram on a favourite route, down High Street past the Goods Yard and along Trongate, up Candleriggs and into Ingram Street, leading back to High Street and home. As they turned into Ingram Street, ahead in the distance Ruby saw the Sheik of High Street in full regalia, accompanied by his vicious hound. The Sheik and his hound had become a fairly common sight these days, wandering the streets righting wrongs and, so far, Tam McVicar had managed not to arrest him. Ruby smiled, remembering that he was supposed to be working; Uncle Jakey was voting with his feet too. The two figures were too far along Ingram Street to be caught and shouting to him, with all the noise of the nearby Fruit Market drowning out her voice, would have achieved nothing, so Ruby didn't try.

When she got back to High Street the bridal party had returned to the McLean home, and it was filling with family and friends, so Ruby could hide in the throng. A fine spread had been laid on by Sarah, using up a large lump of her pre-war stockpile, and it struck Ruby that it was a bit too much; as though Sarah, like everyone else, was compensating for her doubts in case they showed. Ruby shook her head slightly and grinned to herself; like Iris gave a damn what anyone thought, she doubted if she even thought to wonder at Sarah's largesse. In the middle of the room Iris was standing in a throng of admiring women, no doubt looking at the wedding ring, Ruby assumed, passing on her way to pick up the discarded Jamie, who had spotted her and instantly cried with anxiety again, holding out his arms.

'Gus says they're rubies!' she heard Iris say. Everything that came out of her mouth these days started with 'Gus says.' But something made Ruby stand still again and listen without looking.

'I've never seen a bangle like it!' an admiring neighbour said in hushed tones.

'And look at the engraving!' another said. 'It looks really heavy, Iris. What's that pattern called?'

'Gus says it's called scrollwork, and it is heavy,' Iris said smugly. 'It's rose gold, same as the brooch, everything is, my engagement ring as well. They're all family heirlooms, even the wedding ring, though it was too wide, Gus got it cut in half.'

'Och,' said another voice, with that hint of over-egging that had become the norm over this match, 'you've landed on your feet with Gus, Iris!'

In the background she heard Auntie Cissie say 'Told you. In it for what she can soak out of him!' and looked around to see the old sisters watching Iris showing off her booty. They had taken up their usual poses by the fireside, sitting there like a particularly vicious Tweedle Dum and Tweedle Dee.

Bea was in the opposite corner of the room, Dainty Davy by her side, both of them looking glum. Ruby stood with Jamie in her arms, feeling that the room was slightly spinning as she digested the conversations taking place around her sister. Gus Campbell had given Iris Granny Rose's jewellery, Betty's jewellery, and he had even had that lovely broad wedding ring mutilated. All the gems that had been dug out of Betty's death site were now adorning Iris, or nearly all. She expected the emerald locket to appear at any moment, or had he sold that already, as he'd always urged Betty to do? It couldn't be true, it just couldn't, she thought, standing still. Yet it was, it had to be. And Iris couldn't know, she couldn't have taken them if she knew. Yes, she could. She would. What in hell is up with you, Ruby McLean? Of course she knew; it wouldn't matter a damn to Iris where they came from, as long as she got them. She quickly took Jamie to the bedroom where she had deposited Frances a few minutes before. Both children were whiny, it was past their lunchtime and they were hungry and tired with the disruption to their routine. So she went to the kitchen, easing her way through the guests with her eyes down so that she wouldn't be caught up in conversation, then back to the bedroom the same way with food for Frances and Jamie. She changed and fed them, Frances first because, she knew her daughter would never give way to Jamie and would just raise the roof if he was fed before her. Then she put them down for their nap as usual and, catching sight of her reflection in the dressing table mirror, she was taken aback by how completely calm she looked, despite her head whirling with shock and indignation at what she had just discovered. Betty's man – such as he was – and her home already belonged to her slut of a sister, and now her family's jewellery. Just how much was she expected to put up with from these two? She couldn't face going back to the party, so when she heard footsteps she lay down and pretended to be asleep opposite the babies.

'Ruby!' Sarah shook her. 'Ruby, are you coming out?'

Ruby rubbed her eyes. 'My head's killing me,' she said.

'Och, Ruby, I wish you wouldn't behave like this!' Sarah scolded. 'I know you don't like Gus but they're married now and he's been awful good to her. They're about to cut the cake, and people will notice if you don't put in an appearance.'

And so she reluctantly headed for the living room, thinking to herself, 'So this is what they mean by dragging your heels.' George had arrived with Marie and the children, and Agnes, Gerry's sister, was coming through the front door, with Uncle Jakey, minus the Sheik's clothes, just behind. She watched him secrete himself in the chair in the corner nearest the sitting room door as Wee Dug slunk underneath, so she chose a spot on the other side and pulled Agnes down beside her.

'You stay with me,' she whispered.

Agnes nodded. 'What a to-do,' she whispered back, settling herself in the chair beside Ruby. 'Have you heard from Gerry lately?'

Ruby nodded. 'I had a letter the other day.'

'Me too,' Agnes smiled, 'I don't know how he gets the time to write all these long letters.'

Ruby didn't reply. She didn't get many letters from Gerry and, when she did, they were of the short 'Hope everything's fine with you,' variety, but she didn't want to have that conversation today.

'They look happy enough,' Agnes nodded towards Gus and Iris. Ruby shrugged.

'Ruby, Ruby!' Agnes laughed. 'You're an awful lassie! He's not my cup of tea either – '

'Neither is she!' Ruby said bitterly. 'She's definitely not mine!'

Agnes laughed again, putting one hand over her mouth and patting Ruby's knee with the other. 'But what's done is done, and who knows? This might be the making of Iris.'

Ruby grunted. 'Do you realise they'll be living below Andy Morris and his family?' she asked.

'You don't think he's still got a crush on her, do you?'

'I don't really know, but I bet it hasn't even occurred to her to wonder about how he might be feeling,' Ruby replied.

'Now be honest, Ruby,' Agnes nudged her, 'even if Andy said it didn't matter a damn to him, you'd still find fault about something else, wouldn't you now?'

'Aye, that's true,' Ruby admitted, 'but look at them. If there ever two people to find fault with, it's them. What a pair of scunners!'

The cutting of the cake was completed and applauded, with Iris milking it for all she was worth and, as the usual toasts were made, Ruby noticed Gus's hand moving from his new wife's waist to her bottom, where it rested. She nudged Agnes.

'Look at that,' she muttered. 'Big brute.'

Agnes chuckled beside her. 'He was always pretty handy with his paws,' she whispered.

'But in *front* of people!' Ruby replied in a voice dripping with disgust.

'Just imagine what he'll be like in private!' Agnes shot back.

'Oh, Agnes!' Ruby grimaced, turning away, a hand on her midriff. 'That was a horrible thing to say!'

'I'd imagine it's a horrible thing to be on the receiving end of!' Agnes giggled.

'Will you stop it?'

Then it happened. If it hadn't been for a tiny lull after the toasts she might not have thought of it. But there again, maybe she would have, it had been building up for a long time. Ruby had the strange sensation of watching herself stand up and lift a glass someone had put down, booze of some kind, she supposed, she had no idea what.

'I have a toast,' she said in a loud voice, smiling pleasantly. Everyone stopped chatting and looked at her, including the happy couple. 'It's a toast to Absent Friends.'

There was a murmur of approval, everyone had someone away from home that they wished was there, it was a nice thought.

'I've got one special Absent Friend in mind,' Ruby continued. 'Betty Campbell.'

Glasses were raised once more, though a little slower this time. It was an odd thing to introduce the spectre of the dead first wife into her widower's re-marriage, but they had all been fond of Betty, so why not?

'What nobody here knows is that on the day Betty went away, not to Yorkshire, Gus,' she stopped and bestowed a sweet smile on her new brother-in-law, 'but to Clydebank, she paid me a visit and told me why she was going.' She stopped and looked round, pacing herself for full effect. 'You see, the night before she had followed Gus up to Gerry's house, where, as everybody knows, Iris had been living.' She paused and laughed wryly. 'She's moving into Betty's house now, Betty's bed too, I imagine.' From the corner of her eye she caught a slight movement from Gus and, without looking directly at him, held a hand up to stop him. 'Anyway, on that night the door was open and there Betty found Gus and Iris in bed together. How can I put it? At it like knives.' A little shocked intake of breath rippled around the guests and she noticed her father quietly leaving the room. 'You didn't know that, did you Gus?' she asked kindly. 'That Betty had seen the two of you together, very together? Well now you do, now everybody does. Betty was shattered by what she saw, she was still in a terrible state when she came up to see me here the next day. She hadn't slept all night and she was crying all the time. That's why she left, because she was disgusted and couldn't bear the thought of ever seeing you again after finding out what you and the Virgin Iris were up to.' There wasn't a sound now. 'And all that nice, expensive, classy jewellery my slut of a sister is now wearing, it all belonged to Betty, and before her to her grandmother, Rose. It was made by Betty's grandfather, including the wedding ring. Some of you may remember it on Betty's finger, a very broad, heavy rose-gold band. Betty's mother gave her Granny Rose's ring when she married Gus. She thought she would need all the luck she could get. Before Gus got it hacked in half there was an inscription inside reading "Rose, my one true love, Alex." Betty took it off the day she left. She said she no longer felt like a married woman, and she put it in the suitcase she was taking with her, the same suitcase that was dug up in the rubble of where she died. Oh, and Iris,' she said conversationally, 'there's a locket still to come, with a nice big emerald in the middle. It was Granny Rose's birthstone, apparently. Unless, of course, Gus has already sold it.' She turned back to the astonished faces of the guests. 'So now Iris the Slut is wearing Betty's wedding ring, or half of it at least, she's got Betty's family jewellery, Betty's house and Betty's man, though God knows, and Betty knew it too, she's welcome to him. To Absent Friends, then.'

Gus Campbell rushed across the room, his fists clenched, and stopped inches from Ruby's face. She didn't flinch, but raised her glass and looked him full in the eyes. 'Cheers, Gus,' she smiled calmly. 'You betrayed Betty, who was a good woman, as everybody here knows, and then you killed her. The Germans dropped the bomb, but if she hadn't seen what she saw, you and Delilah there, she wouldn't have gone to Clydebank, and if she hadn't gone to Clydebank she wouldn't have died. Congratulations, Gus, you've made it. You've got the slut and much good may she do you, and you her. Welcome to the family.'

'You bitch!' he hissed. 'You fucking bitch!', and even though he sprayed saliva over Ruby's face she still didn't move a muscle, this time it was worth it.

The audience was roused from its silence to utter a communal 'Oh!', not so much at what they had just heard, but because men never swore in the presence of women, far less at them.

'Oh,' Ruby said sweetly, 'I think you've got the wrong sister, Gus.

The one you've just described is standing over the room there. The new Mrs Campbell.'

Gus raised his hand and drew it back to lash out at her, but Ruby stood her ground. Gus hitting her would, she knew, be the final nail in his coffin with everyone. But his hand stopped mid-air, caught from behind by her brother, George, the only man in the room big enough to take Gus on.

'Touch her, Gus,' he said with controlled anger, 'even breathe on her, and I swear to God, I'll kill you.'

Gus tried to pull free, his face red, his bulging eyes still fixed on Ruby, flecks of foamy spittle at the corners of his tight mouth.

'I mean it, Gus,' George said menacingly. 'Make no mistake. I will kill you where you stand.' From behind he put a forearm across Gus's throat, twisted his arm behind his back and dragged him away from his sister. There was absolute silence in the room, then a scream erupted from Iris. 'Well I don't care what any of you think!' she snarled, looking around at the shocked faces. 'At least I could give him what Saint Betty never could! I could give him a wean!'

'Well I think we'll have to see that before we believe it,' Ruby almost chuckled, her eyes still locked with Gus's.

'You have seen it,' Iris replied, her face contorted with rage. 'You've seen it more than most, as it happens.'

Ruby heard another ripple of shock run around the guests and realised they knew something she didn't, a connection had been made for them, an understanding reached. Her mind was still blank, but somehow the knowledge that had changed the atmosphere in the room made her feel as though the floor was slipping away beneath her feet.

'Aye, that's right!' Iris screamed. 'Jamie! Jamie's Gus's wean! You've been looking after Gus's wean, Miss Smartarse, and you've no idea how we've laughed about that, you foul-mouthing Gus every chance you got, and all the time you were being a mother to his son!'

She advanced on Ruby who was still standing stunned in the middle of the room. 'And I'll tell you something else,' she said maliciously. 'We're taking him back right away!'

★

If the room had opened up and swallowed her Ruby would have been grateful. She had been stunned into silence and her brain was refusing to process the new information, not only stopping her ability to think, but paralysing her entire body too. She wanted to run but found she couldn't move and was holding onto the casually lifted glass as though it was a lifebelt in stormy water. Then something else happened, thank God it happened. Bea. As Bea got out of her chair in the corner beside Dainty Davy, the roar that came from her was like her father's loco thundering into the covered approach to Goods Yard and, taking her usual position centre stage, her aggressive whining battle cry reverberated around the gathering, down the stairs and out into High Street. As Ruby stood where she was, most people scattered for safety all around her, while the bravest lunged to get a grip of Bea in what was a well-organised, time-served reaction to her ructions. Her complaints were as loud, familiar and vague as ever, those that could be discerned, and seemed to centre on everyone present being happy, the same old refrain. Everyone in the universe was receiving kindnesses that she alone was denied, that was the gist of it, though all her screeches were now muffled by being sieved through the phalanx of bodies trying to subdue her, or at least deny her access to any innocent body she wished to assault. In another corner of the room the two old aunties voiced their delight with shrieks of laughter.

'Here we go!' Cissie announced. 'No show without Punch!'

'I knew she wouldn't let us down,' Dot replied cheerily above the screams, 'it was the only reason for coming. That and the cake, of course.'

'Aye,' Cissie said, an urgent tone in her voice, 'somebody should get a hold of the cake in case the daft big bugger falls on it or pushes somebody into it and demolishes it.'

Listening to them, though their voices seemed to be coming from miles away, roused Ruby enough to head for the sanctuary of the bedroom under the cover of the chaos. As she passed Cissie caught her arm and remarked sympathetically, 'Nice try, hen, you did well, but you must've known you couldn't beat Bea, she aye wins.'

As Ruby pulled free and moved on she noticed the front door closing. 'Uncle Jakey,' she thought, 'Uncle Jakey and Wee Dug.'

'Ruby! Ruby, hen!' Dot yelled.

She paused in the hallway and turned side on to her.

'Ruby, seeing as you're going anyway, could you grab the cake and take it away before it gets smashed, hen?'

In the bedroom she locked the door behind her and lay on the bed, her face in a pillow. 'Thank God for Big Bea,' she thought. 'Thank every God for Big Bea! Who thought I'd ever say that, but today she has truly been a Godsend!' Gradually her ability to think was restored and she turned fearfully to look at the two sleeping babies. At Jamie. Her Jamie. Her face contorted with grief. He was Gus Campbell's son? It couldn't be. Jamie was a beautiful child, good-natured, affectionate and happy, he was all the things her own daughter wasn't and she loved him with a passion that made her dizzy. No, Iris had been lying, she had just been hitting back at her for her little speech, that was all. He could be anyone's child, he had to be anyone's child, how would Iris know who the real father was? Yes, he could be anybody. She took a deep breath and laughed quietly with relief. She had been taken in for a while there, she had almost believed it, Iris had got her and no mistake. Just then Jamie stirred, opened his eyes and looked at her, but as she reached out to touch his hand she suddenly felt a blow, it was as if a huge, invisible fist had punched her in the stomach and knocked her to her knees. She had seen those eyes before. The resemblance was so horrifically obvious that she withdrew her hand as though stung. How had she ever missed it? The child was looking at her, not, as she had always surmised, with Sarah's or Iris's eyes, but with Gus Campbell's, the paleness of the blue was unmistakable. Appalled, she got up, unlocked the bedroom door, ran down the hallway and out into High Street, tears running down her cheeks.

24

The cold drove her back home. March could be as nippy as it was bright, and she hadn't stopped to collect her coat on the way out. She had followed the familiar route she had taken earlier with Frances, then gone down to the Fruit Market to watch the horses and carts at work. Next she took a wander round the Ramshorn Cemetery to read the ancient inscriptions on the headstones before sitting on a bench and listening to the birds. And thinking. She remembered how Gus Campbell had come over with Betty to admire the new baby boy. She had thought he was looking at Jamie out of curiosity, joining in the neighbourhood's latest game of trying to guess the father, so she had blocked his view. And all the time he knew *he* was the father, he had even brought his unsuspecting wife to admire his son by another woman. And the night of the first Clydebank bomb raid, he had arrived at the shelter with Iris and had said – what was it now? 'I'll take the wee boy,' that was it. She had shrugged him off and told him not to touch Jamie, her precious Jamie, but now she could see the significance of his concern. The pieces of the jigsaw were fitting so well now that she wondered why she hadn't spotted the connections from the start and she felt a fool.

When she got back the party was long over, it hadn't lasted much after the twin performances of Ruby and Big Bea. The signs were everywhere, food trodden into the floor mixed with liquids of various varieties. The wedding cake was smashed, she noticed with slight amusement, the aunties would never forgive her for that.

'There you are,' Sarah said sternly, her closed lips drawn tight. 'And just what kind of exhibition do you think you made of yourself today, then?'

'Me?' Ruby laughed, shaking her head. 'After everything you heard about those two, you're asking about me?'

'Ruby, there was no need for it!' Sarah said fiercely. 'Just who did it benefit?'

'I think it benefited Betty, seeing as you're asking,' Ruby replied casually.

'How could it possibly?' Sarah demanded. 'The woman's dead, and I doubt she would've wanted you shouting her embarrassment to the world.'

'I didn't embarrass Betty,' Ruby countered. 'If I couldn't do anything for her because she's not here any longer, how could I embarrass her? I was aiming at those two!'

'Well, you got them. I hope you're feeling pleased with yourself!'

'I am, thanks,' Ruby said pertly.

'What you put your poor Da through with this kind of thing, he doesn't deserve it!' Sarah fumed. 'You and Iris screaming at each other like banshees and George wrestling with Gus Campbell and threatening to kill him, then Bea like a, like a …'

'Fish wife,' Ruby remarked.

'Aye, like a fish wife!' Sarah agreed. 'Your Da was so affronted by it all that he just sat in the bedroom by himself for ages.'

'That's what Da always does when there's trouble,' Ruby replied. 'He's the only one who hasn't seen one of Bea's eruptions from beginning to end. Well, him and Uncle Jakey.'

'They're both sensitive souls!' Sarah told her.

'They're lucky then,' Ruby smiled, 'the rest of us have to put up with the rough and the even rougher in this family!'

She watched her mother's furious expression as she attacked another of her stress crochet creations as though it was responsible for everything that had happened. She looked tired, she thought, but it had been that kind of day. 'Did you know Jamie was his?' she asked.

Sarah shook her head tightly. 'How would I know? Not that I believe it. Iris was just saying that to hurt you.'

'Well she was, but she was also telling the truth, Ma,' Ruby sighed, 'though I can see why that would be a novelty.'

Sarah looked up sharply and Ruby nodded. 'He is,' she shrugged.

'I've been thinking about it all day, trying to work it out. Remember the day after I got married, the Fair Saturday? Well I saw Gus coming home and he turned at his close and waved to someone further down the street on the other side. I was in Gerry's flat, putting the wedding cake away, and then I came down here and Iris was just in, she'd been to the Shows at Glasgow Green. Remember?'

Sarah put her crochet in her lap and thought. 'I went with Marie and the weans on the Monday because your Da was working all weekend. That's when I won that bowl there. She nodded towards the dimpled glass bowl on the table.'

'That horrible thing!' Ruby laughed.

'I think it's lovely!' Sarah protested.

'Ma, it's orange!'

'Well it's the first thing I've ever won in my entire life and it brightens the place up!' She thought for a moment. 'Betty never mentioned going with Gus, so I just supposed he'd been asked to work a shift somewhere. You know how busy it is over the Fair Holidays. Maybe he just saw Iris coming home and waved to her.'

'Aye, that could've been it, I suppose,' Ruby conceded. 'I'd taken a bit of wedding cake to Betty and she said he was working, she had his tea on because he liked it on the table the minute he came in from work. She never said he should've been off but had been called out, or that they'd had to cancel going to the Shows, and that's something she would've mentioned, surely?'

Sarah and Ruby exchanged a look.

'When I saw him waving he was definitely wearing his working clothes, it was about the right time for him coming home from work, and he was carrying a bag. Not his usual railway bag, a bigger one.'

'You don't think he was at the Shows with Iris, do you?' Sarah said quietly. 'That Betty just thought he was working when he was with her?'

'I do now,' Ruby sighed. 'Maybe he had a change of clothes in the bag, who knows? At the time I just thought it all seemed a bit odd, I had no reason to put two and two together. Who would've thought she'd have entertained him, after all? But it wasn't long after that she was expecting, was it?'

'The thought that it could've been going on all that time!' Sarah's hand flew to her throat. 'Poor Betty,' she said, looking around for a handkerchief. 'Poor Betty!'

'I'm glad she never knew all that before she died, Ma, she was in a terrible state over the one time she did know about. Think how it would've destroyed her to know that big brute was Jamie's father.'

'But that would make it ...' she stopped and began working out the time. 'That's ...'

'Nearly three years,' Ruby supplied.

'I can hardly believe she's been ...'

'Entertaining Gus Campbell all that time?' Ruby said with a dry smile.

'Well, aye,' Sarah said quietly, staring into space.

'So who says it's only been him, Ma?' Ruby asked. 'Even if he thinks it is. She's never been the loyal kind, has she? He couldn't watch her all the time any more than we could. She's been in Gerry's flat on her own for a while and able to do whatever she wanted. Mind you, she always has, hasn't she?'

Mother and daughter sat in heavy silence for a while.

'When did they get Bea under control?' Ruby asked brightly, changing the subject.

'Oh, not long,' Sarah sighed, resuming her crochet. 'The usual, you know.'

Ruby laughed. 'She always picks her moment, doesn't she?'

'Aye, well, Bea thinks every moment is hers, that's the trouble.'

'She's been pretty quiet recently, though.'

'It's her stomach again, she's been feeling really low,' Sarah replied. 'Dr McGill's given her everything there is to give, pills for that and tablets for the other, nothing seems to work. He gave her some pills to help her sleep. I think that's the best thing he's been able to do. She's been walking the floor at night in agony. And she hasn't been dancing much. That usually helps her, the dancing, something to occupy her mind, but she hasn't been able to find a replacement pianist since Betty left. Knowing what she's like puts people off.'

'That's understandable,' Ruby laughed. 'I wouldn't like to be a learner she was teaching either!'

Sarah nodded, smiling, calming down again, Iris and Gus pushed further back in her mind to make way for Bea. 'Davy uses an old gramophone for his lessons, so it hasn't hit him as hard. He's concentrating on Latin American, so Bea says, and Bea isn't fond of that. He thinks he's found one young lad who could be a star. He works on the railway with him, apparently. When he isn't working he's spending all his time coaching the boy, so Bea's on her own a lot.'

'Maybe that's just as well if her stomach's bad again,' Ruby suggested. 'God knows, she's hell even when she's feeling okay.'

'Mind you, I think a wean would solve a lot of her problems,' Sarah said sadly, 'but she's adamant she doesn't want any, so that's that.'

Ruby thought of George's theory about Bea the Preying Mantis and chuckled to herself. 'I can't see her having any patience with a wean, though, Ma, can you?'

'You can never tell,' Sarah said. 'Having a wean to look after changes people, some for the good, some for the bad.' She frowned. 'Let's hope it's for the good as far as Iris is concerned.'

Just then, the new Mrs Campbell arrived, smiling and relaxed, as though nothing untoward had happened earlier.

'Oh good, you're back, Ruby,' she said cheerfully. 'I was thinking that you could maybe keep Jamie for the night, give me and Gus our wedding night to ourselves.'

Ruby exchanged a look with her mother. 'Like it's your first night together?' Ruby asked sarcastically.

'Aye, that's right,' Iris replied happily.

'If you take Jamie,' Ruby said, stressing every word and calling her bluff, 'you take him now,' though she wondered how she would react if Iris just reneged on her plan to take the boy away and she had to keep him after all.

'Och, that's rotten of you, Ruby,' Iris chided, 'but you always were a miserable bugger! Ma,' she protested to Sarah, 'make her keep him for the night.'

'Iris,' Sarah said with unusual anger, 'your lack of shame has always amazed me, but words almost fail me now. Your sister, the miserable bugger here, has cared for Jamie devotedly since the day he was born, as well you know. I'll look after the wee one tonight because I know you won't, but then you will collect him. From tomorrow he will be your full responsibility, yours and Gus's. Is that clear?'

'That's great, Ma!' Irish grinned delightedly. 'See you tomorrow,' then with a conspiratorial wink she added, 'but not too early, eh?'

'God, Ma!' Ruby said when the door closed behind her, 'I've never heard you talk to her like that before!'

'Aye, well, I've been doing a bit of thinking myself,' Sarah smiled shyly. 'Maybe I should've taken a firmer line with her long before this. Cissie and Dot have been telling me that since she was wee. Maybe they were right all along.'

'You haven't told them that, have you?' Ruby implored with mock earnestness. 'Please say you haven't told them that? They think they're right about everything, but if they knew you thought so as well, where would it end?'

'Oh, Ruby!' Sarah said, crying and laughing at the same time. She reached for her hankie and wiped her eyes. 'It's been a terrible day!'

Ruby got up and put her arms around Sarah's shoulders and hugged her. 'Ssh, Ma,' she said gently. 'It's over now, and you have to laugh, don't you? What's the point of crying?'

'You're young, Ruby,' Sarah sniffed. 'The young recover from upsets easier. You'll see that when you're an old woman yourself one day!'

That night Ruby moved with Frances to Gerry's flat, leaving Jamie behind in the care of his grandmother. She could hear his screams all the way down the stairs and out into High Street, but she kept walking, her head down, her eyes full of tears. She couldn't bear to look at him, that was the truth. With each step she felt black, burning shame. Jamie was an innocent child, she knew that. None of this was his doing, he was as blameless of the explosive events of the day as he was over who had fathered him, she knew that too. But when she thought of him now she also saw Gus Campbell's big, brutal, ugly face laughing at her. Her instinctive reaction was to recoil in horror and disgust and there was nothing she could do about it.

So there they all were in High Street, making changes and living different lives, all in the space of one, inauspicious day, Iris and Gus's wedding day. The newly-weds and their son were starting out on a lifetime of connubial bliss in what had once been Betty's family home, though with considerably less goodwill now within the community. Harry and Sarah were officially living in an empty nest for the first time in their lives, or would be once Jamie had left in the morning to live with the parents he didn't know, and Ruby and Frances were starting afresh in the Reilly flat. It was unfortunate in one way that Ruby would have a clear view of Gus and Iris across the road, it meant that she couldn't avoid seeing how Jamie was being cared for. Iris, now a married woman with a young child, was allowed to give up wartime work on the trams to become a devoted housewife and mother, but she had no idea how to look after a child and even less interest.

Two weeks after the catastrophic events of Iris's wedding, Ruby caught sight of her sister from the window, dragging the screaming Jamie out of the close and towards, she guessed from the direction they were taking, the McLean home, doubtless to seek Sarah's help. She had him tightly by the upper arm and Iris, having no aptitude with small children, was walking far too quickly, so that he had no chance of keeping up and was being dragged along. Inevitably, his legs buckled and he swung awkwardly in his mother's wake, ending up behind her on the ground as Iris kept moving, his arm twisting in her grasp. Ruby moved instinctively, rapping on the window and calling out 'His arm! Mind his arm!' Instantly she pulled back as though scalded, as though, in fact, there had been any possibility Iris could have heard her from behind the glass. Or any possibility, come to think of it, that Iris would have understood, or even listened.

So, as they got on with their lives, Ruby studiously avoided any contact with the Campbells across the way. That was the only advantage of having their tenement in sight, she supposed, she could always check that the coast was clear before going out of her own front door. That way there would be fewer opportunities for Jamie to see her, or she him. She told herself he needed time to get used to his parents and his new life and she didn't want him to be upset and confused by seeing her, but in her heart she knew, also, that she didn't want to see him. Maybe in time, she thought, but she knew she was lying to herself.

25

There was a summer haar in Largs, the little coastal town was being protected from the heatwave the rest of the country was enduring by a gift from the sea. The cooler conditions probably didn't please the local shopkeepers, apart from Nardini's, of course; no one passed up a cake, fish tea or even an ice cream from Nardini's, whatever the weather. Walking along the seafront with the water merging with the haar, Ruby was musing on the changes of old age. She no longer liked the heat, that was one of them. Any time one of those grinning ninnies on the TV forecast blistering sunshine she made a note to shop as early as possible and then stay in for the rest of the day. This brought its own discomfort: Paddy. God, but the man must have a sensor that told him when she was in and, even if she ignored his increasingly loud thuds on her door and all that yelling through her letterbox, there was his staying power to contend with. The man just stood there till she opened the door, no matter how long it took. When she answered in a rage he would smile stupidly at her and say 'Oh, you're in!' She had got him today though. She was in but she was going out.

'Where are you going?' he demanded.

'Well, not that you have a right to know,' she replied, locking her door behind her, 'but I can say with absolute certainty that you don't want to know where I'm going, Paddy Keenan.'

He stared at her blankly then understanding, followed by disapproval, dawned in his eyes.

'You're right!' he said, heading back to his own flat with amazing speed, considering he was always complaining about his self-diagnosed arthritis.

'My, Paddy,' she said sarcastically, 'you can fair move on those poor old aching bones when you want to!'

'It just shows how much I want to get away from you,' he replied sullenly. 'I'm in agony, if you must know.'

'So why don't you go to the doctor?' she asked. 'There's lots of things they can give you nowadays.'

'I'm not letting one of they quacks get their mitts on me!' he stated. 'Before you know it they'd be taking bits off me to experiment with or to give to somebody else.'

'Oh, aye,' Ruby shook her head, 'like there's anything left in that old carcass that anybody could use or even want. You're flattering yourself, as usual, Keenan. Sure the rest of you is as decrepit as they apologies for slippers that your bunions and corns are growing through.'

'Here we go with the feet and slippers again!' he protested, his door all but closed. 'Always the feet and slippers!'

'Aye, that's exactly it,' Ruby sighed, 'it is always the feet and slippers. Maybe you could offer them to the doctor instead of your other old bits and pieces. I'm sure they'd like to do a few experiments on how anyone could wear slippers so long that they had to be surgically removed. Do you actually take them off at night?'

'Aye, I do!' he replied indignantly, through the diminishing gap of his front door. 'Do you think I sleep in them?'

'It's possible, Paddy,' she said, shaking her head. 'I mean, there's still the question of how you get them off and, come to that, how you put them on again. Do you use a corkscrew?'

'Och, be quiet!'

'Tell me,' she said conversationally, 'are you being buried in them? Have you left special instructions for the lads at Rarity's about your screwing down? Not that it matters. They won't be able to get them off anyway, they'll *have* to bury you in them.'

'I knew it!' Paddy shouted, opening his door wide again. 'If it's not the feet and slippers, it's death! I knew it!'

'Well, seeing as you've mentioned it, Paddy, I must be going, I've got to see—'

'Don't tell me!' he pushed the door shut with sudden force. 'I know where you're going and I don't want to know! You're morbid, that's what you are, plain morbid!'

211

She walked on as he slammed the door, laughing to herself. She wasn't going where he thought she was, she was going back to Glasgow, but she hadn't wanted to tell him that. If she had, she knew, there would've been a long, pleading conversation from him and abrupt refusals from her that would have led to his feelings being hurt yet again. Then there would have to be a peace offering from her, same old same old, like dealing with a wean, she thought. The lad from the Housing Association, Ian Fraser, had called the day before. He said all of the paper on Jakey's walls had finally been removed and he had a surprise for her. Could she meet him there at 11 a.m. the next day? She could, she decided.

Sitting on the train, musing on her conversation with Paddy had led her to thinking about what he called her 'dying people.' It had started not long after the living arrangements in High Street had changed so drastically, she remembered. Iris, unable to do anything with Jamie, was constantly running over to her mother for help and, it soon became apparent, as everyone knew it would, that she didn't actually want to care for the child. The same people, neighbours and family, who had been watching and predicting Iris's lack of commitment to her child, commented openly that if Ruby hadn't made her little speech on her sister's wedding day, Iris may very well have said nothing about Jamie being Gus Campbell's son, she might well not have taken him from Ruby either. Ruby didn't reply when this was said to her, and made sure her expression didn't betray the slightest concern, but it was like a blade being twisted in her heart each time she heard it. If none of it had happened though, she might still have been raising Gus Campbell's son for years to come, lavishing love and care on him, and that thought was far from appealing. She knew the resemblance between father and son was now widely recognised, prompting people to question how they had ever missed it. So what, she wondered, would have happened, if he grew more like his father as he got older? One day, a few years hence, he might have looked at her with those now unmistakable eyes, and a thunderbolt of understanding could have hit her. Would that have been any better than what had actually happened? At least he was young enough to start again with his parents and, in time, forget that Ruby had been his mother. But for now Iris was tiring

Sarah out, not only running across the road for help, but, increasingly, leaving the child with her for hours that often turned into days.

'I don't understand it,' Ruby told Flora. 'That big beast has waited a long time to have a family, why isn't he making Iris look after him in his own home?'

Flora looked away. 'Who knows?' she asked.

'Do you understand it, Flora?'

Flora shrugged. 'Believe me, you don't want to know,' she grimaced.

'What?'

Flora shifted about in her seat in Ruby's kitchen. 'Well, you asked,' she sighed, chuckling to herself. 'From what I've heard from the Morris's above them, big Gus is a bit keen on his marital rights, he jumps on Iris the minute he gets home and only stops to recover his, um, strength before jumping on her again.'

'Oh my God!' Ruby shrieked, her face twisting with distaste.

Flora laughed out loud. 'I'm told the noise of the pair of them keeps people up at night, and they have to turn their wirelesses up to drown out the sounds!'

'Stop it, Flora!'

'You asked!' Flora said delightedly. 'They say he gropes Iris all the time, even when there's people about. In fact, they think he likes them to see.'

'He did that on their wedding day, during the toasts,' Ruby recalled, 'before mine, anyway. He grabbed her arse so hard in front of everybody she must've have been picking his nails out for weeks.'

'One of the neighbours thought he was hitting Iris there was so much noise, and when he went to the door she answered it wearing not a lot, and he was behind her much the same, grinning. You know the way he does?'

Ruby cringed. She knew exactly.

'But I suppose they are newly-weds,' Flora suggested, 'technically at least. Maybe they'll calm down, but in the meantime I think looking after a child is the last thing either of them is interested in. Anyway, after making you feel sick, Ruby, I have to go. I've got these books to give to Andy.'

'How is he, by the way?' Ruby asked.

'You mean in general or about the lovely Iris?'

'Both, I suppose.'

'Well he's fine in both ways, as far as I can see. He can't get enough of books and discussions. He and Denis talk for hours about politics, religion and that kind of thing, and I don't see any evidence that he's wasting away for love of Iris.'

'That's good,' Ruby nodded firmly. 'He was always far too good for her.'

As the months passed it seemed that the Campbells were not 'calming down' and Sarah was looking after Jamie more and more. She was tired, it was no more than that, she said, getting old and not being used to looking after an active toddler on her own any longer. Then one day she collapsed and could hardly breathe. Ruby found her lying on the floor, drawing heavy, rasping breaths, her eyes watering fiercely with the effort of getting air into her lungs. It turned out to be TB, the dreaded White Plague. No one was surprised, yet, somehow, everyone was shocked. Old Doctor McGill had been replaced by his son, Donald, Young Doctor McGill, and Sarah admitted to him that she had been coughing on and off for a few weeks. She thought it was just a cold she wasn't shaking off because she was tired, and she knew she had a bit of a temperature because she kept sweating. Ruby looked at her and was suddenly stunned by how much weight her mother had lost. How had she missed that?

'You miss these things when you see somebody every day, Ruby,' Donald McGill told her. 'Don't blame yourself for that.'

'But she didn't seem ill, she just seemed tired. Shouldn't there have been something?'

'Sometimes it's like that, no symptoms then suddenly people become really ill,' he explained. 'And knowing Sarah I'm pretty sure she covered a lot up rather than worry the family.'

Ruby nodded. 'I've missed a few things recently,' she said miserably, 'I feel I've been walking about with my eyes shut.'

Donald McGill laughed quietly. 'Aye, well, we were all taken by surprise about wee Jamie. You shouldn't blame yourself for that either!'

He looked exactly like his father must've looked at the same age, she thought, more like a step back in time than a new generation, dark hair, hazel eyes, handsome she supposed, if doctors were ever thought of in those terms. She smiled.

'What?' he asked.

'I was just thinking about your father,' she said. 'I never saw any other doctor when I was wee. It was always Dr McGill. You're very like him.'

'Aye, I know that,' he sighed, 'and I still can't make up my mind whether that's a good or a bad thing. People expect me to be as good as him, he's taking a bit of living down.' He smiled. 'But I don't think anyone's left the practice because the old man's gone, touch wood!'

They sat for a few moments.

'So what happens next for Ma?' Ruby finally asked.

'All we have is bed rest in a sanatorium in the country, well away from the city, where there's fresh air, Ruby, and I have to be honest with you, that's not going to be enough for Sarah, she's past that stage. I haven't told your father yet, but Sarah's very, very ill.'

'There's nothing anyone can do?' Ruby asked aghast.

He shook his head. 'I'm sorry, but there's nothing, Ruby, it's still a terrible disease, though some do recover. There is a new drug available, Penicillin, but it's reserved for the Forces I'm afraid.'

'Huh!' Ruby snorted. 'So we just have to die at home, do we?'

'The thinking is that we have to have soldiers to fight and this drug clears up all sorts of infections that would've killed them in the last war, so we're saving the lives of fighting men so that they can go back to the front line.'

'Saving their lives so that they can get shot and blown up and die,' Ruby muttered. 'Doesn't make much sense, does it?'

'Think how the doctors and nurses on the front line feel,' he said, 'patching them up and send them back out again. I suppose the country is stretched and can only afford to buy enough of this new drug for the troops at the moment. I'm afraid civilians won't get their chance till after the War.'

'It's all we ever hear, isn't it?' Ruby sighed. '"After the War." I wonder what the excuse will be then?' She swallowed. 'So are you saying Ma won't recover? You say some people survive. If I look after her really well, could she get better?' she asked desperately.

'Ruby, you can try, but I don't think so,' he said as gently as he could.

'Well, she's not going away anywhere,' Ruby said firmly. 'I'll look after her at home.'

'You've got Frances to consider,' he suggested.

'We've lived in the same house as Ma for years,' Ruby said, 'if we were going to get it we've already got it. But I'll make arrangements for Frances. I'll ask Gerry's sister, Agnes, to take her while I look after my mother.'

'It's a lot to take on, Ruby,' he said kindly, 'and it will get worse.'

'She's my mother,' Ruby repeated.

'Well, if you're sure, I can give you some advice on how to keep the danger of infection at a minimum,' McGill suggested. 'How to disinfect, that kind of thing. Everything will have to be scrupulously clean, Ruby, you'll have to scrub with disinfectant till it becomes second nature, part of your life. We're not looking at Sarah surviving for long, I have to tell you that, so the usual practice of patients sleeping outdoors isn't important here. We're aiming to keep her as comfortable as possible and the rest of you as free from infection as we can. She'll cough a lot and bring up sputum, do you think you can you cope with that?'

Ruby nodded dumbly.

'That's where the risk of infection comes in, it's spread through the air when she coughs, so you understand the need to for everything to be as clean as possible?'

'Go on,' Ruby whispered.

'Everything she coughs up will have to caught in a swab and every swab will have to be burned immediately, and you must wash her bedclothes all the time. I can't stress the cleanliness issue strongly enough. And your hands too, Ruby, all the time, whenever you touch her or anything she touches.' He looked at her. 'This is going to be hard, Ruby.'

'I know it is, but at least I'll know I'm doing something to help her,' Ruby said. 'I'd hate to be standing there while other people are doing it, people she doesn't know.'

'I understand that, Ruby, and I'll do whatever I can to help, but there must be someone else in the family who can lend a hand.'

Ruby shook her head. 'I doubt that. George is out at work and Marie has the weans to look after.' She smiled wryly and looked at him. 'Bea?' she suggested, arching an eyebrow. 'Iris?'

McGill laughed gently. 'I see what you mean, you are on your own.'

'Is there anything else?' she asked.

'Try to get her to eat, they say lots of milk is good for TB patients, but with everything being rationed ...'

'We'll manage,' she stated firmly. 'We'll just have to pool whatever we have. Anyway,' she said, taking a deep, steadying breath, 'as you say, it won't be for long, will it?'

'No, it won't, Ruby,' McGill said sadly. 'I'm sorry, but it won't.'

After no more than a few months as Mrs Reilly, living in the Reilly abode, Ruby was back in her old home, nursing her mother and caring for her father. Harry was shattered at the prospect of losing his wife and fell back on his usual behaviour when things got too much for him, he simply decided not to take in the news. Turning away and ignoring what was going on was his milder version of a McLean family trait that Jakey took to extremes by disappearing. Sarah was ill and Ruby would be taking care of her till she was better, that was all Harry could cope with. And it wasn't TB, though he knew that would be the rumour, she just had a chest problem. The bad old days were going away, but he understood TB was still a great fear, only it wasn't TB Sarah had, it was something else, something much less serious. In that way Harry McLean could continue to function. Dr McGill, therefore, dealt with Ruby and Ruby dealt with the rest of the family. The first thing she did was to visit her brother and her sisters, they all knew of the diagnosis but she had to inform them of the arrangements she was making for Sarah's care. George, who had taken the news of Sarah's illness stoically, announced that he and his family would still visit her at home. If she had gone to a sanatorium in the country the children would not have been allowed to visit her, but George and Marie took the same view as Ruby, that they and their girls had been exposed to the disease while Sarah hadn't been showing symptoms so they would continue to see her and take whatever precautions they could. Next was Iris, and a visit Ruby didn't look forward to, though she had planned her visit for during the day, when Gus was working. Jamie would be there, but she decided she would just have to harden her heart and go through with it.

'This isn't a social call,' she told Iris in a business-like tone. 'It's about what happens next with Ma.'

Iris nodded.

'Dr McGill says Ma has about six months, so Frances is going to stay with Agnes and I'll be moving back home to look after Ma.'

'Phew!' Iris said. 'I thought you were going to ask me to look after Frances.'

'What?' Ruby demanded coldly. 'You think I'd let you look after my daughter?'

She put a hand up to silence Iris's reply. 'Anyway, I'm here to tell you it's best if you keep Jamie—' she looked around.

'He's sleeping in our room,' Iris said, 'wee bugger kept us up all night again, no wonder he's tired. Screams all night and sleeps all day.'

Several things went through Ruby's mind, the first being, 'He won't sleep at night if you let him sleep all day,' but the major one was a 'Phew!' of her own. She voiced neither but nodded curtly. Her nephew's sleeping patterns were no business of hers. 'It's best you keep Jamie away from her in case he catches it.'

'But he's been with her a lot anyway,' Iris replied, suddenly aware, Ruby realised, that she would now have to look after her son by herself.

Ruby decided to stick to the official line and say nothing about George and Marie's decision. 'It's still better for him,' she continued, 'and it's better for Ma. She doesn't have much strength, wee ones will only exhaust her and, as I've said, I'm sending Frances away.' She looked sternly at her sister. 'I'll be looking after Ma, Iris. I won't let Jamie over the doorstep, is that clear?'

'And what makes you think you should look after her?' Iris asked petulantly.

Ruby laughed harshly. 'Aye, well, I did think of giving you first refusal on that one, Iris,' she replied. 'Maybe I should let you do it instead?'

Iris stayed silent.

Ruby laughed again. 'That's what I thought,' she said and got up to go.

Leaving Iris's house she climbed further up the brae to see Bea, who was restless and almost angry, it seemed to Ruby, as she explained the arrangements.

'I could've looked after her,' Bea said defensively.

'Dear God!' Ruby muttered wearily. 'Not another one! Look, you've got Davy to look after. Who'd iron his shirts and press his overalls if you couldn't do it? Can't have Davy going to work in crumpled overalls, can we?' she asked sarcastically. 'With Frances at Agnes's I won't have anybody but myself, and you don't keep well, do you Bea? This way makes sense.'

Bea glared at her. 'I'm still the eldest,' she protested, 'I should've been consulted.'

'Will you please, for once in your life, stop thinking about yourself!' Ruby shouted at her. 'We don't have time to sit down and consult about this, especially when we know from the start this is the only thing that will work. Ma has to be looked after now, this minute. Understand?' She got up and walked to the door then turned to see a look of disgruntlement on Bea's face. 'And the last thing we need is you hammering down there and throwing one of your usual turns, so if you do, I'll throw you – right down the stairs! Whenever you come to see Ma you will behave, right?'

Sitting at the table by the window Bea looked down on High Street but didn't reply.

'Right?' Ruby asked again.

'Oh bugger off, Miss High and Mighty!' Bea replied, but Ruby was relieved that there was resignation rather than the usual sound of impending battle in her voice.

Next she had to talk to Uncle Jakey. Within the family it had always been accepted that he was a sensitive, easily upset soul and they didn't burden him with things he couldn't handle. He couldn't be protected from this any longer, though. Jakey knew Sarah was ill, but he didn't know how sick she was and how little time she had. Ruby knew what would happen when she told him, he would go off wandering again but, she decided, she would be grateful for that. It was Uncle Jakey's way of coping, his defence system, and it would be one less stunned family member to have to deal with. He was standing in the middle of the room, paintbrush in hand, a new mural half done when she explained what was happening to Sarah. He said nothing when she told him the bare facts as kindly as she could. 'Do you understand what I'm saying, Uncle Jakey?' she asked gently, and Jakey simply nodded his head. Later that day, as she was setting up a sick room for Sarah in the front bedroom, she glanced out of the bay window and saw the two figures walking down High Street in the direction of Glasgow Cross and the River Clyde beyond, Uncle Jakey and Wee Dug, no sign of the Sheik of High Street this time. 'Take care of yourselves,' she murmured, as they faded into the distance, then she turned away to get on with more pressing matters.

So for however long it would take Sarah to die, Frances would be exiled. She had revealed as much emotion at being handed to her Aunt Agnes as she had shown about anything else in her short life. Agnes had two stepsons that she loved dearly but had never raised a baby, apart from her brother, Gerry, of course, Frances's father. She longed to be a mother in her own right and, though Frances's arrival was a complete life change that would turn her existence upside down, she was happy to have a little one about the place. Necessity and the turmoil of fate had forced changes on everyone, but, thankfully, it was all working out in some logical manner. And in the background, somewhere and no longer important, there was still a war on.

It seemed to Ruby that only yesterday she was a carefree seventeen-year-old in a slightly odd, yet, for all their battles and their tensions, close family. Now here she was only three years later, feeling almost world-weary with responsibility, her family fragmenting around her and nursing the most important person in that family, her mother, her mainstay, through the last months of her life. She didn't know if there was a God up there somewhere, but she hoped there was, because one day she had a list of charges she wanted him to answer.

And yet there were moments of magic, namely Cissie and Dot. Those two old harridans who went through life ignoring prohibitions about not mentioning missing legs and pronouncing whores and sluts wherever they saw them, or in the case of the McLean family, saw *her,* and who never sacrificed a brutal remark for the sake of kindness or diplomacy, came through with flying colours where their younger sister was concerned. Ruby had intended taking them to one side before they saw her for the first time after the diagnosis, and explaining to them that she would forcibly throw them out, too, just like Bea, if they made any inappropriate comment on Sarah's illness. She had the list in her head ready to deliver to them vocally: you will not talk about people with TB who have died; you will not tell her how ill she's looking; you will not blame her condition on failings you think she may have been guilty of in the past; *you will be kind.* But in the event she didn't need it because they swept past her before she could deliver her lecture, leaving her in their considerable wake, teetering on the verge of panic. Cissie and Dot did what they did best. They were themselves and saw only what they chose to see. In other circumstances this was a definite recipe for disaster but these circumstances were different and had brought out the best in them.

'My, Sarah, I've always envied you that window!' Cissie exclaimed, as though she had never seen Sarah any place but in her sickbed, the air around pickling her nasal passages with the pungent aroma of disinfectant. 'You can see everything, can't you, Dot?'

'Aye, you can!' Dot enthused. 'Right down Duke Street there and along George Street on the other side, and all the way to the Tolbooth at the front there. I've never had a bay window, but I've always thought how nice it would be.'

'Would you like a sweetie, Sarah?' Cissie asked, leaning forward and holding out a paper bag of Rosebuds. 'Do you want to sit up a bit? Here, Dot, give me a humph up with her on the other side there, and Ruby, hen, sort out her pillows. That's right. You'll be able to see better now, Sarah.'

Watching them, Ruby marvelled that, unlike a great many other people, they didn't keep their distance from the invalid, but leaned in, touching her and speaking to her as usual. She felt like putting her arms round them and hugging them, but that in itself would have been out of place.

'So how's your Iris doing with the wee laddie?' Cissie asked Sarah. 'I have to say, Ruby, hen, I saw the resemblance between him and Gus long ago, I wondered why you didn't. It must've been a bit of a shock to you, Sarah, all the same, was it not?'

Sarah started coughing and, without pausing in her conversation, Dot helped her to sit straighter in the bed. 'But they seem settled enough now,' she said, as though nothing out of the ordinary was happening on this visit. 'And I have to say I'm surprised at Iris, knowing what she's like. I thought she'd have thrown in the towel before this.' She removed the swab containing the sputum Sarah had just coughed up, crossed to the fire and threw it in. 'I mean, she's aye been such a useless creature, hasn't she? Maybe this is her settled now.'

Ruby mouthed to her to wash her hands but Dot frowned at her and resumed her seat by Sarah.

'Aye, well,' Cissie said conversationally, 'it happens to us all, doesn't it?' She looked pointedly at Dot. 'As well you know, Dot.'

'What does that mean?' Dot demanded.

'Well, you always liked a good time when you were young, that's all I'm saying, but you knuckled under and toed the line when you had to.'

'Had to? What are you suggesting?'

'Me?' Cissie said, aghast at the accusation her remarks could have a hidden meaning. 'Sure, I'm not suggesting anything, Dot, if there's something you hear there then it must be your own conscience reminding you of something I know nothing about.'

'Bitchiness isn't nice, Cissie,' her sister informed her haughtily. 'I don't know if you've ever heard that before.'

'Oh, I've heard it said often, Dot,' Cissie responded dryly, 'but I've always defended you. Nobody runs down my sister while I'm around to stick up for her, so they don't!'

Standing at the window looking out, Ruby would have laughed out loud if she hadn't been breathing a sigh of relief. When Sarah tired they saw it but made no mention of it, announcing that they had to go. They had heard there were some sausages due in at the butcher's and would have to rush off. They both hugged Sarah and left the bedroom with a mixture of bickering and bustling, as they always did.

'Now wash your hands,' Ruby insisted.

The two sisters nodded. 'You're doing well, Ruby,' Dot told her, 'keep it up, hen.'

'I will.'

'And let us know if there's anything she needs,' Cissie said.

'Milk, that's what Dr McGill said. But we're fine, we're all giving our rations up to make sure she eats well.'

'She's our sister,' Cissie replied firmly, 'we'll give whatever she needs. You only have to tell us.'

'How's your Da doing, hen?' Dot asked.

'Oh, you know Da,' Ruby sighed. 'He goes to his work, he comes home and sleeps.'

'And he ignores everything else,' Cissie nodded, smiling. 'He's aye been the same, you just have to let him do what he has to do, Ruby, he's a good man, your Da.'

'Aye, not like that bampot, Jakey,' Dot said darkly. 'You can hardly believe they're brothers.'

'Uncle Jakey's upset as well!' Ruby laughed.

'Aye, but he never stays around long enough to get really upset though, does he?' Dot demanded. 'He scarpers at the first sign of trouble!'

'But so does my Da!' Ruby protested.

'Aye, well,' Cissie muttered, 'that's different. Your Da's a good man.'

She heard their familiar noises as they negotiated the stairs then watched them, walking arm-in-arm, up High Street, before sitting down by the fire while Sarah slept in the bedroom next door. There was something about Cissie and Dot she couldn't put her finger on, an odd gentility, a robust honour of some sort, she mused. To them and their generation there was nothing new about TB, it had haunted them as long as they had lived, and haunted their families longer than that. It was part of their existence and they treated it like an old foe they had met and battled with many times and still defied, regardless of its many victories. The only plan they had was to carry on as normal and refuse to let it have the upper hand, that way it could kill them, but it couldn't defeat them.

26

He was waiting outside Central Station just as he had promised, the Housing Association lad, and there was a look on his face, a happy, excited look, as he helped her into the passenger seat of his car, announcing that he had someone at Jakey's old flat he wanted her to meet. Ruby nodded uncertainly; it could be no one she knew, they were all gone. At the close he almost bounded up the stairs then deliberately slowed down for her and she thought for a moment he had been on the verge of picking her up and running up three at a time. The door was open and she could hear noises inside, the workmen, she presumed, but then she came face-to-face with a tall man carrying a clipboard with a camera around his neck. Her heart sank. Surely Ian hadn't brought a photographer to take pictures of her when she had made it clear she didn't want that?

'This is Peter Brodie,' Ian said.

Ruby nodded coolly and pointedly didn't take his outstretched hand, looking back at Ian for an explanation.

'He's from Historic Scotland,' Ian told her. He looked fit to burst.

'So he's not a photographer from the papers?' Ruby asked, looking at the camera.

'What? Oh, no!' he laughed. 'Is that what you thought?' and he laughed even more. 'Mr Brodie here saw the piece in the *Evening Times* about the murals, the one you saw, remember?'

Ruby nodded.

'He called me and asked if he could see them to tell how good they were. I didn't tell you in case—'

'In case he said they were rubbish and I got narked?' she asked.

'Aye,' he said cheerfully, 'that's about the size of it, I suppose.'

'There's nothing like having to deal with a narked old biddy, I know,' she smiled.

'But he didn't say they were rubbish,' he continued, 'in fact – Mr Brodie, you tell her.'

The tall thin man held out his hand again and this time Ruby took it graciously. 'They're far from rubbish, Mrs McLean,' he smiled, 'they're every bit as good as Mr Fraser here told me.' He led her to a pile of flooring timber and sat her down. 'In fact they're quite magnificent.'

Ruby concentrated very hard on not beaming too obviously with pride, deciding there was nothing quite like dealing with a beaming old biddy either. She would treat this news with decorum, she decided.

'Your uncle was a true artist, Mrs McLean,' he said. 'How he managed this level of work and in such extraordinary detail is simply breathtaking.'

Ruby nodded with deliberate condescension.

'What we're proposing to do is take detailed pictures of his work and keep them in an archive in Edinburgh.'

Ruby bridled slightly, the age-old animosity between the capital city and the other one that knew it should be, surfacing. 'Edinburgh?' she asked quietly. 'Why Edinburgh? Why not the Mitchell Library in Glasgow?'

Brodie and Ian exchanged amused glances. 'Just because Edinburgh is our headquarters, Mrs McLean,' the man explained, 'but there will be a file at the Mitchell Library as well. Anyone will be able to see the pictures and we'll have them on our website on the Internet too.'

'And Mr Brodie has given us advice on what we do with the walls,' Ian told her. 'We're not going to remove the murals, we're going to paper over them using a special glue. That way they'll be preserved, they'll always be there. Isn't that great?'

Ruby sat in silence, determined to remain composed. Not only would Jakey's life's work stay where it had been created, where it should be, but he would get recognition for his talents after all these years. He would be somebody at last, the artist she always knew he had been. She was aware of the seconds ticking by and the two men becoming more uncomfortable, but she couldn't say anything.

'We'll also do a press release about it,' Brodie continued, 'and we're working on a TV piece about your uncle and his work. I know from Mr Fraser here that you're not keen on publicity.'

'Not for myself, Mr Brodie,' she said, 'I don't want to be in the papers or the TV and I don't want my name to appear either, but I'm fine about your talking to them about Uncle Jakey's work.'

'Well that's okay then,' he smiled kindly. 'Can you give me some details about him, perhaps? Do you have a photo of him we could use?'

Ruby nodded. 'I've got one at home,' she said. 'He's in the background at my parents' wedding, but I don't know how clear it is.'

'I'm sure we'll be able to do something with all the technology we have nowadays. And he was a fly-shunter, I believe?'

'Aye. When they hear that the first thing everybody says is what a dangerous job it was, but I never felt he was aware of that. Uncle Jakey tended to live in his own wee world, he didn't look at life the way other people did.' She smiled.

'And can I ask, when did he die?'

'Oh, sometime in the 1940s, I think,' she replied.

'Was it an illness?' he prodded.

'Ian was asking about that,' she said casually, 'and I couldn't remember, not sure I ever knew in fact. He was older than my father, so to me at the time that was pretty old, I just accepted that Uncle Jakey had died, and there was a war on.'

'There was still a lot of TB about,' Ian suggested.

'Good lad!' she thought gratefully. 'He was never strong,' she said, 'I do remember that. We always had to look out for Jakey.'

On the drive back to Central Station she was subdued.

'You all right?' Ian Fraser asked quietly. 'I hope today hasn't upset you too much.'

'Och, I'm delighted for Jakey. You've done a really nice thing for him,' she smiled.

'So why the long face?'

She patted him on the shoulder as she got out of the car. 'It's not your fault, son. All those memories, they just come flooding back, all the people I've lost. It's part of getting old, you'll find that out yourself one day!'

Sitting on the train home she felt curiously down, completely at odds with the elation she had felt a very short time before, when she heard about Jakey's work being recognised. It was that old question of how Jakey died that had got her again. How could she answer that? Being reminded of it still upset her, even after all these years, so she skated over it, lied about it. It was family business and no one else's, after all, and lying was a way of life with the McLeans. So many, many lies, and the habit was hard to break. Besides, they were bound to find out themselves, nothing could remain hidden thanks to the damned Internet, yet who would the truth benefit after all this time?

27

Caring for her mother and all that entailed became a way of life, just as Dr McGill had told her. Sarah survived for a little over four months, not six, though by the time the end came Ruby was grateful for that. It wasn't because her hands were almost raw from constant washing or because she barely slept for more than an hour at a time, but because Sarah didn't deserve to linger in a life that had become a painful burden to her. In those months they had become close, the two of them talking more than they ever had in Ruby's entire life. Life outside the bedroom at 252 High Street receded into the distance, even the War seemed to concern them very little. Somehow it no longer mattered, all that mattered was that shortly Sarah would no longer be there and the existence of the McLeans contracted to that and that alone. Cissie and Dot supported both Ruby and Sarah during those months, sitting with Sarah so that Ruby could go out for a walk or see her daughter when Agnes brought her to Gerry's flat for an hour. Harry wandered about quietly getting on with his life somewhere in the background, part of the family yet apart from what was occupying them, though his work kept him away more and more. Neither Bea nor Iris offered Ruby any respite, not that she would have accepted it, but George left the Goods Yard to drop in at various times of the day to see Sarah and to hear Dr McGill's latest bulletin, and also so that Ruby would feel less alone.

'Are you sure you won't get into trouble?' she asked him.

George shrugged. 'Andy's covering for me, he knows where I am,' he replied. 'Besides, there will still be a war on but I won't always have my mother, so just let somebody say something.'

When the air raid sirens sounded at night and others headed for the shelters, Ruby stayed with Sarah. Falling bombs were the least of her fears. Sarah had lost a huge amount of weight, more than Ruby would have considered possible for a human to lose and live, and her mind became more muddled as time went on. She would ramble back and forth about her life, in the past as well as the present tense, then there would be moments of absolute clarity. One bad night, when the coughing was at its worst, Ruby tried to distract her by talking about the family. They were laughing gently about Bea when another kind of bomb hit Ruby.

'It's not really her fault,' Sarah said quietly. 'She's just like her grandmother, so I've been told.'

'Your mother?' Ruby asked.

'No, her father's mother,' Sarah replied, her voice like a distant sigh. 'I never met her, but I'm told she looks very like her, in fact she's like her in lots of ways.'

Ruby was puzzled, she knew her father's mother had died before Harry met Sarah. 'You mean Da's mother?'

'No, her father's mother,' Sarah replied.

Suddenly Ruby's mind was in a whirl. 'Ma!' she laughed, 'are you going daft or what? Da *is* her father!'

'No, not Harry, her father,' Sarah murmured drowsily.

Ruby didn't know what to say. Sarah had moments like this when she was confused, that must be what was going on. She couldn't mean what it sounded like she meant.

'She's always been angry about that, about your Da not being her father too, you see.' Sarah continued, her voice weak. 'It's always bothered her, that's why she is the way she is, she's always been unhappy. She blames me and she's right, isn't she?'

'Ma?' Ruby said gently. 'Ma, are you awake?'

Sarah looked up at her, her eyes bright, her face pale with two points of red on her cheeks.

'Ma, you didn't mean that, did you?' Ruby tried to laugh. 'That Bea isn't Da's?'

'Is that what I said, Ruby?' Sarah asked, surprised, and Ruby felt a surge of relief.

230

'I didn't mean to tell you that,' Sarah said dreamily, 'but aye, it's true. She's never forgiven me. I don't suppose she ever will, will she? And who can blame her?'

With that, Sarah fell asleep, leaving Ruby shocked and confused. There was no one to ask. Certainly neither George nor Iris knew, they would have spoken about it if they had, and she couldn't ask Harry. It simply wasn't the kind of question a daughter could put to her father. Obviously asking Bea was out of the question, though if her mother hadn't been hallucinating, Bea was the very one who would know. And even if Cissie and Dot knew, they wouldn't talk to her about it, there was a loyalty among the older ones that no youngster could breach. They would stonewall any inquiry.

When Sarah awoke the next morning she was alert again, not that these spells lasted long these days. Ruby took her chance and asked her about their conversation of the previous day. Sarah was close to tears.

'Please, Ruby, promise me you'll keep it to yourself?' she begged.

'Of course, of course! So it's true then?'

'Aye.'

'So who knows?'

'Your Da, and Bea of course, and my sisters, and Bea's father, and please don't ask me who it was, Ruby!' Her voice was filled with panic.

'I won't, Ma, shh, it's okay, I won't.'

'The thing I've always thought was that Bea had no real reason to be so angry about it. Your Da hasn't made the slightest difference between her and the rest of you, has he?'

Ruby shook her head. It was true, Harry loved all his children and to him Bea was his child.

'She was only a wee thing when your Da and I got married. He'd just come back from the War, but it says on her birth certificate that her father is unknown and she's illegitimate, there was nothing I could do about that. She wasn't your Da's. He'd joined up without telling me and I was angry, so I told him we were finished and he went off to fight in France. There was no way she could've been his, if you know what I mean ...'

Ruby gulped; she knew what Sarah meant.

'I knew Bea's father was keen on me, so I, well, you know how it is when you're young and daft.'

Ruby knew how it was.

'When your Da came back he said he didn't want any details, he just wanted us to get married and Bea would be his daughter. I swear to God, Ruby, I didn't deserve him. He never once asked the questions any man had the right to ask, never once. And she always has been his, but from the minute George was born she hated him, she hated all of you. The only reason I can think of is that you are all legitimate and she isn't. That's why I was never firm enough with Iris, you see. How could I be, when I'd done what I'd done?'

'But Ma!' Ruby exclaimed, shocked. 'Iris is nothing like you! She's a slut, she's always been a slut. She'll be a slut till the day she dies!'

'And how am I any better, Ruby? Tell me that?'

'Because you *are*,' Ruby said gently. 'Just like me you made one mistake in your life, and you knew it was a mistake, she's just, well, she's just Iris, to her it's a way of life.'

'Is that what you did, Ruby? Was Gerry a mistake?' Sarah asked fearfully.

'Aye, Ma,' she sighed. 'I was just daft, too, that was all. We're two of a kind, you and me, but neither one of us is anything like Iris! At least you didn't let it ruin your life. You married Da and you've brought up a family together and you've been happy.'

'Are you saying you think your life is ruined then?'

'I don't know if I'm thinking straight, that's the truth,' Ruby smiled sadly. 'I mean, we weren't together very long before he went away. Sometimes I forget he even exists till another letter from him arrives, and you know how few they are. And who knows when the War will be over and what life will be like then?'

'Well promise me something else, Ruby,' Sarah said earnestly, grasping Ruby's hand. 'Promise me that if you're sure you have made a mistake when he comes back, that you won't waste your life. I know that leaving your man is a terrible thing, but the biggest mistake, the biggest sin, would be if you wasted your life. I won't be here, Ruby—'

As Ruby opened her mouth to protest, Sarah held up a hand to silence her. Ruby recognised the gesture she often used herself and was shocked, realising for the first time that she had picked it up from her mother, and almost cried aloud.

'Ruby, we don't have much time left together. I'm not a fool,' Sarah said seriously. 'I won't be around to make you see sense in years to come, so you must make a solemn promise that if things don't work out when Gerry comes back, if Gerry comes back, you will not stay with him for the sake of what people might say. You only have one life, I'm more aware of that than most. You have to live it. Promise?'

Ruby nodded and hugged her mother, unable to say a word, and they stayed locked together till Sarah was overcome again with a fit of coughing that broke the spell.

From then on the end came rushing towards them and, even though most of them were expecting it, it still came too fast. The coughing fits, producing blood-streaked sputum, increased, and Sarah's breathing became more laboured. Dr McGill called on his morning visit and told Ruby that the end was very near and soon Sarah would slip into a coma; now was the time to call on the family to visit if they wanted to have a last conversation with her. She decided not to tell Harry. He went into the bedroom every morning before he went to work and kissed Sarah and did the same at night when he came back, whether she was awake or asleep, and these days she was mostly asleep. Whatever words he had to say to her, Ruby was sure, had been said many times over during their long years together. Indeed there was no need for words between them, so there was nothing to be gained for either by distressing them with the finality of the situation.

George arrived and sat with Sarah while Ruby went to talk to her sisters.

'No answer from Bea,' she announced when she came back. 'No idea whether she's out or just doesn't want visitors. You know what she's like. I half expected it. I stuck a note through her door telling her to come down as soon as possible.'

George nodded. 'What about Iris?'

'She thinks it might be better not to see Ma,' Ruby sighed. 'Mrs Campbell thinks it would be too upsetting, she means for her.'

'Thinking of herself as usual,' George said with contempt.

'And what more – or even less – did you expect of her?' Ruby asked. 'She's only ever been concerned with herself. Why would her mother dying change that?'

'Well, at least we won't have to put up with Gus Campbell in the house,' George said.

'I wouldn't have let him in to see Ma anyway,' Ruby said. 'This is family only and he's *not* family. But I'll bet you anything he'll turn up at the funeral, stuffing his face as usual.'

'No way of keeping him out of that,' George sighed, 'he's known Ma and Da for a long time.'

'I don't think there's much point in telling Uncle Jakey, do you?' she asked.

George shook his head. 'What would he have to say to Ma?' he said. 'You know how confused he gets when he's upset, why drag it out for the wee man? We'll tell him when it's over.'

'The word will spread though,' Ruby said doubtfully, 'he could hear it from someone else.'

'Let's play it by ear,' George suggested. 'I've sent someone with a message for Cissie and Dot, so you can try Bea again in a wee while if you like.'

'How kind of you!' Ruby smiled.

'You know how she'll react if I arrive on her doorstep,' George said uncomfortably.

'I'm only kidding, George,' Ruby sighed. 'At least she knows for a fact that I'll slap her if she starts. What about your work?'

'It's okay. I've told them Ma's in a bad way. I'll maybe nip across later, just in case. Da's gone down south with a troop train, he's not expected home till the morning at the earliest, and I've passed the word nobody's to tell him anything.'

And so they sat by Sarah's bed, talking to her when she seemed able to converse, chatting to each other when she drifted off again into her own time and space. They reminisced about their childhood, going over all the incidents that had passed into family lore, and they laughed together, painfully aware that she might not be able to hear their voices for much longer but determined that while she could she would hear only gentle conversations.

Then the front door opened and, leaving George with Sarah, Ruby went out of the bedroom to find Bea in the sitting room. Ruby motioned her to a chair but Bea shook her head and remained standing as Ruby explained the situation. Bea was silent, looking into the distance, deep in thought, before turning towards the bedroom. George, seeing her, got up to go.

'Bea, George and I will step out and leave you by yourself with Ma,' Ruby said gently. She meant it kindly, aware now that there was an issue between Bea and their mother that didn't concern the rest of the family, and Bea was due some private time with Sarah. 'I'll just run down to the Co-op for a couple of things,' she said diplomatically and looked at George.

'I'll go to the Yard,' he said, 'make sure everything's okay there.'

It was Spring again; the air was sharp and cool and it had been raining earlier, leaving the road wet. She was suddenly aware that, like the progress of the endless War, the seasons had become immaterial since the first act of this drama had unfolded. Young Dr McGill's diagnosis had landed like a sledgehammer at Christmas, or was it New Year? It was hard to be sure, time had come to mean very little. She vaguely recalled noticing frost and she remembered thinking at the time that it had nothing to do with her, it was part of another world she was no longer a part of. Now it was April. She watched George running across Duke Street to the Goods Yard, and looked around at the people going about their business, in and out of shops, on and off trams, all inhabitants of that other world. She had loved watching them when she was a child, imagining what their lives were like, where they were going to or coming from, and now she was amazed that they had carried on with their normal lives during these last months. The world of the McLeans had come to centre on the bedroom upstairs and the battle, not for life, but for breath, going on within its walls. Yet all the time this completely separate other world was still turning outside in High Street.

She watched mothers shopping, their brows furrowed with the worries of housekeeping in wartime, planning where to queue next and for what; not that it mattered, if a queue formed you joined it,

235

because whatever was on offer you must need or want it. Children hung onto hands or shopping bag handles, running along complaining as usual, wanting something or just to get home. It had always amused her to watch children as their mothers stopped in the street to chat, obedient and patient at first, then hopping about impatiently before pulling at their mothers' hands. Finally, if all previous hints had been ignored and the chat went on beyond human endurance, they might sit on the ground and scream. This made the mothers affronted at their bad manners, but it usually did the trick and the gossip session would be curtailed as they dragged their offspring homewards, berating them for their behaviour. Somewhere in there, she knew, as in her own day, there would be the eternal and universal threat, 'Wait till your father hears how you carried on!'

Realising she was cold, she crossed her arms, rubbing the opposing upper arms with her hands, wondering how long she had been standing there, before deciding it was long enough and heading back to the flat. The noise could be heard from a full flight below. Bea. Bea in full flood. Ruby rushed up the stairs as fast as she could, her mind racing even faster. Why, she demanded furiously of herself, had she expected anything else of her sister? Bea had taken over every family event in living memory, so what made her think this one should have been any different from all the others? Did she really think Bea had decorum and dignity hidden somewhere in her character?

All she could hear was that whine of hers, that shrieking, screaming, battle-cry. There was no telling what was being said, whether grief was being expressed, over-expressed, or if there was something else going on. It didn't matter, Sarah was dying but she was still at least semi-conscious, how could she – *how could she* – subject her to this? Ruby reached the bedroom door, gasping from her sprint up the stairs and, as she pulled it open, Bea passed her on the way out. She had an impression of the red hair above the red face and the blue eyes blazing, as Bea dashed out without another word. Inside the bedroom Sarah was struggling to sit up, her near skeletal body racked with the pain and exertion of another fierce, cruel bout of coughing. Ruby rushed over to her, holding her up with so little effort that it shocked her anew, as it always did these days, at the same time piling pillows at her back. Reaching for the bowl with the swab inside, she held Sarah around the shoulders and helped her spit into it, praying that her lungs wouldn't explode with the effort. Gradually the spasm subsided and Sarah leaned against her, trying to regain control of her breathing and talk at the same time. 'Shh,' Ruby soothed her, rocking to and fro, 'catch your breath first.' It took a long time though, while every fibre of Ruby's being resisted the urge to run out into the street and up the brae to confront Bea. Sarah stayed leaning against her, trying to breathe.

'She wanted to know who her father was,' she finally said weakly. 'I tried not to tell her, it won't do her any good to know, but she screamed at me till I told her.'

'I'll kill her!' Ruby thought angrily. 'It doesn't matter, Ma,' she said gently, holding a cup of water to Sarah's lips. 'Just forget about it, it's over,' adding silently, 'This time she's dead!'

The front door opened and closed. 'She's come back!' she thought. She laid Sarah gently back on the bed and quickly went through to the hallway, steadying herself to grab Bea by the arm and heave her out of the house. The half-glass inner door to the hallway opened and she was so relieved to see Cissie and Dot bustling through that she didn't know whether to laugh or cry.

'That Big Bea's just passed us in the street,' Dot complained loudly. 'Nearly pushed us off our feet and not a word out of her, just glared at us and ran up the brae.'

'What's up?' Cissie asked fearfully, looking at her. 'Is she …?'

'No, no, Auntie Cissie, come in,' Ruby said, widening her eyes to contain the tears of both emotions.

'Well what's wrong, hen?' Dot asked.

'Bea's wrong,' Ruby whispered fiercely. 'She's just been in screaming at Ma. Ma was in a terrible state, I've just got her settled. Now I'm going to kill Bea. Will you stay with Ma?'

'Oh, definitely, hen,' Cissie said, taking off her coat, 'it's in a good cause after all!'

'And kill her for me as well,' Dot smiled. 'She's been asking for it for years, so she has and you're the very one to do it, Ruby!'

Ruby hung the coats up and stood in the hallway, trying to calm down. She was going to sort Bea out but she didn't want it to descend into a slanging match, she had to be in control. Through the door she could hear the two aunties greeting Sarah.

'There ye are, Sarah!' Cissie said happily. 'You're looking a bit better the day. Isn't she looking better the day, Dot?'

'Let me see? Oh, aye, you are as well. We won't stay long, Sarah, we'll just have a wee cuppa and a bun with you, then we'll have to get back and make the teas.'

'Aye,' Cissie said conversationally, 'so you'll not be angry if it's just a wee flying visit this time, eh? We're due to get our sweetie ration at McLellan's tomorrow though. We'll have a longer gossip then, okay?'

'Aye, and we'll be in a better mood then as well!' Dot giggled almost girlishly.

'Did you hear about that daft bugger Jakey, Sarah?' Cissie asked cheerfully, nothing quite improved the mood of the aunts like someone making a fool of themselves. 'Seems he went into the Co-op up in Castle Street last week dressed as an Arab and waving thon big curly sword Gerry sent back. Had everybody running for their lives, apparently.'

'You'd think they'd know by now he's just a bampot, wouldn't you?' Dot remarked scathingly. 'God knows, he's been at it long enough.'

'I ask you, Sarah,' Cissie continued, chuckling, 'how could it have been an Arab and him with that wee daft dog at his heels!'

'I don't know why the wee daft dog puts up with him,' Dot commented acidly. 'You'd think even a peculiar thing like that could do better than Jakey, wouldn't you?'

'He was in Cochrane's just before that,' Cissie said, 'bought a bag of broken biscuits.'

'Who? The wee daft dog?' Dot asked.

'Don't be as stupid as you look, Dot!' her sister replied. 'The Arab! Since when did any dog go into Cochrane's and ask for a bag of broken biscuits, for God's sake?'

'Could have been dog biscuits,' Dot suggested defensively.

'Will you listen to her, Sarah?' Cissie demanded. 'She's got Wee Dug asking for dog biscuits in Cochrane's now, like that would be okay.'

'It's as likely as an Arab,' Dot murmured.

'Aye, true enough. Daft Bugger,' Cissie conceded. 'You all right there, Sarah? Need a wee hand sitting up?'

Listening outside in the hallway Ruby started to laugh then, assured that Sarah was in safe hands, she turned to the front door. She had Bea to see to.

28

Climbing up the brae towards Bea's tenement, she found herself surprised at the difference a few years had made. As a child she could run up and down the incline repeatedly without even noticing it, now it felt as though being a child was centuries ago. 'First the stairs,' she thought, 'now the brae. I'll be needing a walking stick next.'

There was no answer when she knocked on the door and, as usual, it was locked, so she thumped even harder. When that drew no response, she resorted to yelling through the letterbox.

'I'm staying here till you open the door!' she shouted. 'I don't care how long that takes, Bea!'

'Bugger off!' came the reply from behind the door. 'Get to hell or I'll get Tam McVicar to lift you!'

'That's fine, Bea,' Ruby said calmly, 'but to get to the police station you'll have to open the door and come out, unless you're going to shin down the drain pipe at the back, of course. There are folk who'd pay good money to see that. Me included!'

Eventually the door opened. Bea still looked as fired up as she had when she left her mother's side.

'And before you say anything, I had my reasons, reasons you know nothing about,' she said, standing by her fireside, arms folded, lips pursed.

'You aye do, Bea,' Ruby said quietly, 'and they're aye lousy reasons.'

'There's things she's kept from me,' Bea stated, the characteristic whine rising in her voice.

'Like who your father was?'

Bea stared at her, wide-eyed with shock. 'There you are!' she shouted. 'I knew it! I knew you all hated me and laughed at me behind my back because I was illegitimate.'

'Nobody knows but me, Bea,' Ruby said wearily, 'and I only found out a week ago when Ma was delirious and let it slip.'

'You think I don't know that everybody laughs at me? Big Bea, that's what they call me, I know what that means – Big B, Big Bastard!'

'Except,' Ruby repeated with heavy emphasis, 'that nobody knows but me. If people round about here call you Big Bea in that way, they have other reasons, and I think you know what they are. You caused them after all.'

'You all have your nice wee lives,' Bea sneered, her voice getting louder, 'everything's worked out for all of you. From the day she fell with me everything went worse for me than the rest of you!'

Ruby sat down, still hoping for a sensible if solemn conversation. 'Dear God, not this again!' She ran her fingers through her hair then looked at Bea and shook her head in despair. 'So, you're saying we all have happy, contented lives and you don't, and somehow that's the fault of the rest of us? Have you looked at the lives of people around you? Are you listening to yourself?'

Bea was striding about, pumping herself up for action, Ruby knew.

'Has Da made the slightest difference in how he treated any of us?' Ruby demanded. 'Is there one thing he ever did to make you think he favours the rest of us over you? Has he once mentioned it?'

'He's maybe *your* Da,' Bea spat at her, 'but he's not *my* Da!'

'Just because he didn't father you doesn't mean he's not your Da!'

'Well, I know who it is now, she's finally come out with it, he's—'

Ruby covered her ears. 'I don't want to know, Bea,' she told her. 'It's your business, it has nothing to do with me, don't try to drag me into your wee mad world and I don't know what good knowing will do you anyway, you're a grown woman for God's sake.'

'It'll do me good, all right!' Bea said smugly. 'Just you wait, it will do me good all right!'

'And it was worth doing that to Ma, was it?' Ruby demanded, clutching the edge of the table in front of her and glaring at Bea.

241

'She's dying, and you chose what will be the last time you will ever speak to her to shout and yell at her. That's the best you could come up, was it, to threaten a sick, defenceless woman? She made a mistake when she was young. We've all made mistakes, even you Bea.'

'What do you mean by that?'

'But,' Ruby continued, 'she's done her best for you all her life, she'd have given you her life's blood if you needed it. How can you live with yourself after what you've just done?'

She looked up and the two women locked eyes.

'Just you wait,' Bea screamed. 'This isn't done yet! Just you wait!'

Ruby stood up slowly. She had come to kill her, if only verbally, but she couldn't summon up the words to express her disgust at what her sister had done to their mother. 'Listen, Bea,' she said icily, 'I don't give a bugger who your father was, but let me tell you this,' she paused before going on, emphasising every word, 'you are no longer my sister. You can come to Ma's funeral if you want, I can't stop you doing that, but when this is over, for as long as I live I won't say a word to you or look in your direction. When this—,' she couldn't find the right words to cover Ma's dying, 'when it's over and done with, don't ever approach me again about anything, is that clear?'

In a way, she realised, she had confirmed Bea's belief that she had been rejected, but she deserved it. Now Bea was taking a deep breath and preparing to launch herself at her, and Ruby saw her mouth opening to emit her usual battle-cry. She couldn't be bothered with this any longer, she thought with a sigh, she didn't have time for it, and waved a hand at her in a gesture of weary dismissal. 'I said, is that clear?' she asked again, this time in a louder, firmer voice.

Bea stopped, seemingly paralysed in mid-air, and stared at her, her mouth still open, but noticeably slacker.

'For the sake of trying to preserve some dignity in Ma's passing,' Ruby told her, 'what little you haven't already destroyed, we'll stay in touch till she's gone, but as far as I'm concerned you're no more than someone the family lives beside and knows. We're not related now. We won't be related in the future.'

As Ruby calmly turned and headed for the door, she felt a shift in the atmosphere of the room, Bea was struggling, unsure how to reply. Bea dealt in violent, explosive actions, not considered thoughts and words, she had neither the grace nor the intellect for it.

'There you are!' she shouted pathetically, returning to her previous, discredited claim. 'Just like I said! You all hate me because I'm a bastard!'

Ruby reached for the handle, opened the door then turned back. 'You're wrong as usual, Bea,' she said quietly, looking her in the eye. 'We all hate you because you're hateful. You've made yourself hateful, you've earned it all by yourself.' She went through the door and, as she was pulling it closed behind her, she said firmly, 'Goodbye.'

Walking back down the brae again, her head lowered, her arms crossed and wound around her waist, Ruby was surprised by how calm she felt. She meant every word she had said, there would be no going back on a syllable, and the only feeling she had was one of relief. The aunties were waiting for her in the living room, huddled round the range for warmth.

'Well, did you kill her then?' Cissie asked amiably.

'Kind of,' Ruby grinned. 'Ma?'

'She's fine, hen,' Dot replied. 'Sleeping like a baby now.'

'Don't think it'll be long though, Ruby,' Cissie said gently.

'Aye, I know,' Ruby replied, pulling up a chair and sitting down opposite them.

'What did that mad big bugger say?' Dot asked.

Ruby shrugged. 'She was winding up for a rammy, but I didn't let her,' she said.

'Did you land another fourpenny one across her coupon?'

'Didn't have to!' Ruby smiled. 'Told her a few things. I think she's holed below the waterline!'

'That's a pity,' Cissie grinned. 'There's nothing like a fourpenny one across the coupon when you're really angry, is there?'

The two old aunties chuckled merrily together.

'Maybe I was too tired,' Ruby said. 'Tired of her, I mean, not of Ma.'

'It'll soon be over, hen,' Cissie told her. 'We'll have to be going now, but if you need us, you know where we are.'

'Aye, Auntie Cissie,' Ruby smiled, getting up to help them on with their coats and see them to the door.

243

Cissie turned and unexpectedly hugged her. 'I'll tell you this, Ruby, hen' she said, 'your Ma's that proud of you for how you've looked after her, but not half as proud as me and Dot here. That not true, Dot?'

Beside her Dot nodded vigorously and blew loudly into a handkerchief, then they were gone.

Coming from Cissie and Dot it was the equivalent of a full-scale outpouring of finer feelings and deep emotions from normal people, and Ruby retreated to the bathroom and sobbed for a long time before she could go back out and attend to Sarah again.

That night Sarah lost consciousness and George decided to stay with Ruby. Donald McGill had told them that hearing was the last sense to go, and they should still talk, that Sarah would hear them. So they chatted as normally as they could throughout the small hours, little conversations that didn't mention dying, giving Sarah's last hours no terrors. By the time Dr McGill called on his usual visit next morning, Sarah's breathing was painfully laboured, making awful sounds that felt like physical blows to Ruby as she waited for the next breath to come. When he came back in the afternoon he got as far as placing his stethoscope on Sarah's chest when her breathing stopped.

'That's it, I'm afraid,' McGill said, looking from Ruby to George.

'What do we do now?' George asked helplessly.

'Sit down, George,' he said kindly. 'I'll give you a death certificate,' he reached for his bag. 'Where's Harry?'

'He took a troop train down yesterday. Should've been back this morning but he's been held up on the way. They've probably given him another train to take somewhere else.'

McGill nodded. 'Right. What you do is take the certificate to Martha Street and they'll register the death, there's still time before the office closes, then it's over to the undertaker. It'll be the Co-op, I suppose?'

Ruby and George looked at each other. Neither of them had thought that far ahead, but they both nodded, it was always the Co-op.

'Well you can organise that after Martha Street, George. I'll give the Co-op a call from the surgery to let them know what's happened and that you'll be along directly. It would be good to have it all arranged by the time Harry comes home, I don't think he'd be up to it, do you?'

George shook his head.

'If you stay with Ma I'll run across quickly to Iris and Bea first,' Ruby suggested, as though Sarah might still need something. 'Do I tell Jakey, George?'

'If he's in,' George replied vaguely. 'I haven't seen him for a while, he's likely working, or away.'

She wrote out a note to put through Bea's door, guessing that she wouldn't answer again, then ran across the road to the Campbell house, aware that Gus Campbell would be just home from work. He opened the door in bare feet, shirtless and with his vest hanging outside his trousers. Ruby felt her stomach turn.

'I want to speak to your wife,' Ruby told him.

He grinned slightly. Flora's phrase came into her mind: 'You know the way he does?' He was doing that now.

'Come in,' he said, bowing and making a wide, sweeping gesture of invitation with one arm as he leaned against the door with the other.

'No thanks,' she said. 'If you'll just get your wife.'

Iris appeared then, wrapping a coat around her, and Ruby guessed there was little, if anything, underneath. Gus Campbell stood behind his wife, pressing against her, both his arms around her waist, still grinning his grin at Ruby. She swallowed. 'Ma died a few minutes ago,' she said. 'I thought you might want to know. That's it, I have to go now. Somebody will let you know about the funeral.' She turned and fled into the street without letting herself think. There would time for that later. Lots and lots of time from now on. She swallowed hard, put her head down and headed up the brae to Bea's door. As she had expected, there was no answer. 'Selfish bitch,' she thought viciously, 'everything's got to be about her!' then pushed the note through the letterbox and left. Walking quickly back down the brae she almost forgot about telling Jakey, and ran across the road and up the stairs to his house. The door opened as she turned the knob but Jakey wasn't in and she supposed George had been right, he would be at work. Then she glanced at his armchair and

Ma's crochet thing had gone, which meant Jakey and Wee Dug had too.

'Jakey's away,' she announced when she got back to the McLean house. 'Somebody must've told him Ma hadn't long, that would've been enough for him.'

'Aye, it's maybe just as well he took off, the wee man's better off away till after.'

'I was thinking, could you nip up to Flora's as you're passing on the way to Martha Street and tell her? She'll maybe be at work as well, but there'll be somebody at home.'

George nodded. 'I'll nip into the Yard and get Andy to take a message to Cissie and Dot as well. What if Da comes in before I get back?' he asked fearfully.

Ruby knew George wanted to shoulder his duty as the eldest son by breaking the news to Harry, and she smiled affectionately. 'He probably won't be back before you are,' she said quietly. 'But you've got things to do, so if he is, I'll tell him if I have to.'

He hesitated at the door. 'I wouldn't want you doing that on your own,' he said, 'you've had more to do than anybody.'

Ruby looked up at him. 'Don't worry, George, I'm fine. Nothing could be as hard as these last months have been, not even telling Da. Now off you go, the sooner you get done the more chance of getting back before him.'

Then she sat by the living room range, waiting, aware that with that final terrible breath there was now little for her to do any longer. These last months had been full of chores and tasks that were repeated many times every day; Sarah to be cared for, endless washing to be done, and waiting, the interminable waiting for an outcome she ached for yet hoped would never come. Now that it was over she had no idea what she would do with her time. Watching Sarah suffer, she had become convinced that prolonging her life was a form of passive cruelty, and she had longed for death to relieve her of the burden her ailing life had become. Now, though, she knew she would give anything to have those months back, to have Sarah back. A selfish reaction, she knew.

She would prepare her mother at home, she decided. Sarah McLean wouldn't leave 252 till she was carried out for the last time.

She would sit here in the quiet till the aunties arrived, as they were sure to do, then they would wash Sarah, dress her and have her ready for when the undertaker brought the coffin. It seemed strange that she had been contemplating her mother's death for months yet now it had arrived, everything was happening too quickly and, somehow, she didn't believe it was real. There was a feeling of incredulity about it, intermixed with moments of rising panic. She would never see her, never hear her voice again. How was she to live without her? The thought was impossible.

29

'She aye had lovely hair, our Sarah,' Dot said, pouring warm water over Sarah's head to be caught in a basin below. 'What do you think? Do we put it up in her topknot or leave it loose?'

Ruby thought for a moment. 'When I was wee I used to watch her brush it every night,' she smiled. 'Leave it loose I think. Da always liked her hair long. What do you think, Auntie Cissie?'

Cissie nodded in agreement. 'What dress are we putting on her, Ruby?'

'I thought the blue one. She liked that one, it was her special occasion dress. She said it brought out the colour of her eyes.'

'Aye, well, I suppose we could say this is an occasion,' Cissie sighed. 'And knickers and shoes and everything?'

'Of course!' Dot butted in. 'What do you think of that, Sarah? Sending you to meet your maker with bare feet and a bare arse!'

The three women laughed gently.

'Dry her hair well,' Ruby said, 'she hated having wet hair.'

'What are we to do with her wedding ring?' Cissie asked, looking at Ruby and Dot.

'I don't know, leave it on, I suppose,' Ruby shrugged.

'No, no, you can't do that!' Dot said. 'If you don't take it off some bugger from the undertaker's will just filch it and sell it. It should go to the eldest daughter.'

They all exchanged another look.

'I'd rather leave it on her than let that big bugger Bea have it!' Cissie remarked. 'Besides, she'd likely sell it just to spite Harry, because he bought it.'

Dot shot a warning look at her sister.

'It's okay, you two,' Ruby said, 'I know Da isn't Bea's father.'

'How long have you known that?' Cissie demanded.

'Ma told me a few weeks ago,' Ruby said, 'she didn't mean to, but ...' She shrugged.

'Have you mentioned it to anybody else?' Dot asked.

'Of course not, Ma asked me not to. Bea knows I know, that's all. That's what she was screaming at Ma about the other day. She wanted to know who her father was.'

'And did she tell her? Who was it?' Cissie asked.

'Aye, she told her, but I told Bea I didn't care who it was, I didn't want to know. Don't you two know already?'

Cissie and Dot looked at each other then back at Ruby, shaking their heads in unison. 'When she found out she was expecting everybody thought it was Harry's at first, seemed obvious, and me and Cissie here were getting stuck in, saying what a bastard he was, running off and leaving Sarah to cope by herself. But Sarah jumped in, told us it wasn't Harry's, but she didn't tell us whose it was, so we never asked,'

'So that's why you've always said my Da was a good man?' Ruby smiled.

'Aye, well, he was,' Cissie said quietly, 'he is. He knew Bea wasn't his but he took her on, didn't he? Told Sarah he didn't want to know who the wean's father was, and he never cast it up at her, never. As far as he was concerned he was Bea's Da and that was that.'

Dot sighed. 'I've aye wondered who she took after, mind you, it's none of us, that's for sure!'

Ruby looked at the two of them. 'Well, that's not quite true, is it?' she asked, laughing.

'What do you mean?' Dot asked.

'Well, who else do you know who likes sweet things as much as Bea?'

The two old sisters looked at each other blankly, then recognition registered in their expressions, closely followed by horror.

'Now, Ruby!' Cissie protested. 'I'm sure she doesn't take after me and Dot here!' She looked at Dot who nodded firmly.

'Just coincidence,' Dot stated haughtily.

'And then there's the argumentative streak,' Ruby suggested.

The sisters exchanged looks once again.

'*Us?*' Cissie exclaimed. 'Sure, we're not argumentative, are we Dot?'

Dot shook her head this time. 'I'd say we're kind of pass remarkable,' she mused, 'but that's all.'

'Aye, that's it,' Cissie said, 'we notice things, we take a lively interest, that's us.' She looked up at Ruby. 'If I may say so, madam, strikes me it's you that's trying to start an argument the day!'

Ruby smiled. 'Anyway, maybe we should keep Ma's wedding ring and give it to Da later,' she said. 'What he does with it is up to him. Agreed?'

'You'll get no argument from us on that score!' Dot said firmly, looking at Cissie for a nod of agreement. 'That seems the best thing, Ruby.'

So they worked on, making Sarah presentable, then they stood back and examined their work.

'Have we forgotten anything?' Dot asked.

'Don't think so, she looks fine, doesn't she, Ruby?' Cissie replied.

'What about pennies on her eyes?' Dot asked thoughtfully.

'Och, I've always thought that was a really weird thing!' Ruby replied.

'It's tradition, it's to pay the ferryman,' Dot told her.

'What bloody ferryman?' Ruby demanded.

'The one that takes you to the other side,' Dot said.

'Och, bugger that nonsense!' Ruby said dismissively. 'You couldn't have got Ma on an oary boat never mind any ferry to the other side!'

'I aye assumed the undertakers stole them just like the rings anyway,' Dot nodded, 'greedy buggers.'

Ruby looked at the lifeless form of her mother in all her finery. 'I know,' she said gently, 'a wee dab of her Lavender Water, she aye liked to smell nice.'

Suddenly Dot laughed. 'Know what we should do?' she giggled. 'You know all they crochet things she did? We should get them all the gether and put them in the coffin with her!'

'Auntie Dot!' Ruby reproved her, but she was already laughing.

'Well, they were all bloody awful, weren't they?' Dot giggled.

'Aye, but even so …'

'Tell me this,' Dot said, 'honestly now. Did you ever see anything she did being used?'

'Aye!' Ruby said. 'My Uncle Jakey uses one as a blanket, so there!'

'Jakey? That mad bugger?' Dot giggled. 'That's the best you can up with, that Jakey uses one as a blanket? Sure, you've no idea what it started out as, probably a hat or something!' Dot threw her head back and held her sides. 'Does that not tell you everything? Our Sarah's crochet things were only used by that bampot Jakey!'

'She'd be mad at you two if she could hear you!' Ruby accused them, trying to remain offended. 'She loved her crochet things!'

Cissie sat down, wiping her eyes and heaving with mirth. 'We used to place bets on them, Ruby!' she laughed. 'On whether they'd ever be finished and what they were supposed to be in the first place! My God, but she was useless with that crochet hook, I never understood why she wanted to keep doing it!'

Dot sat beside Cissie, the two of them holding onto each other for support as they creaked with laughter.

'Have you two been round at McLellan's for your sweetie ration?' Ruby demanded suspiciously, and they two old sisters nodded as they shook, mopping helplessly at their eyes. 'So this is what happens when you get too much sugar at one go? You sit laughing like eejits beside your poor dead sister?'

The two old sisters looked at each, nodded and subsided into another fit of giggling.

Ruby watched them, laughing with them and at them. There was something heroic about them, the way they carried on and never allowed life, or death, to get them down; it was hard to be angry with them.

Cissie recovered first, taking in a deep, shuddering breath. 'Come on now,' she admonished the other two, 'we've had a good wee laugh, it's time to get on.'

She looked at Dot severely. 'Get a grip now, Dot. Are you sure Sarah's hair's as dry as you can get it? She's aye been the same, hasn't she, Sarah?' she said conversationally. 'Always leaves a job half-done. You should see her stairs.' Cissie shook her head and tut-tutted. 'I'd better have a wee look, make sure you're all right, Sarah.'

'And we all know *she* never leaves a job half-done, don't we, Sarah?' Dot remarked. 'Everything's over-done, especially her cooking!'

The coffin arrived early in the evening and, as Sarah was placed inside, Ruby had another moment of panic at the speed with which everything was moving and almost cried out 'Wait a minute! I'm not ready for this!' Cissie and Dot were, however, and wanted to get on and put white sheets on all the windows. George stopped them. The last thing he wanted was for his father to find out Sarah had died by looking up and seeing the windows swathed in white. The chances were that by the time Harry came home he wouldn't have seen the windows in the blackout, so it wouldn't have mattered anyway, but it was a risk George didn't want to take.

George sat down by the fire to wait for him as he came through the front door, but the moment his father set eyes on him in the sitting room, Harry McLean knew he was a widower.

'He knew as soon as he saw me,' George told Ruby later. 'I didn't have to say a word. He just looked at me and said "It's all right, son." I just broke down there and then, I've never felt so useless in my life.'

'Why?' Ruby asked, gently rubbing his arm. 'Your mother had just died, you're allowed, you know.'

'I know,' George sighed, looking up at the ceiling, 'but I wanted to do it right for him, to be strong for him, and he ended up consoling me.'

'You've done everything well, George, don't be so hard on your-self, you've made all the arrangements and you've been here every day these last months. I couldn't have managed without you.'

'Aye, I suppose,' George said in a low, unconvinced voice. 'What about the other two? Any word from them? I thought they'd at least appear.'

'I didn't,' Ruby said shortly. Then she changed the subject. 'Why don't you go home and see Marie and the weans?'

'It's okay. I sent word to Marie.'

'That's not what I meant, George,' she explained gently. 'Go home to your family, they haven't seen you for a couple of days, have they?'

'Christ, I never thought of that!' he said. 'But there won't be any buses on yet.'

'So take a taxi, to hell with the expense. Get some sleep and come back tomorrow.'

George nodded. 'How are you holding up like this?' he asked, half laughing.

'I don't know,' Ruby shrugged. 'Because I have to, I suppose. Who knows what will happen when it's over?'

As George opened the door he turned. 'Any sign of Uncle Jakey yet?'

'No.' She shook her head.

'He'll come back when he's ready.'

'Aye, he always does. Now go home, son!'

But it wasn't over, not by a long shot. At eight o'clock the next morning there was a frantic knocking at the door and Ruby opened it to find a bedraggled Dainty Davy standing there, his face ashen. Like her father, Davy had been driving as many trains as he could in every direction, never knowing when he would get home again. Seeing him there, several thoughts shot through Ruby's mind. First, that she had no idea he'd take his mother-in-law's death so badly, and second, that maybe he had come to claim her for upsetting his dear wife. If that was the case, she was surprised he had the guts. He raced past her and shot into the sitting room.

'It's Bea,' he whispered. 'I've just come back in and found her on the floor. She'd fallen out of bed. I tried to pick her up but I can't. I think she's ... I think she's .... dead!'

'She can't be!' Ruby cried. 'Don't be daft, Davy, you're imagining things now! She's probably just taken one of her new sleeping pills. That's why you can't waken her.'

'What do I do? What do I do?' he cried, wringing his hands. 'Can you come up and help me lift her?'

Ruby tried to re-arrange her thoughts. Less than two days ago she told Bea she wanted nothing more to do with her, all relations between them were henceforth and forever null and void. How would Bea react if she came to and found herself face-to-face with her ex-sister? She'd gloat, that's what she'd do, Ruby would never hear the end of it and her future credibility would be shot to hell for all eternity. 'Look, Davy, stop making such a racket, my Da's still sleeping. I'll come up with you,' she said at last, 'but the minute she opens her eyes I'm out of there, okay? You go ahead, I'll get my coat on and be up behind you.'

'Ruby, I don't think she'll open her eyes,' the little man said over his shoulder as he left.

'Christ, here I am again,' she muttered, sticking her arms into her coat sleeves, 'running up that bloody brae, and it's raining, and for nothing. As if I don't have enough to keep me busy, and just because Dainty Davy's got himself in a panic.'

She had never been in Bea's bedroom before and was surprised to find only one single bed there, with, as Dainty Davy had said, Bea half in it, her top half lying on the floor. Davy was trying to haul Bea around, sweat trickling over his head and dislodging his carefully coiffed hair. Ruby took one look at Bea's colour. 'Davy,' she said quietly. 'Leave her.'

'We can't leave her lying like this,' he cried, still pulling on one of Bea's arms.

'Davy, run over to the surgery and get Dr McGill, he'll be there by now, tell him it's an emergency, then go up to the station and get Tam McVicar, if he's on duty. If he's not, anyone will do.'

Davy stopped and looked at Bea, then at Ruby, his face a mask of bemusement and shock.

'Go, Davy,' she said. 'Go now, son.'

As she sat waiting for Dr McGill and PC McVicar to arrive, Ruby didn't feel anything, her emotions were all used up in coping with her mother's death and the aftermath.

'Typical of Bea, though,' she said to herself savagely. 'She always has to be the centre of attention. She was jealous of the bride at every wedding and every corpse at a funeral. Bloody typical!'

30

'It was an overdose,' Dr McGill told Ruby, as they sat in his surgery trying to make some sense out of what had happened over the last few days. Sarah's funeral had gone ahead the day after Bea had been found, with the family in a trance. They had gone through the motions, did what was expected of them by tradition and culture, but it had been a doubly odd experience, Bea had seen to that. She had done it again, upstaged everyone.

'What kind of overdose?' Ruby asked quietly. 'I know she was on all sorts of things for her stomach, Ma told me.'

'Yes, she had ulcerative colitis,' he said.

'What's that?'

'It's a condition that causes the intestines to become inflamed, then ulcers develop. It's very debilitating and there's very little we can do about it.'

'She loved sweet things,' Ruby remembered, 'did that cause it?'

He shook his head. 'What she ate or didn't eat didn't have any effect on this illness.'

'So what causes it?'

'We don't really know, but there's an element of the mind involved, the more upset she got, the worse her stomach was and, as we both know, nobody got upset like Bea.'

'I always knew she was bonkers!' Ruby laughed dryly.

'I'm sure Bea being Bea didn't help, but she was very sick sometimes. There were spells when she seemed to be doing fine, then others when she had terrible diarrhoea and stomach cramps, and she got anaemic from time to time too, I had to give her tablets for that more than once. It was very unpredictable. She never knew how she would be feeling day-to-day. It was hard to know what was causing what, but I gave her anti-depressants—'

'She was depressed?' Ruby asked.

'She could be. That kind of illness really drags people down and the tendency was in her nature, too, I think. Unfortunately the anti-depressants didn't seem to help much, nothing did. I gave her some Nembutal capsules recently to help her sleep, you probably saw them, big blue ones?'

Ruby made no comment. On the few occasions when she was in Bea's house she mainly watched the exit in hopes of keeping it clear should she need to make her escape.

'I'm pretty sure she took too many of those.' He looked at her. 'I'm not suggesting she did so on purpose, Ruby, but she wasn't used to them and with everything that's been going on in the family I know her stomach was in a bad way again. She was probably trying to get some sleep, took a few capsules, wakened again, took a few more, she would've been too groggy to realise how many she was taking. There was a big bump on the back of her head, so I'm guessing that happened when she fell out of bed or that she wasn't very steady and had a fall before that. I'm sure it wasn't suicide and I didn't put that on the certificate. For a start I couldn't, because there was no note. I put the cause of death as Megacolon, that's a very serious complication of ulcerative colitis, and I've had a chat with Tam McVicar to make sure the matter won't be taken any further. He's a sensible sort, McVicar. There would be no point and it would only upset your father even more.'

Ruby thought for a moment. 'Ma always said she would've been better if she'd had a family, but Bea said she didn't want weans. I suppose she couldn't, though, with her stomach?'

'Well, she was *virgo intacta*,' McGill said quietly.

'All these big words,' Ruby smiled, shaking her head. 'Are you saying that last one would have stopped her having weans?'

McGill paused, looking down at the notes on his desk. 'Yes, Ruby,' he said. 'That would indeed have stopped her.'

A few days after they buried Bea, Dainty Davy sought Ruby's help once again. He wanted her to clear his late wife's clothes and possessions out of the flat. Ruby was slightly taken aback. It hadn't occurred to her or anyone else to move Sarah's clothes out the McLean house, but Davy was obviously moving on from his heartbreak faster than they were. So back up the brae with him she went, ready to weed out whatever he wanted rid of, and once again she noticed that Davy and Bea had separate rooms.

'I never knew Bea had her own bedroom,' Ruby said brightly. 'She never mentioned that.'

Davy brushed a hand over what remained of his oil-covered crinkly hair, as though to tame a mane of flowing locks. 'It just made sense,' he said quietly. 'I was coming and going at all hours and Bea was up a lot when her stomach was bothering her. It was so we didn't disturb each other.'

Ruby nodded; it made sense, as he said. 'It couldn't have been easy for you, Davy,' she smiled, 'Bea wasn't easy for any of us.'

'Och, I just kind of let it wash over me,' he sighed, 'I didn't really take much notice. After a while you learn to tune it out, you know?'

'That's more than I ever managed!'

He was wandering about the bedroom, trying to look as though he wanted to be of use but totally unable to pull it off.

'I'm sure this must be hard on you, Davy, so I'll just do it myself,' she said kindly. 'I'll clear the lot out without bothering you, okay?'

He nodded happily, a look of relief on his face. 'Are you sure?' he asked, but he was already halfway out of the door. 'When you're finished, pull the door shut, it locks itself. I'll away. I've got lessons to give.'

She had no idea what to do with Bea's clothes, so she stuffed everything she could find into pillowcases without examining any of it, emptying the wardrobe first, then the chest of drawers. As she worked she decided to give everything to the Salvation Army. They were always looking for donations to help out people who had lost everything in bomb raids. She was emptying the last drawer, the deepest one at the bottom. All that was left was a brown paper parcel that seemed to be stuck. As it came away with a hard tug, the paper ripped and the contents fell out onto the floor. Barely glancing at them she knelt down to pick them up, then something made her look at what she had in her hands. Baby clothes; beautiful blue and pink outfits, full layettes, with exquisitely crocheted shawls. She stopped and unfolded the tiny things, staring at the workmanship. Apart from the crochet-work there were little knitted cardigans with embroidered animals and flowers, all in various colours, and dresses and romper suits with perfect smocking across the front that had obviously been done by some expert hand. They hadn't been made for one particular child, but for any child, boy or girl. Sarah could never have made anything like them and, even if she had, why would Bea have them? She picked up bootees created from minute stitches with ribbon threaded through at the ankles, ready to fit onto the foot of a newborn child. And there were bonnets and mittens and pram coats and leggings – everything a child, or several children, would need. Still kneeling on the floor she tried to work out who had made these things and why, then it dawned on her: it could only have been Bea. Bea had made them. She had made them for her own children, the ones she never had and claimed she never wanted. Looking at them, feeling them, felt like a blow. She thought she knew Bea, she had worked her out years ago, could plot her every move and each eruption before it came. But she hadn't known her at all, that was the truth. What Dr McGill explained earlier had stunned her, she had never thought for a minute that Bea's life was as difficult as he described, and now the little baby clothes, made by loving hands in hopes of one day having a child in her arms to fit them. Bea had slept in a single bed in her own room and there was no sign of a double bed to show that the arrangement had been temporary, so how long, she wondered, had that gone on?

In the McLean home she had been struck by the feeling of Sarah that still lingered everywhere. It was her house, the home she had created and, even though she was gone, a hint of her was still there, her imprint was everywhere. This house was Bea's home, she cleaned and polished every inch of that too, because she had little else to occupy her, yet there was no feeling of her left behind, it was just a house. All those days and nights when she didn't see Bea and was grateful for it, now she imagined her sitting here by herself, making clothes for her imaginary babies and hiding them away at the back of the bottom drawer. When, she wondered, did Bea realise that there would never be a child to wear them? She thought of what that admission could have done to Bea, to any woman who longed for a child, and felt wretched for her.

Ruby quickly bundled together the pillowcases containing Bea's clothes and the baby clothes and piled them up by the door, then she wrote a note for Dainty Davy and left it on the kitchen table. 'Finished, Davy, I'll drop everything off at the Salvation Army.' Then she lifted the bundles, staggered down the stairs and across to Gerry's house and left them there, rather than take them back to the McLean house, though she didn't know why. It was just a feeling.

Sitting on the train back to Largs, she re-lived it again. Had she killed Bea? That was one of the questions she had lived with for more than half a century, and she still didn't know the answer to it. The day before their mother died she had told Bea she was no longer her sister, but after what she had done to Ma she deserved that. Only it hadn't quite been that simple, nothing was. She knew that now. Back then, when she was young, she thought only in shades of black and white, and there were no prizes for guessing which heading Bea came under. It hadn't been an issue for Ruby that Bea wasn't Harry McLean's natural child, but what she had failed to understand was that it mattered to Bea, and who was Ruby to tell her how to feel? She had never thought for an instant that Bea *could* feel, had she? There were all her ailments and illnesses, the pills and potions she took, hoping every day that this one or that one would help her, but nothing could, because there was no cure. And running through it was her longing for a child that she kept hidden from everyone because there was no possibility of that happening either. George, Ruby, even Iris, who didn't deserve it, all had weans, only Bea didn't. She had no friends, her attitude and behaviour scared everyone away, but thinking of her spending her lonely days and nights polishing every surface of her home over and over again, then making delicate garments for children she would never have was heartbreaking, there was no other word for it. Whoever her father was, Sarah was her mother, and despite what the rest of the family thought about Bea, Ruby especially, she must have been as upset as the others at the thought of losing her, even if she didn't show it. Bea was not used to showing any feeling but anger, she

259

had turned it into her own suit of armour, but she did have feelings, and the more she had, the worse her health was affected.

The day before Sarah died Bea had behaved in her usual crass manner and Ruby had disowned her, when Bea's worst fear was being on the outside, the place she had always felt was her allotted space. It didn't matter that no one else was aware of her feelings or why; Bea was. So after Ruby left that day, did Bea think about the great discovery of her father's name and realise that, as Sarah had told her, knowing would do her no good anyway? Was that when she took her 'accidental' overdose, when too many bad things had come together, ending up with Ruby casting her out of the family forever?

As the train pulled into Largs Station Ruby got up. After all these years it was one of the guilty questions that kept her awake and woke her in the middle of the night when sleep did eventually come. Was it her fault? Had it really been an accident or had she tipped Bea over the edge?

31

Ruby was sitting in the living room at 252 with Flora. It was two weeks after they had buried Bea, two weeks and two days since they buried Sarah, and Ruby was experiencing an overwhelming weariness. She was becalmed, unable and unwilling to do or think anything.

'Are you going to stay on here?' Flora asked.

Ruby shrugged. 'Haven't really thought about it, I'm just drifting at the moment, but someone has to look after Da for a while, so I may as well be here as anywhere.'

'What about Frances?'

'Oh, she's back, she's asleep. I thought having a wean about the place might give Da something to focus on, take his mind off the obvious.'

'How is he?'

'Hard to tell,' Ruby frowned. 'He went back to work after the funeral, took time off for Bea's and went back after that, straight into his old routine.'

'I suppose the railways need all their drivers with the War on,' Flora nodded, 'and maybe it's the way he's decided to cope. Have you said anything to him about Bea finding out who her father was?'

'No!' Ruby said. 'Wouldn't dare! He knows nothing about any of that!'

The front door opened and they waited before going on with their conversation.

'Hello, George,' Ruby smiled. 'What are you doing here?'

George looked sheepish. 'I haven't a clue,' he admitted. 'It's like

I've got into the habit of dropping in whenever I have a minute and I can't break it.'

'I know what you mean,' Ruby sighed. 'Flora's wondering why I'm still here and I don't really have an answer either.'

'It'll take a while,' Flora said gently, 'it's been a terrible time for the family. You still won't know what's hit you.'

'Sometimes I wonder if there's a curse on us,' Ruby laughed, only half-joking.

'Now Ruby!' Flora said sternly.

'I know, I know,' she teased Flora, 'superstition is ideologically unsound! What would the comrades say?'

'I'm a comrade and I'm telling you it *is!*' Flora retorted. 'I can't believe you'd even think that, Ruby McLean!'

The two friends laughed, then Flora said, 'So, did Bea tell you who her father was?'

George looked at Flora. 'What did you say?' he asked.

Flora stared wordlessly as a look of confusion passed over George's features.

'What the hell,' he stammered, 'did you mean by that?'

Flora looked at Ruby, her face flushing. 'He doesn't know?' she whispered, as though George wasn't standing there looking at her.

'He does now!' Ruby replied.

'Will somebody tell me what's going on?' George demanded, sitting down opposite Ruby.

'Och, George, it's a long story,' Ruby sighed. 'Seems Ma had Bea before she married Da and that's why Bea hated us all, because we had a father and she reckoned she didn't. See? Nothing to it. That's it.'

'Nothing to it?' George asked in amazement. 'What the bloody hell do you mean? And where does "That's it" come in?'

'Well, it does. I only found out the week before Ma died and she made me promise not to tell anybody.' Ruby sighed heavily. 'But she's gone now and so's Bea, so I don't suppose it matters any longer.'

'So everybody knew except big daftie here? When, precisely, were you planning on telling me?'

'Hardly anybody knows, and I didn't have a plan,' Ruby said

helplessly. 'I would've told you whenever it came up, it just came up now.' She glared at Flora. 'And what's the difference anyway, it's done, gone.'

George leaned forward, his elbows on his knees, his hands clasped in front of him, staring into the fire. 'So Ma had a wean to somebody else and Da just took her on when the got married?' he asked incredulously.

Ruby nodded. 'Didn't ask any questions, didn't want to know anything, he told Ma Bea would be his daughter. And she always was, despite what Bea decided to believe.'

'Good for the old man,' George said softly, smiling proudly.

'In Bea's mind everything that happened in her life was because we knew our father was Da and she knew hers wasn't.'

'That's just daft!' George said.

'I'm not defending her, George, I'm just explaining what she told me, screamed at me, being Bea. We had everything she didn't. Her health was bad, she was sure we looked down on her and laughed at her behind her back.'

'Well that was true, she set herself up for that well and truly!' George muttered.

'That's what I told her,' Ruby said sadly, 'though I wish I hadn't now. She said we hated her and I said she had made herself hateful, she had earned it.'

'Oh, Ruby!' Flora said, aghast.

'I know, Flora!' Ruby said, covering her face with her hands. 'But it only sounds bad because she's dead, doesn't it? If she was still here, making our lives miserable, you'd be saying "Good for you" wouldn't you?'

'Well,' George chuckled, 'if she wouldn't, I would!'

'Shut up you!' Ruby reprimanded him. 'You're not making me feel any better. The other thing was she couldn't have a family because of all sorts of medical conditions with long names I can't even remember now, and we all did have weans, somehow that was our fault as well.'

'She never wanted weans!' George exclaimed. 'She told everybody that, and she sure as hell hated ours!'

Ruby looked down. 'That's what she said, but she did want them,' she said sadly. 'Dainty Davy asked me to clear out her things and there was a big parcel of baby clothes hidden away, things she had made herself.'

'Jesus Christ!' George said thoughtfully. 'Are you sure they weren't for our weans?'

'Now, George,' Ruby said sceptically, 'did she ever give you anything for your girls?'

George shook his head. 'Not even a birthday or Christmas present, miserable big bugger!'

'And she never gave Frances or Jamie anything either. The clothes were tiny, for new babies. She hid them away, she wasn't giving them to anybody. They were for her own weans,' Ruby sighed.

'Have you told Mrs Campbell across the road any of this?'

'No,' Ruby replied. 'It's got bugger all to do with her.'

George nodded. 'Iris would only laugh anyway,' he commented.

'So nothing like you're doing now?' Ruby demanded.

'So Big Bea has become a saint just because she's dead?' George argued. 'Finally resting in peace doesn't make her any less of a bloody nuisance while she was still here, Ruby, and she was, wasn't she? She was a vicious cow as well!'

'But we now know there were reasons, George,' Ruby said.

'Even if she'd told us her reasons years ago, it wouldn't have made her any less horrible. You're acting like you believed her, that all her complaints were our fault, and they weren't you know, that was all in her head!' George said angrily.

'She even thought she was called Big Bea as a sly dig at her,' Ruby recalled.

George looked at her, raising his eyebrows in puzzlement.

'Big Bea, George,' Ruby said. 'Big B – Big Bastard.'

'Och, that was just a happy coincidence,' George laughed. 'Sure Ma couldn't have known what she would turn out like when she gave her the name, could she? Bea just lived up to it – on every level!'

'George, stop it!' Ruby said angrily.

'Will you two listen to yourselves?' Flora said quietly. 'The woman caused ructions all her life, now you're letting her do it from the grave. Let's all calm down, and talk about happier things.'

264

'Like what?'

'Well, the Campbells,' Flora smirked.

'*That's* a happier thing, is it?' Ruby asked incredulously.

'All is not well with Clan Campbell, haven't you heard?'

Ruby shook her head.

'I hear all about them from Mrs Morris when Denis and I visit Andy. Iris's roving eye is roving again!' Flora giggled.

'Now there's a surprise!' George said sarcastically. 'Who'd have thought it? And where Iris's eye goes, the rest of her soon follows!'

'You'd have thought the big beast would've realised that she isn't exactly the steady type,' Ruby said. 'Iris has always tried out what was available and moved on when she was bored. Wonder why he thought he'd be any different?'

'Gus has been heard threatening her with all sorts of things if she doesn't behave herself and she's been screaming at him that she knows he's got money he's not letting her have, so the neighbours say,' Flora divulged cheerfully.

'If he has any money, the minute she gets her hands on it she'll be off like a whippet anyway,' George mused. 'Big Gus isn't daft, he knows that's the only hold he has over her.'

Ruby sat thinking as Flora and George chatted on. If it was true that there was trouble between the Campbells, what effect was it having on Jamie? Her heart turned at the thought of the wee lad hearing them fighting, possibly being caught between them. She knew she could hardly dash over there and reclaim him, but that didn't stop her worrying about him. 'Is Jamie all right?' she asked tentatively. 'Has Mrs Morris said anything about what's happening to Jamie?'

Flora shook her head. 'Not that I've heard.'

'Can't be doing him any good if they're at each others throats,' Ruby murmured. 'Not that it's any of my business.'

Flora and George exchanged a look.

'That's all Jamie was, too,' Ruby continued, 'something she tried out, a new experience. She was never greatly interested in him as a long-term venture either.'

'Did you notice at the funerals that folk were keeping their distance from them a bit?' George smiled.

'I always kept my distance from *him*,' Ruby shivered.

'I remember watching them and thinking how things had changed, when they got married everybody kind of smiled on them,' George recalled. 'It was a bit soon after Betty and, well, Iris being Iris, but folk were still prepared to wish them all the best.'

'Aye,' Flora said, looking accusingly at Ruby, 'all those good wishes went up in smoke after madam's wee speech though, didn't they?'

'Och, be quiet,' Ruby muttered. 'I'm not sorry and I don't feel guilty about it, if you really want to know!'

'I don't doubt that for a minute,' Flora replied tartly.

'Bea blew up that day too, stole my thunder as usual.'

'Oh no!' Flora moaned. 'I was trying to get us off the subject of the late Big Bea, give her – and us – a rest, please!'

'There I was, stealing Iris's thunder and Bea had to snatch it and mine as well from under my nose,' Ruby said, ignoring her. 'She was screaming on about us all having "cosy wee lives", as usual. I was thinking the other night about all those times she went berserk, it was always about family things, weddings, christenings, weans' birthdays. To her, we went on and had lives, but she got married and that was that.'

'Can't help feeling sorry for her,' Flora murmured. 'Who'd have thought anyone could ever say that about Bea?'

'I wouldn't worry,' George grinned, 'she did enough of feeling sorry for herself.'

They sat for a while, each deep in thought, the crackling of the fire the only intrusion on the silence.

'Did you hear Dainty Davy's moved his pal into the flat?' George asked.

'What pal?' Ruby asked absently.

'The young bloke he's been teaching to dance,' George grinned. 'He's a porter at the Yard. They're aye the gether. He's moved in now.'

Flora and Ruby looked at each other.

'Well, maybe the lad needed somewhere to stay,' Ruby shrugged, nonchalantly.

'And Davy would likely be lonely,' Flora agreed.

'Mm,' George said, 'likely. And Davy still has his overalls pressed.'

He threw his head back and laughed. 'Everybody at work has been talking about it! By the way, any sight of Jakey?'

'No, Da was saying last night that this is the longest he's ever been away, he's a bit worried about him.'

'They're asking about him at work,' George said.

'What did you tell them?'

'I said he was ill, what else could I say?'

'He doesn't even know about Bea, does he?' Flora asked. 'So when he does come back he's got more upset to face.'

'He'll be okay,' George said firmly, 'we'll keep an eye on him. And there's nothing to worry about, he'll come back in his own time, he always does.' He looked at Ruby and laughed. 'Besides, he loves dressing up in that Arab costume and swishing the sword about. He'll come back for that alone!'

Only he didn't, of course. A few days later Tam McVicar paid a visit to the McLean home to tell the family that Jakey's body had been found in the River Clyde. It had been in the water for some time, about two weeks they reckoned. A terrible accident, McVicar said. He knew Jakey liked to walk by the river and sometimes he slept out on the banks, he had seen him there often himself and reminded him to be careful. Something must have happened. He'd slipped maybe, or tumbled in accidentally in the dark when he was half-asleep. It looked like that, he had a crocheted blanket around him, one of those things the weans made at school with odds and ends of wool. Wee Dug had been caught up in it too. Constant companions in life, he and Jakey had died together. But you couldn't imagine one without the other, could you?

32

The aunties were to the fore in the tragedy of Jakey and Wee Dug, barbs at the ready. Thinking back on it all these years later, Ruby realised that Cissie and Dot got the family through a lot of their worst moments by simply being themselves.

'Well, here we are again then,' Cissie said, when the family arrived back at 252 after Jakey's funeral. She and Dot had their own seats by the side of the range, where they sat like a couple of poisonous bookends and surveyed the universe. No one had ever dared sit in their reserved spots. 'They must be getting double divi at the Co-op for all the burying business they give them these days, eh Dot?'

'Aye, right enough,' Dot agreed, 'it's like the buses, you don't see any for ages then it's three at the one time.'

Jakey's death had devastated Ruby and, listening to Cissie and Dot, she felt a familiar urge to throw them out, or at least gag them, but, on the other hand, she was also somehow glad of the diversion of the family music hall double act.

'And what a daft way to go!' Cissie chuckled irreverently. 'I mean, men in his line of work get killed all the time, don't they?'

'And there's the War,' Dot reminded her.

'Aye, there's the War, he could've got bombed, you could've understood that, couldn't you?'

'Or fell down the stairs in the blackout,' Dot suggested pleasantly, 'or hit by a lorry or something.'

'Aye, exactly,' Cissie shook her head. 'But to fall in the Clyde and drown, and with that silly wee dog of his as well! I mean, it's just daft, isn't it?'

'Aye, well, Cissie,' Dot said conversationally, 'but he *was* daft, wasn't he? Fair's fair.'

'But there's daft and then there's daft,' Cissie reasoned, 'and that was *really* daft.'

Ruby and George exchanged looks. 'Listen to them,' Ruby whispered. 'They're actually discussing degrees of daftness!'

George took a gulp of his drink. 'Well, they'd know, Ruby!' he muttered.

Ruby chuckled.

'See, even Ruby here can see the daftness of it,' Cissie said, 'and she's been going about with a long face since it happened. Daft, wasn't it, Ruby, hen?'

Ruby nodded, thinking that if she heard the word again she'd go, well, daft.

'I suppose, in one way,' Dot said, screwing her face up in deep concentration, 'that you couldn't have expected anything else of him, could you? Him being like he was.'

'Aye,' Cissie joined her thread, 'right enough. You couldn't imagine their Jakey just dying peacefully in his bed, could you? He was aye a daft bugger, so why not die in a daft way?'

'Makes you think, though,' Dot said philosophically, 'makes you wonder who'll be next, doesn't it? Looking at one or two of this lot, it might not be worth their trouble going home.'

They both looked around the room, examining the groups of mourners talking quietly together, then held onto each other as they giggled. Cissie was the first one to regain something approaching composure, sighing heavily.

'What's up with you? You don't think it'll be you, do you?' Dot giggled, nudging her sister in the ribs with her elbow.

'I was just thinking, that's all,' Cissie said mournfully. 'It's helluva dull, isn't it?'

'Well it's a funeral!' Dot replied, cackling away.

'But you miss Big Bea, don't you? I mean, she was a horrible big bitch and that, granted, but she fair livened things up, didn't she?' Cissie recalled in a fond voice.

'Aye, she did that!' Dot agreed. 'You could aye depend on her to cheer you up by making a bloody fool of herself at these things. It's true what they say, you know, you never know what you've got till it's gone.'

The two aunties sighed in unison.

'Anyway,' Cissie said eventually, 'I know I won't be next, I know I'll outlive you.'

'And how the hell do you know that?' Dot demanded furiously.

'Stands to reason,' Cissie said haughtily, 'I've aged better than you and you know it.'

Dot smiled sweetly. 'Maybe on the outside,' she conceded. 'But inside, Cissie,' she intoned darkly, 'inside you're a cesspool, Cissie. You know that, everybody knows that and, more importantly, the Grim Reaper knows it as well!'

It seemed to those who knew Harry McLean that losing his brother had hit him harder than losing his wife and daughter so close together. Three deaths in less than three weeks was more than enough to devastate any family, so perhaps what Harry was really suffering from was the cumulative effects. Maybe Jakey's death was just the last of the trio, and it was true what people said, each blow cut deeper, compounding the others. He aged quickly, that's what everyone noticed. Not yet sixty, he became slightly stooped almost overnight, as though his shoulders had given way under a burden too heavy to be carried. And in some way he seemed diminished, as though the light and life within him had been dimmed, so that he sank into the background. He even stopped whistling, and you always knew Harry McLean was in the vicinity before you saw him by his whistling. At the three family funeral services he couldn't raise his voice to join in the hymns either, now the music had permanently died on his lips.

Harry was the kind of individual who said little, an amiable man who lived his life at peace with everyone, partly because he walked away from unpleasantness whenever he could, but also because it was in his nature to do so; Harry was everyone's friend. Neither was he given to discussing his feelings or even examining them. For Harry, and many men of his generation, moments of introspection had always seemed pointless; he just got on with his life. But after Jakey's death he couldn't switch off his head and the unaccustomed thinking dragged him down.

Sarah's passing he could handle, surprisingly, there was a logic about it that he could accept. That it was unfair was beyond question, that he was heartbroken beyond doubt, but he had lived all his life with the spectre of the White Plague hovering nearby and his generation believed it would always be with them. It was as cruel and unavoidable as it was random, claiming some, leaving others alone. It had always been like that. So Sarah's death, painful as it was, he could accept in a way, and even Bea's made some sense. She had been unstable even as a child, everyone knew that, forever troubled, though he didn't know why; asking would have taken more examination than Harry's nature was capable of. And she was sick, he knew that, too, an endless sickness that might not kill, but certainly maimed her existence. What she expected or hoped marriage to Davy would bring was beyond him, but he didn't dwell on what attracted one person to another, that great mystery was one Harry just accepted. Like the grass being green, or the sky blue, it was just so. There had been comments at the time of the marriage, he knew, that Davy's mother had just died and he needed a house-keeper, but Harry hadn't taken any notice of them. Even if the hints had been true there was nothing he could have done about the situation, though he had never warmed to Davy and had nothing in common with him, apart from the fact that they were in-laws and drove trains.

Dr McGill had told Ruby, and she had told her father, that Bea had taken too many of the new sleeping tablets when she was going through a particularly bad time. She hadn't been used to them and she had been confused, but even so, she had died from complications of her stomach illness. Harry had nodded when this was explained to him. He didn't believe or disbelieve it, it was built into his character to accept things and, though slight doubts had crept into his mind, he did what he had always done when faced with a situation that made him uncomfortable, he walked away. If Bea, faced with her own increasingly bad health and her mother's impending death, had intended doing away with herself rather than securing a decent night's rest, well, there was a logic to that, too, he decided, then he let his mind go blank again. That had been as much as he could handle, he was satisfied.

But Jakey. Jakey was something else entirely. Jakey was on his conscience, because it had been his job to look after his brother and he had failed to do so. Jakey was Harry's big brother by a few years, but from a very young age Harry had felt that he was Jakey's big brother. Jakey had looked after Harry when they were both motherless children going about on the old horse and cart with their doubly widowed father. He remembered Jakey tucking him into an old wooden box on the back of the cart with a blanket when he got sleepy, and buying him milk to drink so that he wouldn't go hungry, probably doing without himself because there was little money. The old man had little in the way of affection to offer either of them, fate had dealt with him cruelly, as it was used to doing with people back then. After the deaths of two wives, he no longer looked for happiness, all that drove him was the need to provide for his two sons, because he had learned the hard lesson that life was no more than an illusion for people like them. He worked himself to death for his boys, finally collapsing and dying at the age of forty-nine. There seemed to be no particular reason, no acute or chronic illness, his heart had simply stopped one day. Harry had always believed his father had worn himself out.

By that time his old man had realised that there was something different about Jakey, as Harry had, and he left a letter at the Savings Bank of Glasgow, along with some savings, asking Harry to look after his brother. And Harry had tried, though as the years passed he had a feeling like sand slipping through his fingers where his brother was concerned. Jakey became more eccentric as he grew older, he knew that, though he wondered if he was making excuses for his own neglect, if perhaps he wasn't paying him the attention he needed. Harry had his family and his work and sometimes there was little time for watching out for Jakey, but still, he felt he should have tried harder.

And now he was gone and what had he got from life? While Harry had been content with his lot, had he done his usual and mentally walked away from how troubled Jakey was? Even the weans had noticed it, they had grown used to keeping an eye on Jakey and making sure he didn't get too upset with whatever was happening in the family, knowing that the slightest change in routine threw him off-track. Even Ruby, who had spent every moment looking after Sarah during those last months, had found time to check on Jakey, to make sure he had enough to eat, that his clothes were washed, that he was warm and looked after, just as Sarah had done before her.

Now that Jakey had finally gone Harry found himself getting angry for the first time in his life, and fretted about how long it had been since he had talked to his brother. He wondered when he had last seen him as more than a speck in the distance, and was horrified to discover that he couldn't remember. How many times had people told him they had seen Jakey down by the river? Being by the river calmed him, it had always been his escape, where he went when he was upset, and Jakey was upset more often than folk suspected. He had meant to tell him to take care, to impress on him that the water could be dangerous as well as calming, but he never did. It was partly because Jakey had no understanding of danger, he knew that, but also because he just didn't tell him. Everyone laughed at Jakey, in an affectionate way, he knew, but they laughed. They went about their own lives and saw only what they saw, but Harry had worried about him and yet had done nothing about his concerns.

And now it was too late. His father had extracted what amounted to a deathbed promise from him all those years ago and he had silently vowed that he would indeed look after Jakey, and he hadn't, so he had not only let his brother down, but his father too. That was the burden that had prematurely stooped Harry McLean's shoulders and dimmed his life force, though being the man he was, he couldn't tell anyone. Besides, the guilt and the shame were too strong.

33

As the months turned into years and the War dragged on, Ruby and Frances stayed with Harry. There was no discussion, their living arrangements just evolved and no objections to them were forthcoming from any quarter. Since she had married Gerry in 1939, it seemed to Ruby that she had rattled back and forth between her marital and family homes, never really settling in either. The War did that to people, of course, made them feel temporary, as though nothing could be settled till the ceasefire was.

The McLeans were no different, their family life had become just such a temporary routine, but at least no one else died and Ruby's primeval fears of a curse smouldering in the background were laid to rest. After Frances had been handed back to her mother, Agnes discovered that she was pregnant for the first time and took to motherhood with a glee that continued, undimmed, until she had two daughters and a son.

The end of the War in 1945 brought a strange response from the population. There was an air of determined joy, but mixed in with it was a vagueness, a feeling that no one knew what to do or even expect next. Many families had the uncertain prospect of loved ones returning after a six-year absence, while others grieved anew for sons, brothers, husbands and fathers who would not come marching home again. The McLeans had lost no one in the fighting or the bombing, but they ended the War with three less than they started out with, and that thought subdued them.

Getting used to not living with wartime restrictions was odd. The blackout had ended, but power cuts were still frequent and rationing continued. Travel restrictions were lifted, but even so, this post-war life took a bit of getting used to after so long. Sirens still sounded, but only as tests, not that this stopped people, conditioned over the years, from panicking and heading for the shelters again before they could stop themselves. There was a feeling that life should be better, they had won the War after all, but having spent so much on armaments the country was in decline, so in reality nothing much changed.

Frances had started school and Ruby was restless, bored and a little apprehensive about what life would bring when the Gerry came home again. In the months of nursing Sarah she had discovered an unsuspected talent for dealing with illness and chaos and wondered vaguely about becoming a nurse. The Royal Infirmary was just up the road in Castle Street. She would go in one day, she decided, and ask how to go about it. Denis, Flora's non-boyfriend, had taken an entrance exam for Glasgow University's Law Faculty. He had claimed that his education records had been destroyed in the Clydebank Blitz and there was no way of proving otherwise, but as he passed with flying colours, any lingering doubts about how he had got there were pushed to one side. Flora was beside herself with pride and did everything she could to help him, predicting that in due course he would become a friend and defender of the common man.

To Ruby's amusement, the Campbells across the street had indeed become the talk of the neighbourhood, not for their amorous adventures these days, but because of their fights, which, as Flora had said, were loud, frequent and had become legendary. It could be annoying too, when Iris sought sanctuary in her old home and found only a reluctant Ruby to regale with her troubles.

'He's driving me mad!' Iris yelled. 'He follows me everywhere, I don't get a minute to myself!'

'Well,' Ruby said smugly, 'who knows better than him what you do when you have a minute to yourself, Iris? And where's your son?'

'Don't bother about him,' Iris said dismissively. 'Somebody will be looking after him.'

'You mean you've dumped him on someone,' Ruby corrected her.

'Listen to you,' Iris sneered, 'Miss High and Bloody Mighty, you think you know it all! It's all right for you, your man's away, you don't have to escape when you can. You're not the one being groped all the time! Every time I turn round he's waiting there to grab me!'

'You never had any problems with that in the past, from what I can remember, Iris. In fact, it was always the more the merrier. Or is that the problem? That you don't like being stuck with one?'

Iris ignored the taunt. 'He paws me all the time,' she shivered. 'Whenever he looks at me he wants to have me. That's all he ever wants.'

'You mean he no longer wants you for your mind?' Ruby chuckled. 'How awful for you, Iris! I suppose he thinks while you're in his bed you're not in some other bloke's, and if he tires you out you won't have the energy to jump into the other bloke's!' Ruby laughed out loud again. 'Not that I care about him, but you can't really blame him, Iris, can you? Being pawed by any number was never a problem in the past, was it? How was he to know you'd put that on ration as well?'

'Oh, shut up! You're a mean wee cow, Ruby McLean, you always were!' Iris sobbed theatrically.

'So why do you keep coming here with your problems?' Ruby laughed at her, tidying up as she spoke, to make sure Iris didn't think she was being taken seriously.

'I suppose I'm looking for Ma.' Iris blew her nose into a handkerchief and lay across the settee for full dramatic effect.

'A bit late in the day for that,' Ruby remarked tersely. 'As I recall, in the months she lay here dying we couldn't exactly set the clock by your visits, could we?'

As Iris dissolved, weeping and sobbing noisily, Ruby tried to work out which film the re-enactment was from. 'I never understood why you took up with him in the first place,' she told her sister.

'I just thought I'd try it, you know?' Iris said bleakly. 'He was always paying me attention.'

'And you never noticed he did that to every female he met? Every female he saw on the far horizon?' Ruby remarked. 'You didn't see the rest of us keeping our distance from him? Christ, Iris, even as a wee lassie I'd walk a mile out of my way to avoid him, I'd crawl under the lino if I could!'

Iris stared at her blankly.

'Oh, come on, Iris!' Ruby said incredulously. 'Are you telling me you thought it was just you?' Ruby looked at her, chuckling. She did, that was the tragedy, she suddenly realised. Everyone in the family had always said Iris was concerned with Iris and Iris alone, and they had been right after all. She didn't see any situation that didn't have her at its centre, she didn't have a thought for anyone else, *genuinely* didn't have a thought. It wasn't only that she didn't care.

'I thought he would look after me well,' Iris said bleakly, 'but he's a tight-fisted big bastard! I know he's got money stashed away, but he won't admit it, and he checks everything I spend in case I've found it.'

'But you never meant to be a true and faithful wife, now did you?' Ruby teased her.

'I thought, him being old, he'd let me have … friends,' Iris admitted in a childish voice.

Ruby laughed out loud. 'So you thought you'd have the best of both worlds, did you – security and freedom? You are an idiot, Iris!'

'But what can I do?' Iris wailed.

'Nothing,' Ruby said with a bright smile.

'Can I come over and stay here?'

'No,' Ruby replied. 'There's no room here for you and Jamie and there's no way it's becoming a battleground for you and your horrible beast of a man either.'

'What about Gerry's place? That's empty,' Iris pleaded.

'No,' Ruby said again.

'That's it?' Iris screeched, standing up. 'That's bloody it? Just no?'

'Well, no thanks then,' Ruby smiled. 'Is that better? You've made your bed, Iris, lie on it.'

Ruby watched from the window as a furious Iris stomped homewards across High Street.

'Hell mend her,' she said under her breath, 'and hell mend him. Hell mend the two of them, they deserve each other.' Then she fell silent for a moment. 'And God help poor wee Jamie,' she added sadly.

Later, as she sat thinking about her conversation with Iris, she felt a bit uncomfortable. So much of what she had said to her sister could be applied to her. Gerry had survived the War and would be home sometime soon. She, too, had made her bed and would have to lie on it.

34

Gerry came home in late 1946 and when she set eyes on him, Ruby was horrified. He wasn't the boy who had gone away more than six years before, he was a man, and a man she didn't like much either. He had been a drinker before he left. In the few short months they had spent together before he was posted overseas she had worried about that, but she had hoped his stint in the army would do him good, make a man of him. The trouble was that she hadn't thought about what kind of man it might make of him. And Gerry, for his part, came home to a much-changed landscape. The McLeans were now a fragmented family, with Sarah, Bea and Jakey gone and Harry much weakened. The dynamic had changed and they operated in a way that had been established while he wasn't there and therefore wasn't a part of. He couldn't figure out where he fitted in and, as he wrestled with the dilemma he turned to booze, his old and only unchanging support.

In the back of his mind he had thought of his sister, Agnes, as his safety net. If all else failed Agnes would be there for him, as she always had been, but she was now fully occupied with her stepsons, three young children and her marriage. He himself was the father of a six-year-old child he didn't know and who didn't know him, and he felt pretty much the same about Ruby. While he was away fighting he had constructed a version of her in his mind that had become more and more removed from the reality he had known back then, so that he hardly recognised her either and, during the years he had been away Ruby had matured. She was no longer a teenager, she was a woman now, and they were like two strangers, yet they were married and had a child; three strangers, come to think of it. He had lived in the company of men for so long that he no longer knew how to relate to women who weren't prostitutes. Like the others, he had encountered many of them along the way, and at least you knew where you stood with them and didn't have to talk to them. And with the fighting over, he had nothing to do. Once he wanted to be a train driver, but now the very thought bored him. Until he could come up with something else he was at a loose end, and when Gerry was at a loose end he could only think as far as that old, unchanging support once again and while he was being consoled by the bottle, he could think of nothing else. Except a little moaning to his drinking companions, of course, about the fact that his wife didn't pay him any attention and rarely spoke to him and the wean wouldn't even look at him. Being of the same mentality as Gerry, they invariably gave him the same advice: he had to put his foot down, he was master of his own home, he had to lay down the law. He had Rights.

Ruby might have made an attempt to stay on at 252 with her father, but Harry insisted that she go back to her marital home with Gerry and Frances. That was her place, he told her, with her man. So she made domestic arrangements for Harry, she would cook and clean for him, do whatever needed doing, but she would now become Mrs Reilly. Bea's clothes had long since been removed and were probably on the backs of Fraus in Berlin as part of the Allied attempt at kindness to the enemy, to make sure Germany didn't fight on after the War. The baby clothes were on top of her wardrobe though, still wrapped in their original brown paper and just visible from the corner of the eye every time you went into the room. Ruby couldn't decide what to do with them, and so they remained there gathering dust, silent reminders of Bea's lost children, like little, faceless ghosts she couldn't look at yet couldn't ignore.

It was a very disrupted and disruptive time for everyone, that's what she told Frances's teacher when she was called for a chat about how her daughter was doing at school. The young teacher sat behind her high desk in the classroom, using it as a shield, Ruby thought, and seemed so on edge and unsure that she felt sorry for her. The teacher was gripping the edge of the desk so hard that her knuckles were white, and she gave every impression of having practised her speech before a mirror.

'There's been an incident, Mrs Reilly,' she said, smiling the kind of smile that Ruby thought could easily turn to tears. 'We had been finding things disappearing in the class.'

'Disappearing?'

'Yes, disappearing. Everything really, books, pencils, chalk, other people's possessions.' Her eyes flicked back and forth across the desk at Ruby, and all Ruby could think was that for some reason the woman was close to running out of the room, screaming in panic.

'Of course, children do these things when they're little, they don't really understand, do they?' Another nervous little laugh. 'But I think we have to regard this as slightly more serious. You see, the missing things were found in a child's bag.'

'Frances's bag?' Ruby gasped, horrified.

'Well, no,' the teacher said quickly, 'but that's not the problem. You see, we discovered that Frances had taken the things, but she had placed them in this other child's bag.'

Ruby stared at her, for a moment she couldn't think of anything to say. 'How do you know she did it?' she asked eventually in a small voice.

'Well, she admitted it, actually. Quite upfront about it, quite expressionless too.'

'Did she tell you why?' Ruby asked. She felt strangely adrift, as though the ground was moving under her once again as her mind scrabbled for grip. 'Did the other child tell her to do it?' She knew this was desperation; no one told Frances what to do.

'Well, that's the awful thing,' the young woman shifted uncomfortably in her chair, now clenching and unclenching her hands in front of her and refusing to make eye contact. 'You see I made all the children turn out their bags and there it all was in this girl's bag, so the child was a proven thief. She's a very shy, vulnerable child. In fact, I had been concerned about their apparent friendship because Frances seemed to totally dominate her. And the child was in a terrible state, crying and so on, the poor wee mite was so upset she even wet herself. Only she wasn't the thief, as it turned out. Someone had seen Frances with the items earlier and when I asked her about it she readily admitted what she had taken them and placed them in the other child's bag. I asked her why and she just shrugged as if she was bored by the whole thing, and stared at me as though it wasn't of any importance, or wasn't any of my business, I'm still not sure which.'

Ruby gulped. Probably all of that, she thought, recognising Frances in the description. She knew that bored look, that shrug, that emotionless stare. 'She's had a very bad time recently,' she said quietly. 'She had the deaths of three close family members, then her father came home and she didn't know him, still doesn't, and we moved from where she had lived all her life so that we could be a family.'

'And she is only six,' the teacher suggested tactfully. 'I do understand that, but I thought you should know in case of trouble from the parents of the other child.'

The young woman looked closer to tears than ever, tears of relief, Ruby imagined. She would have expected any mother to jump to the defence of her child and cause an angry scene, but Ruby did neither, because she couldn't. She knew Frances, though she was uncomfortably aware she didn't know her as well as a mother should know her child. She was used to her, that was better.

'I'm sorry about this,' Ruby murmured. 'I'll have a word with her and make sure nothing like this ever happens again.'

'She'll have told you that I've moved her to different class.'

Ruby didn't reply; Frances hadn't mentioned it.

'That was partly why I wanted to see you, to explain why that had happened. I thought it best to split her up from the other child, just in case.'

As Ruby left she wondered what 'just in case' meant. In case Frances did something else to her? In case the child got some courage and slapped her one?

Back at the house she took Frances aside and quietly told her what the teacher had said.

'Is this true, Frances?' she asked.

Frances nodded, a disinterested look on her face.

'But Frances, wasn't this wee lassie your friend?'

Frances shrugged.

'Did you want the things for yourself, was that it?'

Frances shook her head. 'I did it to see her crying,' she stated.

'What?' Ruby asked, unsure if she had heard her right.

'She cried,' Frances said, returning her mother's shocked look with one of complete indifference. She shrugged again. 'She cried and wet herself. She's just a baby.'

'But she cried because you had made her look like a thief, Frances,' Ruby said angrily. 'You did that, you stole the things and made it look like she had done it. Don't you see what you did was wrong?'

Frances smiled slightly. 'It was a joke,' she said simply, then turned and walked back to her bedroom.

'Frances, get back here!' she shouted, and Frances dutifully returned and stood before her, staring at her blankly. That was her usual expression, she thought, looking at her daughter, no expression. 'Every day for the next two weeks you will come straight back from school and you will stay in, you will not go out to play. What you did was wrong and this is your punishment, do you understand?'

Frances nodded.

'And when you go to school tomorrow you will tell the wee lassie it was a joke, it was a very bad joke and you're sorry.'

'Oh,' Frances said almost wearily, 'the teacher already made me say sorry to her,' and with that she turned and walked off again. As Ruby watched her go a chill ran through her.

Everywhere she turned there was some worry or other, so she was relieved that marital relations weren't resumed when Gerry came home. He was no more capable of it than he had been before he went away, less so, she thought. Until the night he came home, the booze laced with advice from his drinking companions and demanded his 'rights', though there were few actual words spoken, or slurred. He simply took her as he would the prostitutes he had become used to, as though she was his possession, bought and paid for, before rolling off her, already snoring. Ruby lay in the darkness, curled up in a ball of shock and hurt, and wept as she had in this very bed with this same man, on her wedding night; it was hard to see what, if anything, had changed. In the morning, or the afternoon for Gerry, nothing was said by either of them, and the scenario was repeated several times in the weeks to come. It was no better than farmyard rape, she thought dismally, no better than Gus Campbell. It was almost a relief when she discovered she was pregnant again, not that she wanted the second child any more than she had wanted the first, but maybe now he would leave her alone. The idea of becoming a nurse had faded as soon as he came home, but now she knew she could wave goodbye to it forever. And Gerry's demands didn't stop either, he didn't even seem to notice her growing belly, and he was just as rough, so that she always had bruises that she kept hidden, somehow feeling it must be her fault. When Dr McGill noticed them during a check-up, he was worried that she might have a blood disorder until she explained that they were Gerry's handiwork.

'You mean he hits you, Ruby?' he asked gently.

Ruby put her head down. 'Not exactly,' she whispered, 'he just wants what he wants when he wants it.' She looked up at him, her eyes begging him to understand. 'And how he wants it.'

'So you're still having relations even though you're six months gone?' he asked.

Ruby laughed harshly. 'I wouldn't call it relations,' she cried, 'he has them, I have no say!'

'And do you tell him this?'

'He doesn't ask my permission, Dr McGill. He doesn't say anything and it wouldn't make any difference if I refused him.'

'Is he still drinking as heavily?' he prodded.

Ruby looked up at him sharply.

'Come now, Ruby,' he smiled sadly, 'you know you can't hide anything in High Street. People notice, and I've seen him often enough myself.'

'Aye, he's still drinking,' she whispered, 'and it's worse than before he went away. I know there's nothing I can say or do to stop him. That's when he does hit me, when I try to get him to stop and go back to his work.'

'So he's not working either?'

Ruby shook her head. 'Not regularly, and he just drinks what he earns.'

'So how are you surviving, you and Frances?'

'His sister, Agnes, she's been helping us out, she knows what he's like.'

284

'What about George?'

Ruby looked at him with widened eyes. 'George?' she said, alarmed. 'George doesn't know. If he knew he'd kill him! You won't tell George, Dr McGill? Promise you won't tell George!'

'Calm down, Ruby,' he soothed her, stroking her hand. 'I'll talk to Gerry though. He'll have to listen to me.'

That night Gerry came crawling up the stairs and she heard him trying to get in, but she had locked the door. It was something she did often these days, and he would usually go somewhere to sleep it off. This time was different, this time his manhood had been called into question by Dr McGill's little lecture in the College Bar earlier. Gerry had drunk himself beyond his usual stupor and, egged on by his friends, was in fighting, if unsteady trim, so when Ruby didn't open the door he simply kept knocking on it and yelling obscenities. Getting out of bed she unlocked the door, fearful that Tam McVicar would arrive soon, the last thing she needed was for Gerry to be dragged off in a Black Mariah to jail.

There were different strands to what happened next, and for the rest of her life she couldn't separate them. She had grabbed his arm as he stood on the landing to pull him indoors and Gerry had taken exception to that. Even though he was weaving and staggering about, like all drunks he was of the opinion that he was perfectly sober and could walk alone. He pulled his arm back from her grasp, but in doing so he overbalanced and was about to fall backwards down the stairs. Ruby went forward to catch him as he struggled to regain control by throwing an arm forward and his fist hit her square in the face. 'You bitch!' he yelled, in his mindless, drunken rage. When it happened, she couldn't decide whether the blow was an accident or deliberate. For a moment she saw stars, little black ones, she remembered later, edged in white. She shook her head clear and lunged forward again to hold onto him, but he grabbed her and they fell down the stairs together, with Ruby on the bottom and Gerry on top. And even as she was falling she was absolutely aware that he had grabbed her and deliberately thrown her and had simply followed her down by virtue of the momentum between them. There was no indecision about it, before she even landed with a sickening crunch she knew he had thrown her down the stairs as she was trying to save him. Then, as she lay underneath his dead weight, there was pain everywhere, pain that robbed her of breath to call out for help and then of consciousness.

She awoke in Rottenrow, the maternity hospital further along from the Barony Church. A nurse was sitting by her bedside, talking to her in the gentlest, calmest way as she came to. She was in hospital, she was safe and she wasn't to move.

'Frances?' she asked groggily.

'Is that your little girl?'

Ruby nodded, trying to keep her eyes open.

'She's with a neighbour, she's fine. Now you just rest, everything's under control. Dr McGill will come by shortly and he'll explain everything. Don't do any more talking, just rest.'

Ruby smiled weakly and drifted off again. She was safe, Frances was safe, everything was under control. 'Gerry,' she thought, 'I didn't ask about Gerry.'

The next time she opened her eyes Donald McGill had replaced the nurse with the gentle voice. He smiled at her as he reached for the screens and closed them around her bed.

'How are you feeling?' he asked.

'I don't know,' she replied, trying to laugh.

'Ruby, it's not good news I'm afraid. The baby, we couldn't save him.'

Ruby stared at him.

'The cord had come away in the fall, you see, he would've gone very quickly. One of the neighbours heard the commotion and found you, she sent someone for Tam McVicar and he got an ambulance and the hospital called me at home.'

Ruby still didn't reply. She was safe, the child she hadn't wanted was no more, yet she felt a scream reverberating deep inside her soul that she couldn't release, a scream of grief and loss so intense it made her grit her teeth.

'Do you know what's happening to Frances?' she asked quietly. 'She's not with Iris, is she?'

'No,' he grinned slightly. 'Flora took her to Agnes in Duke Street.

She'll still be able to go school from there, she'll be fine. But Gerry's outside. Do you want to see him?'

Ruby nodded blindly. She wasn't making a choice, he could've offered to bring Dracula to her bedside and she would've nodded.

Donald McGill hesitated. 'Ruby, you don't have to see him,' he said. 'In fact, I don't think you should. I have a fair idea what happened out there on that landing.'

'I fell, Donald,' she said drowsily.

'Well, you can say that if you like, but—'

'I'm sorry,' she said.

'What?' he looked puzzled. 'What are you sorry about? You didn't cause any of this!'

'I called you Donald,' she said sleepily.

'That's my name.'

'No it's not, you're Doctor McGill.'

'Dr McGill was my father, Ruby,' he said, laughing gently. 'When there's no one around Donald will do just fine.'

'Bring him in,' she sighed.

Donald McGill came back leading Gerry and hovered slightly to make sure nothing was going to happen, nothing angry or violent at any rate, before leaving them alone. Gerry sat down. She couldn't look him in the eye but noticed his hands were shaking, whether from nerves, fear or lack of booze, she couldn't tell and found she didn't really care.

'I hear it was a boy,' he said, finally. 'Just my luck to lose a boy.'

Ruby clenched her teeth and closed her eyes; she couldn't believe what he had said. It was as though losing a daughter wouldn't have mattered as much and, furthermore, he was the one who had suffered, he was the victim. Ruby didn't reply but opened her eyes and stared at the ceiling, trying not to think.

'You'll be telling them it was my fault, well I'm not taking the blame for this!' Gerry whined desperately. 'It was you that tried to push to me, so it was! I was trying to get away from you!'

Ruby turned her head, met his eyes and stared at him for a long time. Everything died in that instant. At that moment she couldn't remember if she had ever felt anything for him, but whatever feelings she might once have had for him or about him simply evaporated and were replaced with contempt. He was screeching on as she stared at him, though she had no idea what he was saying, all she could think of was that this was the end. Her mind was absolutely clear and calm. Her mother had made her promise that if it didn't work out with Gerry she must get away from him and in that instant, as she made the mental and emotional journey necessary, all she felt was total peace.

'Get out,' she said quietly, raising her hand in Sarah's gesture to silence the noises coming from his mouth. 'Just get out. I never want to set eyes on you for as long as either of us lives. Is that clear?' She turned her head away from him and closed her eyes. 'Just go away Gerry,' she told him firmly, 'and don't come back again.'

35

When she got out of hospital Ruby took Frances to live with Harry again at 252. 'We're like a pair of shuttlecocks,' she remarked, to her father, but this time she knew they would never return to Gerry's house. Harry, being Harry, asked no questions, accepting the simplified explanation he was given. She had lost the baby when she tried to stop a drunken Gerry falling downstairs. He was drinking all the time and Ruby had decided living with him wasn't good for her and Frances. Harry hadn't been able to avoid the situation at work, though, with Gerry hardly ever turning up and, when he did, being too drunk to be allowed near the engines, ending with his sacking, so Ruby's decision didn't come as a surprise to him.

Even so, the talk among the High Street worthies wasn't universally in Ruby's favour. Some felt sympathy for Gerry, abandoned by his wife after giving his all for his country throughout the War, whereas others, those with experience of hard drinkers mainly, and people who didn't look back at the pre-war Gerry through rose-tinted memory, thought a little deeper and suspected that Ruby's brief married life hadn't been full of bliss and happiness. But women did not leave their husbands no matter how bad things had become; a woman walking out on a marriage became tinged with a stigma, it was something to be ashamed of, and the fact that Ruby wasn't did her no favours.

At the time, she only told Flora what had really happened that night, that Gerry had deliberately thrown her downstairs. It was no one's business but hers, she decided, and it was over and done with, appropriate steps had been taken to ensure he could never hurt her or Frances again. Whether it was a mad action, taken when he was too drunk to know what he was doing, did not matter, and neither was she even curious to know if he could truly remember the incident. The simple fact was that it was in the past and she and Frances were free of him forever. In truth, it was his reaction that finally killed the marriage and implanted in her mind were words she would never be able to forget. 'Just my luck to lose a boy,' he had whined, and 'I'm not taking the blame for this!' It was in that instant she knew that somewhere he recognised what he had done and wasn't man enough to admit it. She never did tell George what had happened, because she knew George would lose his temper and cause Gerry serious harm, and that would do no one any good, particularly George. And there was Frances to consider. Some instinct told her that Frances didn't deserve to know what her father had done. She didn't even tell Agnes when she came to visit. Ruby steeled herself, expecting to be castigated for leaving Gerry, or for some plea to be made in his defence, but Agnes came full of remorse.

'I feel it's my fault,' Agnes wept quietly. 'The drinking, he took to it like a fish to water.'

'I didn't know he drank,' Ruby said simply.

'I should've told you, I know that now, but I thought it was just a thing boys did,' Agnes said hopelessly. 'I thought he would grow out of it, especially when he got married and became a father.'

'Well he didn't quite do it in that order, Agnes, as you know,' Ruby sighed. 'He was too young to be married with a wean of his own, he was still a wean himself.'

'So were you,' Agnes reminded her, 'but I don't remember you behaving like that, Ruby, you just got stuck in and dealt with things.'

'Aye, I suppose that's true, but women and men are different, aren't they?'

'Was it always like that, from the start?' Agnes asked fearfully.

'From the first time I saw him the NewYear before we got married,' Ruby smiled sadly. 'I didn't realise it at the time either, I mean, everybody's a bit tipsy at the Bells, aren't they? It was only when I looked back that I saw it was how he was all the time. On our wedding night he was carried back unconscious and put to bed in the early hours. He lay there throwing up and snoring for the rest

290

of the night. He said all men drank, he was just proving he was a man.'

'I'm so sorry, Ruby!'

'Och, well, how were you to know?' Ruby said sympathetically. 'I thought the army might do him some good, but he came back an even worse drunk and he was harder, thought nothing of using his fists. But don't you tell anybody that, mind. I don't want Frances to hear it in the school playground from some wean who's heard it from her Ma or Da. It's not Frances's fault.'

'I'll look after him from now, Ruby,' Agnes said kindly. 'There's no reason why you should do it.'

Ruby glanced away without replying. It hadn't occurred to her that she should continue to look after Gerry, or that anyone would expect it of her.

'I'll make sure he has clean clothes and I'll pop in to tidy up for him.'

Ruby nodded. 'That's good of you Agnes,' she said quietly, 'especially as you've your own family to look after. I don't think you have to look after him and I doubt he'll even notice.'

'Well he's my brother,' Agnes replied, 'and you can see it as my penance for what I saddled you with.'

Ruby laughed gently, shaking her head. 'You Catholics,' she teased her, 'it's all about guilt and penance, isn't it?'

'Only with some of us, Ruby,' Agnes replied, squeezing her hand. 'Only with some of us, sadly.'

For Ruby the collapse of her marriage was no more than a regret over a mistake and a sorrow for what might have been, but the loss of her son took a long time to get over. She couldn't decide if her reaction was partly caused by her own guilt, as well as grief. She hadn't wanted the child; its conception, after all, had further complicated her already difficult life. As the months of her pregnancy had passed though, the little squirming, jumping creature developing inside her had become as much part of her emotionally as well as physically, he had grown on her as well as in her. His loss affected her in ways the events of the previous years had not; it brought her lower and left her bereft of sense. Every time she dressed or undressed she noticed her flat stomach anew and felt his loss keenly. Had she been able to bury him, she thought, she might have gained some solace in the time-honoured rites. There would have been somewhere to mourn, a grave to visit, somewhere to lay a few flowers, but he had simply been spirited away she knew not where, so it was as though he had simply vanished into thin air.

While the wound was still raw she had an overwhelming urge to find him, illogical though she knew it was, and she took to walking past Rottenrow, the place of her last connection with him, as though he might be waiting there for her. And suddenly the world was full of expectant mothers and babies, everywhere she looked felt like being mocked by Fate. Before she knew the sex of the baby she was carrying, she had intended calling a daughter Sarah after her mother, and a son John, after Uncle Jakey. As she brooded in the months after losing the child, she revisited dark fears of primeval curses once again. Had she cursed the child with bad luck by giving him a name that had done no particular good to Jakey?

In time though, she moved on from the low stages of grief, though it never did go away. In those early months after the death of her boy, whenever she encountered a child called John she entered some peculiar fantasy world and looked at him with more than passing interest, wondering, if the truth be told, if he could be her John, if someone else had him and, even as the years passed, all boys called John still reminded her of the one she had lost. Everyone told her that time was a great healer, but she already knew that was no more than a platitude. The experience of losing three family members in such a short time had already taught her that time only enabled you to cover your loss better, and losing the child underlined the lesson that the healing would only ever be skin-deep.

The last stage in her recovery was to take Bea's baby clothes to Rottenrow and ask for them to be given to some mother who didn't have a lot. The NHS was a fledgling creation in 1948, a huge step forward for the poor particularly, who no longer had to worry about affording treatment for their sick children, but the country was still in dire straits after years of war. There were countless poor mothers with too many children to feed and clothe, so someone, she reasoned, would be glad of Bea's handiwork. Not that she had intended her

John wearing them, she hadn't kept them for that, but somehow she felt the gesture of removing the sad collection of tiny garments from the family would exorcise the last remnants of that primeval darkness.

36

If there was one thing that occupied the minds of the population at large more than any other, and Cissie and Dot especially, it was the continued rationing after the War. They were incensed that it not only went on, but got worse. Naturally, being deprived of sweets almost caused them to combust.

'Who won the bloody War? That's what I want to know!' Cissie exploded. They were sitting in 'their' chairs by the range in 252's living room.

'If you ever find out, Cissie,' Dot agreed, 'just make sure you tell me! They're living it up in Berlin and they started the War, and us, the ones that won it, are still doing without! Berlin Airlift is it? Berlin Airlift? Just don't get me started!'

What had caused their ire was that in 1946, the year after the end of the War, bread had been rationed, and in 1947 the meat ration had been reduced still further. It assuaged their rage not a whit that bread came off the ration list in 1948. As far as they were concerned it should never have been applied in the first place. But the biggest insult, the hugest injustice, was that sweets and chocolate were taken off ration in 1949, only for the nation to go so sweet mad that rationing was hurriedly re-imposed. They had grudgingly grown used to everything else being rationed, but having their sweets taken away once again was just too much.

'I hardly had time to get a bonbon in my mouth before old McLellan was dragging it out again!' Dot complained.

'I'll bet you anything they Germans have got as much as their jaws can chew on, though!' said an incensed Cissie.

'And it's our stuff they're chewing, Cissie, they're taking it out of our mouths and putting it in the mouths of the enemy, so they are! You'd think that Atlee would've done something for us. I mean, he's Labour, for God's sake! What's the good of voting old Churchill and his Tories out if Labour just takes your sweeties away as well?'

'It fair gets my goat!' Cissie exploded again. 'I said all along, didn't I say all along, Dot, that they should've killed that Hitler right at the start?'

'You did indeed, Cissie, you even offered to go over there and give him a damned good shooting yourself! But did anybody listen? No, they did not!'

'And now they're eating our sweeties!' Cissie threw her arms skywards. 'Can somebody just explain this to me?'

'And you can't make a cup of tea the gas is so low!' Dot complained. 'By the time the water's heated the notion's gone off you. And what about sausages? When did you last see a sausage, tell me that!'

'Exactly!' Cissie agreed vehemently. 'And tell me what beating the Germans had to do with cheating decent people out of a sausage? Why are we being done out of a sausage, for God's sake? I thought we fired bullets at them, not sausages!'

'A sausage!' Dot repeated helplessly. 'We won the bloody War and we can't get a sweetie or a sausage!'

They tended to do this, Ruby knew that, when they got stuck on a word very little could shift them, but even so, she thought if they said 'sausage' again she might scream. She watched Cissie looking Dot up and down in the chair beside her.

'Though as everybody knows,' she said with quiet disdain, 'you've scoffed more than your share of sausages in your time, Dot, so you could probably do with laying off them for a while.'

And Cissie and Dot weren't alone in their objections, complaints that the victors in a war that Germany started were doing without while Germany was fed, persisted for years. Rationing would last, in one form or another till June 1954, with clothes coming off the list in 1949, tea in 1952, sweets, eggs and sugar in 1953 and, finally, butter, cheese, marge, cooking fat, meat and bacon the following year. To those born after 1939 it mattered very little, it was all they knew, but to Cissie and Dot's generation it mattered a great deal and always would.

In Ruby's mind the idea of becoming a nurse began to resurface. Harry was supporting her and Frances, but she knew she would have to earn a living for both of them. Harry had reached and, because of the War, passed the age when train drivers took on lighter duties. It took many years to reach the footplate of an engine without shovelling coal, but considerably fewer to be relegated to a minor role, and when he reached sixty-five Harry had to retire completely. She was glad about that, even if Harry wasn't; he was tired and having bouts of irritation that had never been part of his character before, it was time he got some rest.

By then Ruby had applied for a job at the Royal Infirmary as a ward maid. It was no more than skivvy work, keeping the ward clean, washing and scrubbing every surface, but it brought her into contact with patients and that's what she wanted. Her father would be there when Frances came home from school and soon after that Ruby's shift would be over; it suited everyone. Gerry continued to live a few closes up so there was no way she could avoid seeing him, but in a curious way that didn't bother her, he was just someone from the past who no longer played any part in her life. He didn't seek to see Frances, he could see no further than the next drink and, when Ruby did happen upon him he was either collapsed in the street or too drunk to recognise her. The fact that Gerry's situation was worsening naturally caused whispers within the community of High Street though. It was because his wife had abandoned him, some said, he had now given up all hope, as though Gerry was some jilted swain dying of a broken heart. That she wasn't there to make sure he was kept clean and occasionally fed was undoubtedly a factor in his decline, even though his sister did her best Gerry was dying from the slow suicide of alcoholic addiction. There was nothing anyone could do about that but Gerry, and Gerry didn't want to, with or without his wife. Even so, there were those who went beyond whispered criticism, and Ruby opened the door one evening to find the priest from St Mungo's on the doorstep. There was a determined smile fixed on his face, but the over all impression was that seconds before he had been sucking a lemon.

'I don't know if you remember me, Mrs Reilly,' he said smoothly, in a tone that suggested no one could possibly have forgotten him.

'I'm Father O'Hanlon, I conducted your marriage and the christening of your daughter.'

Ruby nodded. She wouldn't have known him from Adam. In fact, she mused silently, she would have accepted his word if he told her he *was* Adam.

'I saw your husband a short time ago,' he announced, striding past her and into the house without invitation. 'I found him asleep in a pew in my chapel. He was in a terrible state. He had,' his face screwed up so much she wondered if it might disappear altogether and she would be left looking at a pair of ears. 'He had,' he repeated dramatically, 'soiled himself.'

Ruby didn't reply. It was, after all, nothing to do with her, so there was nothing to say.

He had obviously been expecting some reaction and, when it didn't come, he glared at her. 'I have been asking around and I've discovered he is frequently in this condition and that you take no interest.'

Ruby didn't contradict him.

'Well?' the priest demanded, in a towering voice she suspected he practised regularly for maximum effect.

'Oh, sorry!' Ruby laughed quietly. 'You got it all so spot-on there I didn't realise you were expecting me to say anything!'

'You are his wife, you have a duty to care for him, do you not?' the priest bellowed.

'Well, you see, that's where we differ. I don't think I do,' Ruby said reasonably. 'I left Mr Reilly some time ago and when I can afford it, I'll divorce him.'

His eyes widened like a character in a silent film. 'Rome doesn't recognise divorce,' Fr O'Hanlon replied dismissively.

'Well, that's Rome's problem,' Ruby smiled, 'not mine.'

'Marriage,' he intoned, striding about the living room, 'is indissoluble, and no decent woman would contemplate divorce.' He said the word as though it equated with cannibalism.

'And what would you know about marriage?' Ruby asked amiably. 'You certainly know nothing about mine, such as it was.'

'I know you are not of the Faith,' he said, deliberately adopting a more civil tone, 'but you did marry in a Catholic church and you agreed to your child being raised and educated as a Catholic. I notice that is not happening either and I'd like to find a way to facilitate it, however belatedly.'

'I married in St Mungo's for Gerry and you're right, I did agree to Frances going to the Catholic school as part of that deal,' Ruby replied.

He smiled broadly.

'But I thought better of it. The deal wasn't fair. I had no idea what I was doing at the time. And besides, with there being no marriage the deal's off too, that's how I look at it.'

He returned to glaring mode. 'But you can't do that!' he cried, throwing his arms skywards, his black cassock flying around him like dark, threatening wings, pretty much the effect he was aiming for, she thought.

'I've done it,' Ruby said simply. 'Now, it you'll excuse me, I have things to be getting on with.' She rose to shepherd him to the front door.

'You should be feeling black burning shame over your behaviour!' he protested.

'Och, don't worry about me,' she said cheerfully, 'I feel fine, so I do.'

'And you still refuse to return to your husband, to give him the comfort and care he needs?'

'That's right,' she smiled. 'He's one of yours, if you think he needs comfort and care, you can always give it to him.'

He was stung, she could see that. He had been accorded neither the respect nor the guilt he had every right to expect from this hard young woman, and now she was firmly seeing him off the premises. Just as the door was being closed behind him he pushed against it to come within inches of her face.

'And don't think I didn't know all along that it was that mad Protestant uncle of yours who did all those things, all those sacrilegious things to my church!' he said angrily.

Ruby laughed and re-opened the door a crack. 'I have no idea what you mean,' she lied.

'He stole my candles and he turned my statues back to front!' he said accusingly. 'I know it was him!'

'Tut-tut,' Ruby said quietly. 'I'm sure you're wrong, sounds just like childish pranks to me.' She pushed the door firmly against him again.

'And don't think,' he yelled, his foot stopping her from shutting him out, 'that I didn't know it was him in those Arab robes either!'

Ruby opened the door yet again. 'What?' she asked.

'He came into my church dressed as an Arab and waving a sword in the air during mass one morning,' he shouted, eyes bulging, 'and he threw some lit fireworks in the aisle and shouted "That'll brighten up your sermon, Allah be praised!" and left. People could've died!'

'What?' Ruby asked. 'From a few bangers?'

'From shock!' he screeched.

'Och, you're exaggerating, surely?' she said calmly. 'Besides, you were right there to give them the Last Rites, weren't you? Sure, they'd all go straight to Heaven anyway, so where was the harm?'

'But I was in shock too!' he replied childishly. 'Who would've given *me* the Last Rites?'

'Well you've got a point there, granted, but I'm sure it had nothing to do with my late uncle,' Ruby smiled sweetly. 'In fact, I think it's awful of you to lay the blame on a gentle wee man who isn't here to defend himself. Besides, my uncle wasn't an Arab. I'm sure I'd have noticed if he was. You should know better than to listen to gossip, in fact, now that I think about it, you're the one who should be feeling black burning shame. Goodnight, now.'

'It was him!' the priest roared. 'He had that dog with him! Everybody knew it was him!'

'Sure,' Ruby replied thoughtfully, 'there's many a man goes around with a dog at his heels. Just look around you, they're all over the place.'

'Not like that one!' the priest screeched. 'No one had a dog like that one!'

'That's true,' Ruby thought, 'can't argue with him there!', shutting the door behind the rabid priest and bolting it as well for good measure. 'Mind how you go now, Father,' she called from behind the door. 'I wouldn't want you to miss your footing and fall and break your neck or anything!' Then she went into the sitting room and laughed till she cried at the mental picture of the Sheik of High Street and Wee Dug visiting St Mungo's with fireworks.

That New Year the old festivities were beginning to be re-established, a kind of enthusiasm was making a comeback. There had been attempts at being festive in the first year after the end of the War, but they were half-hearted. The country was run down, there was no money and, even though they had won the War and had celebrated at the time, nothing seemed to have changed for the better. People were disheartened when it came to New Year, there seemed precious little to celebrate. The lives they had led pre-war had gone for good, as far as ordinary folk were concerned, and families thought back on relatives who had started out with them on those long, hard years after 1939 and were no longer with them. New Year was always a time of joy in Scotland, but it was also a time of sadness, when absent friends were more acutely missed than at any other time. By 1950 the mood was beginning to lift, as the effects of war began to be determinedly put behind them, as people tried to recapture a mood that couldn't, in reality, be recaptured. It had gone because it had run its course, it was no longer part of normal life, but they wished it was and still wanted it be, it was a reminder of happier times that had been taken from them by the War.

George McLean had abandoned New Year entirely. From now on he would celebrate Christmas with his children, but there would be no more first foots from him. Ruby, too, dreaded it, as she would for the rest of her life, but she carried on with the traditional arrangements in honour of her mother. The McLean home had always been full of people at pre-war Ne'er Days, and her mother had adhered strictly to the old customs, but as she repeated each one Ruby was so acutely aware of Sarah's loss that she did little more than skim over them. Somehow it no longer seemed so important to have the house sparkling, the range gleaming and every item of laundry washed and put away. What was the point, what did it really matter? There would be no Sarah to sit smiling with quiet pride as guests arrived to eat and drink the spread she had prepared. There would be no Bea to finish off the night with her usual screaming and yelling

300

performance, that custom, too, was lost forever. Still, she made sandwiches and cut up the various cakes that had been made earlier by Dot and Cissie because, as she readily admitted, she was no good at baking or cooking. The two aunties were seeing in the New Year in their own homes, as was the tradition, but had handed over the New Year bounty earlier on Hogmanay. Sugar, butter and eggs were still rationed, but they had 'come by' a bit extra, they announced with many a chuckle and wink, to produce shortbread, cherry cake, Madeira cake and, the one nobody actually liked but still had to have there, black bun. Black bun was the one you took to first foot other people just to get rid of it.

The sounds of the McCreadies singing 'The Internationale' into the freezing air and mixing with the calling of the women was so poignant in a world changed out of all recognition that they felt like stilettos to Ruby's heart. Still, she went through with Sarah's arrangements, then awaited the arrival of whoever felt like coming, all the while wishing she could just go to bed and ignore the whole thing. That, she decided, was the aim she would keep in mind throughout: she would have to go through with the charade, but it would soon be over and she could retreat to her own bed and pull the covers over her head.

There was no way of refusing to allow Iris and Gus Campbell into the house, so she had already decided to wish her sister a cool 'Happy New Year' without touching her and while studiously ignoring him. They arrived with a very sleepy Jamie who had been woken so that his parents could celebrate, and he was put in the bedroom beside Frances. Then it happened, a glorious thing happened, as far as Ruby was concerned anyway.

It started well enough, as these things always had with Bea in days of old, lots of smiling and exchanging of happy chatter. As usual, as the night wore on, conversations would become incomprehensible, as people shared deep and meaningful musings they wouldn't recall when sober. As the alcohol took hold, though, all bonhomie between the Campbells began to dissolve. The first sign was when Gus tried to stop a tipsy Iris having another drink and she pushed him in the stomach with considerable force, sending him flying across the room to land on his backside. By the way Iris didn't watch his flight and showed no concern when he fell, Ruby surmised it wasn't the first time this had happened. Ruby didn't drink, Sarah had always regarded women who drank alcohol as slightly risqué and, when she tried it, Ruby had found it disgusting. The festivities, though, suddenly promised amusement and she perked up, even without alcohol to give her good cheer. She looked around and saw that Harry had disappeared when Iris had thumped her husband, which gave her full rein to enjoy the Campbells' entertainment.

After disposing of Gus, Iris weaved across the room and engaged a young man in conversation, eyelashes fluttering as much as they could, given that she had very little coordination, and Ruby wondered how many young men she could see. Gus, who hadn't retaliated earlier when she sent him sprawling, picked himself up and went across to where his wife was smiling as coquettishly as she was able at the young man. He grabbed her by the arm and dragged her with some force to the other side of the room and, once again, this looked like treatment Iris was used to, as, without missing a beat, she pulled her arm back and clouted Gus across the ear with the glass she was holding. The tinkle of breaking glass could be heard above the noise of the guests, and blood streamed down the side of Gus's face. Ruby watched delightedly, knowing she should be feeling guilty because this was happening in her mother's house. Sarah, she knew, would have been affronted if she had witnessed this display, but she couldn't stifle a merry chuckle all the same. It was like a ballet, every move was perfectly choreographed and the dancers were hitting their marks with beautiful, if slightly swaying accuracy. Gus wiped the blood from his face and tried again to grab Iris, who was tottering about unsteadily, trying to evade his grasp. Ruby smiled, that couldn't be a new experience for him where women in general were concerned. She looked around the room and sensed conversations becoming more muted, as attentions turned to the battling Campbells. At first the tableau of Iris and Gus had been moving through them, now it was centre stage. Just as it looked as though Iris's attempts to evade her husband were causing her to lose her balance, Gus caught up with her again and she used his grip on her arm as a support for her next assault, by leaning back and delivering a truly inch-perfect kick to his crotch. He went down like a building collapsing and lay on the floor red-faced and panting. Even so, he desperately struggled to hold onto Iris, as she pulled away and departed in search of fresh meat, throwing an arm around some man and sitting on his knee.

'You whore!' Gus Campbell yelled at her, still writhing in agony on the floor.

'Och, shut up, you dirty old man!' Iris said in a deep, dark voice. 'That might stop you looking for your jollies for a while!'

The unfortunate man on whose knee Iris was somewhat unsteadily perched, was trying to look as though she wasn't there. He had his arms crossed and was looking around the room with a desperate grin on his lips, but despite this, Iris was staring into his face with a lecherous smile and trying to engage him in a very one-sided conversation, following him as he tried to put his face anywhere she wasn't. She was talking in a girlish trill, a tone of voice completely at odds with the one she had just used when addressing her husband, the 'dirty old man.' Ruby watched, fascinated, as Gus crawled across the floor on all fours and grabbed Iris's ankle, a bad move, she thought instinctively, as Iris, without looking in his direction, kicked out with the other foot and connected with his eye. He held on though, dragging her to the floor with him, where they continued to trade blows and yell insults, as the unwilling object of Iris's amorous attentions beat a hasty retreat out the front door. 'Who needs Bea?' Ruby thought, watching the floorshow, as the Campbells continued to roll around violently, completely unaware and uncaring of the effect their battle was having on the audience. The fight reached a certain peak that seemed to bring the others to their senses and hands took hold of the couple and pulled them apart. Iris's carefully arranged hair was now in disarray, with tresses hanging about her make-up smeared face. She had lost a shoe and half of the blouse she had been wearing, but seemed completely oblivious to both. Gus's shirt had been pulled out of his trousers and the buttons ripped off, so that his tie hung on the vest on his chest, which was covered in streaks of blood and Max Faxtor pan stick, scarlet lipstick and mascara. As the hostess, Ruby felt she had to do something, though she could have watched the show for an hour more at least.

'I think you should go,' she told them.

'Don't worry, I'm going,' Gus said bitterly.

'Well I'm staying here. I'm not going with him!' Iris spat at him.

'You're coming with me, lady!' Gus said menacingly. 'You think I'm leaving you here so that you can take off with somebody else?'

'And you think you can stop me?' Iris demanded, squaring up to him again. 'I've had plenty since I married you,' she told him, 'and I'll tell you something, even the worst were better than you!'

Gus tried to reach her again, his face red with rage, but Iris, for all her unsteady state, neatly pulled her head back so that Gus fist swung uselessly in mid-air.

'See what I mean?' Iris sneered. 'Couldn't connect there either! You might have the equipment, buster, but you've no idea how to use it! Does that remind you of anything?'

They could still be heard shrieking at each other all the way to the street below, and Ruby watched from the window as they swayed across to their own home, still trading punches and insults as they finally made it to their own close. Neither one of them had given a thought to their son, asleep in the bedroom beside Frances, which was just as well, she thought. If they had tried to take the little boy home with them she would have stopped them. Andy Morris's mother, who lived in the flat above Iris and Gus, came up behind her and looked out on the scene with her.

'I wouldn't worry about it, Ruby, hen,' she said sympathetically. 'It happens all the time.'

'Really, Mrs Morris?' Ruby asked.

'Oh, aye, every time they have a drink there's a rammy just like that and they have a drink pretty often. This the first time you've seen it?'

Ruby nodded.

'Well, you'd better get used to it, that's all I can say, because it won't be the last.' Mrs Morris shrugged. 'You learn to live with it,' she said resignedly, 'but I bet old Cissie and Dot will be disappointed that they missed it!'

304

'I know!' Ruby laughed. 'And they made all the cakes! Still, as you say, there will be other times.'

'I was just saying to somebody there while it was going on, mind the times with Bea? I don't think even she could top those two.'

'But what about the wee boy?' Ruby asked.

'Aye, well, hen,' she sighed, 'that's the thing, isn't it? Somebody usually gets the wee boy away while it's going on, neither one of them even notices. But it's not right, is it? I'll tell you this. I was that glad when she ditched my Andy, but I'm even gladder now.' She looked at Ruby. 'Sorry, hen, no offence. I sometimes forget that she's your sister.'

Ruby patted shoulder. 'None taken, Mrs Morris,' she smiled. 'You've actually paid me a compliment there! And you've said nothing compared to what I say about her! So where is your Andy?'

'Out with pals, that's all I know,' Mrs Morris grinned. 'I'm sure he's got a lassie but he's keeping it to himself, fly bugger! It's just good to see him getting on though, to see him happy again.'

37

When Ruby had been working at the Royal for a year she plucked up the courage to find out about becoming a nurse, a *real* nurse, not just a skivvy. There would never be any money from Gerry, that was clear, not that she had ever asked, she accepted that supporting Frances would be her responsibility. So she made an appointment with the hospital matron and had her arguments marshalled. She had nursed her mother through her last illness, she had been working on the ward and had enjoyed it, but she wanted a career and had decided she could make a good nurse, an opinion shared by the ward sister.

Matron's brief, dismissive glance as Ruby entered should have warned her, or so she thought afterwards, at the time she was too caught up in her own sense of purpose to do more than register it. There was no invitation to sit down, but she did so anyway, and the silence was allowed to stretch, to show Ruby that Matron was in charge and was a busy woman with little time to spare. Ruby waited patiently as Matron studied the papers on the desk in front of her, before clasping her hands on top of them and giving Ruby her slightly impatient attention.

'You asked to see me?' she asked.

'I'd like to train as a nurse,' Ruby smiled.

Matron stared at her as though she had spoken in some obscure, unintelligible language.

'I'm working as a ward maid at the moment,' Ruby explained and was then cut short.

'And why do you think you can step up to becoming a nurse?' Matron asked, giving every impression of being amazed and shocked.

'I'm good with sick people,' Ruby said, 'the ward sister has said that, and—'

She stopped, aware that Matron was looking down her nose at her but unsure why.

'That doesn't mean,' Matron enunciated clearly, 'that you have what it takes to enter the nursing profession. For instance, what educational qualifications do you have?'

Ruby was thrown and made no reply. She had none.

Matron stared at her, a small, insincere smile of commiseration across her tight lips. 'You see, we don't just let anyone into our courses. The Royal Infirmary is a prestigious medical institution and we have very high standards. We only take a particular kind of girl, a very special sort of young lady.'

Ruby felt the colour rise in her cheeks in tune with the anger in her mind. 'What sort of young lady?' she asked politely.

'Well, we do have girls here whose fathers are clergymen, for example,' Matron smiled back. 'And what is your father's profession?'

'My father is retired, he was a train driver,' Ruby replied, a source of pride in railway circles, but she could see it cut no ice here.

Matron nodded wordlessly, then she glanced at Ruby's wedding ring. 'And I see that you are a married woman?' she said uncertainly.

Ruby felt that she had already lost the battle but was determined not to surrender. 'My husband didn't come back from the War,' she said staunchly, which was true to a degree, she wasn't going to enter into any discussion about her private life.

'My condolences,' Matron said. 'But apart from anything else you are a little older than our usual students.' She said it as though Ruby was eighty-two, not twenty-eight, and to underline that the interview was at an end she picked up her pen and looked down again at the papers on her desk.

Ruby sat for a moment. She hadn't come here to ask if this uppity old crone had any scrap metal for sale, she had come to offer her services as a nurse when she knew there was a shortage and, even if this was as far as she got, she wasn't taking this treatment. She sat where she was. 'I may not be a clergyman's daughter,' she said

307

icily, 'but I'm the daughter of a man who fought in one war, came home and provided for his family and drove a train all hours through a second war. We can all pray. I'm sure my father did it often on the footplate of his engine with German planes overhead, so I don't think some man who prays a lot for his living could hold a candle to what he's done.'

Matron looked up at her.

'And furthermore, I am a respectable woman. I have performed my duties here well, better than well, superbly, and I object to being treated by you as some inferior speck of humanity.' She stood up and calmly smoothed her uniform dress. 'I made the mistake of thinking that my ability to deal with the sick would matter, but I see now that I was wrong, snobbery is obviously far more important.' She looked Matron in the eye. 'Good morning,' she said with infinite grace, 'and thank you for your time.' And with that she walked out.

Walking down the corridor she resigned herself to losing her job on the ward as well as any hope of becoming a nurse. She would be dismissed without a doubt, so she turned her mind to other hospitals. Rottenrow was out of the question, she never wanted to see that place again, but there were others, Stobhill and Robroyston came to mind, though she would have to play them carefully as she was sure the miserable old crone would make her feelings known to both and no hospital wanted an insolent ward maid who had given cheek to the Matron of the Royal Infirmary. She shook her head angrily. It was a hospital, not a palace, it was full of patients who were ordinary people just like her, that's why they got on with her and weren't afraid of her the way they were with the doctors and some of those 'particular kind of girls' the old crone liked so much. Who was the old crone to suggest she wasn't good enough to be a nurse? Bloody cheek! At least she had done her a favour by mentioning her wedding ring though. She had only kept it on because of Frances, but she had no actual need of it any longer and no need of Gerry's name either, come to that. Twirling it round and round on her finger she suddenly twisted it off and dropped it in a rubbish bin on the way out. She was done with any ideas of real nursing, and she was done with being Mrs Reilly as well, from now on she would be Ruby McLean, and anyone who didn't know or understand her situation could take a hike.

Next morning she went back as usual to the ward, expecting to be tapped on the shoulder at any moment and shown the door. She was mopping the floor when the message came that she should report to Matron's office and she was prepared for it. She wouldn't give the old crone any satisfaction, she thought, putting the mop and bucket away and checking herself over to make sure she looked presentable. The last thing she wanted was for Matron to hear from a minion in the office that she had turned up for the sack with sweat running down her face and her hair in rat's tails. No, she would go down fighting, she had already decided that, she would resign before the minion handed over her cards. The secretary looked up as she went in and told her Matron was waiting for her. 'Wants to do it herself, does she?' Ruby thought furiously. 'Well, we'll see about that.' This time the old crone asked her to sit down, but Ruby shook her head haughtily and stood where she was.

'Before you say anything,' Ruby said coldly, 'I just want to tell you that I don't regret a word. You treated me as though I had just crawled out of a drain and I long ago decided not to take that kind of treatment from anybody. So I'm handing in my notice, in fact I won't even see it out, I'll leave this minute.'

'My dear young lady,' Matron sighed, 'you must curb this temptation to act on the spur of the moment, if, that is, you intend to be a good nurse.'

'Well I don't,' Ruby replied, her hand on the doorknob. 'You pretty much knocked that daft idea out of my head yesterday and I don't want to be a ward maid in your grand hospital either.'

'Well that's a great pity,' Matron said quietly. 'But I suppose I can always give your place on the nursing course to someone else.'

'Yes,' Ruby said sarcastically, 'give it to one of those well brought-up daughters of the manse you're so keen on, the likes of me has no right to …' She stopped in her tracks. 'What did you say?'

'The place is yours if you want it,' Matron shrugged. 'Of course, I do see your point, perhaps you don't think you are up to it and it's best to find these things out sooner rather than later.'

'No, no!' Ruby cried, sitting down opposite Matron. 'I'm up to it!' She stopped and stared across the desk. 'You're not kidding me, are you? Having a wee joke at the expense of the train driver's lassie?' she asked seriously.

'My dear young lady!' Matron repeated wearily, turning once more to the pile of paperwork on her desk. 'I really don't have time for this!'

Ruby wondered if the papers were the same ones from yesterday, maybe they were always on her desk, props to make her look forever busy.

'If you want this place then kindly see the secretary on the way out, if you do not see her anyway and tell her to take your name off the list. Now please let me get on!'

Ruby sat for a moment, wondering what to say, wondering if she should say anything, then she got up, walked to the door, and shut it behind her. Once outside she stood, thinking, then knocked on the door again, and opened it just enough to speak through. 'Thank you,' she whispered.

'I'm sure you're very welcome,' Matron replied.

The secretary was laughing when she turned round and Ruby's cheeks flushed.

'Why?' she asked, as details of the course were being explained to her.

'She can be a bit of an old bat,' the secretary whispered, 'but she can be fair too. I don't know though, maybe she just isn't used to being spoken to the way you did yesterday.' She covered her mouth, laughing. 'None of us are used to her being spoken to like that. The whole place has been buzzing about it since you walked out!'

'I didn't think I said anything horrible,' Ruby said uncertainly.

'No, not horrible, pithy maybe. I suppose that would cover it. And you were right, if you don't mind me saying so. Maybe she thought about it later and realised that. Either way, you've got a place in the next intake.'

38

They had walked up the slight rise to Safeway's at Paddy's insistence. Every week they bought Lottery tickets for the Saturday draw and, regardless of the numbers, he insisted on having them checked at the supermarket after they had collected their pensions.

'I told you there was nothing on it, the lassie must think you're wandered, me too for being with you!' Ruby shook her head at him. 'Every week we have to do this. I swear to God, I don't know why I listen to you!'

'Well you never know,' Paddy protested. 'You could throw your ticket away and there could be money on it.'

'In which case,' she said sarcastically, '*you'd never know*, would you?'

'Look,' he said peevishly, 'I have enough trouble not checking the Wednesday draw in case my numbers come up and I haven't got a ticket, what harm does it do getting the lassie to check my Saturday numbers?' He glanced at her. 'How did you get on anyway?'

Ruby laughed. 'I got a tenner!'

'Jammy beggar!' he muttered, then brightened up. 'What are we going to spend it on?'

'We?' she demanded, raising her eyebrows.

'Stop messing about, Ruby!' he complained. 'A nice wee fish tea at you-know-where?'

'It won't stretch to that,' Ruby replied. 'How about I buy a couple of slices of haddock and make us a fish tea at home?'

Paddy screwed up his face. 'Aye, well, okay, I suppose so then,' he said.

'Don't force yourself!'

'Would it maybe stretch to a couple of wee cakes as well?' he asked.

'If you buy them!' she retorted. 'You're a right miserable old sod, Paddy Keenan. You've just collected your pension same as me. Your arse is tighter than a halibut's at twenty fathoms!'

Paddy tutted at her. 'Very nice talk, I must say!' he chided her. 'I was going to say that I'd treat us to a wee ice cream down by the front,' he said in an injured tone. 'That would be my contribution.'

'Liar!' she laughed. 'You just thought that up this minute!'

As they sat on their usual bench with their ice creams they looked out across the bay, watching the ferry to the Isle of Cumbrae trudge across the sea.

'Have you ever been across there?' he asked.

Ruby shook her head. 'It's never even occurred to me. Can't be that different from here, a quick hop, skip and jump and you'd be there. You?'

He shook his head. 'No, me neither. Must drive they folk mad, that. The ferry crew, I mean. It's not really like going to sea, is it? Ten minutes there and back every half hour.'

'Maybe they don't want to go to sea,' Ruby shrugged. 'At least they get to sleep in their own beds at night.'

'Aye, but it must be boring, no' think so? It must be like driving a bus back and forth all day long.' He sighed. 'Know what I'd do if I won the Lottery? I'd go on one of they cruises, to the Caribbean or somewhere. Dancing with one of they nice lassies in hula skirts!' He chuckled to himself, waving his arms seductively from side to side.

'Aye,' Ruby grinned, 'I can just see you in a hula skirt and they slippers with your big hammer toes poking through!'

'I meant the lassies in the in the hula skirts and well you know it!' he complained. 'What would you do if you won a lot of money? Buy a wee car?'

Ruby thought for a moment. 'No,' she said finally, 'I've never fancied a car, but I'd get one of they Harley Davidsons.' She nodded her head firmly.

Beside her Paddy choked. 'You'd what?' he demanded.

'You heard,' she replied. 'Saw a laddie on one at Safeway's a few weeks back, never saw anything so lovely, really beautiful it was.' She glanced sideways at him. 'And before you say anything smart, I mean the Harley, not the laddie. I found myself thinking I could shove him off and disappear on it before he gathered his wits about him. I mean, who would believe him if he said a wee old biddy had pushed him off and zoomed away on his bike?'

'You on a motorbike!' he howled, still coughing on his ice cream.

'No,' she said slowly, 'I didn't say a motorbike, I said a Harley. A Harley isn't just a motorbike. Don't you know anything, you ignorant old man? They make this lovely low noise, almost like an engine not working right. A Harley is,' she said thoughtfully, 'a Harley is a dream!'

'Christ, I'd like to see that!' he chortled.

'I'll let you know then, I'll give you a wave as I'm riding past,' she replied tartly.

'I mean, I'd pay to see that!' He slapped his thigh with mirth.

'Then I'll *definitely* let you know!' Ruby snorted. 'I'd pay to see you paying for anything, and before you just have to mention it, buying a pokey hat once in a blue moon doesn't make you the last of the big spenders!'

Paddy took a hankie from his pocket and mopped his eyes and then wiped the dripping ice cream off his hand. 'I've always fancied a wee car,' he smiled happily.

'Can you drive?' she demanded, glaring at him.

'No!' he said, hurt. 'What's that got to do with anything? Can you drive a big motorbike?'

'A Harley,' she sighed impatiently.

'Well a Harley then. It's just a wee notion, isn't it? I've aye fancied one of they wee minis.'

Now it was Ruby's turn to laugh. 'How in hell would you fit in one of they wee things?' she demanded.

'I'm not as big as I look,' he muttered defensively.

'What?' Ruby teased him. 'In this wee notion of yours, do you have your legs lopped off at the knees to get you to a normal size then?'

'A nice wee red one,' Paddy said dreamily, ignoring the taunt. 'All bright and polished up and that!'

'Away with you!' Ruby laughed. 'Even if we managed to squash you in whole, every time you tried to change gear they big feet of yours would hit two pedals at once. You'd end up killing yourself!'

Paddy watched her giggling for a while. 'It aye comes back to my feet with you, doesn't it?' he asked. 'You can't see beyond my feet!'

'Nobody can see beyond your feet!' she howled. 'Sure, the ferry's just arrived across the water there at Cumbrae and the crew can still see your feet! Your feet are one of the sights of the Clyde!'

As Ruby discussed her plans for nursing training, Flora listened quietly.

'I've arranged it with Da,' she said. 'He'll still be here to look after Frances, and there's always Agnes up the road just in case.'

Flora nodded.

'And – what's the matter with you?' she demanded.

'Me?' Flora replied. 'Nothing.'

'Well you might show a bit of interest!'

'Is that not what I'm doing? I'm sitting here listening, aren't I?'

'But you're not saying anything,' Ruby complained. 'You always say something, that's why I talk to you!'

'You're not leaving much space for me to say anything,' Flora laughed, 'you're gabbling on there!'

Ruby looked at her doubtfully. 'So what's happening at work?'

Flora shrugged. 'The fight goes on, as they say,' she sighed.

'Are things no better then?'

'Not so's you'd notice,' Flora sighed. 'Not as bad as during the War, mind. Remember that march where people threw fruit at us in the street?'

Ruby laughed. 'It was the most fruit I'd seen since the start of the War, I aye wondered where they came by it!'

'The men support us now,' Flora said. 'They finally realised that if management got away with keeping us on low wages it might happen to them as well, so that's something. We're missing Denis though, I think that's the trouble. He had this way of explaining the problem in a way people could understand, and he was great at energising them.'

'So how is he doing now?'

314

'He's fine. He was a brilliant student at the Law Faculty, as I knew he would be, and now he's in practice as a fully-fledged lawyer,' Flora smiled.

'Do you see him often?' Ruby asked gently.

'Oh, not as much as when he was in the factory,' Flora said. 'He had so much studying to do at the Uni and now he's busy. You know. But he's finally at a stage where he can help people. He gives legal advice for free to folk that could never afford it, and that's just what he wanted.'

'I was thinking of asking for a bit of advice myself,' Ruby admitted. 'Now that I'm starting a whole new life I was thinking of trying for a divorce.'

Flora looked up at her sharply. 'Does it matter?' she asked. 'Not that I'm saying you shouldn't or anything,' she said hurriedly, 'but it's not as if you want to marry somebody else, is it?'

'No, I certainly don't want to do that!' Ruby exclaimed. 'But here we are, I haven't lived with him since 1948 and three years later I'm still regarded as his next of kin. Whenever he's found lying somewhere it's me they come to. Tam McVicar is always that apologetic, but he's only doing his job, as he says, he has to come to Gerry's wife, so as long as that's what I am he'll keep coming to me.'

Flora nodded. 'I see what you mean, you'll have enough on your plate without that. I'm sure Denis will help you. I'll talk to him and he'll make an appointment.'

'Will you come with me?'

'If you like,' Flora smiled.

There was a subtle change in Denis and it went beyond the three-piece suit and the collar and tie. He was no longer a boy, of course, he was a man now, and a man of education and standing at that, even though he was just starting out on his legal career. His eyes, once his most striking feature, were no longer as warm and friendly, there was a slight distance that hadn't been there when he was younger. And he had a certain bearing, a confidence he hadn't had before, an awareness of his situation. Things like that, Ruby mused, watching his graceful movements as he guided her and Flora to seats in his office, were bound to make a difference. Denis was no longer a laddie from Clydebank or a brilliant engineering apprentice, he had transformed himself into a professional man in a whole other world. He sat back in the chair behind his desk, listening to Ruby in silence as she told her story.

'Up till 1938 the only grounds for divorce in Scotland were adultery and desertion,' he explained, 'but after that cruelty, incurable insanity, sodomy and bestiality were added.' He smiled tightly. 'I think we can ignore most of those and, given the circumstances, alcoholism would certainly be covered by the cruelty grounds. I take it he wouldn't proceed against you on the grounds of desertion?'

'He's not in a fit state to think of that,' Ruby replied.

'Probably better if you take proceedings anyway. If he did he could make a case for custody of Frances. The Courts don't like women who desert their husbands.'

Ruby stared at him in horror. 'Frances doesn't really know him!' she cried. 'She knows that's who her father is, but she hasn't seen him in years.'

'Has he ever asked to see her?' Denis asked.

'No,' Ruby said quietly. 'He saw her just after she was born then he was away for over six years, and not once since he came home in 1946 has her ever looked at her or asked to see her.'

'Does he pay anything towards her keep?'

Ruby shook her head. Gerry supporting his daughter wasn't something she had ever expected and neither had he. 'He's never offered a penny and I wouldn't have taken it even if he had. Everything he gets goes on booze, all he does is drink.'

'Is there anything else we could present?'

Flora glanced at Ruby. 'He did push her down the stairs when she was heavily pregnant,' she said tentatively.

'But he was drunk!' Ruby said.

'He still did it.' Flora looked at Denis. 'Ruby lost her baby because of that. I'm sure Dr McGill would support you on that, Ruby.'

Ruby shifted uncomfortably in her seat. She didn't want to talk about losing John, but there was more to it than that. 'I'd rather not make that public unless I absolutely have to,' she whispered. 'Gerry might be useless as Frances's father. In fact, he is useless, but I don't want her to know he did that.'

316

Denis nodded. 'Do you think he would fight a divorce?'

'I doubt it,' Ruby replied. 'He is Catholic, but he's a drinker first, he's not fit to fight it. I'll talk to his sister though, she's got a family herself but she tries to keep an eye on him. She's been really supportive, I'm sure she'll help.'

'It would be a lot simpler if he didn't contest it,' Gerry smiled, 'but even if he did, I'm sure we'd still manage.'

'Denis, could you give me an idea how much this will cost?' she asked.

'Don't even think about that,' he replied. 'We're friends, I won't take a penny.'

As they sat on the tram home Flora was smiling again.

'You see what I mean?' she said happily. 'He's helping people, just as he always said he would.'

'Aye, but,' Ruby said doubtfully, 'it's an awful big favour, Flora. He has to earn a living, after all.'

'The unions give him work,' she shrugged. 'They'd rather pay one of their own than one of the enemy. Besides, I'm sure he earns well from his other clients who can pay. He thinks of the little people, though, he always has.'

She waited till they were getting off the tram then said 'He's left the Party, by the way,' and walked on.

Ruby caught her by the arm when they reached the pavement. 'He's *what?*' she demanded.

'He had to,' Flora said quietly, 'it's quite logical. No Communist member ever gets anywhere in politics—'

'He's going into politics?' Ruby asked. 'I thought the idea was that he would bring justice to the ordinary people, the little people? Isn't that what you always said?'

'Well politics is how you do that, Ruby, politicians make the laws, solicitors only administer them.'

'So if he wants to get elected ...' Ruby thought aloud.

'He has to join a party that can get him elected,' Flora smiled a little too brightly. 'The Labour Party.'

'Oh, Flora!'

'What?' Flora demanded innocently.

'Oh, Flora!' Ruby repeated.

'Now don't be so naïve, Ruby, it's all perfectly sensible! His ideals haven't changed, but he has to be part of a party with the power to put those ideals into practice, doesn't he? He has to have power in order to change things, and this way he'll get it.'

Flora was still smiling, but it was a desperate smile. Denis's strategy might appear as sensible and logical as Flora was trying to make it sound, in fact, the more Ruby thought about it the more sense it made. But though Flora was putting up a determined defence, Ruby knew that underneath, to someone whose beliefs were as clear and pure as Flora's had always been, there had to be feelings of hurt, of doubt and suspicion at least, of betrayal. And despite Flora's denials over the years, Ruby knew the bond between her and Denis wasn't confined to their shared politics, her friend had deep feelings for him. To say another word would be cruel, she decided, so, putting her arm through Flora's she pulled her close as they walked along in sympathetic silence.

39

'You'll have to do something about that lassie!' Harry shouted. 'I don't like her!'

Ruby stared at him. 'It's Frances,' she said helplessly, 'she's your granddaughter.'

'I know that,' Harry thundered, 'but I want rid of her,' and with that he disappeared into his bedroom, banging the door behind him.

Ruby sat down and tried to gather herself together, but she didn't know how to start collecting the pieces in her mind. Harry McLean never raised his voice. Harry McLean never voiced an opinion. He had spent his entire life avoiding any kind of confrontation, and he didn't have likes or dislikes – apart from Neville Chamberlain, that was. Not that this was a dislike, more a towering rage and his ten-year-old granddaughter was the focus of it. Ruby felt completely confused.

She was three months into her first year as a student nurse and everything in her life had been carefully worked out to the tiniest detail to make sure she could cope. Agnes had explained to Gerry that Ruby wanted a divorce and he hadn't objected so she would soon be free of him, free to concentrate on her course.

Nursing training was more about working on the wards than thinking or learning, she had found that out pretty quickly. It was practical rather than educational, but there were still exams to study for, and passing them would need a clear head. When she came home she cooked, cleaned and cared for her father and daughter, and with Harry retired he had plenty of time to keep an eye on Frances, so she had no worries about either being neglected. And now this bombshell. She got up and tapped on Harry's bedroom door.

'Go away!' he shouted.

'Da, it's me, Ruby,' she whispered. 'I'm coming in.'

He was sitting at Sarah's dressing table, looking out of the big bay windows. Her brushes and lipsticks and her lavender water were where she had left them years ago. Harry was looking down at them.

'I wish I'd gone when she did,' he said quietly. 'Nothing makes sense any longer, I don't like this life without her.'

'I know, Da,' she said gently, sitting on the edge of the bed. 'We all miss her, you know.'

'He turned round and glared at her. 'That's not what I'm saying!' he shouted. 'Everything's changed, it's like I've got somebody else's life, and I don't like it!'

'But what has Frances done?' she asked.

'She's a bad one, that,' he said darkly. 'She steals my money!'

Ruby's mind whirled. 'You mean she takes it out of your pockets?' she asked, aghast.

Harry got up and walked about the room. 'No, no, no!' he said impatiently. 'My money!' He stuffed his hands into his pockets and paced about. 'The money I forget and leave lying around, she takes it!'

'Is that all?' Ruby laughed, relieved.

'It's enough!' Harry yelled.

'Da, she doesn't think like that. You've always left money lying around, half the time you're not even aware you're doing it, or where you left it.'

'But I didn't ever say it was finders keepers, did I? People always gave it back to me when they found it somewhere, didn't they?'

'But Da!' Ruby protested. 'She'll just think it's a few coppers lying around.'

'But she's old enough to know it's not hers so she knows it must be somebody else's, and she takes it just the same.'

Ruby thought for a moment. He was right, she knew that, everyone in the family just collected Harry's little piles of cash from wherever he had deposited them and returned them. But Frances was only ten years old and she had moved back and forth from one house to another, maybe she didn't understand.

'Look, I'll talk to her, Da,' she said soothingly.

From there she went to the bedroom she shared with her daughter and found her drawing with coloured crayons.

'Those look nice,' she smiled. 'Where did you get the money to buy them? Did you get somebody's messages from the Co-op for them?' she asked gently.

Frances didn't look up. 'No,' she said blandly, 'I had my own money.'

'Oh? Where did you get that?'

'I found it,' Frances replied, no expression in her voice.

'Where?' Ruby asked.

Frances shrugged. 'About,' she said.

Ruby swallowed. 'You mean the money Grandpa leaves about the house?' she suggested.

Frances nodded and kept on drawing.

'But that's Grandpa's money,' Ruby explained. 'He's always done that, left money about. We always give it back to him.'

Frances looked up at her. 'If he wants it he shouldn't leave it lying around,' she said. 'If he leaves it then it means he doesn't want it.'

Ruby moved closer to her and put an arm around her shoulders, but Frances went back to her drawing without any reaction.

'No, Frances,' Ruby said firmly but gently, 'you can't do that. This is his house and you can't just take things from him, that's stealing. You don't want people to think you're a thief, do you?'

Frances shrugged without looking up at her.

'So we'll make a rule from now on,' Ruby suggested. 'If you find money about the house, you give it to me and I'll give it to Grandpa. Okay?'

Beside her Frances finally looked up, stared in a neutral kind of way and shrugged wordlessly again.

The lack of any feeling, any emotion in Frances, had always concerned Ruby. There was no closeness between them, between Frances and anyone, come to that. From her earliest days the child had an unnerving way of looking at you, that made you feel you were the one in the wrong, the one in the weaker position and she had just done it again.

'Look, Da,' Ruby smiled, when she had returned to her father's bedroom, 'I've had a word with her, and she just didn't understand. She thought if you left the money lying about it meant you didn't want it so it was okay for her to take it. It was only a few coins each time, wasn't it?'

'It mounts up,' Harry said huffily.

'Aye, but Da, it wasn't as if she was stealing ten-bob notes, was it?' she laughed, trying to convince him, trying to convince herself.

'That'll be next!' Harry said. 'Just you wait!'

'Och, Da!' Ruby chided him.

'Ruby, you mark my words. That one will come to no good!'

'Da, she's just a wee lassie!' Ruby said, her eyes wide with surprise.

Harry looked sheepish. 'But look at that wee laddie across the road,' he said, 'wee Jamie. He's got a terrible time with Iris and Gus, yet he comes over here to see me and he's aye got a smile. He chats away there and he does whatever I ask him. But that one,' he glared towards the door as though Frances was standing on the other side, 'all she does is stare at you and steal things!'

'Da!'

'Ask her where your mother's wedding ring is!' he demanded. 'Ask her about that episode, go on!'

'What do you mean?' Ruby asked, alarmed.

'I kept it in the dressing table here,' Harry said. 'I meant to give it to you, Ruby, but I wanted to hold onto it for a wee while, to look at it sometimes, you know?'

Ruby nodded and looked down.

'You'll get it eventually,' Harry said sadly, 'but I just thought I'd keep it near me.' Then his tone changed. 'I asked her if she'd seen it and she denied it, but I knew she had it. So I waited till she went to school and I looked around and there it was, hidden away inside one of her socks in the chest of drawers!'

'Did you ask her about it?' Ruby said, her hand going to her throat.

'Aye, I did,' Harry replied. 'She just looked at me in that cold way she has and shrugged. Didn't say a word, just shrugged and walked away.' He looked at Ruby. 'I didn't want to tell you, Ruby,' he said miserably, 'but you're going to have watch that one or she'll cause you grief!'

Afterwards Ruby sat in the living room trying to clear her mind. In all her life she had never heard her father express an opinion or say anything negative about anyone. And he was so angry. He got like that sometimes these days, but, she mused, he was getting on. Then she thought back to the earlier trouble at Frances's school. She had told no one about it and had tried to convince herself that it had been a childish prank that got out of control. But what if there had been other incidents she hadn't heard about, things that Frances had got away with? It was hard to separate the wood from the trees but she had to try. Was she to blame? Was she a bad mother, a lax one? If only Sarah was there to advise her. But she had to stay calm and think this thing through from every angle. Harry had gone through a lot these last years, then he had been retired from the job he loved, whether he wanted to be or not. She had noticed him getting a bit annoyed from time to time, but he wasn't a young man any longer, she had to make allowances for a bit of grumpiness at his age. Maybe it was all just too much for him. He hadn't spent as much time with his own children as he was now spending with Frances and not every man was good with children. Men of his generation usually had little to do with them, perhaps she was asking too much of him. Just because her arrangements worked out for her was no reason they should work out for him – or Frances, come to that, maybe Frances needed to be with other children, not a crotchety old man. It was her own fault, she decided, she had been carried away with her nursing dream and that had made her selfish. Tomorrow she had a day off and would visit Agnes and ask if, in future, Frances could go to her house after school and she'd pick her up there after her shifts. That would solve the problem, she thought, smiling brightly. But there was a nagging doubt somewhere, something that made her slightly afraid. She shook her head and poked the fire vigorously to make the thought go away.

Next morning everything changed though. Harry was still asleep when Frances went off to school, being diplomatic, Ruby thought, with a smile, but when she took a cup of tea to his bedroom she found she couldn't wake him. She immediately ran to the surgery for help and Dr McGill lifted his bag and followed her back to the house. After a brief look he returned to the surgery once more to call an ambulance and Harry was taken the short distance to the Royal, where it was found that he had had a stroke and was critically ill.

'He's had a left-sided stroke,' Donald McGill said gently, 'so he's paralysed down the right side.'

'And he's right-handed,' Ruby said quietly.

'It also means,' Dr McGill continued, 'that his speech will in all probability be affected. There's no telling at this stage if he will regain consciousness and, if he does survive, there's no telling what he will be like, Ruby.'

Ruby was listening but somehow she couldn't take in the words.

'I'll call the Goods Yard and get George up here, shall I?'

She nodded.

'Maybe someone can go for Iris later,' he suggested uncertainly.

Ruby's eyebrows shot up sarcastically. 'That's all we need,' she said, 'Lady MacBeth wringing her hands at his bedside! I don't think we'll bother. Did I miss something, Donald?' she asked. 'Surely there had to be some sign?'

Dr McGill sighed. 'Why do you think everything's your fault, Ruby?' he demanded. 'Why has there always got to be something you alone missed? It was the same with Sarah. I bet you still harbour this wee notion deep inside that if only you had noticed something sooner she'd still be alive, don't you?'

Ruby looked down, smiling slightly despite the tears in her eyes.

'You can't go on doing this to yourself, you know. It's, well, it's silly!' He put out a hand and covered hers, then withdrew it again swiftly.

Fleeting as his touch had been, it was long enough. She felt it, too. Whatever it was that had made him take his hand away so quickly had registered simultaneously with her, a burning, stinging sensation that stayed there long afterwards. She didn't have time for it, though, she had her father to think about, so she filed it away in the back of her mind to be dealt with at a later date, or not.

'Do you think he'll make it?' she asked quietly.

'We have no way of knowing,' he replied. 'The longer he's unconscious the worse the outlook.'

'He's been angry at times once or twice,' she told him. 'My Da was never angry, but recently ... I put it down to everything that's happened in the family and the way his life has changed, you know?'

'That can sometimes happen before a stroke,' he nodded. 'A kind of confused rage over something so small no one else can understand it.'

'Aye, it was a bit like that sometimes,' she agreed. 'If he wakes up I'll look after him at home as well,' she said firmly.

'What about your nursing course?'

'To hell with my course, Donald. He's my father,' she sighed.

40

When Harry McLean came out of hospital he was a changed man. He remained paralysed down the right side, his arm and leg stiff, the muscles already withering away with misuse and his right hand contracted and turned inwards like a claw. His speech consisted of noises with the occasional random word thrown in leaving him constantly frustrated and angry. He knew what he wanted to say, but somehow his brain made something else entirely come out of his twisted mouth and anger soon followed. After a while he no longer tried to speak, preferring to retreat into a world of silent, white-hot rage. Donald McGill was the soul of attention, sitting with him and explaining over and over that things would improve, that Harry had to keep telling himself that things would get better if he stopped winding himself up into towering rages. Harry McLean was of a generation that respected doctors regardless of age, so when young Doctor McGill was with him he would nod his head contritely and smile his crooked smile. What Ruby saw was quite different though. If she had thought caring for her mother was difficult, looking after Harry was far harder, as she contended with kicks, slaps and punches from his good side and bile-filled shrieks of raw hatred through the half of his mouth that still worked. And afterwards he would cry with shame, which was worse than the blows as far as Ruby was concerned. The sight of her once big, strong, kind father weeping like a baby broke her heart afresh every time.

As in Sarah's case, there had been no alternative to Ruby caring for her Harry. For a start, she and Frances already lived with him so it would have been impractical for anyone else to do it. Not that there were too many choices; if Ruby didn't do it then George or

Iris would have to move in because they had no room for Harry to live with them. George helped by calling in on his way to work every morning to lift his father out of bed and place him in his chair by the window, and he arrived each night to reverse the process and to carry him to and from the bath. Harry seemed to accept this indignity easier from his son than the chores his daughter carried out. He hated Ruby inserting suppositories, wrapping him in incontinence pads, clipping his nails and rubbing his old buttocks to stop bedsores developing and, with no one else to visit his hatred upon, he took it out on her. She perfected a cheerful way of doing what had to be done but it only seemed to make him feel even more degraded, and so he hit out at her for her cheerfulness too. When she mashed his food and spoon-fed it to him, which she had to do because he had trouble swallowing, he would choke more from anger than the effects of his stroke and she would end up splattered with half-digested food.

Donald McGill noticed the bruising as he helped her move him in his chair so that he could sleep one day. He pointed at her arm and she shook her head slightly.

'I know it's not Gerry this time,' he said in a low voice, 'but does it happen often?'

'All the time. It's like they took my Da away to the Royal and brought someone else back, some nasty old sod at that!' She laughed wryly.

'It's like this sometimes,' he said. 'He's depressed and there's so little we can do for stroke victims.'

'Or their daughters!' Ruby smiled.

'I wish there was some help I could offer.'

'There's nothing anyone can do, Donald, I just have to see it through. He's angry because he's alive.' She sighed, 'I know he wishes he had died in the Royal. He cries sometimes when he wakes because he doesn't want to live, and it's no life, is it?'

'No, it's existence,' McGill said quietly. 'If you let a dog suffer like this you'd be prosecuted, but we're obliged to let a decent man like Harry McLean go through indignity and agony without his consent.'

'Will he get *any* better, Donald?'

He shook his head. 'I'm not going to lie to you, Ruby,' he sighed. 'All I can offer is that he may go quickly or he could hang on like this for years. I could try and get him into some place?'

'No,' she said firmly. 'I'd never let that happen.'

'Some of these places are quite good, Ruby,' he started.

'No!' she repeated. 'Don't mention it again, Donald.'

'But what about your nursing?'

'Oh, I gave that up the day he had the stroke,' she smiled. 'No point hankering after what's gone, is there? I told Matron and she said I could start again when things are clearer. She meant when he dies, but she didn't want to say that. I wish he had though, for his sake more than mine. He doesn't deserve this.'

He reached across a sympathetic hand again but she sensed it coming and moved out of range by getting up and walking to the door.

'Anyway, you've got work to see to, Donald,' she smiled. 'You must have patients lining up at the surgery door.'

'If there's anything you think I can do, just send for me?'

She nodded, but as she closed the door behind him she thought 'Like what, Donald? Like what?'

Donald McGill did help though. Harry was now weakened and prone to all sorts of infections that he would once have shrugged off, and that winter he caught a cold that quickly became pneumonia.

'We call it the Old Man's Friend, because it comes and ends their misery,' he smiled, 'but we have penicillin now.'

'Aye,' Ruby sighed, 'the stuff that could've saved my Ma if she'd hung on a bit longer. That was one of my first lectures – TB is now a thing of the past.'

'Well now that we have it I could treat Harry,' he explained, 'but every time he has an infection it will take more and more to make him better again.' He looked at her solemnly. 'What I'd advise doing, Ruby, is not treating him, letting nature take its course. What do you think?'

There was a long silence. 'Would he be in any pain?'

'No, I'll give him something to make him sleep, but if I do, he won't wake up again. Do you understand what I'm saying, Ruby?

I won't be treating the pneumonia. I'll be making him comfortable.'

Ruby didn't reply.

'Would you rather I talked to George?'

'No, there's no reason he should have to know,' she said, 'it would be better if he thought Da just died of pneumonia, that's enough for him to deal with. What will you give Da?'

'It doesn't matter, does it?'

'Could you get into trouble?'

'I'm his doctor, Ruby, and between the two of us, we do this kind of thing all the time, it's called "the double effect." If we give something to ease a patient's suffering it may well have another effect, if you see what I mean. We're not supposed to strive officiously to preserve life, and in Harry's case that's what I'd be doing if I got him through this only to have other illnesses waiting up the line for him. I see no reason to put him, or you, through a prolonged death. It's all very well talking about suffering being part of life, but Harry has been going through the suffering of a long death since he had his stroke.'

'Okay,' Ruby whispered.

'I'll treat him if you really want me to, Ruby. Do you?'

'No,' she shook her head.

When George arrived that evening Harry was already comatose, so he stayed, just as he had during his mother's last night.

'Like old times,' he smiled sadly to Ruby, 'it's just as well we only had one Ma and one Da, I don't think I could do this again, could you?'

Ruby hugged his arm as they sat with Harry. He was deeply unconscious, his breathing was becoming more irregular and when Donald McGill called again just before midnight he told them it would not be long.

'Why is he breathing like that?' Ruby asked. 'Really heavy then practically nothing.'

'It's called Cheyne-Stokes,' he explained. 'It's a sign of the nervous system controlling the heart and lungs reaching the end.'

'But he can't feel anything, he's not hurting?' George asked.

'No, the coma is too deep for that,' McGill reassured him. 'I'll stay though, if that's all right?'

329

Ruby nodded; she knew what he was saying. There was no sense in trying to call him back in an hour just to pronounce Harry dead. So they sat, the three of them, listening as Harry's body gradually shut down.

'No Iris?' McGill asked.

'No, we've been saved that performance,' George muttered. 'I looked in earlier, both of them are dead drunk.'

'What about the child?'

'He's upstairs with the Morrises,' George said. 'I think he practically lives with Andy Morris's mother these days, and that's all to the good.'

'Odd when you think Gus Campbell wanted a family, though, yet he takes no interest in the boy,' McGill said.

'He's got his hands full with Iris. Too full,' George smiled.

'He always had his hands full of some female,' Ruby remarked, 'might as well be her.'

'I heard that,' McGill laughed quietly. 'My father used to say he was always far too ready with his paws, he claimed he could look at the finger bruises on any female and guess she'd been in Gus's clutches!'

'That was true,' Ruby said. 'He had this way of grabbing you by the wrists to keep you with him. There was no way of getting loose.'

'Nice to have in the family!' McGill chuckled.

'No worse than having Iris in the family,' George replied, 'or Bea, come to that. My God, what a lot! Remember the Bea Battles, Ruby?'

'They're etched into my soul!'

'Then there was Jakey,' George said sadly.

'The Sheik of High Street,' McGill laughed lowly. 'And that wee dog of his, what was it called?'

'Wee Dug!' Ruby chuckled.

'Poor wee Jakey,' George shook his head. 'God, I miss Jakey every day, do you know that?'

'Aye, me too, there was something about him, wasn't there? You felt you had to look out for him. I remember clearing out his flat for the new people moving in. I sobbed all over the place like a big wean! It was the fact that there was so little there, his life amounted

330

to his paintings on the walls. If they hadn't been there who'd have known he existed?'

'Jakey and Wee Dug,' George said thoughtfully. 'Sometimes when I'm working in the yard I look around and I don't know what for. Then I remember, I'm looking for the sight of the two of them trotting about High Street. And do you know the really funny thing?' He chuckled. 'I always think of him in that Arab outfit. He only had it in the last years of his life, but now I can only picture him wearing it and waving that big sword about.'

'Well, he loved it, I suppose that's why,' Ruby laughed.

'What happened to it?' George asked. 'I've thought about it often, we should've buried him in it!'

'No idea where it went. I had a quick look for it when I was clearing out his stuff, but I never saw it.'

'I really resented the new people moving in,' George laughed gently. 'I was so annoyed at them that I felt guilty and went out of my way to be nice to them! It wasn't their fault, they just had no business being in Jakey's house.'

At the sound of Jakey's name Harry stirred. They looked at each other in turn but, even before they returned their gaze to Harry, he had stopped breathing. It was over.

'You know what this means, Ruby?' George said putting an arm about his sister. 'That's us orphans now.'

When Ruby's divorce came through she hardly noticed it, its importance was from another world, another age and it no longer mattered.

'I can hardly remember why I wanted it,' she said to Flora with a smile. 'I mean, what difference does it make? Not that I'm not grateful to Denis, of course.' Somewhere in her mind she noticed that she no longer referred to him as 'your Denis,' and wondered why. 'What's he up to these days?'

'He's standing in the election,' Flora replied. 'You're lucky you've had better things to do or you'd be forced out to canvas for him!' She looked at Ruby apologetically. 'I'm sorry, Ruby, I didn't mean ...'

'Oh, behave yourself,' Ruby laughed, 'you don't have to watch every word, I know what you meant. Do you think he'll win?'

'Yes, he'll win,' Flora sighed, gazing into the fire. 'Denis wouldn't have taken it on if he thought he could possibly lose. Mind you, everyone thinks Atlee will lose and we'll get the Tories back in power, now there's a happy prospect. They're all turning out for Denis, though, everyone he's ever helped. All the railwaymen he's got proper compensation for, all the women he's fought for at work. He's made a real difference to people, Ruby.'

Ruby nodded. He had helped people, everyone in the area knew that, Denis took on battles they wouldn't have contemplated fighting before because the likes of them knew they were beaten before they started. And he had won for them. He was very much the local boy made good, even if he did come from Clydebank.

'And what about you?' Ruby asked.

'I'll be turning out for him, too, of course!'

'No, I meant how are you? What are you doing these days?'

'I'm quite enjoying being a shop steward, even if the men still ask me to make the tea at meetings,' she grinned.

'And do you?' Ruby giggled.

'What do you think?' Flora laughed back. 'A flea in the ear's all they get!'

41

Denis Kelly didn't win his seat in the 1955 General Election, as it happened. Ditching his party and his ethics did him no good at all, but being Denis he put a good spin on his defeat.

'He says he's relieved he didn't get in, there was no point being part of the opposition,' Flora explained. 'Eden's in for the next five years and there's nothing to be done about that. I'd have thought the experience of five years as an MP would've helped him later, but there we are. I suppose he knows what he's talking about. Denis usually has everything worked out.'

Ruby thought she detected a slight hint of disapproval in her voice but decided to leave it alone. 'What's he doing? Has he any plans?'

'He's going to be become a QC and do some groundwork for the next election, apparently.' There was a silence. 'Andy's doing well though, he's through his degree at the Uni.'

'Yes, I heard about that. Is it true he's thinking of going abroad?'

'So he says, he wants to be a military historian. He's thinking about New Zealand or Canada. His mother's beside herself!'

'So why don't you go to Uni?' Ruby asked.

'Too much work with the union and with the factory,' Flora replied, 'Can't do everything. Anyway, enough about me, what's happening with Frances?'

'The truth?' Ruby said glumly. 'I don't know, but then I never have known. I've raised her for fifteen years and I don't know her any better today than I did when I gave birth to her. I'm an utter failure as a mother.'

'She's always been a bit odd, Ruby,' Flora said quietly, 'you can't blame yourself for that.'

'But she must be doing it for a reason, there has to be something I could've done.'

'And what if she was born that way?'

'I've turned that one over and over in my mind too, but maybe I'm making excuses for myself.'

'She didn't show much emotion as a child,' Flora said thoughtfully, 'that's what I remember. She would sit on the floor playing by herself. Jamie would try to play with her, but she was never interested. I can't recall ever seeing her laugh.'

'No, the only time I've seen as much as a grin was when she'd caused someone else trouble,' Ruby murmured, frowning. 'Agnes has never said anything, but I've felt for a while something has happened at her house. If my Da being ill hadn't scuppered my nursing course I was going to ask Agnes if she could go to her after school, but to be truthful, there was an atmosphere, and deep down I felt I couldn't. Besides, she's doing what she can with Gerry. It didn't seem fair to ask her to take on Frances as well.'

'So what's she doing now?'

'She was working at the paper shop just after she left school, but she got sacked from that when stuff went missing, sweets, cigarettes, cash, the usual, you know.'

'Was it her?' Flora asked.

'I'd imagine so,' Ruby sighed. 'She doesn't see anything wrong with it, that's what I've never understood. For her what's wrong is getting caught. It's the same with everything. She sees no difference between lying and telling the truth, she uses whichever gets her what she wants fastest. God knows how she'll end up.'

By the time Ruby could return to her course, the training of student nurses had been re-thought. Instead of working on the wards and attending blocks of lectures, they would, in future, have to live in special accommodation, but Ruby had a teenage daughter at home, a difficult teenage daughter at that.

'What are you going to do?' Donald McGill asked her gently. He had taken to dropping in for a chat whenever he had a free moment.

'Do the Enrolled Nurse course, I suppose,' Ruby replied.

'You don't sound very enthusiastic,' he grinned.

'Well, it's not what I wanted,' she said quietly.

'Ruby, have you thought of making a life for yourself instead?'

'What do you think I'm doing?'

'I mean, you're still a young woman and you're free now. Is there any reason why you couldn't marry again?'

There was something about the way he said it, she thought. He was telling her something, not asking a question or giving advice. She didn't answer for a few moments. 'No, I've got no notions in that direction,' she said firmly. 'I'll do the course and make a life for myself that way.'

'You deserve some happiness, Ruby,' he said sadly.

'And what makes you think marriage equals happiness, Donald?' she smiled. 'I don't see you rushing into it.'

'We're not talking about me,' he protested, picking biscuit crumbs from his knees and placing them on his saucer, from nerves, she thought. 'We're talking about you. You can't dismiss the very idea of marriage just because of one mistake when you were little more than a child, Ruby.'

'It's not something I think about,' she shrugged. 'Maybe when I've done the course things might be different.'

As Ruby was starting out on a new chapter of her life, so was Flora, though a less uplifting one and the cause was Denis Kelly. Despite his positive remarks after the election, his defeat had marked him in ways that would alter the rest of his life. Denis Kelly didn't fail at anything. The bright young solicitor who had been in demand by trade unions who regarded him as a friend of the workers, now became a businessman and, to the shock of everyone who knew him, he accepted offers to represent insurance companies. Worse, he accepted work from the insurers of companies that had supplied asbestos to the shipyards of the Clyde.

Asbestos dust had been known to be dangerous since the 1880s, but no one told the men working with it. It was used to insulate pipes in the engine rooms of boats under construction, water pipes, exhaust pipes, wherever heat had to be conserved and contained. In the late 1950s, suspicions were turning to concerns, as men became ill and died of mesothelioma, a form of lung cancer caused by asbestos exposure. It affected not just those working directly with

the asbestos, but whoever was in the vicinity, as the wet asbestos –
'monkey dung' the men called it – was slapped on the pipes, then
smoothed and evened when dry. After that asbestos cloth was applied,
cut to size and hand-stitched round the pipes. Toilet facilities in the
yards were basic and the men had no way of washing their hands,
so the asbestos dust that caked and covered them could only be
roughly brushed off. They had no canteen either, they ate their
pieces, their sandwiches brought from home, wherever they happened
to be working, their hands covered in dust so thick that, when the
sun shone through gaps in the boats under construction, it was like
a torch beam trying to penetrate smoke.

Now Denis Kelly, the friend of the little people, the defender of
the ordinary man, had gone across to the side of the money men.
The sense of betrayal was so strong even Flora couldn't defend him,
and neither could his own father, who had worked all his days in
John Brown's and knew men who were dead or dying from asbestosis,
men his son had grown up among.

'He says everyone has a right to a defence,' Flora said calmly,
'including big business,' but Ruby could see how shocked and hurt
her friend was.

'I suppose he has to say something, Flora,' Ruby murmured.

'His father's disowned him, but Denis says Mr Kelly just doesn't
understand, he hasn't the education to see that it's just business.'

'What does he mean by that? Prostitution is "just business" but
that doesn't make it right, does it?' Ruby scoffed.

'Exactly,' Flora replied miserably. 'I feel as though I've been made
a complete fool of, Ruby.'

'Well it's not your fault he's turned into such a creep. You can't
blame yourself for thinking the best of someone, Flora,' Ruby said
sympathetically. 'George was always suspicious of him because he
supported Partick Thistle. He said that was just a cover for blokes
who supported Rangers but didn't want to appear bigoted.' She was
trying to make her friend smile, but with Flora the hurt went too
deep to be shrugged off with humour, Flora was one of life's ideal-
istic believers. 'So what are you going to do? Are you going to keep
in touch with him?' Ruby asked.

Flora shook her head. 'How can I? I don't even know him.'

Not long afterwards Denis Kelly, former Comrade, moved down south and joined the Conservative Party. Not that he had a lot of choice. By then he had abandoned the unions and the Labour Party in Scotland and they had abandoned him. Soon he was selected to stand for his new friends in a by-election and this time he won. No one ever had to teach Denis the same lesson twice, the boy learned very quickly.

Ruby felt afterwards that she should have predicted what happened next, but she was too wrapped up in her own life to pay close attention.

'Who would've thought it?' she said to Donald. 'Who could ever have imagined Flora would take the plunge? Flora and Andy Morris, now that did take me by surprise! They're emigrating to Canada, did you know?'

Donald nodded.

'And Flora has always preached against marriage!' she laughed.

'Maybe she just met the right person, Ruby,' he said quietly. 'What happened to the MP chap?'

'The Honourable Denis Kelly MP? Och, he's long gone,' Ruby snorted. 'He wasted no time getting his feet under the right tables once he was elected. We only see him up here when he's in the papers. I feel like punching my fist through his picture when I see it.'

'Is this a case of "I kent his father", Ruby?' he teased her.

'No, I never did know his father, but I know the poor man's as ashamed of him as the rest of us. You have to give our Denis credit though, he knew what he was doing, all those favours for people out of the goodness of his pure heart.'

'But he did help people, Ruby, you have to give him that,' Donald chided her. 'Any time I contacted him on behalf of a patient he did what he could.'

'I know he did, and we were all so grateful we didn't see what he was up to. He wasn't doing it out of idealism, Donald, he had another motive: ambition. When did you last hear from him since he became an MP?'

'Well, he lives in England, sitting for an English constituency and I'm sure Westminster keeps him busy, Ruby,' he smiled at her.

'He had hardly arrived down there when he got himself married to the daughter of a Tory grandee!' Ruby said angrily. 'No flies on our Denis! Mark my words, that's what he's got his eye on as well, and the Lord's daughter was a career move as surely as all his good deeds were years ago!'

'Now, Ruby,' he reproached her, 'don't be so judgemental! Give the man a bit of credit, we can't decide who we fall in love with, can we?'

Ruby didn't know how to respond and a preoccupied silence fell between them that made her feel uneasy. If he were to say anything more she might get up and run and she felt he could, so she had to head him off.

'Flora didn't even tell anyone, the sly dog! I knew nothing about it till they came back from Martha Street already man and wife. Mrs Morris was furious, she was bad enough at the thought of him emigrating, but she was black affronted at being done out of a wedding!'

He smiled but didn't reply.

'Anyway,' she laughed, rising from her chair, 'you must have better things to do than sit here listening to me sounding off. And you'll be getting me talked about, coming up here so often! Don't you think for a minute it hasn't been noted by someone. They miss nothing in High Street!' She giggled unconvincingly. 'Everybody knows there's no reason for you to call here any longer, they'll be pairing us off!'

'Has somebody said something to you?' he asked, worried.

'No,' she replied, 'but they wouldn't, would they? And it's not just me, I'm already a scarlet woman anyway for getting divorced, but you have a reputation to protect as well, you know. You have to be careful, Donald. A young, unmarried doctor and an even younger divorced woman, think about it.'

'I don't care!' he said defiantly.

'I'm still one of your patients, though,' she reminded him.

'You don't have to be, you could transfer to another practice,' he suggested, and instantly she knew he had given it some thought. 'Besides,' he said angrily, 'sod them all! Let them say what they damned well like, I have every right to have friends.'

338

This wasn't going as she wanted, she had taken a wrong turning. The panic returned.

'We could meet somewhere else,' he suggested, brightening. 'See the odd flick maybe?'

'Maybe later,' she smiled tightly. 'You'll have to give me time to get to grips with the course, we're not all academic geniuses, you know.'

Perhaps not academic, she thought, after he'd gone, but that reply had been a stroke of genius all the same. Even so, the uneasy truce of their parting had left her with an unsettled feeling that she found hard to shake off.

So she became a Pupil Nurse, the subtle difference in terminology implying her lower status in the pecking order; Student Nurses became State Registered Nurses, and SRNs were top of the tree. Pupil Nurses, after a compressed two-year course, emerged as Enrolled Nurses, though in practice they were often interchangeable with SRNs. Not that the SRNs approved of this, they guarded their seniority and higher ranking jealously, but there was, as there always would be, a scarcity of nurses and the hospitals were only too happy to rely on Enrolled Nurses. In reality, the course was popular with older and married women who had some experience of life and of organising families, often making them better, more effective nurses. Even knowing this to be true, Ruby had to admit that she felt diminished, second class somehow, but on the bright side, though her uniform was different, she was still able to work with patients. And that was her forte, working with patients. Ruby had a gift many academically-minded, better qualified, ambitious SRNs often did not. In the back of her mind she still harboured dreams of the top qualification, though when she thought about it logically, she knew she didn't need it.

At one point in her training she worked in Gynaecology and Obstetrics and came across, for the second time in her life, the phrase 'virgo intacta.' She was swotting for an exam and the words seemed to jump off the page at her, though at first she couldn't recall where she had heard them before. Then she remembered. Bea. She had been talking to Donald McGill about Bea after she had made the shock discovery that her sister, despite her denials, had indeed wanted children. 'Well, she was virgo intacta,' he had said, and Ruby had asked innocently 'Would that have stopped her having children?' She sat in the library, trying to remember what he had said. He had looked away from her, she now recalled, and said quietly, 'Yes, that would have stopped her.' She didn't know whether to laugh or cry, but imagined him sitting in the surgery chuckling to himself after she had gone. 'I bet he thought that was a great giggle!' she thought angrily. As soon as she got off duty she almost ran down to the surgery. He was on his way out when she dashed in.

'I'm just closing up, Ruby,' he smiled.

'That's what you think, buster!' she said, grabbing him by the arm and pushing him back inside.

'What in hell's the matter with you?' he asked, shocked. 'Are you ill?'

'No, I'm not,' she seethed at him, pushing him into his chair, 'but if you've got any catgut in that bag of yours I'd better get it ready – for yourself!'

He was laughing at her now, she could see that plainly enough. 'What have I done?' he chuckled.

'What have you done?' she demanded, marching up and down the surgery. 'You've made me look and feel like a bloody fool, that's what you've done!'

'Ruby, will you sit down and calm yourself!'

'Don't try your family doctor act on me!' she whispered furiously. 'I wouldn't dare!'

'And you can wipe that smirk off your face while we're at it!'

He wiped a hand solemnly across his face and looked at her seriously.

'Your eyes are still laughing!' she accused him.

He dutifully passed his hand over his eyes. 'Okay, so what's this about?'

'Bea,' she said. 'It's about Bea. Do you remember after she died we spoke in this very room' – she opened her arms wide – 'and I asked you about whether her illnesses prevented her having weans?'

He looked puzzled. 'Not in detail, but go on.'

'You said she was virgo intacta, and like a clown I asked if that would have stopped her having weans. Do you remember what you said?'

He sat in silence for a moment then cleared his throat.

'All coming back to you now, is it?' she demanded.

He didn't look at her and made no sound, but he put one hand over his mouth and his shoulders were heaving. 'Jeez, Ruby, think about it, what could I have said?'

'You could've told me the truth instead of leaving me sitting there like the village idiot!'

'Well, I thought you knew about Bea and Davy,' he explained, 'or I would never have mentioned it. I mean, she was your sister and sisters talk about such things, don't they?'

'*Bea?*' she screeched at him. 'Are you daft or something? Bea talk to me? To anybody?'

He put a finger to his lips. 'Shh, Ruby, calm down, let me explain. When I saw from your reaction that you didn't know, I decided it wasn't my place to tell you. I was young, I'd only just taken over the practice. I'd made a mistake in even mentioning it so I covered up as best I could.' He looked at her, trying not to make his amusement too obvious. 'I take it you've just found out from a medical textbook?'

Ruby sat down. 'Aye,' she said, almost weary now but still trying to hold onto her annoyance even thought it was abating. 'So she really was a virgin?'

'Yes.'

'But how? Why?'

'I don't know!' he said. 'I'm sure my father knew but that piece of information he never passed on. I do have an opinion, though, if you'd like to hear it?'

She nodded slightly.

'I'm pretty sure Davy likes men, not women.'

Ruby let out a long breath. 'One of my mad old aunties always maintained Davy only married Bea because his mother died and he needed someone to look after him.'

'And Bea did that, didn't she?'

'She even ironed his overalls,' Ruby said.

Donald McGill laughed out loud. 'And he got someone else to do that really quickly after Bea died, didn't he?'

'That boy? God, that boy!'

'And no one in the family ever commented?'

'George said Davy must have heard about some big insect called a preying mantis that ate the male as they mated. Some spiders do it too, he said. He reckoned Davy was too scared to go near her.'

'And no one ever wondered about his nickname either, *Dainty* Davy?'

'Well, he was a dancer, wasn't he? Still is,' Ruby said weakly. She looked up at him and slapped his forearm. 'Will you stop laughing! It's not funny!'

'No, not for Bea, I agree, but it's funny all the McLeans didn't think it was funny!'

'Did you never say anything to her? You were her doctor, after all.'

'I didn't know till I read the post mortem report. I mean, I don't inquire into the nitty-gritty marital habits of my patients. If they don't choose to tell me, who am I to ask?'

'Poor old Bea,' she said sadly. 'She had nothing, did she? I always hated the sight of her because she caused so much trouble, but no wonder, she seems to have spent her entire live unhappy.'

Donald McGill nodded. 'It happens, Ruby,' he said softly. He leaned forward, looking directly into her eyes. 'You just have to learn from it and make sure it doesn't happen to you.'

She didn't reply. There was a feeling that they had somehow strayed back onto territory she had excised herself from before and didn't want to be in again. The silence stretched.

'How are you finding the course?' he asked brightly.

It was almost as though he had read her mind and decided to change the subject.

Relief flooded through her. 'It's fine, a dawdle, if I'm being truthful.'

'Well, if you think of anything else I can help with, you only have to run down here and threaten me!' he grinned. 'Now can I get home for my tea? My mother will be wondering where I've got to.'

'They're like that, mothers,' she agreed. 'Frances will be wondering where I am as well.'

Walking the short distance to 252 she felt grateful to him. He had let her off the hook.

42

By the time her two years were up she found herself alone for the first time in her life, when she came home one day and found that Frances had departed; just upped and left without a word. Wherever she had gone she would need money, and Ruby wondered where she had got it or, more likely, from whom and did they know about it yet? Then she looked around and noticed that her daughter had taken with her everything she could find in the house that would be of any use or could be sold. Sarah's wedding ring was safely nestled on Ruby's right hand, that at least was safe, she thought, twisting it on her finger. Frances was no fool, she was born knowing how to get what she wanted and Ruby had always been aware that anything she discovered about her was only the tip of a considerable iceberg. The note on the table simply said 'Don't bother trying to find me, I won't be back.' Ruby sat down and read it again and again, as though some hidden information might reveal itself between the lines if she scanned it just once more.

There had been no particular indication she could recall that this had been in Frances's mind. Frances didn't vary up or down, she just was, she kept herself to herself as she always had. And there were no friends to ask, Frances had never gone in for friends, the word 'loner' might have been invented for her.

At moments like this any mother would be feeling panic and fear for her missing child, would be hopping about crying and trying to think what to do, but it was almost as if she had been expecting it for a long time, or something like it. And, to be truthful, more than any other emotion, Ruby felt relief. That she did made her feel ashamed, but it didn't change her relief. Frances was seventeen years old, the same age as Ruby had been when she was married with a child on the way, and her daughter doubtless felt as she had then, that she knew everything. The difference was that Ruby had been a true innocent, whereas Frances, she suspected, already had more knowledge from her first breath than her mother would have in her entire lifetime. There was nothing she could do about it anyway. In the eyes of the Law Frances wasn't a child, she was an adult who was free and able to make her own decisions and choices in life. No, she just had to take a deep breath and wait for the next development, and there would be one, where Frances was concerned there always was. There was no one to share her thoughts with. George had long ago given up any interest in Frances. Donald? No, she couldn't, wouldn't go to Donald. Flora, who always knew what to do for the best, was in Canada. Agnes, then? Her sister-in-law couldn't help, but she could listen.

'Gerry's not here, is he?' she asked, as Agnes opened the door.

'No, no, come in,' Agnes smiled. 'He's not here often these days, Ruby. In fact, I'm on my own tonight, everybody's out, so it's nice to have some company. Go in and sit down by the fire, I'll make some tea.'

'Where are they?' Ruby called through to the kitchen.

'The father of the tribe and his son are at the football, and the lassies are at night school.' She shouted back cheerfully. 'They're doing embroidery now. They've done dressmaking, they have an idea to open up their own wee place, a bit higher class than I used to do. Weans, eh?' She came through, beaming with pride, and laid the tray before Ruby.

'Aye, weans, eh?' Ruby replied quietly.

'What's the matter?' Agnes asked. 'Frances?'

Ruby nodded and handed her the note. Agnes read it quickly then made to throw it in the fire, raising an eyebrow at Ruby for permission. Ruby nodded and the piece of paper landed in the flames and was quickly consumed.

'Are you really worried, surprised even?' Agnes asked carefully.

'Not really,' Ruby replied, her hands wrapped round her cup, watching the last trace of the note disappearing. 'Relieved in a way,' she sighed. 'I know that sounds terrible, Agnes.'

Agnes shook her head. 'You've always had my sympathies where Frances was concerned,' she told her. 'There's always been something not right about her. I saw it when she was a wee thing.'

Ruby laughed sadly. 'I always thought so too, Flora used to say it as well, but my Ma insisted she was fine, she was going through a phase. I used to think it was a helluva long phase. It lasted all her life.'

'Aye, but your Ma saw good in everybody, didn't she? Your Ma was a kind soul, sure everybody knows that. What are you going to do?'

'Nothing I can do,' Ruby sighed. 'I've never been able to do anything with Frances, have I?'

'You did your best,' Agnes said kindly, 'no one could ask more than that of you, Ruby. Did she tell you I told her not to come back here?'

Ruby looked up at her, shocked. 'No!'

'She was stealing everything she could lay her hands on,' Agnes shook her head, remembering. 'Every time she came here things went missing. I caught her a couple of times with money and bits of jewellery actually in her hands, yet she stood there and denied it. In her hands, mind you. I thought that was really strange.'

'It was the same with George and Marie,' Ruby said. 'I never told you, but they didn't want her in their house either. Marie was in a terrible state, thought we'd fall out over it, but I understood. If I'd been in their place I'd have done the same.' She shrugged. 'Same reason, and she never seemed to learn when she was caught, that always puzzled me.'

'I think she saw getting caught as a kind of occupational hazard,' Agnes suggested.

'What do you mean?'

'Well, like big time criminals, you know, the ones that do it for a living? They accept that they might get found out once or twice out of ten times, and that's a risk they're prepared to live with. Frances is the same. To her it's getting caught that's wrong, not whatever it is she's done.'

'Makes some kind of sense, I suppose. The other thing was that the stuff she took was often of no use to her, it was as if she took it just because it was there. What did she say when you told her not to come back?'

'She didn't say anything, nothing ever shamed her or bothered her, did it? She didn't care. I told her I wouldn't tell you unless she came back, so she never did.'

Ruby put her cup down and covered her face with her hands. 'Oh, Agnes, I'm so sorry!'

'Oh, behave yourself!' Agnes replied kindly. 'It wasn't your fault, there's no reason you should feel sorry!'

'I'm her mother!' Ruby cried. 'Of course it's my fault, Agnes!'

Agnes chuckled, 'What's that saying? "Mother thy name is guilt!" And that's even if you get it right, Ruby! No, this isn't your doing. I remember watching her when she was a wean and wondering. As I say, there was always something about her. She kept herself to herself even as a baby, I always thought that was, I don't know, unnatural, I suppose.'

'I used to wonder if it was to do with me not really wanting her,' Ruby confided. 'Not her exactly, but as you know, she was a mistake. I used to wonder if somehow she knew that and that was why she was so distant.'

'Och, don't be silly, lassie! It was nothing to do with that and you know it! It was just who she was, who she is. You know, I never once saw her laughing or being affectionate to anyone, even as a baby?'

'So many people have said that,' Ruby replied. 'Wee Jamie was always cuddling everyone, but Frances never did and never took a cuddle either. If you put your arms about her it was like you were holding one of they dummies in Rita's shop window in the Gallowgate.'

'In the end I just didn't want her near my lassies,' Agnes admitted, 'and that's the simple truth. Not that it was a problem, they didn't want to be near her.' She looked across at Ruby. 'I'm sorry, hen,' she said sympathetically. 'I shouldn't have said that, I don't want to hurt your feelings.'

Ruby waved a hand. 'No, no, you're family, Agnes, and you did the right thing. I wouldn't have wanted her near normal weans either.'

'Do you see what you said there?' Agnes asked. 'You said "normal weans." That's the point, Ruby, hen, Frances was never normal, she was born like that. You didn't do anything to her. Now you have to believe that, Ruby, hen, as I say, you did your best. Just think how much worse things could've turned out if you hadn't?'

As she walked home along Duke Street she went over everything Agnes had said and knew she was right, though the sense of failure was still there. If she had known Frances wasn't going to stick around, she thought glumly, she could've done a Student Nurse course and become a State Registered Nurse, with the opportunity to advance to the giddy heights of Staff Nurse and Ward Sister. 'But that's life,' she murmured. 'It always throws you a wobbly one.'

Frances's departure to who knew where had the effect of setting Ruby free once again, of letting her decide what to do with her life without having to consider other people. Everything, it seemed to her, had been decided for her; her mistake with Gerry had led to her ill-fated marriage and single-parenthood, then a series of family situations had trapped her in the role of carer. Not that she grudged raising her daughter or nursing her mother and father, but those situations had, at the very least, delayed her doing what she wanted to do. She would leave High Street, she decided, she had to. She had lived there all her life, spent most of it at 252 in fact, but now there was nothing left for her there. Perhaps it was just time to grow up. She had completed her two years and become an SEN, a State Enrolled Nurse and, as nurses of any variety were always needed, she could go anywhere. Where she wanted to go, needed to go, was away from High Street, where she was trapped by memories and by habit. It didn't have to be far at first, but far enough to break the ties that bound her. Once she had made one move, she reasoned, the next would be easier. In the back of her mind lay the fear of Frances turning up again. She knew her daughter well enough to know she would find her wherever she was. Ruby dreaded the prospect. If Frances re-appeared in her life it wouldn't be out of love, but because she wanted something or was in trouble.

The hardest thing she had to do was tell Donald McGill. He had been her main support during the hardest days of her life and had become her, well, her friend, a level she had struggled to keep him

347

at. She decided to see him in his surgery, that way she would be in control of when and how they parted. Donald was aghast.

'You're going away?' he repeated, as though the idea was outrageous. 'Just up and off? Just like that?'

'Well, with a bit more planning than that, Donald,' she laughed, but it sounded brittle even to her. 'I'm moving on, people do it all the time.'

'And you didn't think of discussing it with me first?'

She wanted to say 'Why should I?' but she didn't, couldn't, not to Donald. 'I didn't think it was worth discussing,' she said calmly, 'I can't see what the fuss is about.'

'Yes you do, Ruby,' he said firmly. 'You're trying to present this as a brave new beginning, but you and I both know you're running away.'

She had never seen him angry before and it shocked her. 'Running away?' she asked. 'How am I running away? From what?' Before the words left her mouth she knew she had made a mistake.

'Look, Ruby, cards on the table. You know I have feelings for you and I believe you have feelings for me. We've both skirted round this for years, but I've never pushed it because I hoped you'd come round by yourself and I didn't want to scare you off. I always hoped you'd have the guts to see that the past was a mistake and put it behind you. It doesn't have to be like that between a man and a woman.'

She took a deep, steadying breath. 'If,' she said coldly, 'you're referring to Gerry, I know what a mistake that was, I lived it, remember? But I know about marriages that aren't mistakes too. My parents had a good marriage, so do George and Marie, and Agnes Reilly, I could give you any number. I'm not some scared wean, you know. Who knows? Maybe if I hadn't been caught by Gerry I'd never have married anybody, maybe I'm not the marrying kind.'

'I don't believe that!'

'Well maybe you should try,' she told him quietly. 'It's not what I want, Donald.'

'You mean I'm not what you want?' he demanded bitterly. 'If that's what you mean at least have the courage to say it.'

Ruby stared at him. 'Well, maybe that's what I mean then.'

That night, as she lay in her bed at 252 for the last time, she hurt for the way she had deliberately hurt Donald. He didn't deserve it, he was a good and true friend and that wasn't the way she had wanted to leave him, but she couldn't see him backing off any other way. She couldn't go back and put it right, though, if she did it would leave her vulnerable to persuasion and she had to be strong. What she was doing was right for her. She had to carry it through without any backward glances. Even so, she curled herself into a tight ball and pulled the blankets over her head as she fell into a restless sleep.

43

And so began the itinerant phase of Ruby's life. For the first time ever she had no responsibilities except those she chose to accept, and she enjoyed being free to come and go as she pleased without being answerable to anyone. She worked as a theatre nurse in the Western Infirmary first, across oceans, in Glasgow terms, then she moved to Edinburgh Royal for a few years, across worlds, in Glasgow terms. It was there that she was told of Gerry's death in the mid 1960s. He had been found dead with a broken skull at the bottom of the stairs to his flat, the same stairs that he had once pushed her down and broken her heart. There was a kind of symmetry to it, she supposed. By the time she got Agnes's letter it was too late to attend his funeral. Agnes knew where she was and could've phoned and left a message at the hospital, so she guessed her former sister-in-law chose to write instead and was grateful. She wouldn't have gone anyway, but Agnes had saved her having to refuse, so she expressed regret out of consideration for his sister, who had always been kind to her. He was from another time, a man she hardly knew despite the two children she had borne him. In the same letter Agnes told her that Donald McGill had finally got married to a district nurse. There was a twinge at that, no denying it, however illogical it was. She had still harboured hopes about Donald, carried a candle for him, that's what it was called. Then she smiled. Donald obviously had a thing for nurses.

She was working at Aberdeen Royal another few years down the line when Frances caught up with her. A letter with a London postmark arrived, forwarded several times, asking for a meeting. She struggled for a long time before replying that she would come to the address in Acton at the top of Frances's letter. Agnes was now the proud owner of a telephone, so she asked if Frances could call there to confirm the meeting. If Frances came to her she couldn't get up and go if things became difficult – the Donald principle again – and more than that, she couldn't risk Frances causing trouble in her life, and Frances was always trouble. When she replied to the letter she didn't put her address on it for that reason.

'Aye, okay then,' Agnes said reluctantly, 'she can phone here. But you're making a mistake, Ruby, hen, she can't be up to anything good.

'I know, I know,' Ruby said. 'All my instincts tell me I'm doing the wrong thing, but I just want to know what this is about. Maybe it's over, her letter didn't catch up with me for ages, maybe you won't hear anything and I won't have to go down. Listen to me,' she said glumly. 'This is my daughter.'

Frances, it turned out, had a dilemma, in fact she had two, both under three years old. They peered at Ruby with curious eyes but, she noticed, they didn't seek reassurance by hiding behind their mother, they sat on the floor with a few toys around them. Frances's problem, it seemed, was that she had a new man and he didn't want her children, neither of whom were his. He was off to Australia soon and Frances wanted to go with him, so she needed someone to take the children off her hands.

'It's not for long,' she lied calmly, 'about six months.'

Ruby stared at her, truly dumbfounded. 'You're planning to leave your weans? Even for six months?' she demanded incredulously. 'At their ages?'

Frances nodded. There had been no reunion as she walked in the door, no explanation, it was as though they had last met the day before, and neither had Frances shown the least interest or curiosity in what Ruby was doing now, where she was living or what was happening in High Street.

'And it's taken you a good while to find me,' Ruby reminded her, 'so when does this six months actually start?'

Frances shrugged off the inconvenient question. 'We just had to put it off for a while.'

Ruby looked at her, knowing she was lying. She doubted if there was a man at all, far less a trip to Australia for however long. Her heart sank. The truth, she was sure, was that Frances was fed up with the children and wanted to offload them, and who better and more convenient than her mother? Everyone knew Ruby looked after people, Ruby gave up her own life to care for family and, though she was a total stranger to these children, she would certainly do so again. Blood, after all, was thicker than water, a saying she thought Frances could marshal as an argument without having the slightest understanding of what it meant.

'Well, I'm sorry, Frances,' she said calmly, 'but you'll have to look elsewhere. I have a life of my own now, and they're your responsibility, yours and whoever fathered them.' She deliberately didn't look at the two bewildered children, knowing she had to stay focused.

'That's you all over, isn't it?' Frances almost snarled. 'I don't know why I even thought of you. You were useless as a mother.'

Ruby got up to leave but Frances caught her arm and swung her round.

'Frances,' she said quietly, 'think of your weans. They don't need to be subjected to this.'

'Don't bother about them!' Frances said savagely.

A picture instantly flashed into Ruby's mind of Iris saying almost those words as she dismissed Jamie all those years ago. Was that the connection then? Had Frances inherited the same disturbing gene as Iris, only more so? Looking at her daughter she was shocked, but also bemused, at probably the first real emotion she had ever witnessed from her. Yet there was a nagging doubt at the same time, making her wonder if it was indeed real or manufactured.

'You used to dump me with whoever would take me,' Frances accused her.

'Like who?'

'That woman in Duke Street—'

'She's your aunt!' Ruby almost laughed.

'—and that old man!'

'He was your grandfather, we lived with him!'

'You still dumped me!'

'You were with Agnes while I was looking after my mother, who was dying of TB, Frances. You were well looked after and I saw you when I could during those months. What was I expected to do? And after that I was trying to find a way of supporting you. I had to provide for us, remember?'

'And that's another thing when I think about it,' Frances accused her, 'you took me away from my father, you even abandoned *him*!'

'Your father?' Ruby replied angrily. 'Your father was an alcoholic, Frances, and he was dangerous to be around when he was drinking, which was always. He only lived a couple of closes up the road and you never saw him, did you? He never paid a penny towards your keep either. And I left him after he—' She stopped. She had decided long ago that she didn't want Frances to know about losing the baby she called John, she wasn't going to be tripped into it now through anger roused by a tantrum. She turned to go. 'And this poor father that you were deprived of, can you remember what he looked like? When did you last contact him? Do you even know if he's dead or alive, do you even care'

Frances looked at her with a bored expression, now that it was over, she had lost interest.

'I thought so,' Ruby said curtly.

All the way home on the train she was in turmoil though. Those poor weans, what would happen to them now? And they were her grandchildren, unless Frances had been lying about that too and she wouldn't put it past her. She tried to cheer herself up. Maybe she had hired them, it could part of a wider scam. Now that Frances lived in London she had a bigger stage to perform on, she must have learned a few more tricks. But no, they were her grandchildren, a quick glimpse was enough to recognise one or two family resemblances. The older a child, a boy, looked very like Gerry, and the girl had a look of Sarah about her. She closed her eyes. She had to look at this situation logically. The regret at turning her back on them would stay with her for the rest of her life, she knew that, but if she took them on there was no guarantee that

Frances would leave it at that. Every time she wanted something she would appear with her demands and if Ruby didn't give in she would threaten to take the children, regardless of the effect on them. They, like Ruby, were simply pawns in Frances's games. She had been in that position before, she remembered, when Jamie had been taken away. As in that case, there would be nothing she could do about it. Frances, as Iris had been, was their mother and would have the Law entirely on her side. Even if she returned to dump them on Ruby time after time, that wouldn't change. She could, she realised, come back with more yet children for her to raise. If she had been irresponsible enough to bring two into the world there was no reason why she would stop at that. That was Frances all over, someone else always had to pick up the tab as she went on her cheating way. But what would become of them now? On the way back up north she broke her journey and paid Agnes a visit.

'You couldn't have taken them on, Ruby,' Agnes reassured her. 'I know you'll be feeling that you should, but it makes no sense. You're in Aberdeen now, is your place up there even big enough for two weans? And could you afford to move somewhere bigger and you with no job? You'd have to give up work to take them, wouldn't you?'

Ruby nodded glumly. 'But what will she do with them now?'

'You could've done her a good turn,' Agnes counselled, 'maybe you've forced her to stand on her own two feet, you never know.'

Ruby looked at her sceptically. 'This is Frances, remember?'

'Aye, aye, I know,' Agnes said. 'I was trying to make you feel better, hen!'

'And I know that!' Ruby smiled. 'I was just thinking, if I hadn't given up 252 ...'

'But you did, Ruby, and you were right. Even if you hadn't, who could've looked after them while you were working, and you have to work to earn a living, don't you? No, she's asking too much, she has no right to ask in fact, brazen cow! She's a grown woman, a mother, she has to face her responsibilities. You have to harden your heart, Ruby. It's not a nice thing to say, but it's true.'

'Easier said than done,' Ruby sighed.

'Ruby McLean,' Agnes said sternly, 'just because it's hard doesn't mean it's wrong! You've never taken the easy route in your life!'

Her resolve lasted less than two weeks, her heart may well have hardened but it took its spite out on her mind and visited her sleep with nightmares. When she saw the two children she was convinced she had no more than glanced at them, which made her total recall of their features puzzling. Once, in another time, she had abandoned Jamie, that's what he believed and it was what she believed too, regardless of the bare facts. What were bare facts anyway but a means of disguising guilt? And now she was doing it again, abandoning not just one helpless, innocent child this time, but two, her own grandchildren. She had no idea what Frances was really up to, she never had, but whatever it was there were children to consider. Maybe Frances was tired of being a single parent and just wanted to move on, maybe she was up to no good in some way and the children were getting in her way of that, but Ruby couldn't shake the picture of the two children out of her head.

In her dreams they sat on the floor and stared at her with sad, accusing eyes, and she couldn't shake from her mind the memory that they hadn't run to their mother for protection from the stranger who had entered their home. That's what children did, their mother was the one person in the universe who protected them, the one they always reached out to – even Frances had done so in asking her to take them – but those two had sought no reassurance from their mother. That, she was sure, had to mean something.

She had no clear plan in mind as she booked the train ticket, all she knew was that she needed to see them again. If the worst came to the worst she would have to bring them up to Scotland and work out a way of coping later, but she'd think of that if and when it happened. No use worrying unless and until there was something to worry about. But there was no one in the Acton flat. When there was no response to her knocking she looked through the letterbox and it wasn't just empty, but deserted. Standing outside the silent flat she wondered what to do next, then the next door along opened tentatively and a figure appeared. Ruby looked up at her.

'She's gone,' the woman told her. 'If you're looking for the Scotch lass, she's gone.'

Ruby made a mental note. 'She is a human being, not a bottle of whisky, she is *Scottish*. What does that matter, you idiot, she's still gone!'

'Have you any idea where?' she asked.

The woman shook her head. 'As long as it's far away.'

'She caused trouble?' Ruby smiled. A friendly response might get her a little further.

The woman rolled her eyes. 'And then some!' she said with feeling. 'It was the kiddies I felt sorry for, poor little mites.'

'Yes, that's why I'm here, I'm worried about them too.'

'You from the council?'

'I'm a nurse,' Ruby said evasively, but it seemed to satisfy the neighbour.

'Oh well, you'll know then,' she replied vaguely.

'When was she last here?'

'Moved out just over a week ago.'

'And the kiddies were with her?'

'Oh they were with her, all right,' the woman replied. 'Not that they should've been, she didn't care about them, that's for sure. Left them on their own all day, sometimes more than that, poor little mites.'

Ruby thanked her, not sure whether she should be glad or sorry that the children were with Frances. She stood outside the flats and thought for a while, looking up and down the road as though the two children might come walking towards her at any moment, then she asked for directions to the nearest police station and made her way there.

'I'm looking for my daughter and my two grandchildren,' she explained to the policeman behind the desk. 'I saw them in a flat just up the road a fortnight ago, but a neighbour's just told me they've been gone about a week.'

'And is your daughter over twenty-one?' he asked briskly.

Ruby nodded.

'She's free to come and go as she pleases then,' he told her. 'Doesn't have to tell anyone where she's taken her kids, doesn't even have to tell her own mother.'

'It's just that I'm a bit worried about the kids,' Ruby said. 'I'm not sure she's looking after them properly.'

He smiled at her. He had a nice face when he smiled. 'We all think we know best how to bring up kids,' he said kindly and winked at her. 'My advice is don't get involved, sweetheart, she won't thank you for it.'

Ruby felt about five years old.

He looked at her again. 'You're really worried, aren't you?' he asked.

'Well I've come all the way down from Aberdeen,' Ruby laughed quietly, 'so I suppose I must be.'

'What's her name then? I'll have a look at anything we might have had in the last couple of weeks, put your mind at rest, eh?'

'Frances Reilly.'

He looked up sharply.

'I see you know the name,' she said.

'You might say that.' As he looked her up and down she could almost hear him thinking 'You look like a respectable kind of woman, and you're her mother?'

'To save you the trouble,' Ruby said, 'I know what she's like. She's been like it since she was born, before that actually. When I was carrying her she kicked me once and broke one of my ribs. She's been doing it one way or another ever since, too.' Tears prickled her eyes, taking her by surprise.

The officer came round from the desk and guided her to a bench by the door. 'Look,' he said kindly, 'it's not my place and you'll probably shoot me down here, but I do know this young lady, and that's not her only name as it happens, I know them all. My advice would be to get on the first train home and don't come back here again, don't even think about her again.'

'But she has children!' Ruby sniffled.

'Well, you can take it from an old plod, these kinds of kids tend to get by, they learn ways normal folk don't and they survive. It's not ideal but there it is.' He watched her for a moment. 'I'll have a look and see if we know anything. You sit here. I'll get one of the girls to bring you a cuppa, okay?'

He came back about ten minutes later. 'Nothing's been reported here,' he said, 'and I called the council to see if they knew anything about the children, and they don't.' He changed his tone to one of reassurance. 'So that's good news, isn't it?'

'In what way?' Ruby asked.

'Well, she hasn't abandoned them or anything, so we have to assume that she's got them and is looking after them.'

Ruby looked down at her tea. They knew nothing of the kind, actually. They knew that nothing had come to light in this area, which wasn't the same as saying they were all right. What about other areas? But he was right about one thing, Frances was an adult. This pleasant, sympathetic London copper had already gone out of his way to help her and his hands were tied. She thanked him graciously and got up to go.

'Tell you what,' he said before she let go of the swing door, 'do you have a telephone number? I could take a note of it and if I hear anything I could give you a bell.'

Ruby smiled at him as she searched through her bag for Agnes's number. 'You've been so kind,' she said, 'I'm really grateful. This is the number of my sister-in-law in Glasgow. She can always get in touch with me.'

She heard nothing more, of course, she didn't really think she would. That was one of Frances's traits, when she had run her mile in one area she moved on to another and, even without knowing the details, she knew Frances had run her mile in Acton. What was it Agnes had said? 'Mother, thy name is guilt.' Well, that was true, guilt upon guilt, upon guilt. Why hadn't she seen how things would go, that she would think about Frances's plea for her to take her children and finally agree? What kind of life had she condemned them to by not doing it sooner?

44

Paddy was sitting in her flat devouring the best of a packet of chocolate biscuits by dunking them in hot tea. She watched him, grimacing. His hands were covered in melted chocolate, then half a biscuit broke off into his cup and he fished it out, slurping the dissolving bits noisily from his fingers as he retrieved them.

'So what were you when you were a human being?' she asked

'What do you mean by that?' he demanded, wide-eyed.

'When you were a working man, I mean, instead of an old age pensioner sponging off the state and digusting decent folk with your eating habits.'

He ignored her, partly, one of his favourite tricks. 'I am a senior citizen, Ruby McLean,' he said politely, 'and I worked for every penny of my pension.'

'So what did you do?' she asked again.

'I worked in the shipyards, I was an electrician, if you must know,' he replied.

'My God! You kept that quiet, Keenan! The things I could've got you to do around here, putting in new sockets and fixing plugs!'

'Why do you think I never told you?' he laughed. 'And don't you tell anybody else either, or they'll be queuing up at the door.'

'What would be wrong with that?' she asked. 'You could earn the odd couple of bob.'

'I hated it, that's what's wrong with it!' he said with feeling. 'I had to get a trade and my Da sent me in that direction, in those days you did what your Da told you, didn't you? It came down to a couple of wires, that's all there was to it, always a couple of wires. I was bored out of my mind my entire working life.'

'So why didn't you do something else?'

'Like what?' he demanded.

'I don't know, there had to be something you'd rather have done,' she said.

'I'd like to have worked on the land,' he said dreamily, 'I aye had a notion of living on one of they islands and having a wee croft.'

'So why didn't you?'

'Not many crofts in the middle of Glasgow,' he muttered, dunking another biscuit in his tea. 'And before I knew it I was married with a family. I don't think the wife would've liked it, she'd have thought I'd gone bananas if I'd told her that idea.'

'You've told me, but I see your point, that doesn't matter, I already know you're bananas.'

'What did your man do?' he asked.

Sneaky again, she thought, he seems harmless, but he's a sneaky sod, Paddy Keenan! 'He worked on the railways,' she replied calmly. 'All my family did. My Da was a train driver.'

'Really?' he asked. 'You never told me that. That must've been something, driving one of they big engines!'

'Aye, I suppose so.' She sipped her tea thoughtfully. 'Out on the open footplate in all weathers, boiled alive by the fire down the front, soaked by the wind, rain and snow everywhere else, sweat running off him all year round. He seemed to enjoy it though. My brother ran a Goods Yard and I had an uncle who was a fly-shunter.'

'Oh, they were hardy buggers, them!' he said admiringly. 'Dangerous game, the fly-shunting.'

'Aye, there was always somebody losing an arm or a leg, a hand or a foot if they were lucky. He was fine though, I never thought he understood it was dangerous, he just did it.'

'So what did your man do?

'He was working his way through the lines to train driver, then the War came along and when he came back he was too ill to go back to it.'

'When did he pass away, then?' he asked innocently.

'Oh, years and years ago,' she replied with deliberate vagueness. It was the most open conversation she had ever had with him about her past, but there were limits, she decided. 'And he didn't "pass away", he died, you halfwit.'

'You must have been a young woman then? And you never thought of marrying again?'

Ruby shook her head. 'I could've, but I'm not sure I approve of marriage,' she said haughtily.

'What in hell do you mean by that?' he chuckled. 'You're a helluva woman, Ruby, the things you say!'

She ignored his mirth. 'I think it's okay for men, but I don't think women get as much out of it, that's what I mean.'

'Away!' he said derisively, waving an arm at her. 'Yon women's lib has a lot to answer for!'

'Aye, it has. Mainly that when it arrived in Scotland and saw dinosaurs like you, it ran away in the opposite direction,' she replied, 'we could've done with it up here.'

'I don't see that at all!' Paddy blustered.

'And that's supposed to surprise me, is it? Just for a minute, try and see beyond your caveman mentality and think about it,' she said seriously. 'In our day the man went out to work and the woman stayed at home, right?'

He nodded.

'She took care of everything, shopping, bills, all the housework, and remember back then there were no gadgets to help you, it was all hard work that took all day. Then she had to fit in looking after the weans and cooking, and a thousand other things men weren't interested in as long as they were done. The man came home from work and what did he do? What did you do?' She looked at him. 'The same as you're doing now, lie back in your chair – *my* chair – and wait to be pandered to. Your tea on the table, then the dishes cleared away and washed, and there were still things to be done for the morning, ironing, kids washed and got to bed, the breakfast things put out, clean clothes put out, pieces made up, while you read your paper or listened to the wireless. These days it's the TV, same difference. You see what I'm saying? Worked fine for men, not so well for women.'

'Aye, but there's companionship, Ruby,' he wheedled.

'We've got that and we're not married! We've got too bloody much of it, but that's another story,' she scoffed, throwing a box of tissues at him. 'Wipe your hands, for God's sake, I find one chocolate fingerprint anywhere in this flat and you're for the high jump!'

'And you only had the one lassie?' he said, changing the subject.

'Aye,' she said truthfully, 'only the one lassie, and she was a bad lot. Now that will save you digging any deeper, won't it?'

'That's a shame. And I wasn't digging,' he said guiltily.

'Och, save it, Keenan, as usual you jumped right in there with both big horrible feet! I would've told you about her before but I enjoyed seeing how many ways you could come up with to find out. She lied to everybody, she cheated everybody and she stole from everybody. She took off down to London when she was seventeen and spent her entire life in trouble. I haven't seen her in forty years, and I only heard from her in all that time when she wanted something. Does that satisfy you?'

'Ruby ...'

Just then the phone rang. It was Ian Fraser.

'We've found something,' he said when she answered.

'Oh?' she replied evasively.

'Under your Uncle Jakey's floor. We've found a couple of things, actually.'

'Like what?'

'Well, there's a suitcase. The lads who were taking up the floor-boards had opened it before I got there and inside there's what looks like an Arab costume.'

'An Arab costume?' Ruby laughed out loud.

'Aye, sounds daft, I know, but that's what it seems to be, it's been wrapped up really well and carefully put away, there's a big curved sword as well. It's just like that Arab on one of the walls.'

Ruby was laughing so hard she had to sit down. 'The Sheik of High Street rides again!'

'What did you say?'

'Nothing,' she said, wiping her eyes.

'And there's something else,' he told her. 'A biscuit tin.'

Ruby stopped laughing. 'A biscuit tin? With a pattern in black, red and gold?'

'Aye,' he said quietly, '*the* biscuit tin, the one in the mural.'

She clutched her throat with her free hand. 'You're not going to tell me there's a bar of Fry's Five Boys chocolate inside, are you?'

'Not that I know of,' he laughed, 'but it's still closed! I've got it here beside me, there's an old label with writing on the lid, it's faded so it's hard to make out, but I got a magnifying glass and had a good look under the light. I can just make it out. It says on it "For Ruby". Ruby, you still there?'

'Aye, son, I'm still here.' She swallowed. 'So you haven't opened it, son?'

'No, no, of course not! It's got your name on it, it's yours. You should open it. Besides, it's been soldered shut. If I hadn't arrived when I did the lads would've taken a hammer to it. It's not the first thing we've found under the floorboards during work on these flats, you'd be surprised. People hid all sorts stuff away under there. The tin feels quite heavy, there's definitely something inside. But I was just sitting here thinking, if you hadn't got in touch when you read that wee bit in the *Times,* I wouldn't have known you existed and you'd never have got it. Funny, eh?'

'Aye, funny right enough, son,' she said weakly. Her mouth was dry. 'I don't know what to say.' She was suddenly overcome by emotion. 'I've just this minute been talking about him.'

'Look, this has obviously been a shock. Have a think. I can bring the case and box over to you, years since I've been to Largs, or I can have them sent, or you can come across here again. Give me a call back when you've decided.'

'Aye, fine, son.'

'You okay?' he asked again.

'Aye.'

'No, really, Ruby? I've not upset you?'

'Well you have, talk about a blast from the past! But I'm okay, son, don't worry. I'll do as you say, I'll have a wee think and call you back.'

She decided to ask him to come to Largs. You couldn't trust the post office these days and, if she went over to Glasgow she would have to drag the things home, something she avoided these days.

Ian had no sooner knocked on her door than Paddy appeared. She quickly ushered Ian inside.

'Make yourself comfortable, son,' she said, then, turning to Paddy she asked 'Is there something I can do for you Mr Keenan?'

He dodged back and forth, trying to see behind her into the flat, but she dodged just as nimbly to stop him.

'I saw a boy at your door a minute ago,' he said.

'At *my* door? I'm sure you must be mistaken, Mr Keenan,' she said sweetly. 'Now bugger off!'

'Is there some kind of trouble, Ruby?'

'Aye, there is,' Ruby stated, 'and it's called Paddy Keenan! It's been causing me trouble since the sad day I set eyes on it! Now go away!'

'Well, who is he then?' Paddy demanded, totally unfazed.

Ruby sighed heavily. 'Paddy, I've been trying to keep this from you,' she said sadly. 'But he's my fancy man. All that tosh about sitting with sick people, it was just a cover. I've got myself a toy boy. There it is, the truth, what more can I say? We're going to take off together on his Harley Davidson. If you run down the stairs quick you'll see it outside there.'

'Away to hell!' he chuckled. 'You're up to something. What is it?'

'Bugger off!' she said furiously, and shut the door.

Paddy opened the letterbox and peered through, as she knew he would.

'If you don't remove that ugly mug from my letterbox I'll poke you in the eyes with two fingers!' she said, thrusting her hand at him menacingly. The letterbox closed and, shortly after it, Paddy's front door did the same.

'A friend of yours?' Ian asked, laughing when she went through to the living room.

'A pain in the bloody arse!' she said, shaking her head in irritation. She went into the kitchen to put the kettle on. 'Now, what have you got there, son?'

'Well there's the suitcase with the Arab outfit and,' he said, putting his hand in a paper bag, 'the tin.'

Watching from the kitchen as she got the cups out she stopped and stared at it. 'Aye, the tin,' she said. She laughed nervously. 'I don't know why, son, but I'm scared stiff of that tin!'

'I know what you mean,' he said quietly. 'I am myself and I don't know why either. We'll need a soldering iron to break the seal. I was thinking on the drive down that I should've brought one with me, that was daft. I don't suppose you've got one about, have you?'

'Do I look like the kind of old biddy who'd have a soldering iron about me?' she laughed. 'I suppose that big idiot next door's bound to have one.'

'The pain in the arse?'

'Aye, the very one, but how to get it off him without telling him anything, that's the problem. I like him to know as little as possible about everything on principle, it annoys the hell out of him.'

'Did I hear you saying something about a Harley there?' he asked, grinning.

'Aye, well ...'

'No problem, then.'

With that he walked to the door and crossed the landing to Paddy's flat where, by the speed at which it was opened, it seemed that Paddy had been standing behind it.

'Sorry to bother, you,' she heard Ian say, 'but Ruby said you might have a soldering iron I could borrow.'

'A soldering iron?' Paddy repeated, stupidly, Ruby thought. 'What does she need a soldering iron for?'

'I'm the one that needs it,' Ian smiled, 'it's for my bike. I noticed on the way here that the nipple on the clutch cable is wearing a wee bit, it's not much, mind you, but I thought I'd do a patch up till I can get it fixed properly. You can never be too careful, you have to really look after a Harley.'

'A Harley?' Paddy repeated incredulously. He looked Ian up and down. 'You're not really wearing motorbike gear,' he said suspiciously.

'I've left it all in Ruby's,' Ian said in a friendly tone. 'Can't go sitting in somebody's living room with all that leather on, can you? That's the trouble with leathers, they're just not designed for taking tea and buns in polite company.'

'And it's a Harley, you say?' Paddy repeated.

'Aye, it's a Fatboy, have you ever had one? They're great machines, not much goes wrong with them, but you always have to keep an eye on clutch cables and brake cables. So do you have one? A soldering iron, I mean?'

Paddy seized his chance. 'Just you go back in and I'll bring it over to you,' he said slyly.

Back in her flat, her ear pressed to the door, Ruby scowled and whispered 'Don't fall for that, son!'

'No, that's all right,' Ian replied smoothly. 'I don't want to put you to any trouble, I'll just wait here.'

She put her hand over her mouth to stifle a giggle. There was no way Paddy could get past him without knocking him down and, given that Ian was so much younger, she knew Paddy wouldn't try it. He came back carrying the soldering iron, a huge smile on his face.

'I thought for a minute he'd leapfrog over me to get in!'

'He's harmless really,' she laughed, 'It just makes my life easier if I keep him in the dark. If I gave too much ground I'd never get rid of him.'

He looked at the tin sitting on the table. 'Look,' he said quietly. 'How do you want to do this? I thought I'd maybe remove the solder and leave you to it, take a walk down by the front there, okay?'

She nodded. 'That's nice of you, son.' She laughed suddenly to chase away the tears that were beginning to flood her eyes. 'Daft old biddy!' she scolded herself silently, feeling for a hankie just in case.

They waited in silence for the iron to heat up then he applied it around the ancient solder on the lid.

'Better than the old kind,' he smiled, 'this one plugs in, the old ones had to be heated in the fire or on a gas ring. My Da used to make model engines, that's how I came to be so handy, but this is taking some shifting. He didn't want it opened by a casual passer-by, your Uncle Jakey.'

Finally it was done. 'You'll have to leave it for a wee while, it's still hot. I'll take off for a stroll down memory lane now,' he said, looking at his watch. 'It's just coming up for three. Meet you at Nardini's half-four, five o'clock? I'll treat you to a fish tea!'

'Him next door would go mad if he knew!' she chuckled.

'Make sure you tell him then!'

Outside her window all was calm, the sun was shining and the sea was a sparkling blue. Sometimes she sat for hours watching the changing colours of the water and listening to its different noises. The suitcase was lying flat on a chair and, inside it, Jakey's Arab costume waited to be inspected. She couldn't bear to set eyes on it yet though and, if truth were told, even when the tin had cooled down, she would rather not open that either. She ran a finger over the faded label on the lid that bore her name. Lovely handwriting he had, she remembered, playing for time. Ian had loosened the lid a bit but the stiff hinges still had to be coaxed before it would ease open. When it finally did, the inside was so tightly packed with stuff that she couldn't get her hand in and had to remove the more accessible bits carefully and slowly to make room. Crammed all the way round the tin was a large, bulky, sealed envelope and, inside that, a thick wad of what proved to be bank books. Taking them out one-by-one, she saw that they were from all from different banks, some bearing Jakey's name and some, she realised with a shock, her own. Underneath them, on the bottom of the tin, there it was: a bar of Fry's Five Boys chocolate. Finding it here made her cry out loud and drop it quickly onto the table in front of her as though she had been scalded.

Her eyes were filling, so to stop the tears she pictured Cissie and Dot and wondered what they would have said if they had known he had been hiding that during the War, while they had near starved for want of a sweetie. She looked out across the bay, conjuring up the memory of the hilarious consequences when they discovered a way round rationing by buying chocolate from the chemist, only to discover it was laxative chocolate for children. And somehow that produced more tears. Then came the bulky envelope. Easing it out, she laid it down and stared at it. It had been secured with layers of sticky brown tape, the kind you had to lick, and across the front was written in Jakey's beautiful script, 'To only be opened by my niece, Ruby McLean.' And she would have to open it, she knew that, but she felt afraid, though she still had no idea why she should. This was from her Uncle Jakey. Jakey, who had done her no harm throughout his life or hers, and here he was, communicating with her across fifty years. There was reason for excitement, curiosity, granted, but not fear. Yet that's what she felt, a dread, a foreboding, an urge to leave it where it was and run away.

For some reason it felt as though Jakey was standing in the room beside her, watching, and he had brought with him everyone from that long ago era. They were gone, all of them, she had lost every one of them, the ones she treasured as well as the ones she could do without, like the Campbells.

Gus had lived to a ripe old age, he was eighty-seven when he died and had been bedridden for years before that. Iris never got away from him and their marriage descended into open hatred long years before she was free of him. Once he was dead the second and longest-serving Mrs Campbell finally got her hands on the money he had salted away, Betty's money, her jewellery had gone long ago. By the time she had the money, though, the bitter years had taken with them Iris's looks and she seemed only then to realise it and just withered away. Ruby tried to remember what had claimed her and couldn't, but before her death Iris had spent several senile years, raging at the moon and Gus Campbell and threatening to kill him if he ever came near her again. She would spend her days, the nurses said, waiting, walking stick in hand, for him to appear, and her nights tormented by the same prospect, so that they had to sedate her to allow her a few hours of disturbed, uneasy sleep, unconscious, but still shouting and ranting at her late departed, if not lamented husband. Poor Iris, she thought she had won a watch when she snared Gus Campbell, but her prize had been a life sentence with hard labour thrown in. When she thought of her wayward sister in later years what she saw was a tragedy. Iris thought she was worldly wise and had seemed that way to everyone, confident, in control and blasé. Her plan was to have a grateful and besotted Gus dancing to her tune, but the bright, beautiful, amoral Iris was the one who had been enslaved, caged and worn down by him in the end. There was about Iris's tale a wealth of sadness, of a life unfulfilled and, remembering her in her arrogant, self-obsessed, sassy prime, who would have thought it?

After his mother's funeral Ruby had no further contact with Jamie, the child she loved as her own when he was a baby. Iris hadn't so much delivered him as separated from him, before dumping him on Ruby as soon as she could walk after his birth. Then she left without giving him a backward glance or thought, but he had been Ruby's delight and joy – right up till she was told the identity of his father. With both his parents dead he reproached Ruby for handing him over to Iris and Gus instead of fighting for him. His childhood, he told her bitterly, had been hell, and it had been her fault, because she had abandoned him. She hadn't, of course. There was no way in the world that they would have left him with her. Iris took him away out of spite, she didn't care about her son, didn't want to care about him, or for him, for that matter, and Ruby had never known what Gus Campbell felt. Apart from lust, that was, naked lust. Only once she had seen him in the bed that had become his world in his final years and he still had that look in his eyes, the look of a beast. She winced at the memory. Even all these years after his death the very thought of him still made her feel sick, how was she to visit that on the boy? He wasn't responsible for the sins of his father, but how could she have kept the knowledge of them from him?

There was no way Jamie intended appreciating her position, he was angry and bitter and saw only his own suffering, she understood that. But she knew now, as she had known at the time, that as he grew up looking more and more like his father, the point she had always feared would come when no amount of ignorance, innocence or self-delusion could have covered up the resemblance. She could hardly explain that to him either, nor that she feared her reaction if she should look at him one day and see Gus Campbell standing there. Revulsion, probably. Though it shamed her to even think it, she was truthful enough to recognise the possibility. She hadn't heard from Jamie again after Iris's death and had felt too guilty to contact him either, not that he wished it. Poor laddie, she often thought, a loving boy who saw himself as rejected by everyone, and who could blame him?

So apart from nieces and nephews scattered across the globe, George and Marie's girls and Agnes's family, she was the last of them alive. The last of the Reilly's too, even if she never did consider herself one, and she knew Agnes's weans had never really thought of her as a true aunt, more a friend of their mother's. None of it had ever mattered before, it was just the normal flotsam and jetsam of life, but suddenly everything had been brought into sharp, emotional focus. Seeing the contents of Jakey's tin, all the memories, all the people and their voices, were with her in this room they had never seen, Jakey's tin was Pandora's Box.

Flora was still living in Canada, a widow now after many happy years with Andy, but with children and grandchildren. She still wrote regularly with photos of her family and her life and they called each other on birthdays and at New Year, sobbing as they recalled old times, then laughing at each other for becoming so sentimental.

'Didn't seem so wonderful at the time, did it?' Flora chuckled, with a distinctive Canadian accent.

'Can you still remember your divi number?' Ruby teased.

'14–1092!' Flora shot back. 'How could I forget that?'

'And do you still sing "The Internationale" at New Year?'

'Of course!' Flora exclaimed, immediately bursting into song. She stopped. 'Trouble is, I can't remember all the words now, but I always sing the last line with gusto!' she sang again, and Ruby joined in with her. 'The Internationale unites the human race!' and they both giggled.

'I still believe it, you know,' Flora said sadly, 'I just think it takes too much living up to. You know that saying? "If you're not a Communist when you're twenty-one there's something wrong with your heart; if you're still a Communist after you're twenty-one there's something wrong with your head." That's probably true. My Da, poor big soul, his problem was that he was twenty-one all his life, not that it was a long one. He had a pure heart, Big Ali, he believed the human race was better than it is.'

'Talking of dyed in the wool Comrades, I saw your friend on TV the other night,' Ruby teased her, 'Lord Denis Kelly of Bullshit, quite the elder statesman these days, a revered figure, treated like a national treasure, the old fraud! My God, when you think back!'

'I was amazed when he became a cabinet minister so quickly!' Flora laughed.

'I was amazed when he became a Tory, but he took to it like a duck to water,' Ruby said scathingly, 'straight up the greasy pole.'

'Do ducks go up greasy poles?' Flora asked.

'That one did!' Ruby laughed. 'He might have been born to power and money, he wouldn't come near enough to spit on us once he moved on and, as you know, he moved on fast. You should hear him these days lecturing the working class scum about settling for a pittance for the good of the country, takes me all my time not to kick the TV screen! And when I saw him in his ermine robes for the first time, well, I couldn't stop laughing!'

'Aye,' Flora said wistfully, her Scottish accent reasserting itself, 'hard to believe we were ever that young and innocent, isn't it? We actually believed he was different, didn't we?'

'Speak for yourself, Flora McCreadie! You just fancied him because he was good looking, but we weren't all taken in!' and the two old women laughed at their younger selves.

Flora was always asking Ruby to come for a visit, but she never had, something she didn't divulge to Paddy when she berated him for not going over to see his son. Best to keep that to herself, she didn't want to give him ammunition, he would go on using it against her for the rest of their lives.

She decided to keep Jakey's letter for another time, whatever it contained was too powerful to be dealt with now, especially with a Nardini's fish tea awaiting her shortly. Looking at the clock she realised she had been sitting there for nearly two hours and hurriedly got ready to go. She would take the bank books and the chocolate to show the boy, Ian, that would be enough, and keep the existence of the letter to herself. As she opened her door to leave, Paddy bounded out of his flat noiselessly and appeared at her elbow.

'Dear God!' she shouted, a hand at her heart. 'If I didn't know you were a great hefty carthorse I would've thought you'd been a ballet dancer in a previous life! How come a big noisy creature like you can move so quietly when he feels like it? Creeping up on folk like that!'

'So he's away then?' he demanded.

'Aye, he's away, Twinkle Toes, but he's not gone far,' Ruby turned to lock her door. 'Sure, didn't you hear his Harley starting up?'

'I never heard a sound. Ruby, I wanted to talk to you—'

'Amazing the things you hear!' she said, interrupting him. 'The slightest sound at my door and you're there, great big lugs cocked like radar dishes, but a Harley starting up and you don't hear a sound. Huh!'

'So where are you going now? Will you back soon?' he asked, following her to the top of the stairs.

'I'm going to see a man about a fish, if that's all right with you, and I'll be back when I'm back!' she replied, and hurried on down before he could work out what she meant.

45

'So you got your chocolate after all?' Ian laughed. 'I don't believe it! You realise it's probably worth a fortune, there's bound to be people who collect these things.'

'Aye, but he didn't leave it for them, he left it for me. And he left a fortune of sorts as well.' She tipped her bag up and the bundle of bank books fell onto the table. 'I don't understand it,' she said, puzzled, 'some of them are in my name but I know nothing about them.'

Ian was leafing through them. 'God!' he whispered. 'Most have a few hundred on them, but there's much more on some of them.'

'Surely they'll be out of date by now?' she shrugged. 'Fifty years is a long time.'

'But the banks don't just keep the money for themselves. They put accounts into a kind of limbo after a certain number of years, but the money's still there to be claimed, plus interest. You see it in the papers every now and again, banks asking people who think they might be related to an account holder to come forward.'

'Really?'

'Aye, I'm sure of it!' he said excitedly. 'And didn't you say he'd left some kind of will with a neighbour once?'

'He left it with Betty Campbell,' she said quietly. 'It was just one of those daft kind of things Jakey would do. I kept it because he did it, if you see what I mean, there was nothing to collect.'

'But there is now! Do you still have it?'

'Aye, I've never thrown it away. I suppose I kept it for sentimental reasons.'

'Well we're laughing then,' he laughed out loud. 'Or you are,

Ruby, laughing all the way to the bank, to lots of banks come to that! I'll look into it when I get back to the office. And I meant to tell you, the BBC has decided they do want to make that arty telly programme about him. Is that okay?'

'Oh, fine, son, as long as they don't want me in it.'

'But you can tell their researchers about him?'

'Aye, what I remember at any rate,' she said. 'There wasn't much to Jakey apart from his paintings.'

Walking along the front later she stood for a moment looking out across the bay and thinking. Letting people know about Jakey the artist was one thing, she thought, but who he was, well, that was a different matter and not, she decided, for public consumption. At some stage, she decided, she would have to tell Ian that Jakey had drowned in the Clyde, just fallen in while he was walking along the banks looking for inspiration for his next painting. That would do. And when the time came she would tell him about the Sheik of High Street too, a nice wee funny story. That would do too. As part of that resolve some instinct had prompted her not to tell him about the existence of the letter. As far as he was concerned the tin had contained a bar of chocolate well past its sell-by date and a pile of bank books. The rest was and would remain private. When she got near her door Paddy sprang out again, as she knew he would.

'You're like a jack-in-the box, Keenan,' she told him, 'you'll be dizzy going in and out like that.' She looked at him. 'Or dizzier, I should say.'

'So, what—'

'Now, before you say a word,' she told him snootily, waving a regally dismissive hand in the air, 'I've been to Nardini's for a fish tea with my toy boy. Now goodnight to you.'

'But Ruby, I wanted a word, there's something—'

'I said goodnight, Paddy Keenan!' And with that she closed the door firmly, leaving him on the other side.

After her second visit to Acton she had never heard directly from Frances again, though the memory of the children she had failed to rescue still haunted her. There were calls to Agnes's number every now and again asking for cash, sometimes from Frances herself and, at other times, from a solicitor looking for bail money. He and money were the longest relationships Frances ever had, Ruby mused. It was evidence that her life had played out pretty much as expected. Each time Agnes, as she was instructed to by Ruby, asked about the children, and Frances always replied that they were 'fine.' The solicitor said the same, but added, obviously thinking Agnes knew, that they were happily settled with their foster parents and hadn't had contact with Frances in some time. In one way Ruby felt relieved when she heard that, but in another it deepened her guilt. She was glad the children were being looked after, but they were her grandchildren. She should have raised them, not strangers. Then she would go over again in her mind all the reasons for not raising them herself, the main one being that Frances's disruptive reappearances would have kept everyone on edge and made normal life impossible. That, at least, she couldn't visit on the strangers looking after them, as she could and, undoubtedly, would have done to her mother. Anyway, she had missed her chance where the children were concerned, there was no going back, and she was happy to send the money, it was the price she paid to keep Frances at a manageable distance.

The situation continued until Agnes's children had flown the coop, then she and her husband moved to a smaller house, grasping the opportunity to change their phone number and remove themselves from the telephone directory, thereby cutting off all avenues of contact with or from Frances.

'I decided not to tell you till I'd done it,' Agnes told Ruby, 'but she's been taking advantage of you and me for far too long. It had to stop, so I stopped it, and if you're angry with me then you're angry with me.'

'I'm not,' Ruby said sadly. 'I'm angry with myself, I shouldn't have imposed on you like that. You're a saint for putting up with it.'

'Well, she's Gerry's lassie,' she crossed herself out of respect for her late brother as she said his name, 'so she's my family too, I bear some responsibility. But I think we've more than done our bit, the two of us, don't you think?'

And that was the last she heard of Frances in so many years she couldn't even count them. Until, that was, a letter arrived in Largs with so many addresses and postmarks on it that her current one was barely readable. Had there been a sender's address on the back it would no doubt have been returned to Frances long ago, but Frances knew all the moves. She had thought of that. There would be an address inside, of course, and Ruby had wondered about opening it for that alone and sending it back, unread, from whence it came. For now, though, it still lay in the orange glass bowl Sarah won on Fair Monday, 1939, at the shows on Glasgow Green, a few days after Ruby had married Gerry. That made two unopened letters, she thought. Well, she could halve that number.

The light was just beginning to go but it wasn't yet dark. Ruby turned the envelope up and down, looking for a way to open it without destroying it, then discovered that the adhesive of the brown sticky tape had started to turn hard and disintegrate and came away in her hand with very little persuasion. Inside was a blue-backed school jotter with the times tables and various land measurements on the back, one of the ones she had 'lost' when she was at school. It still had her name on it, scrawled in her childish hand, but Jakey had written above it *'My Life*, by John McLean.' She stopped, remembering the little bits of poetry he had written for her birthdays; she should have realised that his paintings were just part of his creative nature.

I don't really remember my mother but I have a few clear recollections of her, like photographs in my mind. I don't really like photographs. I have many memories of her shouting and waving knives about when there was no one there and of hiding under the table till she stopped. I knew nothing different though, to me it was normal, but raised voices have always frightened me. Then another snapshot when I was about four years old, and she walked into the River Clyde carrying me. I didn't know what was happening. She was my mother, there had to be a reason for whatever she did. A passing river boat skipper saw us and shouted and waved, he was trying to let people know what he was seeing but the river was busy and there was too much noise. I think I waved back to him, but I could be making that up, because that's what children do when someone waves at them. My mother kept walking deeper and deeper till I had to keep my head tilted to stop the water going into my nose, and the next thing I knew the skipper had dived in from his boat and was beside us, trying to get me away from her. She didn't say anything but she wouldn't let go and I remember crying, thinking this man was trying to take me away from my mother. It all got a bit mixed up after that, mixed up and cold and black, because she was holding me under the water.

The next thing I knew I was on the bank, all wet and shivering, with the skipper holding a blanket round the two of us, he was soaked through as well. He had jumped in the water when no one took any notice of his shouting. I could see a crowd, and in the middle someone was lying down. She was on her stomach with her arms stretched out above her head, and there was a man on top of her, moving his hands up and down on her back. Her face was turned to the side towards me and her eyes were open, and through the legs of the people I could see it was my mother and she was staring at me. Only it wasn't her. It was a woman with a grey face who looked like her. I didn't know what the man was doing to her and thought he was hurting her, but later I knew he had been trying to make her breathe again. She was staring straight at me. That's the picture I can't ever forget. I still see that woman with the grey face when I close my eyes. She had drowned herself and tried to drown me, but she had been sick for a long time, my Da told me that later. There was something wrong inside her head, she heard voices and saw things no one else could hear or see, but I wasn't to tell anyone that, he said, or folk would think she was a madwoman and say I might be mad, too, maybe. As long as I understood that she was just sick and that she hadn't wanted to drown me. She didn't mean it, she had just become even sicker that day and didn't know what she was doing. I never knew the name of the riverboat skipper, but he saved my life that day. I don't remember her funeral, maybe I wasn't there.

Later my Da got married again to a nice woman who didn't

shout or throw knives or try to drown me, but she died too when she was having my brother, Harry. Da said she had TB and died of exhaustion after Harry was born. I always felt sad for Harry that he never knew his mother, but I talked to him about her and always told him how nice she was. I thought it was very sad that I knew his mother and he didn't and it felt odd that I cried for her and didn't cry for my own mother. After that Da used to take us around the city on his cart when he was working and when Harry was wee and got tired I would make him sleep in the back of the cart. I liked having a brother, but I always felt I was different from him. Harry had had a nice mother who was kind and looked after me, but mine had tried to drown me, even though she couldn't help it, and I was always worried that she would come back and get me, but I never told anyone that. Even now that I'm a grown man I like to walk by the river, it makes me feel closer to her, even though I sometimes think she might reach out and pull me in. And I look for the skipper, too, because the last time I saw my mother he was there, so he might help me find her. If I find him I might find her. Then I remember again that she tried to drown me and I don't know why I want to find her, but I still do. I get very confused when I think about her and I don't really understand my thoughts.

Ruby put the jotter down and looked out of the window, trying to collect herself. She was thinking so many things it was hard to put them in order. Her father. He had never talked about his mother, her grandmother, so she had no idea how she had died. Poor Da. So he lost both his mother and his wife to the White Plague. His childhood must have been sad, but so many were in his time. Yet he had gone on to make a life for himself, to marry and provide for his children, all of them, regardless of what they were like, then to end as he had, lonely, angry and violent, and upset because his anger was so alien to his character. Life wasn't fair, but some deaths were more unfair. Poor Da. And poor Jakey. Even in his short account of his early life he sounded solitary, and she closed her eyes, thinking of him struggling to come to terms with a mother who suffered

378

from mental illness at a time when it was seen almost as an offence rather than an a terrible condition inflicted on hapless victims. That knowledge, coupled with his father's understandable instruction to keep it to himself, would have isolated Jakey from the start, but compounding that was the horror he must have carried all his life about his mother's suicide and her attempt to take him with her into the depths of the dark river. And he hadn't liked people touching him, she remembered him swerving away from any attempt, nor had he touched other people. It wasn't hard to see why when you knew about his early life. Even the replacement mother who had cared for him was taken away after a short time. Perhaps Jakey decided it was best not to hold onto anything or anyone, or to be held by them. There had always been something about Jakey that made you want to protect him and care for him, they all felt it, Harry, Sarah, George and herself at any rate. Now she knew where that came from too.

It was too dark to read without a light any longer and she was suddenly desperately weary, so she slipped the old blue jotter back in the envelope, made herself a cup of hot milk and went to bed. What she had read tonight was enough, the rest would keep till tomorrow. It had waited for over fifty years, after all. Pressing the play button on her tape recorder she was expecting a restless night, but the next thing she knew it was morning and Jakey's memoir awaited her.

When Da died me and Harry took over the carting and that's how we met Sarah. She worked as a maid in a big house in John Street and when we delivered things to the kitchen she always made us tea and gave us biscuits, and she had this quiet smile that you could see in her eyes. I loved Sarah from the minute I saw her. She was kind to me, like Harry's mother. The trouble was that she liked Harry and Harry liked her. Harry was my brother and I'd always felt bad that I had more of his mother's love than he had, so I said nothing. He was a good brother, I wanted him to be happy and I didn't want to cause him any trouble. When the First World War broke out Harry joined up. Sarah was angry because he hadn't told her, and she told him they were finished. I did a terrible thing then, I'll regret it for the rest of my life. I told Sarah how I felt about her and asked her to marry me, and she said she would. It was a terrible thing because I knew she would have done it, but only because she was angry with Harry, and I still didn't care, I just wanted her for myself. I was taking advantage of her because she was unhappy, and we spent the night together. I thought that if we did she would have to marry me, but the next day she cried and told me it was a mistake, that she loved Harry and couldn't marry me. I went straight off and joined up.

When the War was over Harry and I discovered that Sarah had had a child. We didn't know before because letters didn't arrive very often, and there was no one to write to us. Sarah had called the child Beatrice and when I saw her I was so afraid I could barely speak. The child was my mother, the same colour and look in her eyes, the same bright red hair. I looked at Sarah and she shook her head very slightly. I knew what she meant, the child was mine, but we hadn't to say anything. Harry married her very soon after that, not knowing the terrible thing I had done. He became my child's father and he didn't even know it. Every minute of my life that sin against my brother has been on my mind, but I deserve it because he didn't deserve that. It is like a big, big lie, the biggest lie in the world, and I've told it to my brother, who is the best of men. I know I am a bad man, but I never loved another woman my whole life, only Sarah, that's my only excuse, and ever since she has treated me better than I had a right to expect. She's been better than a mother to me

Ruby threw the jotter down with a gasp and rushed about aimlessly from room to room. Bea was Jakey's child. That was all she could think of. It seemed to be written on every surface she looked at and on the insides of her lids when she closed her eyes. Her mind rebelled against the very idea. It couldn't be, it was obscene. From somewhere close she heard someone sobbing then, realising it was herself, she ran back to her bedroom, lay down across the bed and thrust her fist into her mouth to stop the noise. The tears were coming too quickly and too thickly to be silenced though, and she lay for a long time, crying deep, retching sobs like a child. She had to get out, she decided, dressing hurriedly, she couldn't breathe and she felt sick. Grabbing her bag she hurriedly left the flat, she had to put some distance between her and Jakey's revelations. When she opened the door she found Paddy standing there with the *Daily Record* and pushed past him, locking her door behind her without a word.

'I was just bringing the paper over,' he said.

'Keep it! I don't want it!'

She shoved him out of the way, frantically trying to escape.

'Ruby, what's the matter?'

'Nothing! Go away! Leave me alone!'

'But, Ruby, I need to talk to you …!' he said plaintively.

'Another time, Paddy, I'm busy!'

It was raining, she was glad of that, it meant she could avoid looking at people or them looking at her. All she had to do was keep her head down and hide under her umbrella just as everyone else was doing. Even so, where was there to go? Largs was a small place, she knew every inch of it. Where was there to hide? Oh, God, oh God, none of it could be true! She sat on a bench facing the sea, but if Paddy came looking for her he would go there, it was where they ate their ice creams after collecting their pensions. The last time they sat here watching the ferry coming and going to the Isle of Cumbrae and back, Paddy had asked 'Have you ever been over there?' and she had replied that she hadn't. 'No, me neither,' he said. Looking across the water she wondered if it might be the only place she could be sure of not being found, where peace and quiet were guaranteed. A short trip from home could provide her with the time she needed to think, or not to think, to sort out her head, and Cumbrae was the last place Paddy would think of looking for her, so she headed for the slipway on the merest of whims.

The ferry took all of ten minutes to cross to the island, then she followed the herd, boarding a red and white bus marked 'Cumbrae Coaches' for another short journey to Millport, the main village.

Following everyone else once again she found herself in Stuart Street, heading for the bright green and red fronted Ritz Café. If there was a hot spot on Cumbrae, she thought, it seemed to be the Ritz. Looking around she could see that there had been a deliberate policy to keep the place as it had been for decades, old-fashioned, out of date, and for some reason she felt comforted by that. She had no idea how long she sat there, drinking one coffee after another, cosseted by the low murmur of strangers chatting then departing to be replaced by the next batch, watching the rain clouds move away to be replaced by sunshine and back again, thinking and trying not to think. The paddle steamer *MV Waverley* arrived at the old Millport Pier on her usual summer run, disgorging more customers for the Ritz. She had been right, there wasn't much difference between Largs and Cumbrae. The little island had doubtless been joined to the mainland at some time in the distant past, but the familiar yet alien place gave her the distance she needed.

It was always hard to imagine your parents as youngsters, but even though she was an ancient old biddy now, she couldn't reconcile what she knew of Sarah, Harry and Jakey with the story in the jotter. These were people she knew, people she loved, and now it seemed she hadn't known them at all. So what was real and what an illusion about anything? People made mistakes, she knew that, she had made plenty of her own, and there was that old cliché about not judging anyone unless you'd walked in their shoes, she knew that as well. But ... And there lay the problem, there were so many buts. And just as she thought she might be beginning to see a glimmer of understanding in the distance, like the proverbial light at the end of a dark tunnel, more questions popped into her head and there was no one left to answer them. And there was anger, she had to admit it. She was angry too, angry about everything, though she knew she had no right to be.

What Jakey had recounted was the story of *their* lives, not hers, and it had all happened long before she was born. Anger was not a rational response any more than the petulant feeling that she had somehow been deceived. She walked along the beach and sat down, her mind in turmoil. They were still the people they had been, after all. The way they had treated her had been the way they had treated her, none of that could be changed retrospectively. Yet she felt let down, hoodwinked. Given the choice she could, she thought angrily, have gone to her grave quite happily knowing none of it. And, oh God, poor Bea! Poor hated, reviled, unhappy, jealous Bea! Ruby thought back to the day before Sarah died, when Bea had forced out of her the name of her father. If Ruby felt betrayed, how must Bea have felt when she found out? Years ago she had wondered at the McLean's secrets and lies she had known about, and despaired of them, but she had no idea then, *no idea!* The deceptions had burrowed deep into the fabric of the McLeans, spreading underground like a woodland fungus and, unseen and unsuspected, choking and wreaking destruction on the fabric of the family.

And thinking back she remembered treating Bea with such coldness all her life, loathing her tantrums and her seemingly silly rages. Who was she to have treated Bea like that when she had no idea of the other, more damaging family secrets and lies surrounding her? And Bea hadn't know for so long either. She knew the lies were there, lurking in the background, but didn't find out the truth till her mother lay dying, the day she took her fatal overdose of barbiturates. No wonder she felt low. There was little in Bea's life to feel happy about on a normal day. She had killed herself without knowing about Jakey's mother, her grandmother, which was a blessing of some sort, she supposed. Now it was too late for Ruby to do anything for her unhappy sister, to even say sorry, however inadequate that would be.

By the time she arrived back in Largs that afternoon she was becalmed. The anger had gone, but she felt weak and bruised. Even though she climbed the stairs as quietly as possible, Paddy, her self-appointed guardian, was waiting for her like an over-excited puppy as she put her key in the lock.

'Paddy, leave me alone,' she said quietly. She glanced at him. 'I can't explain, I just need you to leave me alone for a bit. I have things to think through and I need to do it by myself.'

He took a sharp intake of breath, preparing to launch a question, so she held a hand up to silence him without looking at him, then she closed the door behind her and locked it.

'I just want to know that you're okay,' he said through the door.

'Aye, I'm fine,' she said wearily, 'just tired. Now go away, Paddy.'

She stood in her hallway for a few seconds till she heard his door close before she relaxed.

46

A week would pass before she felt able to go back to Jakey's account of his life, and all that time it lay there in full view, threatening her self-control. She had often heard it said that the older you got the worse you were affected by things and the harder it was to recover, she remembered hearing her mother say it, in fact. It was one of those pieces of received wisdom that no one questioned but Ruby had always thought someone should jump up and demand with a snarl 'Who says?' Jakey had unwittingly proved to her there was some truth in it after all and, now that she was experiencing it, she could see what 'they' meant. Still, she was calming down again, beginning to chide herself for being so shockable at her age and after all she had seen, laughing at herself for being a drama queen as she tried to resume her normal routine.

If Paddy had expected a full explanation for her moodiness he was disappointed. She had had some bad news about a friend, she told him, aware that he didn't really believe that was the only reason for her odd behaviour, but it sent the message that questions would not be welcome and he at least had the good sense to keep his curiosity to himself. She was grateful for that. Maybe one day she would tell him, but then again, maybe she wouldn't. Keeping to herself was a habit that had stood her in good stead over the years, she wasn't at all sure she should or even could abandon it.

Not long afterwards Ian Fraser called with details of how she could claim Jakey's money and she was amazed to hear her perfectly normal voice saying she was busy with something at the moment, but she would think about it and get back to him when she had time. Claiming Jakey's money was the last thing on her mind, though.

She didn't need it, she had her pension and a little bit put by, she wasn't rich, but she was okay, so for the time being at least Jakey's money could stay where it had been all these years.

And so she took out the old jotter and began reading again.

The voices didn't start till around the end of the War, but I'm not sure about that, it's all a bit confused. I mean, everybody talks to themselves in their head and it was just like instead of me talking to myself, it somehow became other people as well, but I can't really say when it began or who the voices were. There were lots of voices in the trenches, lots of noise and lots of shouting and I found that hard, it made me feel off-balance, dizzy somehow, as though I couldn't stand up without holding onto something. After I came back from the War I found the voices were still there when they shouldn't be and I didn't want them to be, and it was harder and harder to shut them out. I think that was the difference, and I got tired sometimes trying to. I had always liked drawing and I found when I was concentrating on something else the voices were quieter, so I began to draw and then to paint, one just led to another without any thought. Sometimes the voices went away all together for a while and my head felt so clear and quiet that I was sure they would never come back, but they always did, and soon I wasn't sure of anything any longer. They told me how bad I was, but I knew that already, and they told me everyone knew I was bad and one day they would come and get me. They said Harry knew what I had done, they had told him, and he was coming with a big knife, like my mother, to stab me for my sin. Part of me knew Harry would never do that, but I wasn't really sure, and I would go off and walk by the river and sleep on the banks till I thought Harry wasn't looking for me any longer. Even with what had happened in the river and the fear that my mother might be waiting to pull me in, I felt calmer there than anywhere.

It wasn't long after that people started coming out of photos and walking through me. At first, I knew it couldn't be happening, it was a trick, but the voices told me it was because

I was nobody, that's why people could walk through me, and I began to believe them, I suppose. I thought if I could just get rid of all the photos I found, then the people in them couldn't walk through me, so I threw them all away. The voices had thought of that though, and when I looked in the mirror I saw this horrible monster that came out and walked through me as well, so I had to get rid of all the mirrors I could find. It was the only way I could control what was happening. I started painting really big pictures on the walls to keep me busy, but the first time I painted a face it turned into a monster as well, so I never painted a face again. As time went by I couldn't even look at other people for long before they turned into monsters, so I kept to myself and didn't look at them. When I tried to ignore the voices they did other things to me. Hands would come out of walls and try to grab me, so I went out walking to where there were no walls, but I had to be careful of trees, if I got too close the branches turned to hands and they tried to grab me too.

Then there were other times when the voices didn't tell me how evil I was, but said funny things, or told me to do things, odd things, and instead of people having monster faces they smiled and laughed, and I felt better again. I felt if I did what the voices told me to do they might not get angry with me, they might even go away for good. But soon they were there more often than they were away, and I couldn't tell anybody, because they were my punishment for doing what I had done. It was a long, long time before I began to wonder if what was happening inside my head was what had been happening inside my mother's head, but I didn't believe it, because my mother hadn't told the biggest lie in the world, she was just sick, she wasn't bad like me. But I saw her in the wean, Bea, and that frightened me. She was very like my mother, so like her that even when she was wee I would look at her and see my mother instead, which I knew couldn't be right, but that's what I saw. And she shouted a lot, she screamed and shouted the way my mother had, and a voice in my head would tell me that it really was my mother and she had come back to drag me to the river and

387

drown me. I couldn't make sense of that and I told the voice I loved being by the river, and surely if my mother really did want to drown me she would have done it when I went there. The voice said she was waiting just to torture me, just when I felt safe, that's when she would jump out of the water and grab me, but even if she changed her mind about drowning me, the wean would kill me in some other way one day. So whenever Bea started shouting I would leave as quickly and quietly as I could. I tried not to show I was really frightened but there was a terrible panic in my head and the voices yelled and shouted at me and I couldn't stop shaking for ages afterwards.

Once again, Ruby didn't realise she was crying till she stopped reading. She thought back to how the family had laughed when Harry took himself away from raised voices, it was a male McLean trait, they said. But Harry had simply been embarrassed, whereas poor old Jakey had been terrified. The brothers hadn't shared a trait, though it looked on the surface as though they had. In fact, their reactions were completely different. Jakey, she now recognised, had been schizo-phrenic, his 'wee voices' had been real. All those 'funny' things he had done that had so amused the neighbours around High Street, had been signs of real and terrifying mental illness. He preferred the company of children because they simply accepted without question, whereas adults had to ask why, and Jakey had no answers. There were lucid areas of his life when he obviously knew there was something wrong, but he couldn't tell anyone for fear that he would be branded insane. At a very young age, after all, his father had reinforced the prejudice against the mentally ill by making him understand he must never tell anyone about his mother. His mother had killed herself and tried to drown Jakey, so madness was something to be afraid of and people would be afraid of Jakey, his mother's son, if they found out. So Jakey had reacted by drawing himself into his own ever tighter world, by isolating himself more and more as his symptoms increased.

And Jakey was right to be afraid. From her years in nursing she knew that. He lived in an age when there was little to be done for the mentally ill, the emphasis was on doing something for the commu-nity at large by simply locking the insane away for years, often for their entire lifetimes. They would be banished to large institutions, usually in the countryside, where they got little treatment, less care and no rights or possibility of rescue. There they would be subjected to the barbarism of electric shock treatment without anaesthetic, and yoked to farm machinery like animals, to work the land. That was what would have happened to Jakey, to gentle, sensitive Jakey, who made people laugh and hid chocolate for her in a tin under his floorboards. Was he hiding it from those terrifying, tormenting voices, she wondered?

She had almost found herself hating him after discovering that he was Bea's father, and that made her feel ashamed – had she learned nothing from her treatment of Bea? Her sense of betrayal over Jakey being Bea's father had made her see everything in black and white again and she hadn't considered anything beyond her own hurt, but Jakey had been sick and there was no help and no escape for him. No one in the family had ever seriously suspected that he was in such trouble, though her father and mother thought he was odd and different and tried to protect him, and she and George had taken the same approach. The people he lived among had no reason to look any deeper than his family did, to them Jakey was a figure of fun, a 'helluva character,' she thought bitterly. But there she was again, making judgements. How were they to know? They had their own lives and worries and Jakey had never done anything that had threatened them. He stole a few mirrors and pictures, but that had hardly been life-threatening and they always got them back, and he had harassed Father O'Hanlon at St Mungo's, but if anyone could have done with a bit of harassment it was Father O'Hanlon. 'See?' she said to herself. '*You're* laughing now and you *know*, how can you blame them?'

The jotter was put away once more till she could face it again. To take her mind off it she threw herself into cleaning then painting and decorating her flat and, when no more could be done she baked till the flat was full of more buns and biscuits and cakes than she could use. Paddy was the obvious recipient, the man who lived for cakes. He looked at her sceptically.

'What's up with you?' he asked suspiciously.

'What do you mean?'

'Well, look at this place, it's all done up. Are you thinking of selling up? Is that what's this is about?'

'I wasn't thinking of it,' she said, 'but if you carry on like this I might think of it.'

'And all this baking,' he muttered. 'What's that about? It's odd.'

Ruby shook her head at him. 'It's you that's odd!' she said, lunging towards the cake halfway to his mouth. 'Since when did you question the existence of a cake, Paddy Keenan? Give it back!'

Paddy neatly raised his hand out of retrieval range. 'Since when did you let me have one without yapping on at me?' he asked. 'And now I can have all I want? Have you put something in them?'

Ruby narrowed her eyes. 'Only a wee bit rat poison, seeing as you ask!'

Paddy sniffed the cake. 'I wouldn't be surprised,' he said quietly.

'Well give me the bloody thing back again,' she raged at him, 'if you don't want it there's people starving in Africa would be grateful for it!'

'No, no,' he condescended, 'I'll risk it. Sure, it's not a Nardini's cake, but it would be mouldy before it got to Africa anyway, so I might as well give it a go.'

She took a fish slice from her kitchen work surface, reached up and slapped him over the head with it. 'Don't do me any favours, Keenan!'

The next part of Jakey's tale had dealt with his days as the Sheik of High Street.

I always wanted to be somebody else, I didn't want to be Jakey McLean. Jakey McLean was a bad man. The voices told me what to do. When I was the Arab I felt different and the voices were pleased with me so they didn't threaten me. I was somebody else in the Arab's clothes. Sometimes I felt I was watching him, not being him, but that was fine too. It was like this other person owned the robes and the sword and all I did was let him walk about in them. I called him Lawrence of Arabia, and I'd say to Wee Dug 'Time to let Lawrence of Arabia out again,' and off we would go. I was happy as Lawrence, he wasn't me, happy as

Larry, I suppose you could say.

There were a few blank pages, then Jakey resumed his story with a few desperate lines.

I've just heard that Sarah's got TB. Folk are saying she's going to die. The voices say it's my fault, it's because of what I did to her, I've made her bad as well. They say I kept the TB that Harry's mother died of and gave it to Sarah and it's been festering in her all these years. I don't know what I'll do if Sarah dies. I won't be able to breathe if Sarah's not here. The world will end.

There were several more blank pages, then, turning another she found the same hand, but less well-defined, as though written by Jakey in a hurry. It was a letter, dated on the day before Sarah died.

Dear Ruby,

I'm writing this to you because we have always been good pals. I hope that by now you've read about my life and don't hate me too much, but I know you must be disgusted and I don't blame you. I wish my mother had drowned me all those years ago, then I wouldn't have been there to meet Sarah and she would just have met Harry and everyone would be okay. It's all been my fault. Something's just happened and I have to go away, but I have to tell you everything so that somebody knows I didn't mean it. Bea left a note through my door while I was at work today. She said she wanted to see me. I was really scared. I've always been scared of Bea, even when she was wee. When I went over to her house she told me that Sarah had told her our secret and that when Sarah died she was going to stand up at her funeral and tell everybody. I tried to tell her not to, that it was wrong, that it hadn't been Sarah's fault or Harry's, it was all mine. I couldn't let her give your mother a bad name like that and upset my brother. She started shouting at me, you know the way she always does, calling me all sorts of names, but I made her sit down in her

391

chair. My head was dizzy with her shouting and all the voices were screaming in my ears, but I had to stop her. She seemed to calm down, but then she lifted a knife off the table. She turned into my mother you see, she was going to kill me, so I pushed her really hard and she fell and hit her head on the fireplace. She went very quiet and I couldn't wake her. I tried, but she wouldn't wake up. I didn't know what to do. I've killed her. I've killed her. But I don't know whether I killed my mother or my daughter, my head's not working right and the voices are still all shouting at once.

So I'm taking Wee Dug and going away, I'm going to try to put things right. I should have drowned with my mother. She must've known I was bad, that's why she wanted to kill me. Maybe if I die everything will change and everybody will be all right. Bea will just not exist and Sarah won't have TB and everybody will be happy. I'm going down to the river and I won't come back. When they find Bea they'll know I killed her, but I didn't mean to. Please tell them that I didn't mean to. I was just trying to stop her with the knife and she was shouting and I couldn't think and I only pushed her. Please forgive me.

Ruby ran to the bathroom and was sick, then she sat on the floor, her back against the bath and, thinking how ridiculous she must look, she tried to laugh, but the sound was halfway to hysteria. She hadn't just been reading Jakey's account of his last day, and Bea's and Sarah's, she had been living it too, feeling it. Everything that happened on that day was linked. She could see every part of the chain, retrace every moment of it as though it had been happening in front of her, right there in her living room.

Bea at Sarah's deathbed, but instead of movingly bidding her mother goodbye, she was rowing furiously with her to get the name of her father. She heard the raised voices in her mind, felt Bea pushing past her again and fleeing to her own home. On the street she had dashed past Cissie and Dot and Ruby had left them at the house and run after Bea. She felt her feet pounding up the brae and remembered getting out of breath. Another row had taken place at Bea's

392

home, where Ruby had told her that they were no longer sisters, that after their mother's imminent death and funeral she never wanted to see or hear from her again. It was playing like a film, her mind the projector, as she watched the scene she had known nothing about: Bea visiting Jakey's flat after she had left her. She was no doubt intent on having it out with him there and then, but Jakey had been at work, so she had left a note. In her mind she watched Jakey going to Bea's flat after he found her note, and her third row of the day had taken place, this time with poor, deranged Jakey.

As Ruby sat on her bathroom floor, she imagined Bea's mental state. It had been a terrible day, the worst day of her life as well as the last. Her emotions, which were rarely under control at the best of times, must have had her wound up like a coiled spring about to burst. She pictured her confronting Jakey with what she had been told and heard her threats as though she had been there. Maybe she did lift a knife and maybe she didn't, either was possible and, even if she did, it could also have been entirely innocent. What was just as possible was that in poor mad, hallucinating Jakey's confused mind, the lifting of a knife had connotations no one, least of all Bea, could have guessed. He wasn't even seeing Bea any longer, she had been transposed into the mother who had screamed and brandished knives and come close to drowning him as a child; the mother he always suspected would still drag him into the Clyde one day. She saw him panicking and pushing Bea, watched her hitting her head and passing out, and suddenly recalled Donald McGill mentioning a blow to the back of her head. He said it had probably been caused by her being dizzy after taking too many sleeping tablets by accident and perhaps falling out of bed, or even before that. She followed Jakey as he took flight, Wee Dug, even more terrified than usual, at his heels, convinced that he had killed Bea, and deciding the only way out was to drown himself. In a weird way his voices had been right, Bea had indeed been responsible for his death. There was a logic about it, a twisted logic, but she understood why it made perfect sense in his tortured, mixed-up mind. If he finished his mother's job he could set right the events of years ago that he was convinced had brought the entire family hurt and misery. She watched him, beset by the cruel, persecuting voices, running back to his

393

home and frantically writing his letter to her, then putting it in the box and placing it with the bank books in the tin under the floor-boards. Then she smiled through the tears, watching him place the suitcase with the treasured Arab robes beside the biscuit tin – Lawrence of Arabia, the Sheik of High Street, would bestride the neighbourhood no more.

Only Bea wasn't dead, she had come to and swallowed more than enough barbiturates to prove fatal and taken to her bed, where she was found next morning, half lying on the floor. It was, Ruby had always thought, a deliberate act, but now she was even more convinced of it. There was no way of knowing if she, too, had been hearing voices, but she had certainly inherited the instability of Jakey's mother and of Jakey himself, that had led to the three of them taking their own lives.

Bea's existence was pointless, her health was poor, her marriage a sham and now, on top of that, her mother was dying and she had just discovered who her father was. If Ruby had felt betrayed when she discovered it was Jakey, she could only guess at Bea's feelings of despair, and Ruby knew she had added to them that day. Strange to think that both Bea and Jakey were already dead before the White Plague had finally claimed Sarah hours later, Bea in her lonely single bed, Jakey in the River Clyde, both he and Wee Dug wrapped in Sarah's gift of one of her 'crochet things.' It was all unbearably sad and it hurt as though it had just happened, though the events were more than fifty years old. What to make of it all?

The way Sarah had handled her mistake with Jakey had doubt-less made perfect sense at the time, she had done it to protect the entire family. She and Jakey would keep quiet and she and Harry would raise the child as their own, which she was to Harry in every way. Who could have imagined that Bea would turn out as she had? Her paranoia and unhappiness from her earliest years must have been symptoms of her inherited mental instability, though no one had any reason to even suspect it, no one but Jakey. The family had been driven to distraction by her scenes, her exhausting fighting and screaming had marred their lives and made them hate her, but looking back, Bea had been as ill as her father and grandmother. Had she not been, the story would probably never have unfolded.

A sane Bea would not have forced out of Sarah the name of her father and, in turn, would not have taken her anger out on poor, mad Jakey, who would not have pushed Bea and knocked her out. It was a series of desperately sad, connected events. Reading about them, picturing them, was like following a thread leading, inevitably, to misery and sorrow. Even as her eyes devoured Jakey's story, the illogical thought of making a pact with Fate entered her mind. What if she stopped reading now, at that instant? Would what had already happened all those decades ago, simply not? But it had happened. Sarah's best intentions had set the family on the road to its tragic outcome all that time ago, nothing had and nothing could halt it. If there was one thing she had learned in her long life, Ruby mused, it was that your best intentions always found you out in the end and punished you for them.

She tried to get up from the bathroom floor and found her bones had seized and she could barely move. Her efforts, for some reason made her laugh, the situation was ridiculous! Why did she choose to sit on the floor when she could have sat on the edge of the bath and vomited just as successfully and copiously? She sat back down again to catch her breath before working out a means of getting onto her feet. It was a strange business. Even before she had read the small piece in the *Evening Times* ages ago, she had been thinking of her family and dreaming of Jakey and, after all those years, she couldn't understand why.

Once again, she thought of him going back to his home after he had 'killed' Bea and hurriedly painting the tiny figures on the corner of the River Clyde mural, Wee Dug below and Jakey and Ruby sitting on a bench – no faces, of course – each with a hand resting on the tin box between them. It had been his clue, his final attempt to make her look in the hiding place only he and she knew about. But she had been too upset by his death when she cleared the flat of his few belonging and had missed it entirely. It had been a hard time and she was performing a hard chore, it was the third death the family had coped with in as many weeks and, in truth, all she thought about was getting out again as quickly as possible. The murals had been there, some changing, others remaining as constants for as long as she could remember. They were so familiar that she no longer looked at them closely. The child in the corner wearing the ruby-red dress would have noticed the figures, but Ruby's eyes were adult eyes by then. What was it he had once said? 'Things change when wee people become big people.' A moment of clarity in a life blighted by the cruellest illness of all, one that warped his mind and destroyed his gentle, sensitive personality.

It seemed fanciful to imagine that, from some netherworld, Jakey had somehow known his secret was about to be uncovered more than fifty years later and had been prompting her memory from beyond the grave. Yet, when she thought about it, she decided it was no more or less fanciful than what had happened within the seething cauldron that had been McLean family life. She laughed. The McLeans of High Street had just been an ordinary family, she had always said, before adding, 'But only on the outside.' Thinking of that now she smiled wryly. She had grown up at the heart of the family, thought she knew everything there was so know about them, yet she hadn't even suspected there could be such huge, all-consuming secrets and lies that her own people had hidden every day, year upon year. She had no idea how much there was on the inside of the McLeans. And there was no one to share it with, apart from Flora, of course, but Flora was thousands of miles away and she couldn't have this discussion by phone. Ruby McLean had chosen to live a self-contained, independent life, she guarded her privacy, but now she felt desperately alone and adrift.

From her seat on the bathroom floor she worked out a plan and slowly eased herself over to the toilet, reached for the lid and closed it. Next she hauled herself up till she was lying across it on her stomach, before sliding over backwards to sit on the edge of the bath and turning the taps on. 'I knew one day I'd get some use out of Paddy Keenan's yearly present of bath salts,' she told herself. 'The man has no imagination.' A hot soak, she thought, removing her clothes, would bring back the feeling to her aching muscles and the movement to her stiff bones. If only there was something to take away the pain in her heart.

47

To claim Jakey's money, it seemed, she would have to get a solicitor. The news didn't please her.

'I don't like solicitors,' she grumbled down the phone to Ian Fraser. 'I knew one once. Have you ever noticed the number of solicitors who become MPs? It was bad enough when we had human beings making a mess of our lives, but these days it's all solicitors.'

Ian Fraser laughed. 'I'll find one who's as near human as any solicitor can be. He can tell you what proof you'll need, birth certificates, that kind of thing, but I can collect them together for you if you like.'

'Och, son, you don't need to go to all that trouble,' she protested, trying to shake off the feeling of weakness that had come over her with the McLean family revelations. The wind had been taken out of her sails and she was still trying to get it back. 'Besides, it'll give me something to do.'

'Whatever you think, Ruby. I think I've found out why he opened a few bank accounts for you, by the way. It looks to have started with the Co-op. They only allowed savings of £200, so when he reached that himself he opened an account in your name as well. Maybe after that he thought it was a good idea and did the same at the other banks. Most of them have been taken over but the accounts are still there with whoever bought them up, and you'll get the cash Jakey paid in, plus interest, as I thought.'

'I don't know what to say,' she murmured. 'There was nothing special about me, son, as I said before, I think it was just that I was the youngest, I was the last wean, and Jakey got on better with weans. I still don't think I deserve this though.'

'Think what you've done for him, though. You've got him recognised as a real artist, his name will mean something now.'

She smiled. 'That was you as much as me, Ian.'

'Well, this was what Jakey wanted and I think you'll be surprised by how much you end up with,' he told her. 'It looks like he paid in almost every penny all through his adult life.'

'All he needed was his paint and brushes, his rent and his gas, and he didn't use much gas. My mother bought all his clothes, did his washing and fed him. She fed Wee Dug as well.'

'Sounds like she was his mother as well as yours,' he laughed gently.

'Aye,' she said, closing her eyes and swallowing, 'something like that.'

'What are you going to do with it?' he asked. 'Any ideas?'

'I thought I might take a wee holiday.'

'With this cash you can have a big holiday!' he laughed.

48

It took a few weeks to feel like herself again, but she had survived, her life was on an even keel again and soon she would be back in her normal fighting trim. She sat by her window feeling almost smug. Then the phone rang. It was one of the local GPs, Dr Dolan, and she wanted Ruby to come to the surgery for a chat. She wasn't Ruby's doctor so, she thought, it was likely a request to visit someone who was terminally ill, but why not tell her on the phone? Not that it mattered. she'd drop in later when she did her shopping.

'It's about Mr Keenan, Mrs McLean,' the doctor lass said.

'Paddy?' Ruby asked.

'Yes.'

'You want to talk to me about Paddy Keenan?'

'Yes,' the doctor smiled. 'You are his next-of-kin, aren't you?'

'No,' Ruby said, bemused. 'No, I'm not. He has a son in Canada.'

'Well he's named you.'

'Cheeky bugger!' Ruby whispered, shocked. Her mind was running in various directions. She had seen him ten minutes before, so he wasn't dead. Maybe he had arranged to get something done about his bunions, it was long overdue, and had marked her down as his fetcher and carrier while he couldn't walk. It would be just like him!

'It's about his x-ray.'

'His x-ray?' Ruby repeated. She would have to stop that, she sounded like a daft old eejit, like Paddy Keenan himself, in fact.

'He didn't tell you?'

Ruby shook her head.

The doctor lass look concerned. 'I've been trying to call him but he never answers.'

'He has that caller ID,' Ruby said furiously, 'so that he knows who it is and he doesn't pick up if he doesn't want to.'

'I've written to him too, but he hasn't responded.'

'The surgery address is always on the front,' Ruby shrugged.

'Yes, well, that's why I called you, as his next-of-kin,' Dr Dolan smiled. 'He no doubt told you—'

'The big bugger didn't tell me anything!' Ruby exploded. 'He didn't even tell me I'm his next-of-kin!'

'Oh. Well, you see, Mrs McLean,' the lass persisted, 'I did some routine blood tests a while back and something showed up, a hormone, that made me think he could have lung cancer. I arranged a chest x-ray and I've had the results for a couple of weeks now, but I think he's scared and he's avoiding me so that I can't tell him.'

Ruby felt pole-axed. 'What?' she asked in a weak voice.

'It's okay, honestly,' Doctor Dolan said hurriedly, 'as it turns out he hasn't got cancer. That's what I've been trying to tell him. He actually has areas of calcification on his lungs, areas of scarring.'

Ruby collected herself. 'I know what that means,' she whispered, 'I used to be a nurse.' She took a couple of deep breaths. 'Is this calcification consistent with exposure to asbestos?' she asked.

'Yes, yes it is. I wanted to ask him if he had ever worked with it, because if he did he's due compensation.'

'He was an electrician in the shipyards,' Ruby said, 'he only told me that recently, secretive big galoot.'

'So, I would be really grateful if you would please explain all this to him and get him to get back in touch.'

Ruby nodded and got up to go. 'Just make sure you've got plenty of Plaster of Paris in stock,' she smiled wryly, 'by the time you see him again he'll need it, I'll see to that!'

She thought all day before talking to Paddy. He was scared of the thought of dying, she had always known that, there was no point in frightening him with the thought of the serious illnesses that could follow the scarring on his lungs. There was time enough to think about them if and when they developed and she would be there to help him deal with whatever lay ahead. For now all he had to know was that he didn't have lung cancer and wasn't dying.

At the daily handover of newspapers she grabbed him by the arm and pulled him firmly inside her flat.

'You could always say "Come in," you know, Ruby,' he complained.

'Och, stop moaning, we both know you spend all your time thinking up ways to get in here. Now, sit down. I've had a chat with Dr Dolan.'

His eyes widened and the colour drained from his face.

'Before your daft old head explodes, you don't have lung cancer, you silly old sod. What you have is some old scarring from your days in the yards, it was caused by asbestos.'

'Bastards,' he said quietly. 'The dust was everywhere. I've known that many men who've died of it younger than me. I've often wondered how I got away with it.'

'Well, you haven't, not completely anyway, but you're not dying. I'd be surprised if any of the men in the yards got away with nothing and the doctor lass says you're due compensation. Just think,' she chuckled, 'you might be able to afford a couple of they wee minis you were on about.'

'Why in hell would I need a couple?' he asked innocently.

'One for each of your big feet,' she replied, 'you could use them as roller-skates.'

He shook his head and glared at her disapprovingly.

'But you would've saved yourself a lot of worry if you had picked up the phone or read the doctor's letters.'

'I know that,' he murmured. 'I was scared.'

'I know you were scared, you great lump! And see where it got you! Why the hell didn't you tell me you were going for an x-ray? I would've gone with you.'

'I tried to,' he protested, 'but you were rushing about all the time in a bad mood and telling me to go away.'

It was in the time of Jakey's letter, she realised. She remembered him saying he wanted to talk to her but she had put it down to his usual nosiness. After all that about other people being too concerned with their own lives and worries to see further than skin-deep where Jakey had been concerned, yet she had done the same with Paddy! In those weeks she had become embroiled in a story decades old and well and truly over, and hadn't noticed Paddy trying desperately to get her attention, scared out of his wits that he could be dying in the here and now. Still, Ruby decided, attack was the best for of defence. 'And what's this about making me your next-of-kin?' she demanded.

Paddy shrugged. 'My boy's too far away,' he said, 'it seemed logical.'

Ruby shook her head and glared at him. 'Logical? Since when have you dealt in logic, Paddy Keenan? And that reminds me. Have you got a passport?' she asked him.

'What?' he asked, staring at her.

'It's a simple enough question. Have you got a passport?'

'Ruby, I just never know what you're going to come out with next!' he laughed. 'Why would I need one of yon things?'

'People have them,' she said tartly, 'it's allowed. Have you or haven't you?'

'No, I don't.'

'Me neither, so we'll both have to get pictures taken to apply for one. We'll do that today when we collect our pensions. There's one of they booths along at the pier.'

He stood up, mouth open to protest.

'I've got half a dozen Nardini's cakes,' she said casually.

He sat down again.

She smiled to herself, pleased to see his colour returning with his weakness for cakes.

'Ruby, I never know what's going on in that head of yours, as you well know,' he protested, 'but what in hell are you going on about passports and photo booths for?'

'I've been thinking,' she announced, filling the kettle and switching it on. 'I came into a wee bit money recently, more than a wee bit, in fact.' She stopped and giggled girlishly.

'Did you have a Lottery win you didn't tell me about?' he demanded.

'Aye, I can just see me keeping that from *you!*' she replied. 'No, this is different. Now be quiet and let me talk. I was thinking of buying myself a Harley Davidson.' She ignored him as he choked theatrically on a mouthful of cake. 'But I've decided instead that we're going to Canada. You and me.' She looked at him and laughed as his mouth fell open. 'You're going to see your son and I'm going to see my best pal.'

'Your best pal? Since when did you have any kind of pal?'

'Och, button it! Do you think I tell you everything?'

'And I can't afford a holiday in Canada!'

'I bet you could, you miserable old bugger!' she accused him. 'What have you got to spend your money on? Sure you eat me out of house and home, so you never have to buy a mouthful, and you sit here using my heating till I throw you out! And am I asking you to pay?'

'I wouldn't take charity from my own son,' he protested, 'I'm damned if I'll take it from you, Ruby McLean!'

She watched him whipping up outrage as his hand reached for his second cake. 'It's not charity,' she said. 'If I was giving out charity I'd pick somebody who'd earned it. And if it makes you feel any better you can pay me back when you get your compensation. Consider it a loan.'

Paddy didn't reply.

'Aye, I thought so. Charity doesn't matter a damn if you have to pay for it, does it, Paddy Keenan?' She sat down opposite him, stirring her tea, and fixed him with a look. 'This money only recently came to light,' she said quietly, easing into her prepared explanation. Maybe one day she would tell him about Jakey, she thought. She wasn't sure yet, she would keep it under review for now. 'It's from someone I haven't seen in over fifty years. I just happen to be the last of the family to pop my clogs, so it's all mine. This is my chance not to just rub along.'

'A wee inheritance?' he asked through a mouthful of cake.

'Crumbs everywhere, you messy bugger! God alone knows what your son will make of you! Aye, a wee inheritance, I suppose. I don't deserve it, I've done nothing for it, but there we are, it's mine. I thought we could use it for something besides paying bills.'

'If I'd known you were an heiress I'd have proposed,' he chuckled.

'And even if I'd been an idiot, I'd still have refused,' she countered. 'Now, we have to get passports and you have to phone your son and I have to phone my pal to sort out dates, so we need to get to work.'

'I'll have to think about it, I haven't made up my mind about it yet,' he said grouchily.

'Och, behave yourself! Anyway, there's a condition.' She looked down. 'Them,' she said. 'Your bloody great ugly feet.'

'My feet?' he shouted. 'You always think you can say what you like about a decent man's feet!'

'I notice,' she said quietly, 'that you didn't say a man's decent feet.'

'Well, I can't leave them behind, if that's what you're thinking!'

'No, but we can get shoes that cover them. I'm going to take you to get them properly measured for shoes that fit, and we'll get slippers as well.'

'Now, wait you a minute!' he yelled, leaping to his offending feet.

'In Glasgow,' she said slyly.

He was silent for a moment. 'Glasgow, did you say?' he asked quietly. 'Aye, well, we could do that, I suppose.'

'I know this nice restaurant where you can still get black pudding. If your table manners improve I can take you there.'

He settled back in his chair and helped himself to a third cake. 'Aye, well, maybe you're right, Ruby,' he conceded. 'They don't make slippers and shoes as well as they used to, you know, they make them for the mass market.'

Ruby shook her head. 'The *Reader's Digest* again!' she muttered.

He glanced sideways at her. 'But I'll pay.'

'Aye, well, this is where the charity comes in,' she told him. 'I'll be putting this money to good use by saving decent folk from having to see your feet, so don't worry about it.'

'A man has his pride, Ruby,' he said unconvincingly.

'Really?' she said pleasantly. 'You must introduce me to him sometime.'

She would have to get the lad something. Ian had almost adopted her. They were both railway, of course, and railway folk looked after each other, but still, he deserved a present, something that wasn't a staple of life that he hadn't bought himself and, therefore, had no reason to feel guilty about. Bunches of flowers on all the family graves and a heartfelt apology at Bea's. She chuckled, imagining a pair of hands coming out of the earth and wrapping themselves around her neck. 'Who could blame her?' she thought. Another bunch for Betty's resting place in Dalnottar, but none on Gus Campbell's, of course. Come to think of it, both he and Iris had been cremated, so she wouldn't even have the satisfaction of denying them a bloom or two. 'Can't have everything,' she said to herself.

It would be good to see Flora again after all these years and to let her pour her usual balmy words of wisdom over her raw, jangled soul. Flora had always been Jakey's champion, she remembered, she said he was a sensitive soul who needed protection and consideration. She had been right, and then some.

The letter from her daughter still lay unopened in Sarah's orange bowl. That was a whole other can of worms, though she had long suspected what was in it and why it had been sent. There were grandchildren somewhere, adults now and, as she had many times over the years, she wondered what had become of them. In her mind there would always be a picture of those two bemused weans sitting on a floor in Acton, two more she had failed. She didn't know what to do about that situation other than leave well enough, or bad enough, alone. What had they to gain anyway from some old biddy they probably didn't remember ever seeing pushing her way into their lives now? It was all about her guilt, her need to ease her conscience of at least one thing on the long list and help her sleep at night, she knew that. Well, Tony Hancock and Jon Pertwee had been handling that chore for years now, far better all round to let them get on with it, rather than disturb the lives of innocent strangers, even if they were her grandchildren. Yes, she would leave that alone, for now, at any rate.

And if she had to decide between rushing once again to the belated rescue of their mother, the daughter she never had, and looking after that lonely big fool next door, well, she knew which she would choose. That old saying, 'Blood's thicker than water,' was only as true as you let it be, she decided, you could make water any thickness you wanted. But she would talk it through with Flora all the same when she saw her. Flora always knew the right thing to do.